Singularity
Deferred

Singularity Deferred

Liam R.W. Doyle

Tragic
Press Sans

ISBN-13: 978-0692665763 (Tragic Sans Press)
ISBN-10: 0692665765

First Edition: April 2012
Second Edition: March 2016

Dedicated to the memory of William J. Burling. This story was nothing more than a first chapter, futilely rewritten a hundred times, until he introduced me to a fundamentally life-altering ideology encompassed in this key question to be asked of anything and everything:
"Who uses it and what is it for?"

Many thanks to Dr. WD Blackmon and Professor Brian Shawver. And no less thanks to Liza, Chris, and Angie. Without them, well, this novel would be significantly more painful to read than it currently is.

And more thanks than I can express to my family for their support, their love, their occasional kicks in the pants, and their patience for my grumbles and ignoring of them as I forced the words onto the screen.

CHAPTER ONE

I woke up to what sounded like fireworks going off in a coffee can, and I was in that can. A sound that was less a *sound* than a full-body reverberation. I felt it through the hard metal floor and in my bones. As much as my body kept trying to keep me down, convincing me I needed to keep sleeping, I fought the fog and climbed into that kind of wakefulness where you can't quite clear your head and get a grip of where you are and what's going on around you–made all the worse in this case by the fact I *didn't* know where I was.

Wherever I was, the room was dimly lit by weak and sputtering fluorescent lights hinting at metal walls, floor, low ceiling; smooth, dirty-white crates and bins here and there; and at my feet some unusual piece of machinery that reminded me of three interlocked bicycle tires stuck in the middle of a pile of computer parts. Lying against it was my mother's long, heavy, silver flashlight. *What the heck was that doing there?* I thought. *Forget that, what am* I *doing here?* I sat up, trying to remember anything about what led up to this moment.

Another felt-not-heard explosion caught my attention, and I struggled to my feet. Then struggled to my feet again. I felt unbelievably weak, unbalanced, like right after a too long, too hard weight lifting session (which, as anyone could tell by looking at the hundred and fifty pound me, I did not often commit), and it took a few tries to stagger to the door until I collapsed against the wall. I felt both concerned by my unusual condition and a little disgusted by my physical state, as if I had suffered through a nasty bout of flu, wearing the same clothes the whole time.

I pushed a recessed, oblong "open" button next to the door which slid aside into the wall, revealing a short, narrow corridor that reminded me of movie submarines: exposed wiring ducts and odd pieces of metal frame jutting here and there. All of it painted a dull white. I called out, "Hello?" No response. Narrow doors to the front, left and right. I called out again, and again no one responded. I struggled against the wall, making unintentionally wild steps and over-reaching for portions of the bulkhead, unable to find my balance or completely control my limbs.

Once I got to the door in front, I peered through the little smoked-glass window set at eye level. Inside looked like the cockpit of a plane, and my confusion started to solidify into a needling anxiety. *How in the world did I get into a plane? What in the world did I do last night? Why is there no one in the cockpit?*

I pushed the open button for this door and a loud, rhythmic beeping flooded out. I examined the three windows in front. Black. Very black. I figured it was the darkest night I'd ever seen, or something was covering the glass. The cockpit was tight and cramped–I had to literally climb into the single large, black chair. I looked over my shoulder out the door to see if anyone had come yet (no one had), then turned my attention to the console of . . . controls that didn't look like any airplane controls I was familiar with. Instead of toggles and dials and a yoke, the console was covered with all manner of computer screens and small clusters of buttons. Some smaller monitors showed images I couldn't make out: circles, lines and curves, scrolling numbers and words. Some looked like animated navigational charts, in full color 3-D even, while others looked like calculators gone insane. One of the main monitors in front caught my eye:

–HULL DAMAGE: undetectable. (.0045 stress factor)

Course deviation corrected - minimal energy usage

–COMMUNICATIONS HAIL (23.2.88)

–COMMUNICATIONS HAIL (23.5.40)

–Incoming object (q67754)

—SRS Identification: energy based (factor 7)

–NEAR PROXIMITY ENERGY RELEASE–

—Gauss Barriers inactive -4-

–HULL DAMAGE: undetectable (.016 stress factor)

–Unidentified Craft: distance at 66k (5-5-7)

Course deviation corrected - minimal energy usage

–COMMUNICATIONS HAIL (23.16.82)

The last line appeared as I read, causing the first line to scroll off the top of the screen. If this was what was currently going on, I assumed someone was trying to call us. I craned back around and yelled again, "Hello? Anyone out there?" and again received no reply. I looked around the console at buttons and words that were just too many to take in. A small monitor off to my right had one flashing label on its face, in a couple of rows of touch-screen icons. The flashing one read "Communications." *Why not*, I thought.

I touched it and the other icons disappeared with a set of new virtual buttons replacing them. I could make sense of most of them. I did what seemed most obvious and pressed "receive Xmission." Instantly, the loud beeping turned into a slight background noise and, while the control screen I was paying attention to didn't change, the main one in the middle showed some movement. Turning my attention to it, I was surprised but relieved to see a person looking back at me. A man of some exotic ethnic decent I couldn't place. No hair on head nor face, angular structure, dark complexion.

"How good of you to answer," he said in a gravelly baritone. "It took some work getting your attention." Actually, what he *really* said was something like: "*Masayang* proper *tú* comeback *la sig-wei. Nulij'yu tú* ears up." I never got proficient at speaking the mix-up of Spanish, English, and various Asian languages that formed the predominant tongue spoken by most traders, haulers, pirates, and the like, but I eventually got good at understanding it. Not at that point I wasn't, though.

"Uh, I'm sorry I have no idea what you just said." He looked right at me through the screen, examining me as I was him. I glanced up and around quickly for the lens of a camera but saw none.

He continued, but in a simplistic English still peppered with slang I had to guess at. The conversation went more or less like: "Who are you? You're not Jarrod. You do look a lot like him. . . . Where is he?"

"I, uh" I began most eloquently, "I don't know any 'Jarrod'. In fact, to be perfectly honest, I don't even know where I am. Could–"

"Humorous," he interrupted, "We detected only one person on board, so either he's dead, or you've taken his ship, or both." He had a creepy smile: "As much as I would appreciate that, I'm going to guess it's more likely he's run off, as expected, and you're covering for him." (That last bit, he actually said the figure of speech, "y tú fuzzfacin' dachi." I could never hear that and keep a straight face. I had to constantly have him rephrase what he said, which certainly contributed to his bad attitude.)

"Look, I'm sorry, I really am, but I'm in some trouble here. I honestly don't know how I got here–I woke up, and here I was. No one else seems to be here, and I'd really like to know where I am and why."

He continued as if I hadn't spoken, "To come to the point, Jarrod, you, both of you, I don't care, there's something of mine Jarrod took from me, and I intend to get it back. I'm willing, for old times' sake, to ask nicely and forget this happened. Maybe. But the more I'm delayed, the more apt I am to simply take it back. At whatever cost, to whoever has it."

"Okay, go ahead. Seriously. Come aboard and get it, whatever it is, and then tell me how to get back down or up or, uh . . . over, or what-the-heck-ever. Better yet, take me with you, and we can find Jarrod together and get some answers. I like that one, actually."

He snorted, "Funny. We already know it's not on your ship. If you really don't know what you're doing there, I'd say that's *your* problem. Since neither Jarrod nor my property is currently on board, I'm going to give him one chance. And you give him this message: He's to meet me on Sandiki in ten seds. If he doesn't, I won't come politely knocking next time. Understand?"

"Hey, I–"

"Hao." The monitor clicked to darkness, followed after a pause by:

–Communication terminated (23.42.7)

–Ship Identified – NT: *Tsaul Ki* (revenant class)

–*Tsaul Ki* distance +5.33k -> (5-5-7 . . . . . . 5-8-7+)

I sat in silence, uncertain what exactly just happened. Who was that? What in the heck was that all about? The only thing that came to mind was *I'm back where I began.* Except, now I had some communication controls, at least. I felt a little more collected despite my situation, what with having some human contact–even if weird and belligerent.

I turned my attention back to the little monitor on the right for clues as to how to reach anyone else on it. Some labels on buttons and panel sections on the console started to catch my attention. At first, I couldn't quite make sense of the words, as if the odd lettering made the word unreadable, then I realized I was reading things I simply couldn't have expected to see: "Shield control," "astrogation," "artfl. gravity control. . . ."

I started looking around more closely, reading everything, becoming increasingly curious, then disbelieving, then nervous. "Orbit modulation," "anti-matter drive control," "dark-matter focal control," and finally my eyes happened upon and stopped at "fore-window opacity." That set had an oblong button with "+" and "-" symbols on either end. I looked up at the three blackened windows in front of me, separated by thin strips of hull structure just barely keeping the triptych of glass from being one long swath of ebony. Without looking away from the middle window, I depressed the

"-" end of the flat button and watched as the dull black steadily dissipated to allow what was outside become visible, like window tinting fading away. What came into view was a similar yet deeper blackness filled with pinpoints of light. Just to the right and below, the size of an orange held at arm's length, was the most beautiful and terrifying image of what could be nothing other than an alien planet. Not the blue of Neptune or Uranus, or the orange-striped Jupiter, ringed Saturn, red Mars, or blue and white Earth–but something I'd never seen in any astronomy text or television program. It was a disk of green, brown, and yellow stripes slowly but visibly grinding against each other as they moved across the surface, causing little eddies of storms at the meeting places.

A planet. Stars and a planet not just out and forward, or above, but *below* my eye-level, where if I were in a plane I should have been able to see land. I felt dizzy and nauseated, weak and light-headed. I put my head between my knees for a few minutes and controlled my breathing. It was a while before I could convince myself to look back up.

CHAPTER TWO

I became aware of my bladder screaming in agony. Strange how a very basic need can actually drive away mind-boggling questions like, oh . . . how and why was I in *space*! By the time I'd willed myself to look back up into the impossible, the planet had already passed from sight. All that remained was a field of pitch black awash with stars. A gorgeous sight, really. Something that can be rarely seen anymore from Earth, where standing in a rural field, the light pollution from towns and cities miles away still prevent people from being able to see the stars in the same way our pre-industrial ancestors were able to. This view of space was not at all intimidating, but rather hypnotizing. I left it only out of necessity.

I climbed delicately out of the chair, woozier than when I first sat down, and exited into the small passageway I came through earlier. I hoped the toilet was behind one of the other two doors. The one now on my left was big, solid, intimidating. Air-lock, or, the-door-to-not-good-results, probably. The door opposite it was more like the one to the cockpit but without the window. I opened it and found a sleeping cabin. The disheveled bed and stale smell gave it away. My hope of finding what I was looking for was rewarded by the small, sliding partition off to the side that opened just wide enough to allow me to sidestep into what could generously be called an alcove containing a toilet and shower, of sorts.

After having dealt with one pressing matter, I felt more capable of dealing with the present situation . . . which I still couldn't really grasp.

Space? How is that even remotely possible? And that's when it hit me: *virtually* possible. I had to be in some sort of simulator. Why I woke up in a simulator was equally beyond me, but it was light-years more reasonable than being in *actual* space. That ominous door was probably the door-to-a-warehouse-and-laughing-jerks.

However, as I lumbered to the hallway with the air-lock, two and two suddenly made four. The reason why my movements and my balance were off since I woke up: less gravity. Of course, I'd never experienced less than Earth gravity before, so the thought never occurred to me until that moment that would be the cause for my awkwardness and, well, light feeling. It certainly wasn't zero-gravity, but as I started walking around in a tight circle, making little hops, I guessed it was probably more than moon gravity (one-sixth if I recalled) but still less than what I was used to on Earth. I didn't semi-float like the astronauts in the videos from the moon walks did, but this feeling was unmistakable now that I could associate it to something. Was this even possible to simulate? I didn't think it was, at least, I'd never heard of anything like that. Even NASA had to use water or short and vomit-inducing arcs in a DC-10 to simulate weightlessness. I went back into the sleeping cabin and sat down on the cot jutting from the wall, my head swimming.

I couldn't understand it. It made no sense. I was just a techie for an Internet service provider, a small local one at that. How could I possibly be in a spacecraft? Last thing I could remember was . . . I couldn't remember. It was odd, like trying to remember a dream you just had–you know you had it, you remember having had it but can't remember the dream itself. I couldn't remember yesterday. I remembered pouring over server logs at work; I felt as though it *should* have been yesterday, or maybe the day before, but seemed more like a couple weeks ago. I tried to think and felt certain I worked the day before, and the day before that, and all week, but my memory told me I hadn't been to work in many days. What did I do, then? I couldn't recall. *Was* it a party? Was I slipped something to knock me out? I seriously doubted it, since I hadn't been to a party since college and my friends really weren't the partying kind. And I certainly didn't know anyone who would play with chemicals that knocked people out and screwed with their memory.

I felt my anxiety building, my "lizard-brain" telling me to flee instead of fight. I knew that if I didn't have something, anything to grasp hold of, I'd panic.

I stood up, a little more used to the altered sense of balance, whether from experience or new acceptance, and again stepped gingerly toward the hatchway. I looked back through the little window in the door to the cockpit, command cabin, or whatever it should have been called. Bolted down bucket chair, wide console filled with little screens, buttons, and lights–but dominating the room were the three windows. I looked back out at the void, held away from me by the glass in the ship's hull and the glass in that door.

The thought came to me that there was glass, transparent sheets of glass, filling three good-sized holes, where otherwise all the air would be almost instantly pushed out into vacuum. I wondered how that was possible. The space shuttles had small glass windows, and I'd not heard of any emergencies arising on a mission because of cracked glass. I stood fascinated by that thought before finally realizing I felt better. Thinking about the glass in the windows of NASA's space shuttles actually subdued some of my anxiety. Perhaps it was from thinking about something specific and not trying to grasp the enormity of my situation in general, or possibly from feeling like if the shuttles could spend hundreds of hours in space without any failed windows, I felt somehow I was fine and was going to remain fine.

I tried not to think of problems with valve seals and insulation debris.

I retained my newfound calm as I turned back around and faced the more solid door I came out of earlier, into the room I'd woken up in. I opened the door, and it whispered aside. I gazed around to take in all that I missed earlier in my haze of first waking up. Boxes, crates. Mostly white, off-white, scratched and scuffed up, with various labels and logos I didn't recognize. Cargo boxes, I suspected. Strange device in the center of the room: It was a hodgepodge of parts stuck together obviously using function over form as a design philosophy. It reminded me of the time I had to jury-rig a computer together in a case that was not meant for upgrading. I had drives and parts laying on static-plastic on top of the case and on the table, ribbon cable and wires in all directions, and cooling fans attached in strategic places using plastic-coated twist-ties. This object at my feet reminded me of a much bigger version of that.

Except, in addition to electronics that had no recognizable purpose, there were the large parts in the middle of all the wires and circuitry and unusually placed buttons and toggles. The inner-tube looking tori I saw earlier were the largest of the parts, set directly in the middle, intertwined amongst themselves like the rings of a gyroscope. I touched them, ran my fingers along them, tried gently to make them move. They didn't yield but certainly looked like they were meant to. They weren't rubber, as I first thought, but some kind of matte black metal. Much colder to the touch than they should have been. I picked up the flashlight and turned it on. In the dim illumination of the room, the sickly yellow light from the ancient flashlight was even dimmer.

I looked at the floor around the device . . . and noticed the blood. I saw it in very fine dots on the floor not far from where I had been lying. Of course, I know for certain *now* that it was blood, but somehow I also knew it *then* as I looked down at it. Dark brown, dried, but unmistakable. Blood splattered on a floor is something I think most people recognize immediately, and, if not, if their first conscious guess is paint or stain, they're simply lying to themselves. We living creatures recognize the leaving of blood where it shouldn't be found. I didn't have a good feeling about it.

I knelt down and slowly scanned the floor for clues as to what it was doing there. It was a fine mist. No, not even really a mist, just a lot of tiny dots that got fewer but larger in size as they got closer to a particular off-white cargo box. I shuffled over to it in a crouch, following the trail, and stopped when I recognized half the blackness on the bottom edge of the container was not a shadow but a thick rivulet of blood along the line where the crate met the floor.

The container's door faced me, opening outward. It bore a faded, scratched label for something called "Syr-Synergy," below that some Asian characters, and then a line of dots in what I figured was some kind of shipping code. I looked at it for a while, unmoving in the glow of the light-strip situated at shoulder level along the walls–casting shadows at unusual angles. Of course I had to open the door, of course I had to see what was in the crate, and of course I was frightened to petrifaction at the idea of seeing what I knew was in it. Nothing good is ever seen where pools of blood are involved. I considered remaining ignorant. What would be better, to stay inside a mysterious spacecraft I had no idea how I got into or where it was going, with what I was sure was a dead body–or stay in said spacecraft with the unknown bleeding and likely dead creature constantly calling to me to look at it? Nagging at my mind, knocking like a monkey-paw-created aberration at the door of my consciousness, rapping and demanding entrance until I finally swung the door wide.

I clutched the recessed handle on the door and in one quick move pulled it open. No reason to play shadowy peek-a-boo with whatever was inside– best to get it over with, like removing a bandage on a scraped knee. Yep, exactly what I feared and worse than I'd thought it'd be. A man, dressed in some kind of jumper or flight suit, crammed with no dignity into the small space. Bloated, discolored, skin around the eyes pulled back and shrunken, making them appear to bulge out. Dried blood soaking the stomach of the jumper and pooled on the bottom of the container. The odor was an unbelievably putrid, gassy, sour smell that I will never, as long as I live, forget.

I'm certainly not proud of losing it like I did. Manly-man image and all that. But I also don't think, considering the circumstances, anyone would blame me for it. Growing up in a middle-class, suburban environment, video games are the closest you tend to get to dead humans and a pound of hamburger a couple days beyond its freshness the closest you get to that kind of smell–and then that's only a sliver of the impact. The olfactory evidence of a human being reduced to spoiled meat. Add to that the fact I was once again acutely aware of being alone in a box floating in unknown space: well, I let myself break down for a while.

I ended up staying in the cockpit, or control room, for quite some time. I distracted myself with the console, displays, and readouts, finding some innocuous-looking button and switching it on and off, overly interested in whether the indicator light was an LED or some other technology I didn't know about. I was in there so long playing around with whatever I could, to keep my mind occupied, that I found a few games on one of the consoles: word and number games, puzzles, solitaire-type games. Those ended up being a great time-and-attention waster until my thirst became so great that it had become more of a distraction than anything else I could come up with in that tiny room.

After some out-loud discussion with myself, I finally worked up the nerve to exit the control room, keeping an eye on the cargo door as if it was poised to betray me in some evil-door manner, and entered the bedroom/bathroom/who-knows-whatall room.

The more I looked around, the more I got the impression of a dorm room. Clothes drawers, foldaway desk, well-hidden and diminutive kitchenette devices. A mini-pantry filled with both dried and tubed foods and boxes and bags of foodstuffs that probably would have been quite the no-no on a space shuttle. Stuff that was in the form of flakes and pieces and grains. Fortunately, aside from a couple of containers of liquid in a small fridge, all of it smelled perfectly edible. Although, the moment I smelled what I think was some kind of milk, the sense-memory of the cargo box hit me full force and I found myself dry heaving into the toilet for a while.

I tentatively nibbled, munched, and sipped on stuff that didn't seem bad, or capable of going bad, while I examined the containers they came in. Much of it appeared to have been repackaged into plain storage containers, but there were a few products that were still in colorful commercial packaging. Most of it was in English, though there were many sections on some packages, and some entire packages, that were obviously Spanish (although I couldn't read more than a word or two), and some that had Asian characters. I know now that it was a conglomeration of the once disparate languages of Japanese, Chinese, Tagalog and Hindi called, uncreatively, "Asian," but at the time I couldn't guess what it was.

I was comforted to see stuff that made sense, even if I didn't recognize it specifically. A cereal box (with a crazy cartoon character I'd never seen before but was as familiar to me as all interchangeable cereal mascots throughout my life) with a panel of unpronounceable nutritional information, a slew of marketing hyperbole, and a smattering of legalese on consumer assumption of responsibility for use of this product, and I felt right back at home and that all was going to be well.

So long as I got to wherever I was going before the food ran out.

I stopped munching when I pondered the idea of having to search the cargo boxes for any stored food once I'd gone through this cache.

I remembered what that creepy-looking guy said earlier: I looked just like this Jarrod. I made myself remember what the guy in the crate in the next room looked like. It wasn't hard calling up the image, it'd been lingering in the periphery of my consciousness for the last two, four, however many hours it'd been since I saw it. I hadn't kept track of the time I spent trying to not think of it. Now, thinking of it, I was certain that if the guy who was supposed to captain this ship looked like me, then it wasn't that guy in the crate. Even with the state he was in, his blond hair, receding jaw, and wide nose didn't look at all like me.

I spent a lot of time looking around the bed-and-breakfast room, trying to get a sense of what kind of ship this was and who owned it. What kind of person *was* this Jarrod that guy had spoken of? He was undoubtedly bi-orderly: the room was in a general state of disheveled, but there were individual things that were well-organized. The clothes created a mess somehow bigger than what few articles there were. Then there were books, several, maybe twenty or so, of varying shapes and sizes, organized on two shelves with an elastic strap keeping them firmly in place. While I'd never heard of most of the authors represented, I recognized a couple books like the seemingly ubiquitous *Moby Dick* and a collected works of Shakespeare in faux leather binding.

Seeing these books, I thought about my own book collection and how much of it has migrated over to e-books. Surely, in a spaceship, there must be an e-reader with countless books. I looked around for some kind of handheld device, a slate or tablet, but couldn't find anything. Well, surely, if the proper pilot of this craft is Jarrod, and Jarrod's not that body, then if there's a handheld he likely took it with him. I hoped to God I wouldn't be here long enough to need a library of books.

Though, I was glad that, in this spacecraft, familiar paper books were around, and it suddenly occurred to me what other information these books could provide. I fingered through the various books I'd never heard of and tried to find what looked like the most recent, newest one. They were all somewhat weathered and used, well-read with creases in the spines and dog-eared pages. None of the covers were glossy, none of the pages crisp. So, I just started pulling them down one at a time, flipped to the second or third page in each book, and looked for the small, bunched up writing each one would have behind the title page.

I found that the last book to have a familiar publisher's info page had a copyright date of 2026 (there were actually only six or seven books in this collection published before that one), the others had decidedly different formats. A couple had "professional" looking (but very different from what I was used to) publishing info on the first or last page, or inside cover, and some even had End User License Agreements, while a few had printed statements expressing more or less the opposite intent: use and copy and change at your leisure. But most had little more than title, author (if even that), and maybe what looked like a year. 2214, 2265, 2177, 2031, 2271, 2240, 2276. . . . I pulled each book from the shelf, and the highest number I found was 2301. Is that what year it was? 2301? Nearly three hundred years . . . in the future? I don't know why I hadn't really thought of it before, why I hadn't really, consciously, considered the fact that it might not be the same year I last remembered anymore. I mean, when you wake up in a spaceship and don't know how you got there, being in a different time really isn't outside the realm of possibility.

I supposed.

I sat down on the bed, the novel *Exponential Threat* hanging open in my hand. I looked at the front: some military sci-fi story to judge the book by its cover. How did it get to be 300 years in the future? I entertained the thought of having slept in that cargo room for three centuries. That was exactly as absurd as the situation I was in, no more, no less.

I sat there for a while, absently fingering the pages of the book in my hand, thinking. When I got tired of thinking, I lay down on the bed and tried not to think anymore. I fell asleep eventually.

CHAPTER THREE

I was surprised I could sleep at all, much less as soundly as I did, that night . . . day, whatever the time period was. The sleep did me good. However, when I awoke and acknowledged I was still there and it wasn't a dream, a wave of despair washed over me. I seemed to have accepted where I was on some significant, subconscious level. It felt like when I stayed at a co-worker's cabin a couple of summers ago, where I was in a strange and uncomfortable place I couldn't leave until the Labor Day weekend was over. I guess I adapt well. What pained me the most, now that I truly accepted my situation, was my separation from my family—my wife Lori and sprite-like daughter Chloe. Five, almost six, and just started first grade. I imagined those mornings when I'd lie in bed, no Saturday morning alarm. I could hear them in the kitchen down the hall: muffled, unintelligible speaking punctuated by laughter. The clink of dishes. The clack-clack-clack of Boosh's paws on the tile as he followed them around while they made breakfast. I'd lay there in the soft sunlight, tinted orange and red by the pattern of the thin bedroom drapes, and put off getting out of bed until Lori sent Chloe to jump on the bed until I got up, smiling.

Finally, I don't know after how long, I wiped my face dry on my sleeve and took some deep, controlled breaths. Yeah, I could be a putz and do nothing but weep and moan about what mysterious hell I'd found myself in, or I could be proactive. Or, as my manager would say: "Synergize my resources and action plan my positives." Well, I imagine he said things like that; I didn't really listen to him all that often.

The light in the room had auto-dimmed to a night-light level during my sleep. As I moved around, the room slowly illuminated to a soft glow. If I was going to actually *do* something and move forward, I was going to need to get out of my foul clothes, and possibly my own skin if the stink didn't wash off. I figured out how to use the surprisingly convoluted shower stall and its trickle of a water spray. I found some clean clothes that fit me remarkably well, then I went back to the control room, munching on a handful of Fruity Flavored Cardboard Oh's (and if that hadn't been their actual name, then "truth in advertising" was still non-existent these centuries later).

With a determined spirit and mission, I began a concerted effort at trying to figure out where and when I was and where I was going and when I'd get there. Eventually, with significant caution lest I accidentally vented the air into space, I hunted and pecked the controls and until I figured out I was five days out from some destination called "Gadreus." After a little happy-dance I went directly to the living-sleeping-dining room and made sure I had enough food. Confirming that, I had myself another happy-dance. Little favors were all I was counting on right then, right there.

By the time the fifth day rolled around, I had passed stir-crazy and was well into blended-into-a-puree-crazy. It's amazing how quickly the novelty of being in space can wear thin when there's nothing to do or look at. If it weren't for the display that kept a constant and unswerving countdown to arrival, I'd probably have gone nuts with fear that I'd never see any civilization again, not just my family. Space, after all, is pretty big and empty. My mind often pictured scenes of a gnat flying around the Sahara in search of another gnat. I figured that'd be a close approximation of what it'd be like to randomly run into something else out here.

When I awoke the morning of the last day, I saw in the distance a point of light that was brighter than the other stars in the black field. Within a couple of hours, it had grown to the size of a pea. I guessed it was a planet, and most likely Gadreus. My boredom quickly turned to elation, and swiftly evolved into impatience. I watched the dot become a small disc, and by the time it was as wide as my extended thumb, I could see it was primarily a cream-colored white with thin bands of orange and yellow and swirls of soft brown. When it was half as large as the view window, I decided with a good amount of certainty that the coloring and swirling was not atmosphere on a rock planet, but that it looked more like a gas giant like Jupiter. (I started to get concerned about just where I was going to be landing, if at all!)

Fortunately, after another couple of hours of mixed impatience and awe, when the planet had grown well beyond the size of the window, I saw a dot directly ahead, appearing black against the white of the planet. It grew slowly bigger and became obviously separate from the planet and not a storm on it. It was a moon. I figured *that* must be Gadreus. When I had gotten close enough to see specks of light against its black face, indicating technology, I literally jumped for joy. I was in space and couldn't remember how, I was near a planet that as far as I knew wasn't in my home solar system, and I had no idea where I was or how to get back home, but I was positively ecstatic at seeing signs of other life.

I straightened myself up, then wondered with some alarm: How exactly was I going to land? It would be just perfect if I were to come all this way to smash head-on with a colossal rock. I sat, chewing on fingernails, watching the growing orb that was the moon take over the view. There were flimsy whips of light gray streaks laced out over the surface here and there. They resembled clouds in some loose way, but were closer to descriptions of formless ghosts than any Doppler radar weather image I'd ever seen. Finally, after getting close enough to see that the black land was dotted liberally with black pools of liquid and lines that looked like canals, something changed on the main monitor screen.

–Guidance Beacon theta-theta-mu acquired 3.5.39

–Navigation Lock initiated. . . . Course Change engaged (1-1-9)

I watched the view move and slide as the ship changed from perpendicular to the surface of the world to almost parallel with it. I had no idea what the scale was because, while I could see lights on the surface, there was nothing I could judge size against. A number on a display next to a wire-frame graph of the moon got smaller as we got closer, and slowed down perceptibly as the course changed. I got an idea it was altitude, but I had no idea if the number was a measure in feet, miles, kilometers, or what.

The surface features, the lakes and canals, hills and clouds slid past until a large grouping of lights came from out of the horizon and stopped directly below. The course changed again, and the ship started to head directly down to the surface.

–Local SVN Beacon acquired

–Low-M Atmosphere entry procedures initiated. . . .

–FREQ .003 registry scan detected

–SVN Inner Sphere/Aerial Flight permission granted

<>– Verification Tracking Number Z-667422\876-HH2 –<>

–COMMUNICATIONS HAIL (3.16.71)

That one I was familiar with. I reached over to the communications display and hit the touch-screen. The main monitor cleared and the image of a very normal-looking fellow in what looked like service station coveralls came into view. He was looking away at something over his shoulder as he began saying, "Jarrod. 'Bout time. A whole sed late and–" he turned finally, and his sleepy look slowly melted into one of curiosity and suspicion. "Who're you?" (Well, actually, he said, "*Tú shéi?*" but you get the idea. This guy didn't speak as heavy of a dialect as baldy a few days earlier, but I still had to ask him to re-phrase himself until he found a level of English and Spanish I could make sense of. For the first time I was glad for those required Spanish semesters as an undergrad.)

"My name's Mitch Creek, and I don't belong here. On this ship I mean."

I'd practiced what I was going to say when I finally met someone, but I could already tell it wasn't going to come out right. "I need to speak with someone from uh, the American government, space program, or military, please. If you would." He stared at me through the distance. "If uh, someone from one of those is available, of course."

"Where's Jarrod?" I wondered if this Jarrod knew how much he was missed by people who keep expecting him.

"I don't know a Jarrod. I told some guy named . . . actually, I never got his name, from the *Tsaul Ki*, I believe it was, the same thing. If Jarrod was here, he's not now. I'm here alone, well, sort of, but I have no idea how I got here. I could use some help."

"*Tsaul Ki*? You spoke with Farrius? What'd he say? Where is he?"

"I don't know. Something about telling Jarrod to meet him somewhere in ten seds. I have a feeling Jarrod isn't going to be happy to see this guy, judging by his attitude. I don't know where he is. After giving me the message, he ended the communication. I haven't seen anyone since, in about five days, until you."

"Are you related to Jarrod?"

"Huh?"

"Never mind. Look, we can figure this all out once you get down here." He looked down at something for a moment. "Take pad K-three. I'll meet you there."

"Wait! I don't know how to fly this thing."

"You're serious?"

"Yeah."

He furrowed his eyebrows and gave me an odd look, something between amusement and perplexity. "Okay," he said, looking back down and typing something, "I see you're still in auto-lock; I sent the procedures to your SVN receiver. Just input the remote override authorization, and then once you land, stay inside. I'll be right there."

"'K, thanks." I looked down at one of the smaller displays. Some kind of navigation display had been replaced by an authorization request and an input field. "Oh yeah, what's the remote override authorization?"

The guy looked at me. "You're kidding. You have control of the ship and you don't have the codes? Well, you'd better come up with it in a couple minutes or else your trajectory is going to put you into the sea. After the atmosphere turns you into a streaming ball of fire, of course."

"Is there some kind of override-override code? Some default manufacturer's code or something?"

"Well, Jarrod usually uses r-r-five-o-nine-x-*ma.*"

I paused my finger over the nine, "Wait, what was that last one?"

"*Ma.* You know, *ma.* It's the one on the same key as *mi.*"

"You're just making those up."

"Look, the *katakana* should be on the same keys as the Anglo. See? You only have a minute or so; hurry up."

I huffed in frustration. "I don't speak, whatever, *katakana.*" The Asian characters that shared the keys with letters I recognized were the same kind of hodgepodge I'd found throughout the ship.

He impatiently drew something on a piece of paper and held it in front of the camera. "Looks like this."

I quickly scanned the keyboard and found the character he drew. I continued with the nine, x, ma and submit. The display admonished, "Incorrect code. Enter authorization."

"No good, that didn't work."

"Must have reset them. You get to work guessing, I'll work on trying to crack it from here," and he began typing furiously.

Guessing? Thirty-six numbers and letters, plus capitals, plus symbols, plus a couple dozen or so *katakana*, what chance did I have of guessing? I tried "Jarrod." Nope. Tried in some various capitalization forms. Nope. I tried the name of the ship itself (which I had discovered on that second day), "*Lysander.*" Nope. I tried various words and numbers I'd seen the last few days, yet nothing worked.

"How close are you to that code crack? Some rather scary lights and displays have just come up on the console here, and a sound that I think is meant to really get my attention." I wiped my forehead.

Without glancing up, "Hang on, I'm working on a multidimensional algorithm designed for that ship's A.I. matrix. When it's done, it'll only take seconds to find the right code."

"Doesn't seem like a very secure code, then."

"What was that?"

"Oh, nothing. Mumbling"

I looked at the waiting "Enter Authorization" request, orange writing on a black and red display background. Pulsing slightly and urgently. I'd thought of a possibility, though it seemed too absurd to try; but then, what *hadn't* seemed absurd to me the last few days? I pressed the "submit" button on the keyboard without entering in any characters. The display changed to "Authorization approved," and quickly changed to show various navigation and ship status controls working at making serious automatic changes to my course.

The bearded guy paused what he was doing, looked at something, and then looked at me. "Good job. Figure it out?"

"Yeah, I did, I guess. Not sure what it's supposed to mean. Was pretty easy."

"Well, you have an inside scoop. He's usually impossible with his pass-codes."

"Huh," was all I could think to reply.

"Your ship's picked up my reentry and landing commands, so it should be only a few minutes before you're safe and sound. We'll probably lose communication briefly. See you soon." The screen went black, then refilled with little graphics and numbers related to the moon I was approaching. I noticed from the way I could better see the relative change in distance from the clouds and the ground that I was approaching quickly. I had no idea if entry was going to be rough, but I'd seen enough movies to anticipate it would likely be. I searched around the base and back of the bucket seat for straps, and found them. It only took a moment to get the harness strapped around my chest and waist. I felt secure, but also a little trapped.

The ship started to vibrate. The shaking increased and leveled off to a bearable level. Certainly nothing like I expected–I waited for the other steel-toed boot to drop. A thin, luminescent film, like a layer of northern lights, played over the view-ports as I continued to descend to the moon surface. I gripped the chair's armrests and felt my jaw tighten. I wasn't a fan of amusement park rides; I tended to get a little nervous about unexpected dips, swirls, and loops. And those were all professionally built contraptions intended for safe enjoyment. I had no idea what might happen here, and I didn't think there was a regulation committee that oversaw safe planetary reentries.

It only lasted for a minute before the ship's speed decreased and I was less falling than gliding through the atmosphere. I unclenched my clawed hands and felt a little embarrassed by what ended up being an over-reaction. I was still on a gentle angle with the ground, yet I could now see buildings and structures: a large town clustered on lake edges and large islands in a central gathering. Both the land and the water were indeed black; it hadn't been a trick of the light due to the distance I was when I first noticed the blending obsidian. I was perhaps a few thousand feet up and had a pretty good idea of scale now. The splatter-shaped lake that included dozens of islands of various sizes, fjords on the mainland, and large tentacles of water spread out in all areas, was more of a sea than a lake. The small city occupied just a tiny speck of a corner of it. The expanse of water took up most of the moon's surface as I got closer to it.

As details and shapes defined, and the relative distances of surface objects got larger, I saw I was headed toward one of the island clusters in particular. Short buildings and other structures scattered around, and cars that, while they didn't look at all familiar, didn't look too unusual, either. I saw trucks, vans, and cars moving around on narrow roads. There were boats in the water–all cargo and haulers by the look of them, no pleasure craft. Most of these vehicles were nondescript and very similar in appearance, but the important part was there were people! People driving cars and piloting boats, and as I glided closer, perhaps just a couple of hundred feet from the surface, I saw people walking in and out and around buildings. As a self-professed socially inept geek, I was never so glad to see people in my life.

There was a small grouping of buildings on the edge of one of the smaller islands that circled around expanses of tarmac. Single-engine-looking planes and a couple of odd-shaped craft sat unmoving in various positions. It reminded me of a small town's local airport. I glided over one of the open areas and continued to descend the last hundred feet or so to touch down softly. It became perceptibly quieter. I hadn't realized that all this time there was some constant low frequency sound, but when it cut out after landing, its lack was noticeable. It made me feel like I had to pop my ears though the pressure never changed.

I noticed a new yellow tint of light in the room. A band of yellow had appeared around the top of the cabin's wall about two inches wide. On the main monitor:

–Environmental Assessment complete

<>–N2 79% O2 18% CO2 .08% Total Trace Elements 3%–<>

<>–Atmospheric Pressure 0.91kg/cm2–<>

<>–Ambient Temperature 291.4K–<>

–BioSafety Assessment <>–Level 1.5–<>

–Matching local pressure

–Matching gravitation

Now the pressure changed. I had to make some extreme faces and force air into my nasal cavities before my ears finally popped. The yellow band of light turned green, flashed a few times, and stayed on at a low intensity. As quickly as I could I unstrapped myself from the chair and stood up. And sat back down. I was just a bit heavier and a lot more awkward now. I got back up and made my way through the cockpit and into the entry vestibule. I stood in front of the outer door and noticed the panel next to it had a small green light that read "ACCESS READY."

"Well," I said aloud, with butterflies in my stomach and a light head, "here we go," and reached out and touched the OPEN button. The door slid open; the revealed sun (planet) light bathed me in harsh white light and back-lit a very large man nearly nose to nose with me. I felt something hard jabbed into my stomach, and the guy pushed me back until he was inside, and closed the door behind him. "Hey!" was all I could manage to say.

It was the bearded guy from earlier, who'd got me landed. "Okay, look at me." I did. "Did you kill Jarrod? Do you know where he is?"

"No!" I felt both indignant and shocked. He was pushing his considerable mass against me, hiding the gun he had in my gut. "No, I don't even know who Jarrod is!"

He studied my face. I could smell some odd citrus odor on his breath. He had flecks of gray in his brown eyes. His staring was making me very uncomfortable. Finally, he said, "What's your name?"

"Mitchel . . . Creek."

I don't know what it was that changed things for him, but he said, "Okay, I believe you." He backed up and quickly put whatever he had in his hand in one of the large pockets that were all over his orange overalls. "We only have a couple minutes before the ISR rep gets here. We need a straight story."

"Huh?"

He examined me for another beat. "You really have no idea?"

I shook my head and shrugged. "Until last week I'd only been in a plane a couple of times. I barely even believed there was life on other planets, much less civilizations of English, and whatever, speaking humans beyond my own solar system! We'd even recently shelved our only space shuttle program. In fact, I'm pretty certain I'm a few hundred years into my future, and have no idea how or why."

He blinked at me. "Oh . . . kaayy. Where are you from?"

"Earth," I chuckled. "Also, until last week, my usual answer to that question had been 'Iowa.'"

He seemed to think for a moment. "Hmm. Earth. Here's the thing–the guy from Inter-System Registry is on his way here. Any ship that comes in from outside the system is investigated by an assessor. He's going to link-up to the ship's manifest, and if we're lucky, he'll be too lazy to ask more than a couple questions. But hopefully not so bored he'll have nothing better to do than be too nosy."

"Uhm, listen, why don't we just tell him? That I found myself on this ship a few days ago, no one else was on here, etcetera? I mean, I do have to talk to *someone* . . . official, about what's going on here. And how the heck I'm getting back."

"Now is not the time. Or place. Obviously you really don't understand what's going on here, because bringing up topics that would prompt an investigation just now would not be wise. Not for Jarrod, or you. Not only would you likely not get sent back to Earth, but you'd probably get brought up on charges."

"Charges? For what?"

"Well, arms trafficking, espionage, conspiring with seditious intent, just to name a few."

I felt dizzy again. I'd had a friend who had a brother whose uncle's friend, or something like that, was picked up by local police in Bolivia for some reason as he was just passing through. He wasn't doing anything illegal, but because of a suspicion and a clerk error, he was in prison for five or six years in horrible conditions before the State Department could affect his release. And that was on my home planet! I was who-the-heck-knows how far away from home without so much as even a passport. I wasn't comfortable about doing anything that had the feeling of deceiving some kind of government official, but I also didn't want to get executed for some huge mix-up. I was going to have to trust someone to lead me around here, get me going in the right direction, and it looked like this guy was going to have to be it.

"Okay. So . . . what do I do?"

He had moved to the entry of the cockpit and was looking out the front windows. "Great. For starters, you're Jarrod. Jarrod Sagson, actually–he may ask. You're carrying a shipment of . . . " he looked down at some hand-held device he was carrying, "medical spore protegens. For the far colonies. Your bill of lading looks in order, so I don't think he's going to doubt it. Unless he's an idiot, I seriously doubt he's going to open up the crates to check. Okay so far?"

I was trying to remember Sagson, spores, far colonies, and don't-open-crates. "Yeah, I think so. But uh, I think we really don't want him looking in on the crates, more than you know."

He swung around to me, eyebrows raised, "Why, exactly?"

I went over to the cargo bay door I hadn't touched since that first day I saw the body. I opened it and the lights came on, slowly flickering to life. I gestured for the big fellow to go on in. He stepped past me and walked right up to the strange device that came up to our chests. He leaned down, hands on his knees, and peered at the collage of parts, almost as if he could suss out its meaning. "This is fascinating. This, right here," pointing at something blue and striated, "is a prototype phase converter. I read about it on one of the underground tech journals. This thing is capable of multiplying the energy from minute gluon disruption to. . . ."

"Yeah, even better," I pointed to the crate nearby. He looked up at me, stood, and followed my gaze.

Keeping an eye on me, he walked over to it. "What's in there?"

"I'll spare you the shock *I* had. It's a body." His eyes widened, and his face began to contort. "Hold on, I had nothing to do with it! It was in there when I woke up on this ship. And I'm pretty sure it's not Jarrod. I think."

He reached down and pulled open the crate. I kept in a position that allowed me to avoid being able to see inside. The guy stood there for a moment then leaned inside and worked around at something.

I had stayed back at the bay door, but the smell came at me as bad as I could have imagined. I flew to the main ship's door and opened it, letting back in the glaring light, and the fresh air. I leaned against the edge and took in deep breaths.

The sound of scraping caught my attention. I looked back in the cargo bay and saw the guy moving crates around. He'd rotated the one with the body around so the door wasn't visible and was pushing another in front of it. I went back in and helped him move a couple more of the beaten up boxes. He then went over to the device and tried to pull it toward the back of the bay. It didn't budge. He tried to push it while I pulled, and there was no give. "We don't have time for this," he huffed, and started opening various crates until he found a large empty one. "Help me lift this." We lifted the crate up and over the device, then moved a couple of crates next to it so the open door of the one over the contraption couldn't be seen.

He then moved, faster than would I have thought a person with his girth could, to a computer console in the wall. He pushed a few graphics on the screen and I felt air rushing through the bay. "That can't get rid of it, but it might make the smell less noticeable."

He took a breath while looking around the room, examining it for any visible incriminating signs, and nodded. He looked at me then offered his hand. "I'm Frankletti." I took his sizable fist. "When we get a moment, after he's gone, we can discuss what to do about getting you out of all this. But, for now, we need to get past this roadblock."

He squinted his eyes at me and asked, "Sure you and Jarrod aren't related?"

I sighed. "Like I said, I don't even know him."

"Oh, that reminds me, speak as little as possible. You sound like either an ancient past recreationist or a hick who'd just walked out of the mines of one of the Proxi-Cent reservations." I just gaped at him half-comprehending, but in retrospect, I figure that's about what he said.

Just then, a voice called up from outside the main door, "Hello?"

Frankletti said, "Okay, let's do this." He winked at me. "Good luck." The fact that needed to be said made me feel more uncomfortable.

I bounded to the door and met a short, middle-aged man wearing a rumpled shirt, slacks, and something like a Mississippi string tie. Around his neck was a long lanyard with an ID badge at the end showing the same tired face that sat atop a very similar-looking rumpled shirt. "Officer Rice, ISR. And you're . . . ?"

Jumping right in with nervous energy I said, "Jarrod," and nearly forgot the last name. I was about to try to say it but knew almost instinctively, in that fraction of a second that I'd delayed in mentioning it, it would look odd if I added it, so I went with "Captain." And a wan smile. Rice must not have detected anything unusual in my response as he was looking at his handheld as he walked into the ship. I looked over at Frankletti, and he raised an eyebrow at me.

"What's your cargo? Where's it stored?" Rice continued.

I turned back to him and said "Spores. Er, medical spores meant for the far colonies, right in here," I said, indicating the open door to the hold. It occurred to me just then that Frankletti had said something about arms trafficking. Aside from one body and one strange device that could have been a weapon, or a food processor, I really had no idea what was actually in those boxes. They really could be weapons for all I knew. Officer Rice was scribbling something on his handheld's display, and then looked up at Frankletti.

"Who're you?"

"Max Frankletti. Plat-sys sub-manager. I came on board to check a possible xenon gas leak initial scans picked up." Rice gave him a furrowed eyebrow look. Frankletti continued, seeming to intuit his question, "We met a couple of weeks ago at the comptroller's office. I was filing a claim for equipment reimbursement. You were waiting in the one comfy chair. We briefly spoke about the fluoro-blasts on Cygnus-2. Stunning display and all."

"Oh that's right. I thought you looked familiar. I just transferred here last Cycle and haven't gotten used to all the center's employees."

"Well, no problem. You all work in the complex mainly, and I stick to the platforms." Frankletti smiled charmingly. While I was actually a little miffed at being left out, and I wanted to get this over with quickly, I figured the banter was fine. All the better to get Officer Rice to not think anything suspicious.

Rice stepped into the cargo hold, "Well, let's get this over with, then. By the way, *is* there a gas leak?" He looked to Frankletti and me alternately.

Frankletti answered, "Oh, no. It must have been a glitch in the scan." In the vernacular, he added, "Careful's yesterday's wish, *acuerdo?*" Which I interpret to mean: "Never can be too careful, am I right?"

"No, guess not." He sniffed the air, curling his lip. "What's that smell then?"

Frankletti stepped forward, "That's that refrigerant coil you'd mentioned, Jarrod?"

"Oh, right," I said, taking the hint. "Yeah, one of my food cooling storage coils went out on the trip. A whole day's worth of food, bad. Been pretty dodgy there for a while, thought I'd have to eat the spores," I chuckled. Frankletti closed his eyes and lowered his head.

Rice cocked his head at me, then shrugged and blew air out his nose a couple of times in annoyance and continued over to one of the crates. Frankletti exhaled and mouthed "Stoppit" at me. Rice lifted his handheld up to the sticker on one of the crates, and a thin red light like a grocery checkout scanner's reflected off the solid black strip on the crate. The handheld beeped, and Rice read the results. "Twenty crates?"

"Yeah, twenty," I said with certainty. Rice started counting himself, pointing at each one with his handheld's stylus as he went. I leaned against the doorway and tried to look casual while he counted. I looked back at Frankletti and he shrugged noncommittally. So far so good, I guess.

After he finished counting, he wrote something on his handheld's display and then stopped to read something. After a moment, he started looking around the hold, at the walls, the ceiling, the large hatch in the floor. I kept my eye on the area of the floor where I had first noticed the drops of blood. It had been days ago so I wasn't exactly sure where the visible pattern was, and I was pretty sure the crates we had moved around now covered it, but at any moment I expected him to lean over in that area like I did.

Finally, he turned to me. "Is this hold certified to transport potentially dangerous bio-material?"

I ignored my prickling scalp and continued to lean casually on the wall and gave a calm look around. He'd said that almost entirely in plain English, so I risked a reply, "Yeah. It was uh, retrofitted not too long ago." I hoped the addition of some information would sound more credible, but short enough that my ign'ant "hick" English wouldn't be too obvious. (I had as much of an idea if the hold was certified as I did that I wouldn't wake up tomorrow on some strange spacecraft in some unknown part of space.) I repressed the urge to glance at Frankletti. I also had considered throwing a little Spanish in, but I figured my ridiculous English would be better than partial and possibly incorrect use of the lingua franca. I hadn't yet figured out how Spanish had taken over many of the function words while many Asian languages infused the verbs and nouns and many short phrases. Sounding archaic was probably better than ending up sounding as if I was making up a dialect.

"You have the ship's dry dock log?" he asked.

I could only shrug and nod as if saying "Well yeah, of course," because I just didn't trust myself to actually speak anymore.

Officer Rice looked at the hold's walls again and said, "Well, that's alright. Everything looks in order." I was incredibly relieved to hear that; I didn't think my body could handle another adrenaline dump and remain standing still. "How long will you be staying on Gadreus?"

"Oh," I glanced over at Frankletti; he remained stoic. "A couple of days only. Need to resupply, uh, stretch my legs, you know." I tried Frankletti's charming smile. I don't think it worked as well on me, but it seemed to satisfy Rice.

"Alright." Rice started for the main door. "Be sure to check in with the B-of-T office for your permit if you plan on leaving the pad complex. Welcome to Gadreus; enjoy your stay." And, like that, he disappeared into the light outside.

"Well, honestly, that went a hell of a lot better than I could have expected," Frankletti said. "So," he said, turning back to me as he closed the cargo bay door behind us, "we have some work ahead of us." He went forward into the cockpit. I looked out the entry door, blinking at the bright light. I realized it wasn't all that bright out there, not compared to a sunny Earth day. The light was actually about the same as a cloudy day and was coming from the planet that dominated a quarter of the sky. I had no idea if it was generating the light or reflecting it from a sun, but it was much brighter than the very dim, perhaps cozy, light of the inside of this ship.

As my eyes adjusted, I looked at the low buildings that surrounded our landing pad and the handful of other landing pads that formed a giant honeycomb shape on the ground. There were trucks and carts and four-wheelers speeding around from place to place. People in coveralls, some with hard hats, here and there loading and unloading and doing unknown things underneath ships. Other people in various dress doing their own maintenance on ships or speaking in animated gestures to people in coveralls. I noticed a few people in dark uniforms carrying some kind of gun on a strap strolling around or standing by a door.

A static-y, roaring sound above me caught my attention, and I watched as another ship, a couple of pads away, descended from the sky to land gently on the colorfully marked pad. Small jets of steam or gas exploded out of holes along the bottom. A truck with a cargo bed trailing behind it drove up to the newly arrived ship.

"Hey, Jarr–, I mean Mitchel, come in here," Frankletti called from the cockpit.

"Mitch," I said joining him.

"The ship's logs are pretty *completa baka*."

"What do you mean?"

"I mean, here, look at this."

I leaned over to the screen he'd indicated. It was some kind of three-dimensional display of squares with text in grids with colored cells layered on top of each other with various transparencies. "That's very nice, but I have no idea what I'm looking at."

"See," he said, pointing to one of the layers, "The ship left Pertha-4, a colony about four systems away from here, a few standard weeks ago. It took a twenty-sed trip even farther from the civ-core to some place marked in the log only by its galactic coordinates, then left the same day. It travels for about two days, and then the next entry is for about five days ago, at a position impossibly farther away than it should have been able to travel in that time."

"That's when I awoke in the cargo hold."

"Well, what happened?" Frankletti leaned back in the chair with the sound of creaking leather. "According to the logs, the *Lysander* took what should have been a four week trip in a couple of days. There's about twenty or thirty missing days in the log. Nothing in the captain's log, nothing in the systems' logs. There should be thirty days of hundreds, if not thousands, of entries indicating fuel levels and power levels and atmosphere status checks and sensor checks and about a hundred other automatic events that get logged–and they're not here."

"Were they erased?"

"That's just it, I don't think so. See, look at this," he pointed to a monitor filled with numbers and letters in regular-spaced intervals.

"Again, no idea what that is."

He looked at me a little shocked. "That's standard Uni-SLOL. Even kids not forced to attend CASS regulated schools learn what this is."

"Hello, remember, Earthling, hundreds of years in the future, don't belong here."

He sighed. "Ah yeah, okay, this is the core data collection for the logs. According to the galactic standard timestamps, the missing days don't even exist. It's like one minute the ship is one place, then a day or two of missing data, and then the timestamps come back in sync but for a position that should be weeks away, not a couple of days. See this section here shows the presence of data for that period. Data was collected, logged, but doesn't appear to exist."

"What's that mean?"

"It means, I need to analyze the data to see what this information is. It could be encrypted, it could be misformatted, it could just be garbage. But it whatever it is, it can provide us with an idea of what happened."

I looked at all the characters on the screen, seeing if I could make some sense out of it. It was completely random gibberish to me. "What about the guy back in cargo? How can we find out who he is?"

"His name's Jon Ronald," Frankletti said distractedly as he typed furiously.

"What? How do you know?"

"Name badge." He reached into one of his large pockets and drew out a plastic card with a small picture of the living Jon Ronald and the name "Ronald, Jon H." along with a thin black stripe, the title "Research Technician - Level 6," and a symbol that looked like three intertwined triangles in cobalt blue. "That was on him. I didn't find a wallet or anything."

"Great! Maybe we can search some . . . what do you have? I mean, does the Internet still exist? Some kind of network of interconnected computer systems providing unlimited data access?"

He paused to look at me curiously, "Yeah, something like that. It's called, 'The Net,'" he said ominously, then cracked a smile and chuckled. He turned back to resume typing. "Actually, the local systems are called 'Nets'; the connected Nets are called 'Pansys.' But, anyway, we can't just go asking about a Jon Ronald. The Net is generally monitored. And if he's been reported missing or connected to a crime, and since he doesn't look like some anonymous *pulube*, he probably has been and we go making information requests about him, it could get us involved in uncomfortable ways."

I plopped back against the door frame of the cockpit. "Great. So what do we do? He obviously has answers. Well, okay not he himself, being dead and all. But, maybe, I don't know, where he worked, last place he was seen, all that detective stuff.

"In fact, speaking of which," I continued, "why *not* go to the police or law or whatever about this?" I stood up next to Frankletti and made sure I had his attention. "I haven't done anything wrong. I didn't kill anyone, steal anything. I'm caught up in something weird and not my doing. The . . . law, government, whatever, will have the resources to figure this out and send me home."

Frankletti slowly turned and penetrated his stare through my eyes, making sure *he* had *my* attention, "Are you absolutely certain about that? Absolutely sure? You have no idea what happened, so you say?"

I nodded weakly. "In fact, I can't quite remember very well what the last thing I do remember is, before the waking up here part. It's kind of a fog."

"Then you can't be certain that you *didn't* have anything to do with killing that guy, or making Jarrod missing, or whatever else illegal is wrapped up in this, can you?" I shook my head. "And even if you are one hundred percent guiltless, you don't know what the officials are like. At best, you'll be arrested just for being in a suspicious circumstance, and the bureaucracy will probably keep you in a cell until there's some agreement about what they should do with you–which may never happen. Even if the right people hear about your story, they probably won't be able to get past the system to convince the CASS that you're not either a criminal or insane, and nothing will happen to explain your circumstances or get you home." I was deflated. I leaned back against the wall with my arms crossed, looking at the floor. He continued, "And to be honest, I'm not convinced you're *not* a criminal and/or insane, but I'm giving you a bigger chance than the officials ever will."

"Alright. I get it. *Entiendo. Verstanden. Je* freakin' *comprends.* So what do I do?"

"Well, I need to send this data to my system in the office to better work on it. I'll get a couple of guys to clean out the cargo bay. In the meantime, you browse the gift shop. Maybe you can find a nice mug to take home with you," he said, smiling. I deigned a courtesy smile.

Frankletti wrapped up some business at the keyboard, got up, then led me out. "Jarrod and I go way back. I want to know what happened to him, and his ship, almost as bad as you'd like to go home." We started down the short set of stairs to the tarmac. The smell of fresh air mixed with oil and a surprising hint of coriander, of all things, was a nice change from the stuffy ship. "I've ways of asking questions, getting information, that doesn't risk drawing unwanted attention. Well, a lot *less* risk."

I turned around to look at the ship I'd been inside of for five days. It wasn't much: a few odd shapes with odd angles and juttings somehow stuck together to form something that looked a lot like a foil-wrapped semi truck. Nevertheless, I had gotten so used to being inside of it, imprisoned more or less, that the welcome taste of being outside made me surprisingly uneasy. It was a starkly fresh reminder that I'd never been here before, didn't know where I was, and had no idea how to get home. I half considered running back inside the ship and grabbing Mom's flashlight.

We went into one of the rough, weather-beaten buildings and I could smell ozone and electricity. It was also much warmer than outside, which had felt like a cool autumn day. We went past a desk where a woman wearing her blond hair in a ponytail appeared to be helping someone open a crashed program. I guess some things never change. Frankletti led me down a hallway painted gray-green, past people with whom he'd exchange a nod and quick greeting, through a door and down a flight of stairs. The last door had "Systems Control – Area K" stenciled on it, along with what was probably the same thing in Asian characters.

"Say," I asked Frankletti, "on the ship and around here, that *katakana* you mentioned? It's not Japanese, is it? I mean, I don't know any Asian languages, but I'm sure I've seen characters from like Korean, and I think Hindi and Filipino. Tagalog, or something like that."

"I have no idea what you just said," he replied as he opened the door and led me into a large dark room divided into many cubicles and partial offices.

"The stuff that's not English. What language is that?"

"It's called 'Asian.'"

I looked around at the various people, many wearing earpieces or headsets, typing at computers and gesturing on holographic displays.

Frankletti appeared to be leading me to a row of doors at the back of the room.

"What I'm saying is it looks like a mixture of various Asian languages."

"No, it's simply called 'Asian.' I guess most people you'll meet talk like Rice and I do, but some people speak in all Asian."

"Actually, that Farrius guy spoke a lot more thickly than you do."

"Yeah, I suppose it's different depending on what systems you're from and how much you travel. Some colonies and settlements speak languages no one anywhere else knows. Usually some otherwise dead language from the time of Earth."

Oblivious to the implied meaning of what he'd said, I asked, "I guess I can see Spanish and English merging, but how can several such diverse languages become one?"

Frankletti shrugged, "Who knows. Not my thing."

He opened the door labeled "M. Frankletti – Platform Systems Sub-Manager." He said, "Alright, here we are." Then said, "Light," and the room went from pitch black to slightly above regular black. He sat at a semi-circular desk with a couple of monitors and a bank of small screens. He began typing and gesturing away.

"You guys like it pretty dark down here, huh."

"Hm-hm."

I eased myself on the old pleather couch against one wall. "So, I was just thinking: You'd mentioned 'arms trafficking' earlier. Seemed like a rather specific example of something I could get in trouble for."

Frankletti looked at me sidelong. "Hey, this might take awhile. Actually, it might take all day, or two, depending on whether it's just garbage data or encrypted. Why don't you get some real food, look around a bit."

I sat up straight, "Is that safe? I mean, you convinced me about the danger of getting noticed by the . . . officials; should I just be walking around here?"

"Safest thing. You're just in an industrial supply hub, people all over minding their business, waiting for loads. No one's going to pay you any attention. Wear this badge and don't make any trouble, and you won't *see* any trouble." I took the plastic badge he'd retrieved from a desk drawer. It said "Class A Transient Permit."

"Uhm, where can I go around here?"

"Pretty much any place that doesn't say 'Do not enter.'"

"Like this room?"

"It's keyed to let you in here, of course."

"Of course." I examined it for some kind of bar strip or chip or anything that indicated it somehow could control where I was let in. "Oh, I don't have any money," I realized. "I mean, I do, but, not that I think would be good here."

He sighed and began typing something. Presently a small sheet of paper whispered out from a machine in the corner. "Take that up to the Receiving Office. First door past where we came in. They'll issue you a credstick with the refunded deposit for the equipment you just returned."

"But I didn't return any equipment."

"They don't know that," he smiled. "Then ask how to get to the caf' from there. Just come on back down here once you get bored."

I stood up and took the paper from the printer. It looked like an excellent example of a Standard Form. "Alright, back in a while, I guess."

"Mm-hm."

CHAPTER FOUR

I made my way back up to the first level and found the right office. I hesitated at the door, sure that a couple people who passed me looked back, curious about the guy standing in front of a closed door. I knew in my gut that I'd go in there, a question would be asked, and I'd answer wrong, and the Jig would be Up.

Instead, I went in and handed the guy behind the desk the form. He asked me to sign a slate that was nothing more than a piece of clear plastic with a rendering of a form (I remembered just in time to sign Jarrod's name instead of my own), and I was handed back a small square of plastic. He gave me directions to the café and I was out of there in under three minutes.

I found the café in a connected building that you could get to either from the outside pad or a corridor a short way from the Receiving Office. It was larger than I expected, probably servicing several pad terminals. It had floor-to-ceiling windows along one wall, an automat-like region along most of another wall, and a small area of fresh food at the end. It smelled of mostly fried chicken with an undercurrent of something like cabbage, or was it Brussels sprouts? And cumin. The lighting for the dining area came mostly from the windows. There were about twenty or thirty people in there in various dress–a lot of overalls, flight-suits, and work clothes. A lot of casual clothes that looked just like what I'd expect at what was the equivalent of nearly every large interstate truck stop. Trousers, jeans, t-shirts bearing various unfamiliar designs or slogans, hats that were a lot like ball caps and a couple that looked like Greek fishermen's caps. There were a few people in nicer looking clothes, more suited for an office environment, seated at a couple of tables.

I grabbed a tray and some utensils and passed a couple of people browsing the automat on my way to the mini-buffet. A man dressed in kitchen whites was busy stirring a fresh batch of some pasta into a large bowl of green-tinted pasta salad. The guy looked up at me, nodded, and said, "*Ganda su tali*, hey?" Which, literally meant, "Can I dirty your dish?" But, at that point, all I heard was meaningless syllables. I gave what was becoming my standard stunned look and said, "I'm sorry, I don't understand."

In a thick accent, he replied, "Oh, you're a light year or two from home, aren't ya?"

"You've no idea."

"I haven't heard that thick a' old tongue since I took a stay at Proxima C'. That where you from?"

I shrugged. "Near there. So, *you* speak . . . English . . . fluently."

"Well, it's good for me to exercise the old Earth-speak, you know. It's not like it's a dead language or anything! I mean, sure, some of your anti-social runners and haulers will tell ya Earth-speak is dead, or at least just for rock-rooted scum in the backwood worlds–but you'll never find a trader or pirate worth their salt who doesn't speak it fluently, know what I'm talkin' about?" He smiled and adjusted his cap. "So, I was sayin', what can I getchya?"

"Oh. Just looking for the moment." I scanned the display of dishes and found many recognizable ingredients. Breaded chicken pieces, (and come to find out, it actually was a species of chicken), a few pasta salads with different combinations of vegetable pieces, a steaming tray of meatballs swimming in a gravy, a dish that looked just like green beans and bacon pieces (although I found out later that it contained neither), and a few dishes that were quite unusual and seemed to have a preponderance of creamy paste and tofu chunks.

"You know, that chicken looks pretty good. I haven't had any in a long time." The sense recall of hot chicken grease and crunchy breading, the smell of it, made my saliva glands ache from over production. "I've been eating cereal and pastes and cardboard for the last week; all of this looks so good."

"Yeah, I hear ya. I started out on a CASS transport, never saw planet-side for months, but we got real food a couple times a week. Then I worked on this dark hauler for a few years; saw more barren rocks than I could count, and went months between meals that didn't smell like molten carbon-pulp. I tell you what, that's a smell that never gets out of your skin, know what I'm talkin' about?"

"Oh, yeah, absolutely." Of course, I had no idea what he was talking about, then. I would eventually.

"So," I continued salivating, the smell, pungent though it was, making my stomach rumble so that the table full of mechanics at the far end had to have heard it, "gimmie a couple pieces of the chicken, a few of the meatballs, a couple scoops of . . . that, and . . . that."

"Hey, payday, huh? Yeah, real meat and girls, usually in that order, when a guy from off-world gets a cred'fill. Say, if you want to know a good joint, check out Moonlights about five k's down 2nd Street. They got this one dancer, Jasiqua . . . man oh man."

I looked up from the fragrant gravy soaked meatballs he'd just placed on my tray. "Uh, yeah, sounds great, but, not here long. You know. Gotta get right back." I tried to smile.

"Ah, I hear yeah. You can be on a run that takes a whole month, but the corp won't let a guy have an hour's break."

"Yeah, well, ya know. So, thanks," I gestured with the tray as I moved to take my leave.

"Hey, have a good run, guy!"

"Yeah, you t– heh, you know what I mean." I walked away from the counter, shaking my head at my social gaffe, and moved toward the checkout island. The whole place reminded me so much of a hospital cafeteria, I had almost forgotten exactly where I was. A quick look out the wall-length windows revealed a band of pale blue sky above the buildings, and the faded image of a color banded alien world hanging above us. I remembered quickly.

A youngish kid, maybe early twenties, late teens, was manning the register. He was ringing up someone else who had gotten a couple of items from the fresh food bar. I was able to see on the display "32 CR" before the customer waved a credit stick, similar to my own, across a pad to pay the balance. When I got there, the kid dutifully tallied the items on my tray, "Two chicken pieces, meatballs, fugu salad, veggie medley," and hit the total button: 68 CR.

I doubted a meal could possibly suck my credstick dry (but I was a little nervous after what the cook back there had said about it must have been payday), so I asked, "Is that a lot, really?"

"Huh?" The kid looked unused to being noticed and acknowledged by customers.

"That amount. I'm new to this . . . region, and really don't know the exchange rates." I thought that'd be a pretty safe non-lie.

"'Exchange rates'? You're paying with a credstick, right? We don't accept local currencies."

I'd gotten the stick out by then and waved it where the person before me did. Thankfully a little green light indicated all was good, and the display changed from "Payment Pending" to "Thank you!" I stammered, "Yeah, sorry. A little confused. No, I was just wondering if sixty-eight credits is a lot for this food?"

"Hey, I don't set the prices, my manager does. It's what it is here. It's probably a lot less elsewhere; we have to ship most of our fresh stuff in."

I picked up the tray and headed out to the tables. "No, it's okay. I was just curious. Thanks."

"Oh, hey, if you want something to drink, use bay fourteen. Fifteen's kinda off and on."

"Great. Thanks again." I'd just realized I hadn't gotten anything to drink and looked around. I felt a little self-conscious, standing there, like I was back in school and looking for a place to sit that wasn't either going to offend one group by my nearness, or associate myself with another group I didn't want to be associated with, and so I'd just stand there while critical eyes looked me over. Fortunately, I was just being paranoid. No one in the cafeteria was paying me any attention. The two groups of office workers were discussing something in hushed tones, some guys who reminded me of truckers were laughing at something one of them had said, the people sitting by themselves were mainly looking at their meals.

I sat my tray of tantalizingly fragrant food down at a smaller table and looked back at the automat wall. The last couple of sections were drinks. I walked up to them and waited for a woman in a light gray dress suit to make her selection. It gave me a chance to look over the couple dozen palm sized buttons with names and brands to choose from. I didn't recognize any of them, although their logos looked strange and familiar at the same time. Like companies from my time that had simply evolved and mutated into new marketing images. Some of the selections were just a word or two in striking colors, but there were a few buttons that were holograms, 3-dimensional images, and animations. I found one that said in a type smaller than the brand name "Sparkling orange soda." A description so un-alien and normal it had to be good.

I inserted my credstick in the slot and hit the button. Nothing happened. I was certain that's what the woman before me had done–simply insert credstick and push selection. Nothing. I looked around the credstick slot for any kind of "exact coins only" kind of display, and found a label with the number 15 on it. I sighed and moved down to the next bay of beverages and looked for the orange soda on that machine.

Not finding it, I decided on another item and was about to inset the credstick when I heard someone behind me say, "Mister Sagson? Jarrod Sagson?"

I turned and faced two men and a woman dressed in uniforms like that I saw earlier on the pad. These three had pistols on their belts and not the submachine gun looking things the ones outside were carrying. They had very serious expressions.

I hesitated for a minute. These were the law in these parts, and I've always believed you never lied to the police. Ever. They would find out, if they didn't already know, and everything would get much worse for you. The results could be even worse, here, where there might *not* be such things as Miranda Rights. Or, perhaps it was not so bad in that these might just be security guards and have no real and lasting power. They didn't have sleeve patches, though the guns didn't ease my mind any. I decided to ride the fence. "Why?" I replied.

"Mister Sagson, you're to come with us, please." The "please" didn't sound sincere. "We have some questions for you."

"Has something happened? Officer?"

The apparent leader of the trio grabbed my upper arm, not gently, and urged me toward the doorway. "Don't make this difficult."

"But, my food!" I had no idea what else to say. I didn't know what was going on, but I did know that I paid 68 credits for the first real meal I could've had in a week, and there it was, going to go to waste. The other patrons who hadn't noticed me earlier certainly did then.

"Okay, okay, I'm going. Easy." I stumbled forward and started for the double doors leading back out to the corridor.

CHAPTER FIVE

We walked through hallways and through a couple of doors and around a few corners, one of the officers in front and the other two behind. Everyone we passed would step aside, sometimes pretending not to notice us, sometimes stopping to watch us pass.

My surprise eased into a sickening fear. I'd never been arrested before, or even "politely" asked to answer some questions by any police. Once, in college, I attended an impromptu party in the woods just outside of the city. Some cops came by and asked the group of us some questions, what we were doing, how long we were planning on being there, were there any minors among us, and the like. Even at the time, I was certain that our complete and utter silence and funereal appearance, aside from the two guys who were doing all the answering for us, was extremely suspicious. However, the cops must have had better things to do because they just told us to be careful and went along their merry.

This was quite a bit different. My mind was racing, on only a couple of pistons, trying to think of how much I should tell them. Should I tell them everything? Nothing? How much did they know? Was Frankletti somehow involved? Did he turn me in? Was there something to turn me in *about*? Was he caught, too? Was there something he was worthy of catching for? I kept trying to come up with ways to answer certain questions and constantly stopping myself with the advice: *just see what happens.*

We came to another attached building (it appeared as though the entire complex was made out of attached buildings, and not just one giant building like your standard airport terminal, or dozens of unconnected buildings like a sea port), with the sign over the ante-corridor reading "Bureau of Transportation – Management Enforcement Division," and eventually to a door marked "Holding Room B."

Evidently, holding rooms across the universe must all look the same, and they all look like the holding room from your average basic-cable cop drama. One of them told me to sit down and wait. I did. And I did some more. I kept thinking of that chicken I was missing, punctuated by thoughts of prison rape.

Eventually, the door opened and in walked a middle-aged man in a slightly better-looking version of the same uniform as the previous three. He sat in the chair opposite me and pressed a couple of buttons on a small set of controls at the table's edge. "This is Captain Escatado comma Jonah of the M.E. Division of the Bureau of Transportation. It is . . . fourteen fifty-two local time, zero three zero three eff tee, on the third of Tenthmonth, one one two local, twenty-three sixty-two dash zero two dash sixteen CASS Standard. This begins the interrogation. Please state your name."

"What? Sorry, I wasn't listening. I mean, I'm sorry. What?" So many numbers, I kept trying to replay the sentence in my head, trying to suss out the individual parts. Local, standard, CASS. The cook earlier said something about CASS.

"What is your name. For the recording." It didn't sound like a question.

"Oh. Am I under arrest?"

"You are being confined for questioning." Captain Escatado casually sat back and crossed his arms. He was being the patient officer who wasn't going to say more than he had to.

I leaned forward, "What did I do? What am I being confined *for?*"

"Let's get the formalities out of the way, get the tedious stuff done, what do you say? Then we can have a nice conversation, and I can answer your questions. Just state your name."

"There are some who call me Jarrod."

"Jarrod what."

"Jarrod Sagson."

The captain sighed, "And is that what you call yourself?"

I had no idea how far I was ready to play this game, nor how much further it *could* be played. "On occasion." All I knew was when I screwed myself into this terrible situation, getting worse by the minute, I could give myself points for not lying. If that counted for anything.

"Okay, so friendly isn't going to be the option, eh?" The captain leaned forward to match me. "Your ship has been impounded. It's secured, and I have officers combing every inch of it. And you know what they have found so far?"

I didn't move a muscle; my pounding heart may have made it appear as though I did. I could feel my head pulse and blood rush through my ears. He stared me down for seconds, maybe a minute. I didn't say a word. I didn't think I could speak at that moment if I wanted to. So soon. Everything was boiling over so soon. Five days of interminable purgatory, and then within a couple of hours everything was blowing up.

Maybe this was it. This was what had to happen. There was no need to deceive; I hadn't done anything wrong. And I was certain, as always, the government would have the resources to make things right. Right? "My name isn't Jarrod. It's Mitchel Creek. And I had nothing to do with that dead guy, I swear!"

The captain sat back in the chair looking pleased. "There, you see? A conversation." He pulled out a cigarette and offered me one from the foil-looking pack. Of all the things I'd seen so far, that may have been the most unexpected. Being an ardent non-smoker, I had been certain that one day cigarettes would be eradicated. Within my own lifetime perhaps. Here they were, centuries later, still hanging on. Tenacious little buggers. I shook my head.

"So, now." The cigarette seemed to self-light as he initially drew in on it. I had to admit, that was somewhat clever. "The image analyzers didn't pick up on you right off, since you'd changed your face, obviously. And a good job, too–the analyzers didn't pick up on any remnants from the alterations. So, Jarrod, what brings you to Gadreus?"

"You're not listening to me. My name is Mitchel Creek. I found myself on that ship five days ago, with a dead body, and no idea how–"

The captain interrupted, "But what I don't understand is why you were so careless, when surely you must know you're a wanted man."

"I'm from the past, dammit!"

"What did you say?" I seemed to finally get his attention.

We were then both interrupted by a loud, oscillating siren and the flash of a strobe light hidden somewhere in the ceiling tiles. "What the holy–" the captain began, looking up and around.

"Your attention please," came a pleasant and calm female voice from some speaker that also couldn't be seen, "please make your way calmly and quickly to the nearest building exit. Illuminated arrows should be visible along the floor directing you to the nearest exits. A fire has been detected inside the building. This is not a drill. . . ." She began to repeat the recorded message.

"Mother of–" the captain stood up, torn between following this new line of conversation that suddenly piqued his interest, and checking on this alert. He started for the door with a window of frosted glass. "Wait right here."

"If there's a fire, shouldn't I–"

"I said wait here. If there's a fire, you'll be escorted out."

I took long, deep breaths, trying to detect any trace of smoke. Was that smoke? Or the lingering cigarette.

I twisted around in my seat to get a look out the open door. The captain was in the corridor talking to someone. I saw his hand still on the door, holding it open, and his and someone else's silhouettes through the frosted glass. The recorded announcement recommended avoiding elevators. No reference to avoiding being held by the police during a fire. They should really look into that.

Finally, Captain Escatado leaned back in the room, "You, these officers will take you outside the building. Don't make things worse by giving them any trouble, understood?"

"Aye, aye, Cap'n."

He sneered and disappeared down the hall as the door opened and two uniformed officers I hadn't seen on my way here stepped inside. "C'mon, let's go. Think we can do this without using cuffs on you?"

"Yeah, yeah, no trouble. No problem." I got up and started out the door. The officers got in front and behind me.

"So," I said casually, "what's the hubbub? Something blow up? We in any danger?"

"I'm sure everything's fine. Just keep moving. Quickly now."

We started a brisk walk down corridors different from the ones that brought me there. We passed a few people on their brisk way out, but no one paid us any attention. Finally, we came to a maintenance door with a security pad. One of the officers punched in a code on the keypad, and the door unlocked with a serious click.

"Uhm, the floor arrows are pointing that way." They ignored me and escorted me past the door. I caught the one behind me making a furtive look up and down the hallway we exited before closing the door behind us. A long row of thin, rectangular lights, partially hidden behind pipes and wire conduits as wide as my leg, lit the length of the passage. "I don't mean any disrespect, officers, but . . . this seems a little odd."

"Not yet," one of the officers cautioned in a hushed tone. I was having doubts about the intentions of these police officers.

They led me on down the hallway to a descending vertical ladder off to one side. One of the officers climbed down, then the other urged me to follow. I gave him a quizzical look, and he responded, "Go on–we only have a few minutes." Continuing to look at him, I climbed down the ladder. It went down a tube maybe twenty or thirty feet, then opened into a much larger passageway. It was a maybe fifty-feet tall semi-circle, and on the ground below the ladder was a motorized cart with someone in an orange jumpsuit behind the wheel. "Hurry up! Let's go!" he called out to us.

We finished the descent and barely sat down before the cart went from zero to sixty in the time it took me to land on my butt in the seat. We practically flew through the cavernous passage, banks of fluorescent lights streaking past. I looked over at the officers: one had taken his cap off and the other was holding his on his head. He caught me looking at him, and nodded at me. Confused only began to describe how I felt.

After maybe a minute or two, we entered the rear of a hangar. Larger, more lights, the smell of grease and burning wires . . . and something like burnt Brussels sprouts, again. There were about three or four ships, similar in size or a little larger than the one I came in, in various stages of being dismantled throughout the hangar. Men and women in jumpsuits were here and there doing various things involving lifting something, drilling something, ratcheting something, or filling the surrounding air with sparks. They didn't pay us any attention as we barreled past and around them.

We came to a ship about two or three times larger than the *Lysander* and it appeared to be the only one put together. I saw someone standing at an open door at the rear of the ship, waving at us. It was Frankletti. We came to an abrupt and squealing stop at the end of the metal gangway leading up into the ship and the two police officers hopped out and trotted into the waiting ship. Frankletti called to me, "Hey, are you coming or staying? Prison, laboratory, padded room–they're all fine alternatives to getting on this ship, now."

I vaulted over the side of the cart and looked down the way we came.

Sparks, smoke, the sound of heavy equipment. Through it all I expected to see a cadre of police or soldiers speeding along to catch up with us, but there was nothing like that. I turned and ran up the ramp, the sound of my heavy steps banging against the metal and echoing above the din in the hangar. I ran past Frankletti, who yelled something to the cart driver, and then closed the ship's door, leaving us in a dark alcove illuminated by various flashing colors from controls on the wall beside us.

"Okay, just what in the world–" I started, but he pushed past me and pressed one of the buttons, creating a weird underglow on our faces.

"We're on. Launch now." he commanded someone on an intercom and then ambled deeper into the ship through tight and narrow passages. I stayed close behind him, amazed at how dexterous and light on his feet a man of his size could be. We came to a bare metal door that slid aside at the press of a button and opened into a room that looked a lot like the cockpit on the *Lysander*–if it were five times larger and all the walls, floor, and ceiling were stripped of covering to expose metal struts and wiring. One of my police officers sat in one of the three chairs situated in front of a massive console.

"So let me guess, he's not a cop," I said, indicating the uniformed guy who was now engaged in reading off numbers and statuses while pushing buttons.

"No, he is," Frankletti corrected. "He just happens to be my brother."

The officer paused long enough to nod at me and say, "Officer Joseph Frankletti, second class, at your service. But just call me 'Joseph.' This ship's only big enough for one 'Frankletti' on board." He winked at his brother and went back to work. A slight hum and vibration became more pronounced. I heard the hiss of a release of gas from somewhere in the ship.

The elder Frankletti said, "The other guy's not, though," jutting his chin at the slighter rescuer. "He's Ian, a docking mechanic from Area J, and an on-again-off-again member of my crew."

The other guy who I'd not seen come in and strap into a chair in front of the long console, pressed a button and said to no one in particular, "Stand by for atmo-burn in twenty seconds." His voice echoed, amplified, through the ship. Out the window, I saw the hangar moving away from us and realized we were the ones moving, though I couldn't feel a thing. We were moving out into the open.

Frankletti motioned to a couple of large padded chairs with straps against the wall and said, "You'd better get ready. The first couple of miles can be pretty rough." I sat in one of the bucket seats and messed around with the straps until I finally got the wide strips of what I later found out to be a material called steelprene (still not sure if that's a product name or a scientific name) buckled over my shoulders and around my waist.

I looked around and saw Frankletti had left the room. One of the pilots started speaking through the ship again, "Burn in five, four, three, two . . . and mark." It was surprisingly anti-climactic. I had expected to be pushed back in my seat, smooshed into it, with the skin on my face waving around my skull like in a wind machine. Instead, all I felt was a little vibration and rocking like the first section of a roller coaster as it ratchets up the initial hill. The scene outside the windows belied the rather sedate experience I had inside the ship: The ground rocketed away from us at an amazing, dizzying, gut-dropping speed. The relative lack of expected vibration and movement made the scene out the narrow window that ran around the front of the room seem like a video instead of reality, and that probably saved the floor from getting the contents of my growling stomach.

This reminded me of my poor, carefully selected meal, possibly still sitting untouched, in the cafeteria.

CHAPTER SIX

"I had Kara go get you soon after you'd left the office," Frankletti explained to me after we'd successfully entered Q-thrust. "I'd discovered that the officials had an all-system alert out for the *Lysander* and knew the second it'd landed. It just took some time for the left hand to tell the right hand to find you."

Karayitri, or Kara as she preferred ("Unless you want to swallow your teeth"), was sitting in the chair opposite me in the dingy kitchenette area of the ship. She had her feet up on the table, leaned about as far back as physically possible in the chair before it'd break off its base, and added, "You're lucky Joseph and Ian got to you when they did. An entire detachment of fed Protectors was on their way to you. Then we'd never have been able to get you out."

"Well, thanks, guys," I told them. Ian grabbed something crunchy from a cabinet behind me and went back to the control cabin. "But, you faked a fire alarm, probably breaking some laws there, at least one of you impersonated a cop, and you broke out a prisoner in police custody who was about to be handed over to . . . government officers."

"Don't forget launched a Haz-Mat transport ship without B. of T. authorization, stole five kilotons of earmarked power cells, jammed CASS sensors, and some of us left work without permission," Frankletti smiled.

"Yeah, that, too," I swirled the velvety, yet surprisingly crisp and light, purple drink in the cup in my hands. "But what I mean is, why? Why do all that? Why put yourselves at so much risk?"

"Just the desire to screw with the officials, especially in anything that has to do with Jarrod or his ship, is enough for me to consider breaking a couple laws. Well, I'd consider it," Frankletti grinned large. He leaned forward, "But I found something particular when I saw the alert: Red level. All passengers of the *Lysander* wanted in connection of political terrorism, sabotage of CASS property, and theft of vital intelligence and dangerous experimental research."

"Wha– I– what? That's what?"

"Yeah, I thought so, too." He leaned back in his chair. "I didn't think you were any more a political terrorist than you were an expert pilot." He said, winking.

"So," he continued, "that just seemed to make the mystery of the Jarrod-less *Lysander* all the more intriguing, and all the more reason to keep it out of CASS hands. I knew that once you and the *Lysander* were in their control, especially with charges like these, I'd never find out what happened."

"You have the *Lysander* stored in this?"

"Well, one out of two–it could be worse," Frankletti sighed.

"Oh."

Kara spoke up, "The only way Max here got me to risk my neck like this," she said, pointing a thumb at Frankletti, "was with some going-on about you and time travel or some nonsense."

"Uhm, not to be a jerk, but if it's 'nonsense–'" I started.

"Max here is about as solid a guy as I've ever known. Unless he got a hold of some rancid poly-prot juice, he's not one to go spewing fantasies about time travel. I don't really believe it, mind you; but, if Max says it, I want to see what it's all about."

"So," I turned to Frankletti, "You do believe me, then."

He shrugged. "Look, I'm not one-hundred percent convinced myself."

He gave a look at Kara, who gave a look back. "There's just . . . something going on that's obviously outside 'normal,' know what I mean?"

"Yes. Yes, I very much do."

He chuckled. "Yeah. Well, I'm also not one-hundred percent convinced that you're an angel in all this, either." I started to interrupt, "But, I'm also pretty sure that if you're a party in jacking with the officials in a major way, I want to see how it turns out. Or, kill you myself if I discover you *did* off Jarrod."

"Look! I told you–"

"Yeah, yeah, I know. I'm messing with you," he said, smiling. I wasn't so sure he was.

Ian leaned in through a doorway to the control cabin. "So far so good. Not a blip of anything with wires or fires as far as we can sense. We have enough cells to get to New Torment in four seds." He popped back out.

"'New *Torment*? Sounds nice. But, what about that place that, uh, that guy said to meet him?"

"Farrius and Sandiki? Eh, not important." Frankletti stood up. "We're on our way back where you came, see if we can figure out what happened. We're heading to that location marked in the *Lysander's* log, but we have to make a stop first. Get some things, meet some people."

He stretched his neck side to side and said, "It's pretty late; get some sleep if you can," then walked through one of the other portals out of the dining room-slash-kitchen, his footsteps hardly making a noise on the metal floors.

I looked over at Kara; she looked at me and said, "All I have to say, is you better damn well be from the past, or I'm gonna be real pissed."

She got up and followed Frankletti, whom I heard call back to Kara, "Technically, we're all from the past. . . ."

"You know what I mean, you big *culo.*"

It was suddenly quiet and I had no idea where I was supposed to sleep.

* * *

I sat in the kitchen ("galley," as I was reminded) later that night, munching on a rather dry and colorless yet tasty sandwich I'd made from various ingredients I found. According to the clock in the room I was finally told I could crash in, it was about two a.m. I had no idea according to what planet that time belonged to, but everyone in the ship appeared to be asleep–so I guess time is relative, in a manner of speaking.

That first week-like period of days I'd spent back on the *Lysander* proved to me I wasn't dreaming all this oddity, and that if I was insane and delusional, insanity is tedious. However, just as soon as I was over the shock of that situation, I was suddenly thrust into a whirlwind of moons and spaceports, inspectors and cops, escape, and space again–all in the span of a few hours, reigniting the anxiety and displacement, fear and uncertainty I tried to work through those first few days.

I couldn't sleep. In the dark, with nothing but the quiet hum of the ship, all I could think about was Lori and Chloe. Did they know I was gone? Is time moving on for them as normal? When I get back, *if* I get back, will it be the same time I left or will the same amount of time that has passed for me have elapsed back there? Even more, what with the whole relativity of time thing, I had nothing to relate to. I didn't even know what happened; how I could possibly imagine what conditions surrounded going back, if that was even possible.

If I'd woken up on a ship in the South China Sea, I could plan and consider viable options: Find a way to make it to a port, get a map, find someone who speaks English, find an American embassy or military post, use my credit card to buy a ticket back home, get myself on morning talk shows to tell about my strange journey. The world, *well, better start being specific*, I reminded myself, Earth, was finite. Somehow, some way, I could get back home if lost on Earth. I had nothing I could be so certain about in *this* situation, aside from the fact I was certainly lost, confused, alone, and scared.

In the dark with the quiet hum of the ship, acutely aware of the fact there was the infinite vacuum of space below me, above me, all around me, I felt the fear and uncertainly of cosmic insignificance. I, this whole ship, was *nothing* in the cosmic sense, and there was nothing that required that I should find myself back on solid ground, much less back home, nearly three centuries ago.

So instead of lying there half-asleep with fear amplifying that feeling of one's body being weightless but jerked around with unexpected muscle twitches, I got up and found the kitchen. Galley. Getting my feet moving on something solid, my mind away from drifting thoughts and spirals of anxiety that aimed toward panic, made me feel a bit better. More substantial and less an ephemeral plaything of the infinite. Besides, for being something that was probably ninety-nine-percent preservatives (and please please please not Soylent Green), the faux-ham wasn't too bad.

I sat at a round, off-white table in the roundish, off-white chair of the room-that-wasn't-impressive-enough-to-be-called-a-"galley," finishing my off-white midnight snack, when Ian came in. He was still in his clothes from earlier but this time covered in patches and swaths of grease and grime.

"Hey, you're up late," he said in his slight Spanish accent as he ran his hands under the utility water. I'd later find out that in many ships, they tended to have a system of pure water for consumption and a less-stringently-pure recycling system for water used just for things like cleaning. Recycling water evidently took a lot of ship's energy.

"Couldn't sleep."

"Mmm," he replied.

The sound of chewing in my head, the running water, the hum of the ship.

"So," I said after a while, "what have you been doing?"

"Hmm? Oh, finishing some of the rewiring of the secondary Fabric Tear System. *The Bluerock* was in for maintenance back on Gadreus, and we left kind of in a hurry." He was leaning back on the cabinet and wiping his hands on a rag that was almost as dirty as his hands still were. "Lots to get done, and hopefully before we need to use what isn't finished."

"'Fabric Tear'?" I asked.

"Yeah, the system that tears space for interstellar travel."

"Whoa. 'Tears space'?" I asked.

Ian sat down across from me, excited to be discussing something of interest to him. "Yeah, you know. The FTS. It creates a tear in the fabric of space micrometers in front of the ship."

My head was swimming. "Oh, yeah. Of course," I smirked. "No, no no no. Back up. We're falling through a rip in space?"

"Well, not quite. More like a million-gazillion tears in space in a row," he said.

I raised my eyebrows.

"As you know, tears in the fabric using current technologies last only milliseconds, but that's just enough to get the ship to 'fall' into it at faster-than-light speed. Well, relative to an object *not* falling through the tear, of course." My expression hadn't changed. "Didn't you learn this in a school or anything?" he asked.

"Uh, time traveler here, remember."

"Oh yeah, sorry." He continued, "Okay, it's like this: the anti-matter. . . . No, that's too complicated. Okay, phased neutrinos which we force to interact with dark matter, we. . . . No, that's even more complicated." He sighed and looked pained. "You know what? It doesn't really matter how it's done. What matters is that it results in a tear that lasts only for a millisecond, but that's long enough for the ship to fall into the tear and appear on the other side of it instantaneously. Relative to where we were a millisecond ago. It's the only way, as far as we know, to get past Einstein's speed limit for energy."

"A millisecond isn't instantaneous enough?"

"Oh God no. Not when you're talking about moving a five-hundred meter ship ten or so light years across space. A millisecond is an eternity."

I was balancing on the fence between being fascinated about something I could just grasp (like late night college dorm conversations about the meaning of life) and being overwhelmed (like early morning college math classes). "Okay, so, we move to the other side of a tear in space instantaneously. A gazillion times or so."

"Million-gazillion," Ian smiled.

"Heh, yeah, okay. So, what's that mean? I mean, what does that do for us?"

"Well, it allows us to make the Procyon run in only ten parsecs."

"What?"

"Sorry," he chuckled, "old space navigator's joke." Ian got up and grabbed a bottle of warm fruit juice out of the cabinet. "But that's not too far from the truth. We're in essence making our path to wherever we're going much shorter by constantly falling through tear after tear after tear each microsecond after the next. Put this way, Procyon is about one-and-a-half parsecs, or five light years. Before FTS, the fastest that trip could be made is about, I don't know, a thousand years or so. But with FTS that trip becomes a ten-thousand kilometer fall through space taking only about a week."

"Oh my God."

"Pretty amazing, huh."

"I'll say." I thought about that for a moment, sandwich in my hand completely forgotten. Falling through space. Trips between stars taking only days.

"Wait," I started, suddenly excited. Things had been going so fast the last day or so I barely had time to breathe, and now here was someone that could give me some definite answers–give me some much-needed grounding, so to speak. "Where are we? Right now? Where exactly are we coming from and to? And, God, where the heck is the Earth in all this?"

"Well, we're coming from the Sirius system and heading toward Procyon, actually. And Earth, hmmm," Ian thought for a second, "is somewhere around there," he said, pointing to a spot on the wall of the kitchen.

"Cute," I said.

"Seriously," he laughed. "Yeah, okay, sorry," he said as he slid open a panel on the galley table, revealing a control panel. "Let's see," he pushed a couple keys then sat motionless, except for his eyes, which moved around as if he were looking at something I couldn't see inches in front of his face. "Here we go." A three-dimensional image of a spiral galaxy appeared in the air over the table in front of me, with a little sign reading, "You are here," pointing to a dot in one of the spiral arms. I gave him a look. "Oh come on," he pleaded, "that never gets old."

"You know, it actually does," I chided, but smiled, anyway. As anxious as I was to get some answers that I knew I was so close to, a little humor may be what I needed to take the edge off. But I was still impatient. "So?"

"Yeah, yeah." He continued to move his eyes about in small, almost imperceptible twitches. "Okay, here we go." The galaxy faded into a plane of concentric rings with lines emanating out to the outer edge from the center. The circle was in the middle of a faded and barely visible sphere. At the center point was a tiny set of numbers and letters. Around the plane of circles and in a sparse scattering through the sphere were dots of various shades of yellow and red and white with splotches of alphanumerics accompanying them as well. I peered at the display, trying to understand.

"Oh, sorry," Ian said. Eye twitch and the labels changed into words. At the center was *The Bluerock*. "Okay, we're that, in the center. Over here," he made a white dot floating on the air in the circular grid, about three or four feet away from the center, flash slightly, "is Procyon. It's actually two stars, a binary system. Behind us," another white dot, this time a few inches away from the center, flashed. "And that's Sirius, another binary system."

"We were just there?"

"Yep. That's where we came from. Gadreus, Alpha Sirius-Four's third moon."

"I didn't see two suns," I remarked.

The reply came from the doorway, "Sirius Beta's a dwarf. It looks like just another star from where we were." Kara was standing there in her shirt and pants disheveled in a way that looked like she slept in them. She walked over to the thing that made coffee. I'm tempted to call it a "coffee maker," but it was as similar-looking to a coffee maker as a cube looks to a Bundt cake. Joseph, equally disheveled, came in behind her and collapsed with a sigh into one of the molded plastic chairs.

"I got the new navigational array programmed," Kara informed Ian as she poured a mug of the black oil. "It's running diags now. When it's done, I'll start the swap-over process."

"If we can stabilize the feed," Joseph mumbled.

"We don't technically need the array online for another couple of days," Ian told them. "You really should get some sleep."

Kara flopped down into a chair and took a long drink from the mug. She shrugged, "Better sooner and work out any bugs."

"So," she continued, "Giving our . . . guest here some astronomy lessons?" I couldn't tell if her pause was ironic or derisive.

"I'm sure you can imagine I've been pretty curious as to just where the hell I am, you know." My tone was probably a little harsher than I intended. She nodded but avoided looking at me.

Ian played around with making the holographic image of our place in the galaxy rock and twirl listlessly. "Okay, well, there we are. . . ."

After a pause I asked, "Here's what I don't get. We're in space. In my opinion that's pretty, far out. No pun intended. I mean, real far out. Where

I'm from, or *when* I'm from, we barely got to the moon. But we're already playing around with cyberware and genetic manipulation and things like that." They were looking at me blankly. "What I'm saying is that in three hundred years or so, in a time where we can literally tear holes in space . . . I don't know. Everything else seems so, normal. I mean, clothes, buildings, the smell of gasoline–with the exception of, oh, flying through space, it's really not so different from where I came from."

Joseph chuckled, "What'd you expect? Foil clothing and crystal buildings like on the show *Slip Star*?" Kara snickered at that. Joseph continued, "Functionality never goes out of style, my friend."

"No no," I searched for the right words. "I just figured we went from horses to space craft in less than a hundred years; we should, three hundred years later, I don't know . . . be cyborgs ruled by an artificial intelligence life form, or something." I chuckled at myself, but only so I could say I was half joking in case they laughed at me. I was serious.

"Ah," Ian said. "Yeah, I can see that, I guess." He leaned back in the seat and stared at the floating image still in the air between us. His eyes darted from white dot to white dot as he thought. "Well, I guess there are limits to some things," he said finally. "Not everything can advance faster and faster year after year. I mean, I guess computers got as fast as metal, glass, and bioneurofibers can make them go–and after that, it's basically a matter of tweaking it. Computers can think, if that's what you mean. But I guess it's a matter of how far God lets us develop things."

"Or more like war and scarcity," Frankletti said as he walked into the galley, running a big hand through his tangled hair.

"How's the cell containment holding out?" he asked Ian.

Ian twitched his eyes for a second and replied, "Twenty-seven fifty at the moment. There's some degradation from the relay I had to replace–the sync delay may be caused by something further in." Frankletti grunted as he leaned against the cabinets and yawned. Ian continued, "I can check on that when we port. Until then, I just have to tweak it every few hours or so and we'll keep from blowing up."

"Good to know," Frankletti yawned again.

"What were you saying?" I asked.

Ian answered, "Oh, a section of the anti-matter cell containment's been throwing–"

"Uh, no," I interrupted. "That, I think I might be interested in hearing about, later–but I mean the comment about 'war and scarcity'."

Ian looked at Frankletti. The big guy shrugged. "When the only human planet is set back to the Dark Ages for a century, constant war destroying half the planet, and natural resources scarce . . . probably makes for slow progress out of the cradle of ash."

"The Tribulation," Kara mumbled from out of where she was laying her head on her arms atop the table, just under a cluster of holographic stars.

"Wait a minute: you're not talking about like a religious 'tribulation,' are you?"

"Yes," Ian said.

"No," countered Frankletti, who gave Ian an exasperated glance. "Although religion had no small part in creating it." He poured himself a glass of drinking water and continued after a long gulp. "Thought it started around when you were from," he nodded at me, "but guess it's some time after. In short, old Earth's ecosystem went crazy, fast. Religious fundamentalists went crazier, and, between the two, the web of Earth's economies and governments collapsed. Half a century or more of half the world killing itself while the other half tried like mad to get out of the way from both the fundamentalists and the planet itself trying to kill them."

"Not all the religious were crazies," Ian protested, as if he'd said the same thing to Frankletti many times before.

Joseph shook his head, perhaps amused, and Frankletti said, "No offense." Ian rolled his eyes. (I'm sure that for an instant I felt the ship lurch when he did that, but I could be wrong.)

To me, Frankletti said, "In any case, the two most important goals for everyone who wasn't flinging bombs at each other, was fixing the planet or getting away from it. Terraforming and faster-than-light travel. All other development had to take a number."

"Hey," Ian said, perking up, "right back to what we were talking about! The FTS. Once the Anhouse-Mortsen principle was discovered, it was just a matter of one or two or hundred failed attempts before the first working FTS drive was developed. Then, zwoom!" He made a shooting motion with his hand, "Off we went to the stars!"

"Sort of," piped in Kara from the crook of her arm.

"Yeah," explained Frankletti, "enter the religious nuts again."

Ian's expression took an uncharacteristically serious visage as he said, "Look, some of us tried to stop them, and you know it. Not all of the religious were nuts; there were many who worked on helping the Exodus happen and you know it."

Frankletti continued to look straight ahead, Kara raised her head enough to look at Ian. Both Joseph and I looked back and forth among them.

Quietly, I said, "Look, I know I'm the new guy here, and I don't want to walk into any old minefields, but I just want to put it out there that . . . I have to agree with Ian." Ian smiled again, but looked like someone waiting for the punchline to a joke. "I mean, obviously I don't know how it all happened, but, while no one could ever accuse me of being religious, I grew up Christian. Most everyone I know is as well. I don't . . . didn't? No, don't know any zealots or fanatics. I would think most of the religious people in question in this situation you're talking about weren't, I don't know, mad instigators?"

Ian looked to Frankletti for the punchline. Frankletti said, "May be, may be. But let me ask you: Between the everyday ordinary believer, like yourself, and the fundamentalist–which type made the most, and the most drastic, changes in *your* society?"

The path of progress in history and culture came to mind and I started to say, "The billions of ordinary believers," but stopped myself. I couldn't help but think of the tiny handful of Muslims with a fringe minority view of Islam, who have flown planes into buildings, and how that resulted in such a fundamental change in the way my country became. I thought about the minority of fundamentalist Christians who have loudly hijacked the discussions in politics and culture, turning every issue into one of some war between faith versus secularism. The world, my world, may have been made up predominately of believers in one religion or another, going about their lives and making the world turn, but it was the most violent or divisive and outspoken of them who seemed to change the course of society in stark, and usually negative, directions.

Everyone was looking at me, waiting. Finally, I said, "Okay, so, yeah. I guess the zealots do tend to out-shout and out-kill the liberal and moderate of us."

Frankletti gave a half shrug and said, possibly ironically, "It's the fundamentalists and 'true believers' who make things happen."

Ian smiled humorlessly. "There's only a couple fundamentalists on *this* ship."

Joseph propped his feet on the table and leaned back in his chair, saying, "And they're dragging the rest of us along for the ride." He winked at me. My thoughts would return to this conversation many times in the days to come.

Ian relaxed back into his seat, seeming to shake off the earlier wave of darkness. He turned to me and continued, "Anyway, my family stayed on Earth while those who could, left."

"And continued to leave as fast as ships could be built," added Frankletti. "Cities, already falling to scrap, were used for raw materials."

"Finally, I guess even the most patient of people can get fed up," Ian said, shrugging. "My great-something grandparents made it off the planet and headed out for the colony on Centauri. That's where I'm from."

"Okay," I spoke up, "what happened to the whole terraforming thing? Obviously the getting off the planet thing worked."

Frankletti replied, "Well, turns out, in the century it took to develop the FTS, they also figured out how to adjust ecospheres on a grand scale. Unfortunately, it was all theoretical. Nothing could actually be done without a lot of resources that weren't available. By the time the survivors of Earth had gotten out far enough and found enough resources to make it work, no one wanted to go back and fix the planet they came from. The planet that, as they saw it, was the source of all the problems in the first place." Joseph chuckled at that and Frankletti passed him a look of agreement. "There were enough near-habitable moons and planets that could be transformed so that Earth could pretty much be forgotten."

"Except by those who stayed and tried to make a difference." Ian shot a glance at Frankletti.

I asked, "So, when *was* all this, anyway?"

"Well, like I said, I think the worst began sometime around your time. Early twenty-first century, yeah?" He nudged Kara. She shrugged and mumbled what I think was, "I guess." Frankletti said, "The famine and plagues and what. . . ."

"Tribulation," Kara mumbled.

"Lasted a century or so, and the Exodus finally got going, what, late twenty-first, early twenty-second?" Frankletti looked up in the air, and I was certain he was examining his own thoughts and not some unseen computer display that Ian referenced.

"The first colony ship that successfully left Earth, The *Nova*, was in twenty-one twenty-four. You know, all this should have been on the *Lysander's* computer. You didn't look?" Ian looked both incredulous and amused.

I stammered, "I, really didn't know what I was doing on there. I mean, I tooled around a bit, sure! But didn't want to take the chance of screwing something up. So, I slept a lot, read a lot–would have loved to have found the . . . wiki or encyclopedia online, or something, but. . . ." I shrugged, a little embarrassed. All the hours I spend on that ship wishing I knew what had happened, clues or news, and I never found anything that seemed helpful. It was very much like a boat in an endless sea cut off from everything. But now, I smiled as I thought, that wish was coming true.

Ian said, "Well, I can set you up to access the computer here. You might find it better than *our* versions of ancient history." He smirked at Frankletti and I felt more of the lingering tension drift farther away.

"Tomorrow," Frankletti said gruffly. "Ian, take a quick look at the containment, and then let's get some rest. We have a lot more work tomorrow to keep this thing together if we're going to reach New Torment."

"I'll set up a maint-macro to keep an eye on containment." Ian was already staring out at the invisible, eyes darting nearly imperceptibly.

Frankletti gave Kara's chair a little kick, "Bunk it, Kay" Kara got up and walked right out as if sleepwalking. Joseph plopped his feet back on the floor and groaned as he stood up. He clapped Frankletti on the shoulder and shuffled off without a word. Before he followed, Frankletti said, "You too, not-Jarrod. I'm going to be putting you to work on this boat. We don't take mere passengers."

I smiled, "Doesn't being three-hundred years old give me some elderly dispensation or something?"

"My mother's a hundred and sixty and is still working an asteroid ore extractor," he said and walked out.

CHAPTER SEVEN

And put to work I was. I learned enough about menial labor over the next few days to earn a mail-order degree in it. I was tasked with everything from "Stand there and hold this for a minute," which would often mean half an hour, to, "Strip and re-insulate that leg-thick bundle of wires with matching f-block resin or else we all die!" Although I can say one thing about it: It was a lot more interesting than those days of catatonic uncertainty aboard the *Lysander*.

However, the most valuable benefit of those days was getting to use the ship's computer. And one of the many things I learned is that if I thought the Internet of my time was a jumble of mis-matched facts and information, it had nothing on the eclectic quasi-informative chaos of the pan-stellar information system, or Pansys. At least with my familiar Internet, changes and additions and connections between data happened nearly instantaneously. When you're dealing with a system of networks that can take days, weeks, or even months to sync-up or respond with new or counter-information, it makes for a lot of confusion and contradiction. The ship's computer apparently syncs up and caches data from the Pansys node on whatever system it's docked at—which is itself usually a cache of static data it's received from other nodes on other ships, bases, and distant planets. Very rarely does it maintain any kind of live connection as distance outside of a planetary system, and its particle-to-laser signal accelerators, means having to deal with regular ol' radio frequency speeds. That doesn't tend to work very well when the ship is traveling faster than light through space-time rips.

Much of the interface with the Pansys was familiar, and the frequently necessary 3-dimensional interfacing using holographic displays wasn't too difficult to pick up on. Although, I was constantly plagued with problems of missing data implied to exist from various sources. Ian informed me that often links from one node-base would refer to data located on another node-base that would be blocked by local security. Sometimes node A would allow connections to node B, but not C. Yet C can access B. So when C is told there's data on A, it's blocked. This also happens when the node-base happens to be destroyed, but that's rare. You also had to know what node-base applications and tools were the best to use, yielding the most info in the quickest time: something I was very slow in picking up. What would take me an hour to look for, Ian could find in seconds–and not just because of cybernetic implants. The others were also adept at navigating the Pansys, they just didn't bother all that much with it (aside from technical manuals, navigation guides, and astronomic news).

I did learn some more surrounding the events of the last three hundred years, although I was never sure how much I could trust. A lot of the information was conflicting and contained obvious slants. Sometimes specific dates and names would conflict from one reputable-looking source (a quality that was shaky-at-best to deduce) to the next. Yet, the general story told by Ian and Frankletti seemed to bear out: The Earth went through ecological and political melt-down, creating massive refugee problems, resource shortages, disease epidemics, and social chaos despite what appeared to be valiant relief efforts from public organizations and individuals working together. Religions seemed to bear nearly universal condemnation for either encouraging the strife, or preventing efforts at finding the solutions. Although, at the same time, I learned religion was still a viable subject out in space. It seems many people still believed in radically changed versions of the traditional religions I was familiar with. (Interestingly, Buddhism changed not so much.) And then there's a religion, or, more a faith, called "Theoversism," which is some kind of pantheism that worships the universe itself as a divine being. It has few elements of traditional religion and much of what I saw as "New Age" spiritualism. Some things never die.

I was in the medical alcove, taping gauze over a new burn on my calf, when Frankletti called on the intercom that we were approaching the Procyon system. I made my way up to the control room and found Ian and Joseph arguing about something under a floor panel in front of the main control console. If the *Lysander* was my idea of what the inside of a spaceship should look like–gleaming white with rounded corners, *The Bluerock* was something of a kid's flying clubhouse, complete with odd pieces of metal, of seemingly no purpose, tied to the wall.

Joseph was on the floor on his stomach, head and shoulders down the hole, saying, "I told you it wouldn't last. It wasn't rated for that kind of current."

"Look," came Ian's voice from the floor, "those spans are always underrated. They're used to transfer five times as much current as we're putting through it!"

I'd become used to these exchanges after the first day. If I moved just right, I could just make out Ian lying on his back under the semi-porous metal floor tiles. I ignored them as I sat in the co-pilot's chair and looked out the windows. Just off center was a star brighter than the rest: Procyon. Well, Procyon A, most likely. I had been informed that the Alpha was a bright, young star, while its companion was a semi-visible brown dwarf. A star so cold, relatively, that it could actually have a planet-like atmosphere. One made of mostly ammonia, I believe, but an atmosphere, nonetheless.

"How long?" I had to ask twice.

"Huh?" Joseph pulled his head up out of the floor.

"Until we reach New Torment, how long?"

He torqued his torso and neck around to look at one of the consoles without having to actually get up off the floor, and said in a comically strained voice, "'Bout a coupla hours."

Ian added, "We'll drop the FTS as soon as we replace this span, then go in on Q-thrust the rest of the way."

I hmm-ed and sat back in the chair. If I kept my eye on the back edge of where the window met the bulkhead, I could sometimes catch a star inch across the black and disappear beyond the edge. Just a speck of light, now and then, barely discernible amidst the field of sugar spilled on a black cloth, separating itself from the others to move independently behind us. At home on a planet in fixed orbit, I was so used to traveling and turning so that the entire collection of stars moved as one across the sky, like the inverted bowl with pinholes moved around me as a unit. Here, to see the star field move and shift in such a way as I'm literally tearing through space, so fast that we cause the closest stars to individualize and move in parallax, made me a little lightheaded. Made me forget where I was for a moment–I was out there. I was in awe.

I was tired.

I glanced over at Laurel and Hardy. Ian had come up from the floor and was talking to Joseph about safe FTS drop procedures in light of some change in this or that equipment. I didn't realize until I sat down and dozed off how much the last week was catching up to me. The physical activity, the constant active process of wrapping my mind around some new task or Pansys finding or just waiting to get on to the next stage of . . . whatever all this was . . . whatever all this was going to end up being.

At times, I was simply waiting for the 6:00 p.m. bus to take me home. Other times I'd break out in a sweat, and my gut would turn to water as I realized this could be it, I might not get home. I might not even make it to Procyon. This wasn't a vacation. How easy it was for my mind to fool me into thinking it was. How easy I avoided thoughts about my wife and the way she liked extra pepper on her eggs but hated it on anything else, the way she liked to trace my jawline when we'd lie in bed, the way she got upset whenever someone in a city council meeting said something stupid to her (which was often). Or my daughter and the way she'd tell me she wasn't sleepy even as her eyes were closed, or the way she'd talk to herself in the voices of the cartoon characters she was drawing. How easy it was to avoid thinking of these things . . . too often. To keep me sane, I suspect. Good, mind. Good.

I found it interesting that one couldn't tell, by looking outside, whether one was in FTS flight or not. You would think that tearing holes in space would cause some visible effect, but, no. Evidently, if one could see in a couple of the other seven or eight dimensions invisible to humans, it'd be a horrific nightmare scene outside those windows. However, with my humble three-dimensional sight, the only way I noticed we slowed from FTS to Q-thrust was a significant increase in the underlying hum and vibration of the ship. And a sudden appearance of a flashing light right next to Procyon Alpha.

"That's New Torment," Ian told me, seeing my notice of it. "Mining and manufacturing outfit in an asteroid belt."

"Huh. What's it mine and manufacture?"

"Enriched deuterium, heavy erbium, and other elements hard to find outside certain planets of newly formed stars. They also make the ballistic-absorbing alloy used for ship hulls."

I peered around the area of the distant flashing light. "Where's the planet?"

"What planet?"

"The one you said that stuff's found on."

"Oh," Ian shrugged, "that's the asteroid belt. Seems Procyon B hates planets. It's a *way* off-center orbit around A, so its planetary system eventually destabilized and broke up any planet large enough *to* break up. Everything else it either pulled out of orbit or forced a fall into the belly of A."

"Nice."

Ian, Joseph, occasionally Kara, would approach a console and do a little of this and some of that, and eventually we got close enough that I could just make out a large object behind the flashing light, blocking an increasingly large patch of stars behind it. The flashing light, a beacon, or lighthouse of sorts, was certainly bright; being seen from so far away, it took a while before I could make out more lights on the asteroid that was itself beginning to gain more visual definition. Dots of light here and there: most stationary, some moving. Huge swaths of light shining out on the black rock.

"Where's the rest of the field," I wondered.

Joseph was the one who answered this time, glancing at a console screen's nav display, "Next closest rock is . . . about five thousand K to the two o'clock and three degrees from GC north. There's some rocks and tiny stuff floating around, but no worries. We could be going max Q and with the shielding and hull we won't even feel a tap."

"Not much of an asteroid field, huh?"

"Hmm? What do you mean?"

I shrugged, "I don't know, I thought you had to like, maneuver through asteroid fields."

"Heh, where'd you get *that* idea? A field that dense wouldn't last a year; they'd all get drawn together and collide and grind up. Not a stable place to do any mining."

"Oh, yeah, makes sense." The number of times my romantic ideas of space were crushed was almost half as many times as I saw or learned something that made me gasp in awe.

When I landed on Gadreus nearly a week ago, the light from the nearby planet and its sun diffused through the moon's atmosphere made the view of the small port town look like it was a cloudy mid-day on Earth. Here, though, the distant, cold white light from Procyon A was too faint to have any effect on the airless asteroid. The approach to the cluster of industrial buildings was marked by a sparse patchwork of harsh lights with sharp edges that barely illuminated towers, spots of walls on certain sides of buildings making a perforation of white spots down roads from building to building and across the surface of the craggy rock. A rocky surface that became barren immediately beyond the outside edge of the outermost factory-like building. Vehicles that looked like crazy collisions of Legos and erector sets crawled and glided to and from the lonely cluster of mechanized life.

We drifted toward the second largest of the buildings. Ian got clearance from a base traffic controller and we were told which hangar bay to land in. The building had several open squares in its ceiling, like monstrous skylights. Ian told me the bay openings were shielded to maintain air pressure inside while the approaching ship sinks through the shield, conforming to the ship's contours like dipping a model ship through the surface of a tub of water. Once inside the hangar, the view was not any more cheery looking than outside.

"De-con' and environ-sync should only take a couple of minutes," Ian said once we had gently settled in the hangar. His eyes were rapidly flickering at invisible data and interfaces; his hands seemed to move and do things at the console of their own accord.

Kara leaned around the bulkhead into the control room. "ISR's on the way."

Ian looked confused and swung around to look out the windows, which provided a decent view of straight ahead and slightly above but gave no view of the floor of the hangar. "There shouldn't–"

"And Max wants you to secure the cell containment module and prep for repairs. He wants to get fixed and back out ASAP."

Ian got out of the chair and squeezed past Kara, "Yeah, sure. On it." He gave another look over his shoulder out the windows that showed nothing but dim hangar walls.

I was glad I wouldn't have to be the one running point with the ISR officer this time–now it was all Frankletti's responsibility to fool the bureaucracy. He soon appeared and made a scowl at Kara, who nodded back. The two of them moved off to the smaller exit door situated beside the cargo compartment and its giant descending ramp. Frankletti gestured at me, "Not-Jarrod, why don't you come on down here with us."

"Uh, but, I. . . ."

"Safer with us than if you're lurking around aimlessly. Suspicious."

"Oh, okay." I caught up with them as Kara opened the outer door with a hiss and blast of visible steam or gases. A ladder descended and, from around the edge of the door, I watched as graceful and sure hands climbed the rungs, followed by a head of soft brown hair that was bound up with a haphazardness that was both purposeful and oddly attractive. This ISR officer was as beautiful as the one on Gadreus was unexceptional. Once on the ship, she gave us all a steady look and put on a pair of glasses she pulled from a shirt pocket. The image of "smart-girl beautiful" was complete and I had to remind myself to breathe.

"Max Frankletti?" she asked. Frankletti nodded. "You're the registered owner and captain of this craft," she expressed more as a statement than as an inquiry as she looked at a handheld tablet she had at her side.

"Yeah, that I am."

I heard steps behind me. Joseph came around the corner with a smirk and asked in a too loud whisper, "Did I miss anything?" Ian emerged behind him looking concerned. I shook my head at Joseph, and he winked at me.

I turned back to the ISR officer. "Well, let's get this over with," she huffed and started in my direction. I flattened myself against the wall to let her pass, and she glanced at me as she did so. A few steps toward a scowling Ian, then she stopped and turned back to me. My heart skipped for a couple of different reasons–both originating from nervousness. She gave me a long look. I glanced sidelong to Frankletti at one side, who remained stoic, and Joseph at the other, whose eyes were wide with interest. The officer looked down at her tablet. I tried to look at it without being obvious, but I couldn't make anything out.

"Is your name Jarrod?"

"No." I said too fast and surprised myself. Shit. "I mean, yeah," I tried to laugh, embarrassed. Too shrill. I looked for some clue from Frankletti, who hadn't changed. "Sorry, long . . . flight. Little tired." I smiled. I wanted to vomit.

My beautiful angel of doom asked Frankletti, "This is him?" He nodded, all seriousness. To me: "Mister Creek, will you come with me, please." Again, not a question. She gestured to the exit.

I shrugged and tried to smile. The blood rushing through my ears muffled all sound; my voice was hollow and distant to me, "I . . . don't know what you mean."

Her hand went to her jacket pocket. "Don't make this difficult. I can fill out arrest papers, or cause-of-death papers. Your choice."

Shit!

I searched for some hint of help from the others with whom I just spent a better part of a week in close quarters. Frankletti was stern. That nod. That look earlier between himself and Kara. Did he sell me out? Kara only looked down, her lips pursed. Joseph was also looking back and forth from one to another, expectantly. That's right, he was a cop! But he helped rescue me from his own back on Gadreus. Did he know about this? He wasn't making any move to support the ISR officer. Ian stayed distant with a look of disdain. For who? Her, or me? "'This is him?'" she had asked. I couldn't believe it.

I started to move involuntarily toward the door, expected at any second to be prodded or shocked from behind by some terrible device, and pleaded to Frankletti, "Why?"

I heard a choked snicker behind me. Joseph. The jerk! Laughing at me. Shock or not, I turned around to glare. His hand was over his mouth, and his chest was jerking from suppressed laughter. The ISR officer was smiling, pleasantly, not cruelly, as I would have expected her to smile in this situation, were she compelled to do so. Ian still looked disgusted.

I swung back around and now Kara was stifling giggles, and Frankletti had a self-satisfied smile. No. Way. "You– She– You. . . ." Frankletti nodded and shrugged as if to say, "Who, me?" Kara and Joseph stopped trying to suppress anything and just let it out.

The officer stood, pleased with herself, but raised a concerned eyebrow, "Hope we didn't get you *too* bad." She extended her hand, empty. "Tabitha Kim, Intersystem Security Rep."

I shook her hand. It was warm, soft. "So, you *are* an ISR, then?"

"Oh yeah. Civilian contracted, more or less. I was Frankletti's assistant on a communications relay base some years ago. We go back."

I wondered why Kara seemed to be the only person who called Frankletti "Max." I confronted him, "Is there anyone in this galaxy you don't know?"

He shrugged, "I just go to the places that have people I do know."

Kara and Joseph were getting themselves under control. Kara started to scare me; I'm not sure I saw her crack a smile the last few days. Joseph looked positively gleeful, but not in a mean way, "Oh, he so got you! *Usted* hung *baligtad*, man! I'm glad I got to see that."

I smiled despite myself and leaned back against the bulkhead. My legs were weak and shaky. I wanted to be so angry; I deserved to be. However, reassured all was well, I had to admit, that was a good get. "I don't know how, but I'll pay you back," I chuckled, trying to sound evil. "Someday, somehow."

Ian huffed. "Is it over? Can we get to work now?" He started to walk away. Odd. I would have thought Ian, of anyone, would have loved to be in on a joke like this. But then, over the last couple of days he seemed to be more stressed and distant. I know it was taking a lot of work to keep various systems from shutting down or throwing errors more serious than just annoying. Being the lead tech on the ship, he had a lot of responsibility. I hated to see the lively and good-natured Ian, who was the first to clue me in on where in the universe I was, change to a dour Ian, though.

"Yeah," Frankletti agreed as Ian disappeared. "We have a lot to do. I want to get as fixed up as we can and restocked in twenty hours, twenty-five max, and get on out toward the unknown."

He nodded at Joseph, "Get the supply list parsed and send the standard stuff to the base requisitioning system. Send the rest to Tabitha."

"Aye, Cap'n," Joseph said jauntily, then saluted and followed after Ian.

"Kay," he said to Kara, "keep working with Ian on the FTS. Every system and subsystem and redundant system. Where we're going, that's the last thing we want failing."

"More than life support?"

"If the FTS goes permanently down light years from anything and off all regularly traveled routes, we're going to *want* life support to fail."

Off went Kara.

Turning to Tabitha, Frankletti said, "Do you have any available crew that we can get to help us? A few extra hands could really help."

"Mmm, I can see what I can do. Maybe Xander's team; they were supposed to do work on repairing platform twenty-one the next few days, but an explosive fault took out the entire rig yesterday. Tore the asteroid into pieces. No one was on it at the time, thank goodness. I'll talk to Sandy; she's the Mech' union supervisor this quarter. I bet she'll have no problem."

"Great, whatever you can do, Tabitha. I appreciate it."

"Hey," she slugged Frankletti's large arm, "anything for my old boss-man, mister boss-man, sir."

"You," he said to me as Tabitha descended the ladder, "come with me. I'm going to start teaching you a thing or two about astrogation. Need to change underwear first?" he teased.

"Har-dee-har, mister boss-man, sir."

* * *

Well, I can't say I had the promise of being an expert space navigator—nor a mediocre one. Though, I did learn a thing or two in those hours about general ship controls and how not to blow up too easily. I learned from Frankletti one of the problems with figuring out the story of me and the *Lysander.* "Not enough dark matter."

"What," I asked.

"See, where the *Lysander's* logs seemed to restart, where you woke up far out away from anything, and the navigational point in logs where it last was before the jump . . . between those two locations has very little dark matter."

"Wait, I remember something I came across on Pansys . . . something about the FTS using dark matter to do the tears, right?"

He nodded and leaned back in his chair. We were in the galley, using the holo-display to go over system charts. "See, dark matter kind of comes in clumps and threads throughout the universe. And where the highest concentrations are, regular matter kind of stuck to and gathered and made the known universe."

"Yeeaah. . . ." I said raising a brow. "How's that work?"

"Okay, imagine a giant cobweb. It's stringy and without any apparent order or symmetry. It has holes, and it has places where the strands group together in clumps." To illustrate his metaphor, he leaned forward to the recessed table controls and brought up a three-dimensional image of something very like what he was describing.

"So, that's dark matter," I said.

"Right."

"Why's it look like that?"

Shrug. "Don't know. Just a property of it. Spread out as fast if not faster than the fabric of the universe itself."

He did something else with the controls, and now very slowly an overlay of yellow that lightly covered the entire display appeared and began to gravitate toward the greater concentrations of dark matter. "As normal energy cooled and formed matter, it started collecting at the dark matter clumps. Which is why there's galactic neighborhoods."

"Oh yeah. Whole clusters of galaxies found in groups."

"Yep, like ours, like most of them. Wads of galaxies." As we spoke, the yellow sand formed eddies and swirls and knots of galaxies in distinct clumps with large areas of nothing between them.

"But what happens at the macro level, happens in the micro." He zoomed the image in toward a single galaxy. Strands of dark matter and knots of galaxies flew at my head to disappear past the edge of the hologram as we seemed to fly into a spiral galaxy. Farther, until it no longer had a discernible shape, and the component stars became individual, and we stopped when there were just several white and yellow and red dots floating above the table. "See," Frankletti continued, "as we zoomed in, we can see that giant splotch of dark matter our galactic neighborhood is stuck to is made up of smaller threads and splotches. Smaller and smaller, layered within layers."

"Like a fractal image."

"Yeah, okay." He pointed to an area between two of the stars. "You can see strands and clumps between the stars, between most of the stars."

"Sure."

"Where they're thickest, those, in essence, become the roads between the stars."

I had to think back to earlier conversations of how the FTS worked. "Because . . . the harnessed neutrinos from the anti-matter engine are phase shifted to interact with the dark matter. And we use that interaction with the help of a graviton accelerator to create the tears in space, which we fall through."

"Exactly!"

"Okay, I get it. So where the dark matter is thickest, the FTS is the most efficient and effective."

"Right again."

"Which means," I shifted the display to center on a virtual dead-pool of lack of dark matter, "where the *Lysander* had to have traveled: no dark matter."

"The shortest space between the two points: virtually none, right. Space, even so-called 'empty space,' is technically filled with dark matter. It makes up a quarter of the entire universe, whereas all the stuff we can see and touch makes up less than five-percent. But there are places where the concentration's not enough for the cascade we need to make FTS work. Sometimes it doesn't work well, sometimes not at all." The display shifted again. A three-dimensional grid appeared along with names next to the stars. I saw Procyon, Luyten, Sirius, Proxima, Thaedrus, Sol, Kipfer, all connected by computer generated ephemeral strands of dark matter. One strand that connected Luyten and Procyon to Sirius glowed brighter than the others. "That's the dark matter highway that must be used to get from those systems to this."

"Dang. That looks pretty far. How far is that?"

"Oh, about two hundred light years."

"And, how long to get there?"

"It takes weeks because of the arc. If you tried to just go in a straight line, you're off the highway and the trip will, at best, take months, actually. More likely years, though."

I scowled. "Wait. Wait a minute. Didn't, didn't you say that the logs on the *Lysander* indicated in only took a couple of days to travel that course?"

"Actually, *not* that course." He made some more adjustments and now two additional points lit up. One was in the emptiness past Luyten's Star and Procyon, and the other was in the emptiness past Sirius. "Where the *Lysander* was, is that nowhere up there past Luyten's. Where it ended up and you awoke, is down there past Sirius. To get from that point to the other–"

"That's another, what," I squinted at the three-dimensional grid lines and estimated, "five light years added on?"

"Not bad. About that, again, in a straight line. But you can't travel in a straight line. So, we're talking, nearly eight light years and two standard weeks."

The impossibility of the history of the *Lysander* just kept adding up. "I . . . how–"

He smiled and leaned back. The chair creaked. "I don't know, but we'll see."

I gave him a suspicious frown. "Do you know something?"

"I know a lot of things, Not-Jarrod, my friend. On this, however, I'm not quite sure. Not yet at least." He smirked self deprecatingly. "But, I may be privy to some *kaalaman secreta* that could shed some light on all this."

"Hello?" came a familiar voice from down the passage.

"In here," Frankletti called.

Tabitha peeked around the doorway. "Hey. How's my fugitives from the unlawful law?"

"Only hours away from being more fugitive." It wasn't often that Frankletti made jokes as bad as that–he deserved my groan. "A couple of Xander's guys are helping Kara make some final modifications, and Ian's about done with what he's doing. We're taking off the moment the last screw's back in place. We can sleep once we're on our way."

Tabitha was looking more casual than when I saw her several hours ago, when she was in a blouse and slacks. Now she wore long, pocketed shorts and her hair in a loose ponytail. She was idly peeking into magnet-latched cupboards as she said, "Well, I was wondering if our time traveler would be interested in a little tour of the facility. Just around the complex here."

"Sure. Love to."

Frankletti called "school's out for the day" and told Tabitha to get me back before dinner—there's a lot more manual labor needing done. Tabitha led the way out the ship casting a "Yeah, yeah," behind her. I followed her, smirking. I could get to like her, I thought.

The main cargo hold was open and we left down the ramp. There were crates and devices surrounding the ship, cables and hoses running hither and thither. Joseph had some kind of computer tablet and was working amongst the clutter with a guy and a woman from what I guessed was Xander's crew. The hangar was cavernous, and the shielded hole in the ceiling was almost as large as the floor space. Evidently, some massive ships have been known to dock here. Our hangar was just one of several in this building; the other hangars were independently walled with connecting airlocks.

"Have you been off-world much?" Tabitha asked as we passed through an airlock into a personnel corridor that ran between hangars and connected with a smaller building Tabitha would show me was for maintenance, metal shops, a foundry, and some offices.

"Actually, not at all before my time trip. We civilians didn't get to go to space." As we started astrogation lessons, Frankletti let me know that Tabitha Kim knew all about my situation, being someone he trusted and had connections around the star systems as well.

"You mean the military control space flight on your planet?" She seemed disgusted and not surprised.

I chuckled, "Well, sort of. I mean, my planet was Earth, you know. A long time ago."

"Right, I get that."

I looked at her askance. "I mean, back at the beginning of the space age. No one but the government had the ability and resources to build rockets and stations." I thought for a moment. "I guess that was changing by the time I . . . left. Was taken," I shrugged. "Come to think of it, there were rich guys and corporations beginning to get into the game."

"But the government dissuaded them?"

"Hmm? No, actually, I think NASA was promoting them to get involved. Guess they weren't getting enough resources from the government to do the work and progress." I smiled, "But scientists are scientists and adventurers are adventurers, and they're going to aid discovery and progress through whatever means, I suppose."

Tabitha smiled and nodded. I got the sense she was pleased I learned a lesson of some sort.

"You seem rather anti-government for a government worker."

She glided beside me, her hands in her pockets. "Civilian contract. I have that position, and I send appropriately expected communications and reports specifically so that CASS doesn't put an official presence on here."

I was starting to get used to all the acronyms I'd been hearing the last couple weeks. "Cooperative Association of Sovereign Systems, right?"

She nodded, "Mm-hmm."

"Now, I gathered, from stuff I'd read recently, on Pansys, that that's a sort of loose . . . bureaucratic thing. Like the United Nations. I mean. . . . That's, I'll have to explain that later. But that it wasn't a government. More like a union of systems."

We had come to a corner in the corridor that jutted out from the building we were in. Continuing on would make a right turn into another pressurized building. The walls at this corner were made out of the translucent micro-poly-bond "glass" that was used in ships. There was a well-worn couch and molded plastic chair and side table placed against one wall.

It had the feel of an auto service shop's waiting area. The corridor lights, dim in the first place, stopped before the glass. We'd have been in the dark save for one of the complex's outside lights, aimed to illuminate what looked like a cluster of sheds just below us, casting some residual light up into the corridor.

Tabitha sat on the arm of the couch and nodded at the view. "What do you see?"

I looked. "Those sheds."

"Okay. What else?"

"There's another building over there. With the flashing light on it."

"Mm-hmm. And?"

I shrugged. "Not sure. I mean, I guess I can see the asteroid, the blackness where there's no stars. The stars, too."

"Do you know how many people are on this rock?"

"I think Frankletti mentioned something like a hundred or so."

"There are three-hundred seventy men, women, and children on this rock. Another fifty working a rock out that way, twenty out there, and another twenty on one that way. And do you know how many military or government personnel on here?" I shook my head. "None. Why? Because the CASS is a myth."

"I was arrested and detained by the myth last week."

"You were arrested and detained by *believers* in the myth."

"*I* believed the guns they carried."

"And that's how the myth is maintained: the guns."

She paused. We looked at the stars.

She continued, "Nearly five hundred people, alone in a barren, desolate region of space. Circling a cold star buzzed by another that can barely be seen. No planets. We're visited by supply ships now and then dropping off essentials, picking up materials. We're not on the way to some frontier world, no resort world. We're untouched by the hand of government, save for a charade. To us, government is a myth as distant and unconnected to our work and our lives as the ancient gods of old Earth."

"It seems like a myth to you, out here. But it's not to those where the CASS have bases and officers, right?" I asked.

She smirked, but it wasn't unfriendly. "And that is the dual nature of a myth that people believe in, and not one that has passed into antiquity. Here, it is an abstraction, easily dismissed. Elsewhere, too many places, actually, the myth drive the actions of believers."

"Wait, are we talking about religion now?"

She paused, then said, "Not in the sense that it involves deities or supernatural elements. But the belief in the right of the monopoly of violence held by a few who steal the title of 'leaders'; the right of wealth to buy power over people; and the belief in selling yourself, mind, body, and soul, in a manner of speaking, to people who use you for their own benefit and at the same time make you think it's the right and natural way of things–that all is accepted by people and forced upon others very much like a religion. That is the power of the myth: at the same time it's a creation, a fantasy, a fiction–it's powerful enough to cause people to kill and die for the protection of the myth."

"Whoa, hold on there." I couldn't help but scowl. "That was a lot of concepts you just smooshed together that I need to parse."

She chuckled, "Okay, okay. Sorry." She shifted on the couch and considered me. "Let me put it this way: You come from a world of government, you indicated it earlier. I don't know what it was called, but it might as well have been called the CASS. The name is different but the practice is surely the same. We, here, without the coercion of government–well, not direct coercion, anyway–we're not an aberration, this community. We're the norm. There are other communities, colonies, worlds out there that live exactly as they did when humans escaped the legacy of Earth.

"The CASS *did* start out as a benevolent and powerless council," she continued, "helping aid communication across the disparate new worlds, providing mediation services among interworld merchant unions. But those who didn't learn from the past forgot the reasons why we *fled* Earth like animals out of a burning forest, instead of being able to gently branch out from it, and found the benevolent bureaucracy to have a unique position in the galaxy. A gathering of information on the worlds and their people, a privileged access to these worlds and people–an assumed position of ethical superiority originally based in service and peace. A government infrastructure, grown out of perceived necessity that only needed central leaders to take control and the firepower to maintain it."

I sat in the chair and leaned forward. The soft light of the corridor on the other side silhouetted her. "I think I understand what you're saying. I'm not saying I agree–I have no ideas, especially about any . . . post-Earth history: an organically grown collection of, what, mediators and diplomats, joined forces and created an interstellar government?" Tabitha shrugged as if to say, "More or less." I took that as encouragement to continue, "But after what happened on Earth, with all these new opportunities, how could they, whoever 'they' are, who transformed the CASS, do it?"

"Years had passed, generations, since Earth, before the CASS in its benign state even formed. Generations before the CASS reorganization. Pre-life-extension generations. People forget. New concerns and problems arise, helping people to forget what'd come before."

"But everybody followed along."

Tabitha leaned back and put a supporting arm across the back of the couch. "Nuh-uh. There were some worlds that made remembering the lessons of Earth a part of their cultural ideology. My family's from one of those. Others found perfectly good ways to manage themselves and their resources without the need for an outside, disconnected mediator, and so weren't as susceptible to CASS's assumption of control."

"Without governments?"

"Some. Some were able to start right off without issues of wealth-based power. Didn't have to deal with other worlds that did. Others developed all ranges of local government systems, but wanted nothing to do with an off-world group involving themselves in local interests."

"Were they . . . what, overthrown? Invaded?"

Tabitha laughed gently, "Hardly any. There were enough worlds the CASS was involved with that those in power had a good galactic empire right from the first month. Only a few worlds that realized the implications of the change in CASS bucked it. A few were let go, a couple had some influence exerted on them. The CASS didn't have anything to worry about regarding the isolationist worlds. They left alone those who left them alone. Unless it was a world rich in certain resources, then, somehow or another, they joined the cooperative of systems."

"So, you're on a mining base far from CASS, in order to leave and leave be." Another "more or less" shrug. I paused for a moment. "But wait. You're an ISR agent. Sort of. In an 'uninvolved' system. Such as it is. I don't get it."

"We've been talking about the past. Live and let live used to be the way of the benevolent empire. It was the way they got so many systems to acquiesce and support the CASS. But when does power ever stay satisfied with what it already has?"

"They're spreading their control?"

"Mm-hmm. But slowly. Quietly. They exert various forms of pressure, whatever works for the world in question, to get some form of eyes and ears there. Usually it's locals, at first. If everything goes passively, they start finding ways to simply insinuate their control into the local governments. Then the CASS officials start arriving. Bureaucrats, ambassadors. But bureaucrats and ambassadors need protection. And that protection needs a base, a garrison."

"It started here, on New Torment."

She nodded. "For us it was the need to protect our manufacturing from other mining or alloy production firms. Never mind we're part of a self-regulating trade guild. It's for our protection," she said with a sneer. "'Oh, we got reports that your last food shipment went missing. Sorry, but you know how those independent cargo shippers are. Have you considered that request for an ISR office on your base yet, by the way?' After that, they got their officer, me, and an agreement to cut our use of organized independents for shipments in half."

"Is there anything being done to stop it?"

By the gleam of light from the outside spotlight, I saw she gave that gentle, approving smile again. "Let's walk a bit; I have some people for you to meet."

That's when Ian arrived, looking relieved to have found us. "Oh good! Listen, we should be getting back to the ship."

"You shouldn't be ready to take off for a few hours, I thought," Tabitha said.

I asked, "What's up? Something wrong?"

"Hmm? Oh, no. We just have a lot to do to be *able* to leave in a few hours."

"Drat." To Tabitha I added, "Do you have to go back to, whatever? Can you hang around, maybe tell me more about that stuff?" Ian looked annoyed. Maybe he didn't like Tabitha, I thought. Maybe they had a history as well?

She said, "Sure, I can do that. Maybe I can lend a hand. I *was* one of Frankletti's master electricians and comms officer extraordinaire." We started walking back.

When we got about halfway back, the corridor came alive with an undulating yellow light.

"Odd," Tabitha said.

"What's that?"

"Come on, let's get back," Ian urged.

"If something's happened, there's supposed to be an automated message broadcast and sent to our comms." She touched a spot behind her ear. "Nothing at all."

"You have an implant?" I wondered.

"What? No." She pulled back her wavy hair to show me a tiny device hugging the back of her ear. A nearly invisible wire or tube came off it, went around the top, and into ear. "Can't do implants–they're unstable. It's a multi-channel transceiver that uses my skull as the mic and stims the canal. Perfect signal and doesn't affect my hearing."

Ian was edging on down the corridor without us and gave Tabitha glare, "Come on, let's go."

"'Perfect signal,' 'til now?" I said.

"Yeah, I need to find a terminal. Let's try the fuel manager's office, down here. I hope it's not some kind of seismic activity, not after what happened last week. We lost so much time and equipment from that."

As if on cue, a sharp shudder passed through our feet and I felt my ears pop from a change in pressure. Down the corridor in both directions, about every hundred feet, a long, thin compartment opened up in the wall.

"*Punyeta.* That's not good."

"What was that?" I asked, hoping the concern in my voice wasn't as obvious to everyone else. Ian looked positively worried.

"A breech most likely, in both the complex structure and shielding," Tabitha answered. She jogged the remaining few meters to the fuel management office and pushed the door open. Inside were two men standing in front of a desk, talking to each other in urgent tones. One of them spoke, "Kim, you know what's going on?"

"No. I came in to see if I can find out."

The other one leaned over and pressed some virtual buttons that were projected on the surface of his desk. "Everything disconnected a couple of minutes ago. The network went down."

The first guy said, "That never happens."

"Mitch," Ian tugged my sleeve, "we should get back to the ship. I'm sure we can find something out from there."

"Yeah, okay. Tabitha, we're going to get back."

"I'll go with you. Hold on." To the guys, "Can you get anything on your comms?"

One wiggled an ear with his hand. "Nope."

"No."

"I'll see what I can find out," she said as she walked out the door with us.

Before reaching the hanger airlock, Tabitha paused at one of the openings in the wall. "Are either of you lunged?"

"No," Ian replied.

"Huh?" said I.

She pulled out clear face masks that dangled a hose with a short cylinder on the end. There were orange suits in the cabinet, as well, but she ignored them. "Put these on."

I watched as Ian and Tabitha strapped the masks over their faces then followed their lead. As soon as the mask covered my nose and mouth, it sealed itself to my skin, and I could feel a slight current of cool, fresh air blown into my nose. She approached the airlock and examined the display next to it. She glanced back at Ian and me, and said in a muffled voice, "Atmo breach on the other side, but shouldn't be bad. Hold onto the wall rail just in case." Ian and I grabbed hold of the metal handrails that ran up to the airlock.

Tabitha punched some keys on the panel and grabbed the rail herself as the door hissed open, very slowly at first and causing a faint whistle as air from the corridor was sucked through, then opened quickly the rest of the way.

Half of one of the hanger walls was missing. I could feel myself being gently pulled in that direction, but not much more than as if in a strong wind storm. The mask tightened a little more on its own over my face and the air pressure being forced into my lungs increased slightly. It was almost like being suffocated with a pillow of air, while breathing it at the same time. It was also extremely chilly–like my body heat was being drawn out of me. Many of the crates and boxes, hoses and cables, had gathered around the hole, although they seemed blocked from going all the way through by an invisible force.

Also among the debris, bodies. The people from Xander's crew. Their clothes were soaked in blood and some left large swaths of blood along the hangar floor as their bodies were slowly dragged toward the breeched wall by the pull of the vacuum of space.

"What? Explosion?" Tabitha asked above the rushing air and muffling mask. She staggered over to the closest body. Ian was stunned in place as he looked frantically around.

I rushed, carefully as the air current tried to pull my feet from under me, over to Tabitha. She was looking down at a woman in workman's overalls. "What happened?" I looked at the person she crouched over and saw holes in the overalls with blossoms of blood soaked around them. I'd never seen any industrial accidents before, but I was pretty sure they didn't cause bullet wounds.

"There," she said, pointing over at a crate that was wobbling on an edge, trying to roll over. I recognized the trousers on the legs under it. I ran, stumbling once or twice, over to the crate. Joseph was dead. Similar holes.

I turned around. Tabitha was tapping at the device behind her ear. Ian seemed to be looking at something in the air in front of him. "No," he said, nearly too soft to hear. "No. No no no *no* NO!" He ran, scrambling, toward the ship.

"What?" I said as he flew past.

"On the ship, *now!*"

I turned to Tabitha; she was looking at me. Ian was already inside. We ran, having to nearly jump over the lip of the bay door as it was already closing behind Ian. Tabitha and I stood in the cargo bay, raising eyebrows at each other. Seconds later, *The Bluerock* lurched and shook and we were thrown to the ground. I'd learned enough in the last week to know that Ian was making an emergency takeoff–bypassing the gravity compensators and guidance assist. He was going full manual.

Tabitha and I stumbled our way into the ship proper when a violent lurch threw us a foot off our feet and against the bulkhead. A conduit coupling ripped my leg open and I banged my head against the wall. My vision blurred and my hearing faded for a moment. Tabitha grunted in a scary way and clutched her shoulder. I grabbed her around the waist and helped her up as she hissed and groaned. Blood ran down into my shoe. We had to get strapped into something.

We heaved and limped up the steps to the control deck and stumbled around the doorway into the control room. Ian wrestled with the controls, still intoning "No no no" under his breath. I wrapped the chair's straps around Tabitha and, as they clicked in place, she too exclaimed "No!" over my shoulder.

I turned. Outside the windows, seesawing in the view as Ian tried to control the rebelling ship, was a cluster of white explosions illuminating an asteroid as it broke into countless pieces.

CHAPTER EIGHT

"She wasn't ready, dammit. Not ready." I'd never heard Ian angry and careless with his words before.

Tabitha still held onto her shoulder, which I was sure was dislocated, but it seemed forgotten as she stared out at where New Torment used to be. Even after the last flash of light faded and there was nothing but a star field to look at. "What was it?" she gritted. Her eyes were wet but no tears fell.

"Meade class battleship."

That pulled Tabitha's gaze away from the windows. She scowled at Ian. "What?"

He didn't look at her. His hands were a blur of urgent activity, his eyes moving and vibrating more frenetically than I'd ever seen. "In the hangar. I saw, I got a scan of ships above the asteroid. Leaving. One of them was a Meade class battleship. It had opened its weapons locks. I knew what was coming." His voice was unaffected.

"Everyone," groaned Tabitha. "Dead."

It hit me. "Frankletti!" I bolted toward the door and crashed into the edge of it as my wounded leg gave way from pain, nearly causing me to dislocate my own shoulder. My head was filled with glass and knives and tied with barbed wire. "Frankletti!" I called out as I limped down the corridor, clutching at any purchase along the walls.

I got to the galley. Some cabinets had opened despite the magnet latches. Plastic dishes and food containers had scatted about the floor. I heard Ian say, "No one else is here." I spun around. He'd said it over the ship's comm. "No other life signs." Still unaffected.

"Dead?" I asked.

"Someone in the engine ancillary is, but it's not Frankletti or Kara."

I stumbled my way back across the galley and down the short corridor to the medical alcove, Ian's voice following me. The ship kept jerking and bouncing like I'd never experienced before. My gut felt like I was riding a roller coaster. "How do you know?"

After a pause, "Neither of their marker sigs are showing up."

"What are–"

"Look, can we discuss this later? I'm holding the ship together by mind control. Literally. We're going to need to make some emergency repairs outside if we're going to stay alive longer than twenty minutes."

"Alright, hold on." I tied a compress around the gash in my leg and started feeling the pain reducers, antiseptic, and blood coagulant mixture bubble around the wound underneath the sterile padding. I searched through the packages and bins for what I needed, dropping supplies to the floor. At one point I noticed a package of eyewash drift as it fell in slow motion while at the same time my stomach lurched. Then it fell normally: Artificial gravity was kicking on and off. I got what I was after and scrambled back to the control room.

Ian was scrambling into one of the emergency space suits, his arms and legs moving quick and sure while his eyes darted around, focusing on nothing I could see.

Tabitha was still strapped in her seat, her face ashen and dripping in sweat. "I can't unbuckle," she said very matter-of-factly. Her right arm lay limp in her lap.

I unbuckled her seat straps and she winced as the tension against her torso relaxed. "Don't worry," I assured her, "I had a friend on the Lacrosse team back in college who would dislocate his shoulder at least once a season." I unbuttoned the top two buttons on her shirt.

"What's lacrosse?" she asked through clenched teeth.

I pulled back on her shirt collar as firmly but gently as I could, exposing her shoulder. The bulge of bone was pushing forward, which was a good sign. "It's something I probably won't be teaching you to play any time soon." I smiled at her; she smiled back. My friend told me the first time he had dislocated his shoulder the pain was so bad he ended up passing out before they could reset it. Tabitha appeared to be doing a good job dealing with it, but even her shoulder felt clammy. I opened the blister pack I brought with me, unpeeled the dermal patch of muscle relaxer and pain inhibitor and adhered it to the back of her shoulder.

Ian had finished climbing into the nearly skin-tight suit and was about to leave the cabin. I said, "Wait, you said we were attacked. The asteroid was attacked. Are they still out there? Why aren't they finishing us off?"

He pulled out some equipment from the cabinet. "They Q'ed out of here as soon as they launched missiles. I don't think they thought anyone would be able to survive. And we're *not* if we don't get out there and start shutting exposed systems down, closing vulnerable panels, making her space-worthy. Half the liquid hydrogen has already leeched out of open valves. The ship wasn't in any state to take off when we did; we're lucky we made it. We never would have if we had to cut through any atmosphere." He considered Tabitha. "Is she going to be able to get out there?"

"No, I don't think so."

"Get suited up and head out to the port-side anterior. I'll tell you what to do." He bolted. From down the corridor he yelled, "Bring a kit!" and was gone.

"It's working," Tabitha said. "My fingers are tingling."

"Okay, this is probably going to hurt." I gave her an apologetic look.

"Hey, I can deal with a foot reattachment, I can deal with this."

"Huh? Really?" I gently lifted her forearm to make her arm into an Lshape and started rotating it to the side.

Tabitha closed her eyes, her face and neck muscles tightened, but it didn't seem to hurt as much as I would have expected. The pain-derm was working pretty well. "Yeah, was an accident with an ore loader. Few years ago."

"You worked the asteroid?"

She opened an eye to give me a reproving look. "Of course. Everyone on New Torment has to do some time working the ore in some way or another. Even us administrative types." She opened her eyes and looked out at the view of empty space. "*Had* to."

I looked away from her face as it melted in a way the physical pain hadn't been able to do. I placed a hand firmly on her shoulder as I lifted her arm by the wrist up and away from her body. I pulled hard on her wrist and pushed steadily on her shoulder. She hissed through clenched teeth and gasped in wide-eyed shock when I felt the ball of her arm bone re-seat into the socket. She looked at me with her mouth open, unsure. I slowly released her arm and she was able to ease it up and down. "Ow," she finally said in a conversational tone.

Another lurch, a shudder, and a grinding sound reminded me of my next task. I grabbed another of the suits from the cabinet Ian left open. I had seen him and Kara put them on before, during the trip to New Torment. I stripped down to my underwear and stepped into the thick, black material. It felt stiff and unyielding but moved freely once it was wrapped tightly around my body.

"Don't forget the power pack," Tabitha said. She got out of the rear seat and moved up to one of the control seats, all the while massaging her shoulder. I pulled out from the cabinet what looked like a fanny-pack. On the suit-ward side was a patch of tiny black fibers that matched the patch that was at the small of the suit's back. Once I got the pack situated, it adhered to the suit and stayed in place (the smart-fibers becoming both an anchor and a data port) as I connected the strap around my waist. The front of the strap had a console section that fed me numbers and symbols I didn't understand. With the connecting of the pack, strips and patches along the arms and legs illuminated, making the wearer and his or her movements readily visible against the blackness of space.

"Is this all right?" I asked Tabitha. She nodded and turned back to the console.

"From what I can tell, we're running on emergency power and life support. Inertial dampeners are still on maintenance mode. How in the world did we lift off without falling apart?"

I grabbed a mask and gaspack and started out the door. "Well, this is my first spacewalk. If I don't come back," I hoped I sounded as jocular as I wanted to feel about it, "you can have my stuff."

Tabitha smiled, "But you have to come back. You can't die without hearing about toe-moving disembodied foot."

"Ugh. Looking forward to it." We shared a look.

I walked out the door.

* * *

I stood in the port-side airlock, looking at the shallow concave plate in my hand. From the convex side it was just a sheet of opaque blackness. Turn it over, and from the side that goes toward the face, it was clear as windowpane. A tiny bundle of tubes and wires fed from the bottom of it to the pack strapped to my back. Around the edge of the plate was a wide plastic strip with "REMOVE" printed multiple times around it.

I tore the strip off and immediately a thick clear gel developed and grew around the edge. I took a breath, and raised the mask to my face. It smooshed around a little as it pressed against my head until it finally took a comfortable position before sealing itself from forehead to chin. I let out

my breath, expecting the inside of the glass to fog up. It didn't. A cool flow
of air flowed gently into the mask and I breathed easily.

The appearance of figures and numbers surprised me as they formed in
front of my face. A heads-up display with what I took to be indicators for
air quality and pressure, heart rate, and my location, which was currently:
"Port Airlock."

While it felt as hard as glass in my hand, as I moved my mouth I could
feel some give. "Hello, hello," I said. It wasn't uncomfortable. I heard a
buzzing down near my collar. The earplugs. I inserted them into my ear
canal, and Ian's voice filled my head, "Mitch . . . are you there? Mitch?"

"Yeah, yeah. Sorry. Almost suited." I pulled the hood of the bodysuit
over my head and ears and overlapping the edge of the mask. The edge of
the hood chemically bonded with the edge of the mask and I was now
contained in a single piece of material that would protect me from death.
Well, protect me from space, but what's the difference, really.

As soon as the hood sealed, a message popped up in my vision that said
"PECS Activation: Confirmed. PECS Systems: Stable." In the panel next to
the outer door, a red cartoon outline of a person changed to green when my
suit sealed up. Next to it the words: "All Occupants Ready," and a touch
area under that which read: "Airlock Open S-1." I touched it. The lights
inside the airlock, already dim, slowly faded out while a red glow brightened
steadily. I heard gas escaping and the pressure on my suit start to change. It
became slightly more rigid (although still not cumbersome), and gently
pressed into me from all directions. My ears wanted to pop and I force-
yawned to try to get them to. I also felt the suit start to warm up slightly. A
tiny display in the HUD, next to my heart rate (which was slightly fast, I
noticed), showed "37.1 / 18.3C".

After a moment, the escaping gas stopped and two new touch areas
appeared: "Airlock Open S-2" and "Re-Env Airlock." I pushed the first and
held onto the bar bolted next to the door, which separated and rotated away

into the wall in three pieces. I stood a moment, transfixed, while the ship shuddered unnoticed beneath my feet. With my free hand I reached out through the hatchway into space, breaking the imaginary plane that separated "inside" from "outside." There was no more difference than when one reaches inside a house to the outside, no give, no pull, no anything. Somehow, I still could tell a difference. I felt that I was touching space through my suit-encased hand. I felt it; I know it.

"You coming, or what? I need you at that port access area. If you don't get the sub-system shut down and sealed off, the inertial dampeners won't stabilize and the ship'll break apart at the next smallest G-change."

"Yeah, I'm on my way."

I leaned out and over the edge of the hatch, where I could see nothing but more star field below me. An acute, though brief, feeling of vertigo hit me; I pulled myself against the edge of the opening to steady myself. The feeling passed, but I knew it was there at the edges should I look out (or down or up) with even the least apprehension.

I looked down and up and to the side of the outside of the ship and could find no hand holds or anything to grab onto. "Ian, how do I get down there? There's nothing to grab onto."

A pause. "Just touch the hull; the suit will hold you."

Well that's convenient, I thought. I reached around the edge and placed my hand flat against the hull and, in that instant before it touched, I felt my hand become attracted to the metal like a weak magnet. Yet, it stayed firmly attached to the hull. I had to roll my hand up from the wrist to the fingers in order to disengage my hand from the ship. I placed my hand on the inside wall . . . nothing happened. I reached back outside and firmly planted my hand, took a deep breath, and swung my leg out and against the hull so that I was hugging the ship, edge of the hatchway against my chest and face-mask. Once I was certain my outside hand and leg weren't going anywhere, I stretched and placed my inside hand on the outside, then pulled my body out and quickly hit my other knee against the outer hull, and I stuck fast. I gradually wiggled my body more and more forcefully, but my hands, leg, and knee were secure. *I can do this*, I assured myself.

I started inching down and away from the hatch and made it about ten feet before I realized I forgot the tool kit back in the airlock. The crawl back up and awkward return through the hatchway boosted my spacewalking confidence, though, so when I had the kit strapped around my body, I found it a lot easier to get out and back against the ship. I crawled on my hands and knees, backward, down the hull as it curved away. I could still feel the ship shudder and bump under me, but the urgency lessened as the feeling minimized without the stuttering artificial gravity. Once I got to the point where I couldn't see the hatchway any longer and I had no sense of being what I thought of as nearly upside-down, I rotated around so I could see where I was heading and pretty easily adapted to the idea of there being no up or down, top or bottom. I crawled around bulges and juttings and odd pieces of the ship toward where Ian wanted me.

My heart rate was quick, but stable, and what I was sure was the indicator for my skin temperature had fallen and stayed steady at sixteen degrees Celsius.

I crawled over a section that jutted out came upon a large section of the ship without hull plating, revealing about ten feet by thirty in which mechanical and electrical parts were exposed to space. A jet of vapor was silently geysering into the void and sparks shot from various places.

"Ian, whatever else is wrong, should this area be uncovered like this?"

"No. Without the plating there, here, and a couple of other places where maintenance was being done, all it will take is a pebble to enter one of these areas while we're in Q-thrust to tear the ship inside out. Fortunately, most of these open areas are in the aft, and we can set up some temporary localized shield generators in those areas. You ready?"

"Yeah," I said.

"Okay, I'll lead you through getting started, then come over when I'm done here. You're going to need to throttle any leaking gas first, before the main antimatter containment fails. Then you'll need to close the port dampener relays. . . ."

* * *

For hours, perhaps an entire sed, the three of us battened down the hatches, stored the mainstay, and swabbed the poop deck. Ian and I spent much of that time on the outside, refreshing our airpacks a couple of times, before moving inside and working on systems and equipment that had been disabled or open for maintenance when we took off. Tabitha had found a sling for her arm and worked inside the ship doing whatever Ian couldn't do with his remote control. We became space-worthy and safe from immediate disaster, capable of FTS flight–though worse off than we were before we landed at New Torment for repairs. After getting enough done to not worry about falling apart, we each crashed in various locations of the ship and slept.

Artificial gravity shut down sometime after we collapsed. An alert woke Ian up; my hitting my wounded leg on the ceiling woke me up. We finally got it working, for over half the ship again, at least.

Finally, when we were relatively rested and could think about what to do next, we discussed what to do next.

"Hide. Run and hide. Find somewhere to stay for a while under the scanner," Ian suggested. "Manatili que hacemos itim-itim."

Tabitha sat up in the galley chair, "You said they were gone. If anyone wanted to find us, they'd have known we'd survived already and have been back. We've been drifting here for two seds and haven't seen anything."

Ian shook his head, "The CASS will know; they'll find us."

"Why?" I asked. "Why are they even after us? What I mean is, I know why they're after me, sure. And I suppose this ship and everyone for helping me escape. But why blow up a whole mining facility? And us? Why not arrest us? I don't get it."

Tabitha furrowed her brows and looked to Ian and me and then back to Ian.

Ian shrugged. "I don't know."

"I have to admit," said Tabitha, "CASS is capable of a lot of things. They've exploited, extorted, and have even followed through on threats in the effort to spread their hegemony, but this does seem awfully odd. It was just wanton murder." She made a pained expression. "Are you sure it was CASS?"

Ian nodded, looking sullen: his normal state since the urgency of wrapping the ship up in duct tape subsided.

"Maybe it was someone else who wanted to make it look like CASS, and we just happened to be at the wrong place and time," I offered. Tabitha nodded thoughtfully. "Is there any reason why someone would want to do that to New Torment?"

Tabitha considered and finally shook her head. "We've had some trade rights disputes with another mining co-op, but that was worked out amicably some time ago. I hate to say it, but I'm sure it had something to do with you. It only makes sense."

I tried to detect any hint of anger or resentment in her tone; I just heard sadness and exhaustion. "Tabitha," I said, meeting her eyes. "Listen, I'm really sorry about what happened. I . . . I realize all your friends and coworkers and . . . everyone. . . . Knowing that what happened was, because I just happened to be there, god. I just . . . I'm sorry."

She gave me a tired smile and looked down. No one spoke. A hum, more perceived because of the knowledge that a change in tone or timbre could mean trouble, seemed to emanate from everywhere. A beep, a ting, a quiet chime from here and there.

Tabitha took and let out a deep breath and seemed more resolved, "We need to contact someone. Someone from the synd."

Ian looked stunned. "What? No. No, we can't do that."

"It's our best option. Maybe our only option," she countered. Tabitha stood up, moved around the chair, and leaned on its back with her free arm. "Look, Frankletti and I are both principals in the synd. If he's alive and able to do so, he's going to get a message to them, knowing I'll do the same."

"It's not a good idea. Even if our comm was working perfectly, which it's not, it will take years before a regular send from us reaches anyone. And we can't use the nodes; they're sure to be monitored."

"What's the 'synd'?"

Tabitha said, "Syndicate. It's the . . . trade collective, of sorts, Frankletti and I belonged to. We helped facilitate free trade, collective ownership of property, and subversion of CASS influence around various systems. At least until some years ago. There were some disagreements, some splitting off to form other groups. And eventually Frankletti and I ended up working to subvert the system from within the system."

"Subvert the CASS?" I shook my head, "Tabitha, don't take this the wrong way, considering, you know, a moment ago, but is there a chance that the CASS may have done what it did to New Torment because of *you*?" Now it was Ian's turn to look expectantly between her and me.

She said in a small voice, "Maybe." Ian scowled, accusative. "But, honestly, I hadn't been all that active lately." She looked disappointed at the admission. "Nothing that would warrant destroying New Torment, at least. I'd been on Torment for three years, and I hadn't done anything . . . provocative, in the synd, for a couple years before that. Besides, like I said, CASS is a lot of things, but they're not murderers of innocents. At least not directly, and not like that. Their mode of operating is through their own form of subversion as they gain political and ideological control of a place and people. When they use force, they use it where it's seen as a military necessity. This kind of thing, too messy and crude and no obvious benefit to them, that I can see." She looked at Ian.

"Look: I know what I know, alright? They were CASS ships. Don't ask me to explain it."

I asked, "What could this synd do to help us?" hoping to get the conversation back to something productive. I was a little upset that Tabitha may have thought she herself could have been the cause of the attack and left me to take all the guilt–but if what she said was the truth, I agree that doesn't seem likely. Plus, she'd been on the station for some time, then I arrive, and we're attacked before we even had time to take a breath. The weight of responsibility settled right back on my sloped shoulders.

"Aside from possibly relaying a message, I'm not sure," she said.

Ian snorted. "Figures. Bunch of criminals, anyway."

Tabitha turned on him. "What did you say?" she said in a low, dangerous voice.

Ian seemed to puff himself up. "Criminals. Insurgents, trouble makers, smugglers, and instigators of chaos."

"Wrong! Criminals do what they do for their own profit, without a care about who they harm and possibly even with the intent of harming. We took nothing for ourselves and worked to help others to shake off imperialism. What would you know about it?"

Ian stood up to match her. "I happen to know my brother and his family were victims of your synd's busy-bodying where they didn't belong. Ten years ago on AC Beta Prime he and his family bought into your group's garbage about fighting imperialism, fighting ideology. Fighting stability and security and prosperity is what it was! You don't think CASS is capable of what just happened? They nearly eradicated the entire settlement. Killed my brother, his wife, their kids."

Tabitha tried to keep a low, steady voice. "I'm sorry for what happened, but doesn't this just prove to you the evil CASS is capable of? Why it's important to fight their control over the systems?"

"It proves to me not to look the gift horse in the mouth. They had a good life, but your synd's rabble-rousing threw it into chaos, caused unrest where it didn't exist before. People were happy, and now they're dead, when they could have lived securely."

"If they were happy, how was the synd able to get them to believe in fighting for their independence? I wasn't there, but I know what happened. Those settlers weren't living happy and content lives. They were working more than half the day to farm and manufacture goods that were all shipped off to other systems by an unfair and brutal trade agreement those settlers had no say in. They didn't agree to be slaves when they established their colony there. Synd didn't have to work hard to convince the people there that they deserved better. They deserved to own their own labor. To see some benefits of their work instead of living in virtual shanty towns while the CASS-kissing politicos supposedly *leading* the colony were reaping all the rewards."

"Lies. Propaganda. My brother, Jenny, Mark, and four-year-old Saray died because of it."

"I'm sorry, but they, and the twenty synd members who helped them and encouraged them and fought with them, died trying to make a better life. The reason all of our ancestors risked their lives centuries ago to explore the most hostile and deadly environment any human is fool and brave enough to venture through."

Ian stepped toward Tabitha. "*You're* a fool for wanting to get your old playmates involved in this. You're going to get us killed."

She planted her left hand on her hip. "There's a Pansys node maybe four AU from here. We can reach it in just a couple of days. I can hack it and send a message without CASS knowing a thing about it. We have no choice, and you know it." Ian remained silent in the face of her challenge, and glared. "Where do you suggest we go, Ian? What do we do? You have some ideas?"

Ian lowered his eyes and looked distracted. I finally said, "Obviously I don't know what options there may be, but Tabitha seems to have a plan, and, Ian, well, unless you *do* have something better, something is better than nothing." I shrugged. "I say we head to the node and take it from there."

Tabitha relaxed but Ian looked positively disgusted. "What right do you have to say what we do?"

"What? Ian, settle down. I'm just trying to help out here."

"Help!?" He was nearly apoplectic, "You're the reason we're in this situation. You and your damn time device. I'd still be on Gadreus, Frankletti and Kara and Joseph wouldn't be dead, and I wouldn't be trapped on a dying ship with this whore!"

"Hold it right there, friend," Tabitha's voice took a quiet, deadly serious tone. "You have issues with the synd, fine. But I've never done anything to you personally, and I damn well am not going to let you call me that to my face and get away with it." She approached Ian and I was certain, wounded arm or not, she could take Ian out without getting winded.

I stood up and put my hands out. "Look, we just all of us need to calm down. We're in a bad situation. No doubt about it. But, Ian, this isn't you. This isn't the good-natured guy who joked around with me at the start of the trip. I don't know what the deal is, but it started before New Torment, and it's going to have to get resolved somehow, or else things are just going to get worse. Tabitha, he didn't mean it. We're all running red-lined, and we need to chill, and cut each other some slack. We all three need each other to get out of this." The two of them stared each other down, but their shoulders slackened some. "Can we get past this? Move on and find solutions, not excuses?" I couldn't believe I said that last; it just came out. I blamed too many corporate motivational seminars.

Tabitha shot me a glance I couldn't read. She put her hand in her pocket and looked at Ian. "Well?"

"Fine."

"That's it?" She looked ready to coil back up.

"I'm not going to apologize if that's what you're getting at."

I had to move in to defuse the situation before the break in tension evaporated completely. "We can all apologize to each other for a lot of things later. Let's just call a ceasefire and move on. We're the crew now. Let's take a breath and get moving. Okay?"

"I said, 'fine,'" Ian replied through clenched teeth.

Tabitha kept her glare on Ian as she sat down. She looked away and nodded.

"Good; it's a start."

Ian said, "We'll go to the node. You'll send your message. Then one way or another, we're parting company." He stormed off.

I watched him go and waited for the sound of his thundering against the metal-tiled floor to diminish. "Seriously, I don't know what the deal is. He's like a completely different person from when I first met him."

Tabitha stared a hole in the bulkhead.

"So, wait, I don't get something," I began. "Both you and Frankletti were in this synd thing. Why's Ian taking what happened to his brother out on you, but he's all buddies with Frankletti?"

"Frankletti saved his life before he knew who Frankletti was or what was in his past." She shrugged. "I guess, he just put that little bit of information in a mental compartment and threw it away."

We were silent for a moment.

Then I said, "This message: think it'll work?"

She sighed and seemed to shake off the last several minutes. "Yeah, I think it will." She shrugged. "I've done it before. It's actually not too hard. The problem is not knowing if it does get to the intended recipient, and, if so, when. Could be a day, could be a couple of weeks . . . all dependent upon what that node's package schedule is. I used to know the schedules pretty well, of the nodes in the systems I used to operate around. What gets lasered as slow and encrypted transfer, what gets sent off with regular trade or CASS ships to get FTS'ed to the next system. I've been next door to this node for a few years, and I've never actually been to it." She sighed and lowered her forehead to the table. "Maybe I *am* sinking into the mire of being a good little drone for the system."

Without anything to say to that, I hmm'ed.

After a moment, she furrowed her brow and asked, "What's it mean to 'cut slack'?"

CHAPTER NINE

The two-sed trip to the node ended up taking five as the Q-thrust system kept shutting down. Evidently, the lesson learned was that going from zero to ten thousand kilometers per second without working inertial dampeners makes things prone to not work properly. Ian, when he didn't have to work on some repair with his hands, spent almost all of his time in the cabin he had shared with Joseph and Kara. I stayed in the small spare cabin I'd flown to New Torment in. And, to Ian's endless disgust, Tabitha ended up staying in Frankletti's cabin.

At the end of the fourth day, Tabitha caught me wedged under the floor of the galley fixing a leak in the water system. Over the last few days I had become very intimate with the ship's computer schematics and systems repair documents. Tabitha was wearing some sweats and had her thick wavy hair tied back in a ponytail. She had been able to go without the sling after the first day thanks to fantastic pain relievers, muscle relaxers, and tissue repairing supplements. She leaned over where I was under the perforated metal flooring and asked, "Mitch, can I talk to you a minute?"

"Sure," I grunted. Centuries in the future and they still had wrenches that killed your knuckles in tight places. Flying cars: no longer a problem, however.

"No, I mean up here. Private."

Intrigued, "Oh, yeah, sec."

I shimmied and shook my way out of the ship's guts and crawled back up top. "What's up? Where's Ian?"

"Sleep, far as I can tell." She led me to her cabin. I admit to having felt both weird and excited about where this was going. I'd been in her cabin and she in mine the last few days, but always for business or casual conversation–not with an air of conspiracy and secrecy. When we walked in, she slid the panel closed behind us. I suddenly felt self-conscious about what I was doing with my hands. In pockets, to the side, pocket and side. . . .

"Do you know what this is?" She handed me a slate: a five-by-eight inch piece of paper-thin clear plastic computer. The entire surface was filled with text. I took it and used my finger to move the virtual pages around.

"It's ship's logs."

"See anything unusual about the time of the attack? I've been curious about it for days now, needing answers, looking for details. It just doesn't sit right to me."

I scrolled to that section of the log. Over the last couple of weeks I had gotten good at reading logs and data dumps, since being stymied over what Frankletti tried showing me about the *Lysander*. After all, in my day-job back in my home-time, a significant amount of my occupation was going through server logs and network traffic. These ship logs were in many fundamental ways not that different–just have to learn a different vocabulary, basically. "Hmm, well, some of these times seem out of sync. And . . . that's odd. Am I reading this here right?" I pointed to a section of the log.

"Yes, you're reading it right. For some reason the ship IDs fluctuate."

"Almost like . . . they were one ship and then another and back. That doesn't make sense. Some kind of . . . I don't know, cloaking or masking technology?"

"Possible. But not with some of these other anomalies, like the times and the missing entries."

"Hmm, that seems to happen a lot."

"What?"

"Nothing. What do you mean?" I sat on the bunk.

"When I checked the data integrity cycle records, there are indications of log entries that aren't there."

"Hacked?"

"That's my guess."

"They couldn't have done it at the time of the attack, could they?"

"Not likely, no."

I sighed, knowing where this was heading. "Why do you think Ian would do this?"

Tabitha sat at the other end of the bunk and crossed her legs. "I don't know. It's sloppy work, I can say that. And I think Ian could do a lot better than this."

"But you still think it was he who did it?"

She nodded.

"What could have happened he wants to hide? Does he want us to discover it?"

She shrugged. "Thing is, the edits seem to go back to even before the attack. I'd say maybe as much as an hour before. Missing sensor readings, missing comm log entries. It's made to look like nothing's missing, sort of like holes covered over with cloth. Thin, worn cloth. Maybe he is trying to make us see something. Or maybe he's just gotten incredibly sloppy and careless. You said it yourself. He's changed the last couple of weeks."

I nodded. "Should we confront him about it?"

She considered it. "No, not yet. We've kept a peace by avoiding each other; I don't want to rock the boat before we've had a chance to send the message. I don't think whatever he's hidden is going to make any difference now. Let's just get this part over with, then we can deal with this," she said indicating the slate.

"What about since?" I asked. She raised an eyebrow. "I mean, do you know if anything else has been altered in the logs since then?"

She furrowed her brows. "I don't know. But I can set up some processes to start doing cycle to entry comparisons and hope if he has done some more editing he hasn't cleaned up his act any better."

"Were you and Frankletti a couple?"

She actually shook her head in confusion. "Sorry, what?"

"I was just . . . I know, personal question. Sorry. I was just wondering if you and Frankletti ever had a . . . relationship. You just seem really fond of him and all."

She chuckled, "Yeah, we had a relationship. He was my boss, my mentor, my peer, and my friend. Pretty much in that order."

"Okay. I'm sorry; that was too personal, wasn't it?"

She cocked her head to the side, regarding me in an amused curiosity. "No, it's okay. He's not really my type. As a partner."

I smiled, "I see."

She leaned back against the wall at the head of the bunk, legs still crossed in front of her. "Your wife, Lori, right? How long did you say you've been married? Ten years?"

Reality-check time: as effective as a cold shower. I felt guilty for what I had been thinking, and had thought maybe a couple of times each of the last four days. "Yeah, ten next November. Er, that's still a month name, right?"

"Yeah, colloquially," Tabitha chuckled. "I don't get the marriage thing."

It was my turn to cock my head at her. "You know, the whole religious ceremony thing most people do. What's the point, really?"

"Well, tradition for a lot of people, I guess. I suppose that's why we did. It's not like Lori or I are religious people or anything. I mean, sure, I was raised Lutheran; she was Episcopalian. Neither of us practicing. But when it comes to something huge in your life, like, pledging to live it with another person, religious traditions suddenly become what's normal. Right?"

"Because it's what you've been convinced to believe as 'normal'."

"No one convinced us; it just *is*."

"Exactly." She sat forward. "Ideology is what is so ingrained into everything about your life that you're made to think it's what's 'normal' or natural. Why the ceremony you had? Whatever kind of ceremony you had. Why not a . . . " she thought deeply, "well, I don't recall other Old Earth religions. Why not a ceremony from another religion than yours?"

"I don't know . . . we're not part of the other religions."

"But you already told me you weren't really a part of your *own* religion, right? You don't really believe in it, you don't practice it. So, why is your non-practiced religion's marriage ceremony the only normal option? Why not a different religion's, or none?"

"I don't know, I guess I just never thought of it. *We* didn't. It's just . . . tradition."

"It is, it *is* tradition. Don't you see? Tradition thought of as what's natural and normal without even thinking about an alternative, or the negation, as possibly being equally natural. That's ideology. That's cultural mind control."

"By whom? This 'hegemony'?" By this point on our five-day-tour I had started getting used to hearing and saying that word.

"Exactly. What's easier to control than a flock of sheep?"

"Yeah yeah," I smiled, "a flock convinced to control itself by believing the will of the shepherd is the flock's will, right?" We'd had a few of these conversations, and she had gotten used to my good-natured skeptic playfulness, and I her earnest didactics.

She smiled back and sighed, leaning back against the wall. She unfolded one leg and brought it out in front of her where her pale foot, full of little curves and with well-kept nails, sat a couple of inches from my leg. "Trust me, by the time we get through this trip, I'll have you converted to a good anarchist. You're not the first I've had to work on, and you won't be the last."

"That sounded like a threat. I think I feel threatened."

She started to look serious again. "Do you miss her?"

I forgot about Tabitha's foot, but found myself staring at it anyway. "Yeah," I said quietly. "So much." And I did. Every day. "It's hard, you know. Sometimes I feel like I'm just away on a business trip, at a conference, and I'll be flying back to her in a day or two. Sometimes I feel like . . . she's dead and gone. Most of the time it's a weird, horrible combination of the two feelings I can't define or make sense of." Tabitha looked at me, quiet. "My daughter, Chloe–I keep thinking, 'I have to get home before her sixth birthday,' and I keep thinking I'll never see her again. And all the time, as far as I know, it's a crap shoot. A coin toss. For all I know I'll be going back to the moment I left and not a thing will have changed for them. Or, for all that I know, I'm here forever. And I'll never know which it will be, you know? It's that same coin toss in my mind today, tomorrow, the thousandth day I'm here, and beyond. Any day I'm here I could be back as if nothing happened, back when Chloe is herself fifty and a grandmother, or never. How in the hell do I live like this?"

Tabitha shook her head. Her eyes were a little glassy. She whispered, "I don't know."

"I guess we're all good at compartmentalizing when we have to, huh?" She nodded. We sat there, each in our own thoughts for a few minutes.

Then I said, "Well, if anyone's going to get a shower tomorrow, much less, oh, I don't know, have anything to *drink*, I better get back on that broken filter line."

"Yeah, I need a shower," she said, smiling.

"So, silent about the log thing, right?"

"Right."

I stood up, leaving Tabitha sitting pensive on the bunk. "Night."

"Night," she said.

* * *

The next day, after our respective showers, the Pansys node registered on shortwave scan. The three of us collected in a rare détente in the control room. "Well, there you go. Your node. Better get your suit ready," Ian told Tabitha without looking at her. In the field of stars out the windows, I could see a pulsing green light.

"Just wait. We still need to get through the security perimeter."

Ian looked surprised. I asked, "What security?"

Tabitha explained, "All Pansys nodes have a standard security perimeter a kilometer or so in a sphere out from them, to detect any ships intent of tampering with the node."

"Like us," I said cheerfully.

She smiled, "Yeah, something like us."

Ian turned from surprised to quietly upset. I'd given up wondering about his shifting moods.

"Ian," Tabitha said, looking at a sensor readout from her seat at the co-pilot's console, "I need you to stop here." He didn't appear to do anything, and the readout didn't reflect any changes. "We need to stop now before we set off the security alert." He made a couple of moves, positioning engines fired without sound, and we remained motionless inside the ship. It was looking to be a good day, techonology-wise.

"Okay, this shouldn't take but a minute. Unless they've changed their standard security protocols over the last few years . . . which I highly doubt." She had started typing furiously at the console.

Ian was sulking in his command chair. Several times the last few days I had tried to talk to him. At odd times, when we had to work together to fix something, I would catch him in a decent mood, and we'd actually have a conversation. He had an interest in "ancient" computer technology, and at those times I could see the old Ian. Stupid jokes, a bit of goofiness. But most of the time he was sullen, and much of the time he seemed anxious and nervous. I couldn't help but began to be concerned about our safety. He never seemed violent, but my years of movie watching warned me to keep my cabin door locked the last couple days. I just hoped that after this we could part ways, and, as Ian suggested, he could go to wherever he'd get some rest and downtime. Giving him the benefit of the doubt, I couldn't actually blame him, after what happened on New Torment with Joseph, Frankletti, Kara.

But it was weird–I would think given any chance to possibly find Frankletti and Kara, he'd take it. Tabitha had assured me that Ian was loyal to Frankletti and looked up to him, and on the trip to New Torment I could see that. However, I could also see how much Frankletti could get under his skin about religious issues. Not that Ian seemed like a fundamentalist by any means. Though, he did take what he believed quite personally. Don't we all? Maybe Ian was secretly glad not to be forced to be loyal to the man any longer.

"That should do it," Tabitha finally said. "I've essentially made the node think its security sphere was still up and running, but we should be able to get in close now and not set off any alarms." She got up while Ian wordlessly set the ship to close in on the node. She had readied her suit and equipment next to one of the now ever-present tool kits that seemed to be needed in nearly every part of the ship at random times, and started suiting up. She strapped her own kit of electronics and computer parts around her torso and paused to watch the crescent-shaped Pansys node grow in size. It was difficult to estimate how large it was; at first it looked like it could have been the size of an entire station, then I could see it as being the size of a couch–but then it got too big for that, and I finally settled on it being the size of a small house. It had markings here and there, some looking like official identification, some cautions or warnings, and that green beacon jutting out on top, flashing in a hypnotic pattern.

"Good," said Tabitha, breaking the silence. "If you could spin around so it's outside the starboard hatch, that should get me close enough to just hop over to it and get to work." Again, without a word, Ian set the ship to gently rotate so the node drifted off to the right of the windows.

"How long do you think it'll take?" I asked.

Tabitha was preparing her face-mask, "Maybe thirty minutes, tops. I just have to remove a couple of access panels, patch into the circuitry, do some of this and some of that, and send the message."

Ian sat stiffly. I said, "Well, good luck." She smiled and started out of the control cabin. I called after, "And don't forget to bring back milk and eggs!"

I got into the co-pilot's chair, adjusted a couple of settings, and saw the airlock indicators for the starboard hatch. Saw the processes of decompression and the seal opening. After a moment Tabitha came on the comm, "Alright, I've reached the node and am getting to work."

"Roger." I sat back in the chair and stared off into the star field. I could see a pulsing shine of green light off a section of the ship out the right, or starboard, window panel. On . . . off. Five second pause. On . . . off. Pause. On . . . off. I was uncomfortably aware of Ian staring at the console, not moving. I was afraid to move myself, thinking it would just point up *his* not moving, and make my awareness of it even more uncomfortable. On . . . off. Pause.

After some time Tabitha came back on, "Okay, all's good. Message being sent. I should be back on in a few."

"Roger, dodger."

Back to the silence.

Until I saw the console indication that the airlock had closed. "Huh," I said in the comm, "That was fast."

Tabitha replied, "What do you mean?"

"You're not done?"

"No, I still need to cover my work and get unpatched. Just a few."

I looked over at Ian. He hadn't actually moved, except his eyes, which were now darting around in his remote control way. "The security sphere was a disappointment. I had hoped she wouldn't have known about it. But I forgot. She's done this kind of thing before."

"Ian, what are you talking about?" I felt a shiver down my spine.

"Forgetful. Heh, I've been so forgetful lately."

I tried to reopen the airlock from my controls, but they didn't respond. I tried to chuckle, "Open the pod bay door, HAL."

"It started with my forgetting how important my role was to be. I got caught up in the superficial, and forgot the purpose. The greater purpose." Then the lights cut out and switched to a dim red glow. An insistent chime began to ring. The ship's hum changed.

"Hey," asked Tabitha's distant voice in the comm, "Everything alright over there? What's going on?"

"Ian, what are you doing?" I tried to use the console, but most of the screens and buttons and controls had gone dark. A white strobe light somewhere in the room started breaking the enveloping red.

"I thought to save myself, save the ship. It was reflex, really. A forgivable lapse of humanity, I hope. I'm making up for it now. I know my role."

"Ian, seriously, I don't know what you're doing, but surely we can work this out, right? Ian?" Something blew in the ship and rattled the floor tiles. Ian's humorless smile was alternatingly awash in red and harsh blinding white.

"Mitch, what's going on over there? The hatch is closed. I can't open it."

I crouched next to Ian and grabbed his shirt, turning his chair around to me. "You don't have to do this. Is it her? Are you wanting to get rid of her? Look, it's almost over. You can take off as soon as her friends come. It'll be fine."

"It *is* almost over, Mitchel. I'm okay now. God has been telling me what

I needed to do. I thought my job was to just hand you and the device over to the Priory. But I was wrong."

"Device? The time device? It was here on the ship, all this time?"

"I was to lead them to the device, but it was my duty to destroy you myself." The ship groaned and shuddered, and something else blew. I could smell something burning and hear the distant sound of spraying fire-suppression foam.

"Ian, no."

His eyes unfocused and he continued to move them around at unseen controls as he started mumbling something ritual sounding. I shook him by his shirt. "Stop this! Ian, stop, please!"

"Mitch! What's wrong with the ship? It's shaking."

"Stop, please stop." The tool kit was next to me.

"It's okay, Mitchel. Almost done. Maybe you'll have a reward waiting for you as well. I understand, I really do. You're not evil, you're part of His Plan, just like me. Almost done."

The wrench was in my hand. "Stop!"

"Almost. . . ."

I hit him across the temple as hard as I could. His head jerked without resistance. He slumped forward, head lowered, as if in reverence. Blood streamed from his hair and through the slots in the floor.

His voice, croaking and small, "Almost. . . ."

I didn't even feel myself hit him again. And again. He was on the floor. I felt ice water flood my muscles, and then I could feel. The wrench was poised to hit again, and I so wanted to. God help me I wanted to keep hitting him into and through the floor. I dropped the wrench.

I tried to stand, but my legs had no strength. I clawed myself into the chair and fumbled at the console. I had control back. The containment was failing and antimatter was at risk of a critical cascade. I hit every automated emergency process I could find. Another shudder nearly shook me out of the chair. I gripped the console and ripped my palm open trying to stay upright. I did everything I could to try to stop the cascade, but I couldn't. I cursed myself for not knowing what to do. I cursed the ship. The acrid smell of some fumes hit me hard, and everything went soft and pale.

The specter of death reached out for me. I didn't want to go, but it made me get up.

Death's face was shiny.

CHAPTER TEN

I woke up, cramped, freezing, with a horrible headache and a sick stomach.

"Don't, don't move. Lay still." Tabitha's disembodied voice was in my ear. Everything was blurry, but I could make out a black human-like shape with a bright halo for a face. After a moment, the glare eased up, and I could see the reflecting mirror set in the center of the ring of light. Tabitha in a PECS suit and mask.

"You rescued me." I saw blurry numbers and symbols dancing in my vision. I was in a suit and mask as well.

"Maybe. That's yet to be seen, actually."

"The ship–"

"Gone. Wish I could have seen it blow; an antimatter micro-singularity is a sight not to be missed."

I moved my head around, blinking, trying to focus. I still couldn't see anything else but the black against dark shape of Tabitha looming over me. Something was pushing into my back, and my legs were numb. My hands, too. I could feel something akin to pain, significant pain, but not a part of me. Like it belonged to the suit, and I was just touching the pain. "Where are we?"

"Inside the node. I got a mask on you just in time. The ship was filled with toxic fumes and smoke. I set the ship to Q-thrust away as fast as possible, with a delay. It actually took off just as I got you to the hatch, and it took us maybe a thousand meters out before we were scraped out the hatch into space."

"I'm hurt." I wasn't sure if I asked a question or made an observation.

"Well, you had a mask on. I thought we were going to be able to just hop from the ship to the node before it left. I had to use personal navjets to get us to the node. You got frostbite by the time we got inside, but luckily the medkit has a dose of metabolic boost. The suit's warming you up and we can check later if there's any permanent damage. You're going to have a full-body bruise for a while, though."

Ghostly numbers started to become clearer. 36.0 / 11.1C. In the dim light of a portable lamp I saw we were in some very tight space, like a wiring closet. Conduits of cables ran along us into the darkness. Tabitha lay next to me in what amounted to a crawlspace. "What do we do now?"

"Well, once you feel like moving, we crawl along this access tube until we reach the emergency maintenance cabin. I've already been up and back–it's where I got the medkit. All of these nodes have a little space in case Something Bad Happens and a maintenance worker gets stranded. Kind of handy, don't you think?"

"Yeah, handy."

The body temperature display continued to slowly rise, and with it the pain in my extremities. It started to move from being something spectral to belonging very definitely to my body. "My hands and feet . . . really starting to hurt."

"Well, I can give you a little more pain killer, but we need to get moving as soon as we can, and you're going to need to be conscious and aware."

"A little more," I said, my voice level.

Tabitha reached above her head into the floating medkit she'd tethered to a conduit. She pulled out a bundle of small clear envelopes, each with a disk of various colors about a half inch in diameter. She held the bundle close to her mirrored face mask. "My glasses were back on the ship. Hope they used standard color-coding on these."

"Wait, what?"

"I'm kidding." She sounded like she was smiling. She selected a yellow one, opened the envelope and "popped" it by pushing its center until it clicked. Then she felt my suit around the neck and pulled out a light blue disk that was already there. She inserted the yellow and pulled out a tab of plastic film. "No, actually, I can't even see colors well." Before I could panic she said, "Still kidding."

A second or two later I felt warmth move through my arms and legs, my head began to feel light, and the pain receded to background noise. "Better than ibuprofen gelcaps," I quipped. I couldn't tell what expression she made.

I relaxed, clenching and releasing my fists while Tabitha folded up the kit. I noticed the discarded disk floating languorously, bounding from pipe to conduit, off Tabitha, to ricochet off the metal grill we lay on.

"Ready to go?"

With gentile motions, I squirmed around to get in a good position to pull myself up, or along, the conduit. My leg, which had begun to feel perfectly fine the last couple of days, was aching and sore. My hands and feet still felt burned and were a little numb, but all the pain was dull and manageable. "Yeah, lead the way."

With the kit pulled along by one hand, the halo of light projecting from the edge of her mask leading the way, she started snaking forward: worming her way past me like a lithe black cyborg serpent, then crawled on. Her body blocked my vision of anything in front of us, save for odd glimpses of heavily shadowed wires and cables and panels whenever her head and rear moved in such a way as to let me see past. We slithered this way for a few minutes, my leg becoming increasingly stiff, until Tabitha stopped. I realized my mask's external microphone was picking up no sounds as she released the manual seals on a panel and pushed it into a space beyond. She gripped the edge of the hatch, not much bigger than she was, and pulled herself through in one move. I pulled myself up and looked through into a room, maybe fifteen feet by ten, and five feet high. A faint blue light that reminded me of the bioluminescence of some sea creatures cast a pall over the alcove.

I pulled myself in, somewhat more clumsy than Tabitha had, and floated to the far side. Tabitha replaced the panel and twisted the seals closed. "'Scuse me," she mumbled as she floated around me to reach a panel on the wall. A couple of button pushes, and the blue light faded from barely there to somewhat there, and I felt a slight change on the pressure my suit was exerting against me.

"Should be just a few minutes, and we can take the masks off. The atmo' is almost ready but it'll take a bit to warm up in here."

"No artificial gravity?"

"We're lucky these things even have canned air for an amenity."

I nodded. The blue room contained a handful of cabinets, one of which Tabitha was returning the medkit to, and the odd strap and handle here and there to aid in moving around–or keep *from* moving. Opposite the panel we entered through was the official hatchway that led out to space. It wasn't much bigger than the ersatz door we made.

Tabitha reached up and unsealed her mask. The ring of pin-lights faded out and I could hear the brief Velcro-like tear of the mask pulling away. Her face was odd and spectral in the blue glow. She took a deep breath. "Home sweet home," she said, smirking.

* * *

"So, it could be a day, maybe twenty, maybe never." I said.

"Yep, that's about right." She was half lying in the bedslot. A narrow, cushion-lined space in the wall meant for sleeping, lounging, waiting for death. I was below her (according to the arbitrary directions I established), lying against the wall, occasionally nudging myself back against it with the use of a recessed handhold. She continued, "I know the message was sent successfully, but I've no way of knowing if anyone from the synd will receive it, and, if so, how long before they arrive."

"What about, like, an emergency beacon? Surely if the node has this room, it must have that." She was silent. "Tabitha?"

"Yeah, it does."

"Okay. So, what? It activates automatically, or you had to do it?"

She paused. "No."

I sighed and rubbed my eyes with the palms of my hands, which caused me to drift slightly. My fingers and toes felt like they'd been burned, but there was no permanent damage from the exposure to empty space. Apparently, it can take a long time to freeze to death in a vacuum. "Alright. You don't want to set the beacon. I can understand why. We just renovated. Property value is up. Our neighbors are nice, and it's so hard finding a neighborhood with good schools. Why should we want to leave?"

"You're feeling better," she said. From my angle, I couldn't see more than her arm disappearing under her drifting hair as she rested her head on it, snug in the bedslot.

"Yeah. So what's the deal?"

She rolled over to look at me over the side of the slot. "Used cautiously we have maybe as much as twenty days of rations. Air shouldn't be a problem. Once the beacon is set off, a CASS cruiser, or some CASS-contracted repair or recon ship, could get to us as little as five days. Maybe less. Let's see if the synd arrives in fifteen days. That should be ample time."

I thought for a moment. "'As little as.' But maybe more. So we could wait the fifteen days, no one comes, we argue and fight, and I finally convince you to set off the beacon. What happens when it takes six days? Seven? Another fifteen? Maybe the closest CASS-contracted ship was supposed to come from New Torment? How long before they figure out there's been an unanswered node beacon and send someone from the next closest system a week or two away? Are you prepared to die with a whimper from starvation along with your ideological hatred?"

She just looked at me over the edge of the bed. She may have been trying to figure out a way to say "yes" and believe it herself. Finally, she said, "Considering New Torment was CASS's doing, I think they may already be aware. In fact, they may still have a ship in the vicinity just waiting for emergency beacons."

I shook my head, "I don't think it was CASS."

"Of course it was. We already figured–"

"No. Remember when you showed me the logs the other day?"

"Yeah."

"It fits now. What we suspected, it's real."

She furrowed her brows in the dim blue light, "What do you mean? Ian? What happened back there?"

I thought for a moment to straighten out what I could remember–put it in order. It was only a few hours ago, but the unconsciousness, the shock, left my memory of those last minutes on the ship a jumble I had to sort through, sitting there in the node. As we were warming up, I had told her an overview: Ian went crazy, took over the ship and started it toward a destructive cascade. However, I hadn't yet told her what was said. "He told me he was leading someone to the time device. That he was to be an instrument in my death."

"An arrangement with CASS? To also lead you to where Frankletti and his old synd friends were, maybe? Perhaps your escape from Gadreus was easier than it should have been?"

I sighed. Her obsession was starting to grate on my nerves. "No no. He said something about . . . a priory, I think."

"'Priory'? That's like a monastery or abbey or something, isn't it?"

I nodded. "Yeah, I think so. Something like that. Doesn't sound CASS related."

Tabitha was gazing off at the wall. Finally, quietly, she whispered, "No, I guess it doesn't."

In the blue silence, I thought about what happened on the ship and the feeling of being out of control as I realized Ian was destroying the ship around me, murdering me. How he was able, in a sense, through mere thought, to kill me, and I couldn't reason with him. Ian was gone and was replaced by some fanatic that couldn't be talked to, couldn't be diverted from his task. I was scared. More scared than I'd ever been, more than the time I went tandem skydiving for my twenty-fifth birthday. More scared than the time I'd broken my arm in the back of a system of caves my Explorers troop was exploring and I didn't know if I could get out of the crevice I was stuck in. That feeling of being utterly out of control (and facing imminent death, leading me to do what I did to Ian) made my stomach turn. The image of Ian turned from a living human into a bashed inanimate object by my hand–I felt the blood drain from my head and my stomach lurch. I reached for the plastic bag I had nearby for when the pain medicine started to fade and the zero-g combined to make for a roller coaster in my guts.

After the violence of my dry heaving (my empty stomach serving me well), Tabitha asked, "Still getting used to weightlessness?" She looked at me with concern.

I shrugged. "I dunno, maybe."

It's a cliché, the whole blood-on-your-hands thing, but it's also surprisingly true. I felt like my hands were dirty, covered in something that had to be scrubbed clean. I didn't feel compelled to crack into a whole Lady Macbeth scene, but the urge to wash my hands clean was strong. I cinched the bag closed and just tried to breathe easy.

What if I had to do it again, I wondered. I had liked Ian at the beginning; he spoke to me as a friend, was the first to really teach me about where I was and how to get answers from the unfamiliar technology. I had no idea what stressors caused him to break, caused his underlying ingrained ideology to fester and transform into something deadly. What if Tabitha turned? Her own, separate ideology was already closer to the surface. She's fought for it, had maybe even killed for it already–is possibly willing to die for it. What happens in fifteen days or so when our choice is to call for help or die . . . will she make the call? Will she prevent me from doing so? Will I be forced to kill her to save my life?

In the cold, harsh light of reason, the idea that I could contemplate killing another person, in order to save my own life or not, startled me. I had already done so, only hours ago, and here I was debating with myself if I could do it again. I looked at Tabitha. She was staring up at the top of the bed slot, pensive. I watched her eyes occasionally squint, chew her bottom lip in thought. She had locks of hair, auburn-turned-blue in this light, float lazily around her head. Could I imagine her becoming dangerous? Could I see her threatening to kill me if I stood in the way of her ideals-driven goal?

Yeah, I could. It frightened me in the way the last moments with Ian had: I was not in control. I hadn't been in control for days–not since I got here. I had been buffeted by a sea of forces acting upon me, pushing me here and there, having me do this or that without my knowing what was going on and why.

What's the alternative, I thought. *Stranger in a strange land,* and all that. Surrounded by people I don't know, at their mercy for my survival, at the very least. And for helping me possibly, maybe, *hopefully* get home. Back where I have a daughter who sleeps with her arm above her head and collects lizard-themed toys, a wife who stays up when I stay late at work and smells like strawberry and vanilla shampoo, a job, friends, regular television programming, poker night twice a month, and a cedar deck I'm building on the back of the house. Back where I have control, or at least a semblance of control. I am in an impossible situation, looking for an improbable answer, doing formerly unimaginable things.

It was time I took back some control and guided my *own* path. Whether it landed me in a future-world prison, stranded on a remote planet, had me do things I didn't think I was capable of–it was time I stopped being so helpless.

CHAPTER ELEVEN

It happened on the eleventh day. It probably saved our lives.

I can't even begin to describe ten days of mind numbing boredom and tedium while locked in a sterile room that was not even large enough to do a cartwheel in. We know: on the fourth day we had a zero-g cartwheel competition, despite the low height of the ceiling, and Tabitha won. I think. I won the room laps competition, and a few others. She won most of them, though. It gets kind of blurry in there, those several days. I can imagine that only prisoners, in jails in which they are forgotten by the guards, could truly appreciate what we were going through.

We continued on the first day to talk about Ian, CASS, what this priory thing must have meant–but we eventually gave up because we had nothing to go on. Then we took turns reading stuff on the node's Pansys archive. That kept us occupied now and then, for a while. Nevertheless, eventually, the need to *do* something would accelerate the stir-crazy. After the first day, we took to challenging each other to various competitions: throwing paper airplanes (and paper shuttles and paper probes and paper satellites and paper planets that looked a lot like crumpled balls of paper) into various receptacles around the room, who could come up with the most rhymes for a word, who could touch the wall longest without floating too far away, who could count the furthest in prime numbers, most cartwheels. . . .

And we learned a lot about each other. Floating about or strapped to a wall or taking a turn in the bed slot, during the quiet moments between sleep and competitions tinged with a hint of desperation, we would talk in the blue glow about our pasts, becoming more candid each passing day. I learned about her estrangement with her family, her sister's murder, her own brutal rape at the hands of a supposed friend years ago. I told her about my dashed dreams of being an artist, my wife's first miscarriage and the way I sobbed like a baby when Chloe was born.

We also got on each others' nerves, a lot. At first, it was the big differences: roles of government, use of economy, tolerance regarding different political or religious views. The irony is that we both fundamentally believed similar things on these accounts, but where we differed we felt compelled to convert the other person. During the first couple of days, we tended to ignore the differences or make light of them. Joke about them or shrug off a conflict, knowing that there would be no sense in arguing. But as the days creaked on, we stopped caring about decorum or manners or politeness when we would bump against a philosophical difference. The little things would turn into arguments, which would turn into verbal fights, and, if we were lucky, would turn into icy silence for hours until one of us would come up with a new challenge that we would both embrace wholeheartedly as a change in the temperature of our mood.

On the ninth day, we had been discussing something ridiculous–the best method of routing around binary star system Lagrange points (I had been keeping up with my astrogation self-training) and it turned into a shouting match. In retrospect, what we had been arguing was absolutely inane; but, at the time, it was the most important subject in the world. Undoubtedly, we were projecting all of our tired, anxious, cramped and sweaty frustration into this ridiculous argument; and, during a peak of the shouting match, I made the regrettable mistake of yelling, "If only you'd fucking listen to me, you arrogant bitch!" and she hit me. It was a good punch to the jaw, despite the awkwardness of zero-g giving her little leverage. I'd never hit anyone

before (well, except when I killed Ian), so, fortunately, my first instinct
didn't include doing that. I grabbed her arm, but the lack of gravity caused
us to pretty much flail in opposite directions. I landed against one of the
walls, and Tabitha deftly righted herself and glared at me with a look of
disgust. My blood was pounding in my ears, my hands felt numb–there was
a part of me that was dying for an all-out fight, but most of me was chilled
back into sensibility by her glare.

I spat, "Look, I'm sorry," at her. I was, too; but, for some reason, I
couldn't sound as sincere as I actually was. She called me the equivalent of
"asshole" and glared for a while longer while I tried to ignore her. We
steamed like that for a few hours, and then we both fell asleep at some
point.

I woke up afraid. I woke up with a sickening feeling that I'd offended her
beyond repair. I woke up with an image of Ian in my mind calling her a
harlot with true spite in his voice and on his face, and I felt disgusted with
myself. I looked around and saw her in the bed slot already looking at me
with a completely blank stare. I immediately said, "Please, I *am* sorry. I
didn't mean it."

She blinked, sighed, and nodded. But didn't speak for a few hours more.

After a while, she put on her PECS and stepped outside for a bit. I had a
silly fear that she'd somehow catch a passing ship and leave. When she came
back in and accepted my earlier apology and apologized for hitting me, I
told her this, and she laughed and called me ridiculous. We were good for a
while after that.

We verbally tiptoed around each other for another day, staying on light
topics, but eventually we found a land mine and tripped upon another
similarly innocuous disagreement that quickly exploded into name-calling. I
honestly don't recall who hit whom first. I regret to say it could have been
me, and, despite everything that has happened between Tabitha and me since
then, I still regret the possibility that I may have started it and hit a woman–

an action that fills me with self loathing despite the fact that Tabitha would later chide me for condescension to her gender by feeling like that. But we've since decided that it doesn't matter: we were both on a course toward a fight, and it didn't matter who threw the first punch.

We had grabbed onto each other in order to land blows in weightlessness. We grabbed each other by the hair, around the neck. It was disgusting how brutally we fought each other. At some point, we separated, floating away from each other. We were both panting in ragged, strained breaths. Tabitha's pony-tailed hair had been torn loose from its binding, and her visage of rage, tear-wet face and mouth in a grimace, peered through her tangled hair. There was a dark blue-black stain on her teeth and lips I could tell was blood. I felt blood run from my nose and float away as shiny black spheres that would eventually get caught by the air filters. My throat was sore, probably from screaming at her through the fight, but I don't remember. We had both gripped onto wall straps at opposite ends of the room, panting at each other. I think I started crying, angrily. I knew even at that moment it wasn't Tabitha I was really mad at, but she had to be my only target. I wanted to tear her apart in righteous anger. I wanted to die from self-hatred and disgust for feeling that way.

I don't recall either of us apologizing. At least not then, nor the next couple days. In a strange way, I think we both silently understood the inevitability, and understood how we both really felt. It was like a ritual of sorts: a rite we both had to participate in and pass in order to move on to the next stage. One doesn't apologize for participating in a ritual. It was an understanding that came over us minutes after we had stopped.

When I could see again through my burning, wet eyes, I saw her on the other side with her face in her hands, sobbing. I floated over to her. I wasn't sure what to do, I wasn't thinking. My hands had taken her by the upper arms on their own accord. She tensed and looked at me. I think I looked at her with confidence–at least, that's the best way I can describe it. She saw me in that moment. She closed her eyes and wrapped her arms around me, viscously, and hugged me tight. I did likewise. We didn't say anything for some time.

After a while, maybe a couple of hours–I don't recall, we treated each other's wounds in our underwear. Tabitha was already unburdened by excess modesty, having grown up in a fraternal environment of freedom fighters, but it had taken me a few days to get used to the idea that constantly wearing our clothes was making our increasing personal fragrance a little worse. We could clean ourselves with our limited water–to a point, but our clothes were out of the question. I make no excuses for the fact that I found Tabitha rather attractive from the beginning, so the idea of our running around half-naked was probably more intimidating to me than I would admit. However, after the first few days of feeling unclean, as well as somewhat brotherly to her after hearing the story of her past, and occasionally angry at her for disagreements both slight and serious, the sexual tension I personally felt was reasonably suppressed.

Until we were drifting next to each other, our still elevated body heat palpable between us. She had once again bound her hair back and I had carefully, gently, put a tiny bandage under her bottom lip, then she had set a strip of tape across my nose. When she reset the cartilage in a single, painful, skillful move, I felt something sexy about the act of her strong, sure movement, barely muted by the explosion in my face. I held onto her hips to give her leverage and stability as she made the repair on my nose. Her skin was moist and warm. My hands were still there after she finished with the tape. Her hands were still on my face. As with the first hit, I don't recall who moved toward whom first for that kiss. We agreed later that it, too, was inevitable.

* * *

We alternately made love, had sex (there's a difference, of course), dozed, and talked in quiet tones for a few hours before finally falling into a deep sleep.

There were moments during those first few hours when guilt clawed at my consciousness; but, fueled by endorphins and desire, happiness and comfort for the first time in weeks, I wouldn't allow it. When I woke up, my defenses were down. We had somehow sleepily attached some of the wall straps to a thin blanket so we could lie underneath without drifting around. Tabitha was still asleep, spooned in front of me, her hair in my face warm from my breath. I thought of Lori. I rolled on my back and wept silently, my chest so tight I understood the idea of a heart breaking.

I finally slipped out from under the cover and drifted to where tissues were stored in a cabinet of personal hygiene afterthoughts by whoever stocks these emergency pods. My head felt like it was going to explode, my fists ached from clenching. Images of Lori, Lori and I, Lori and Chloe, kept flooding my mind. Thoughts of betrayal wracked my consciousness. I didn't hear Tabitha approach: I felt her wrap her arms around me from behind and rested her head on my shoulder. She didn't say anything and I was glad. But I put my hand on hers to let her know I accepted her comfort–even though she was a part of the reason I was in pain.

Lori would understand, I finally convinced myself. I felt that if the situation had been turned around I would have understood. The place and time, the aching need for comfort and affection, the very real near-certainty that I'd never return home. On the flip-side, a voice kept telling me I was a terrible person for not being able to control myself like the romantic paragon of virtuous loyalty to my love and wife I was supposed to be, and refrain from the vile temptations that beset upon me on my quest to return to her. I felt pathetic.

"I'm sorry," I said. I think it was meant for Lori, who couldn't hear it, as much as to Tabitha for my appearance.

She gripped my hand, "It's alright." She didn't mean my appearance. She lifted my head to look me in the eyes. Her face was both soft and strong, confident. "It's alright," she said again. It was consoling, and matter-of-fact. She meant it, and she wanted me to believe it. It was okay. I had to understand that whether what I did, what we did, really was acceptable or forgivable or not, didn't currently matter. It was okay for no other reason than because it *had* to be.

* * *

Obviously, things were different after that. We didn't necessarily argue any less (we were still two humans locked in a tin can), but the passion in the arguments wasn't nearly as inflamed as before and never came close again to becoming violent. We found we were a little more cautious of our words and would either choose to cut the argument short and not talk for a while, or channel the aggravation into sex. Which we did a lot the next few days: sometimes out of boredom, sometimes loneliness, sometimes for what seemed like a guerrilla movement of affection and care for each other. I think that last one was the reason that scared both of us equally. For Tabitha, I think she'd had so few intimate relationships, spent so much of her life in the service of an idea and not individual people, she didn't know where something like this could take her–and that frightened her. She had always been in control of what drove her, and this *thing* between us was an unknown element.

For me, it wasn't lack of control of my feelings that was a problem–I'd felt these feelings of affection before, and that was the problem. I knew what this could lead to for me. I could accept a purely physical relationship. I think, given the circumstances, even Lori would, too. I hoped. Two people, alone, forced to interact for days on end, uncertain whether they'd be alive in another few days–it might have even been unusual if nothing happened at all. I could accept it if this is what we had there, in that emergency pod, and, once we were rescued, we'd go back to being . . . well, whatever it was we were on *The Bluerock*. However, there was something else developing that I didn't like, and it had to do with the way I watched her sleep. The way she'd crinkle her face when she got aggravated. The way she'd put her hands on my shoulders and press herself against my back as she looked over my shoulder at what I was reading on the five-inch monitor set in the wall. The way I would sometimes forget to analyze what she was saying, for any holes in her position about whatever, and just listened to her talk, enjoying the tone and cadence.

On a couple of occasions, she would stop talking and cock her head to the side. "Well?"

"Hmm?"

"Do you disagree?"

"Mmm, uh, no, that sounded good."

"Were you even listening?" she'd say as if what she had been saying may have been crafted to force me to take a counter-view and express it in no uncertain terms.

"Sure I was," and I'd repeat more than just the words she said, but illustrate I knew the intent.

She'd squint and look at me sidelong, "Okay, you're weirding me out."

I'd make a goofy face or something, and chuckle, and we'd talk about something else. Or have sex.

I didn't know if this could last. Did I want it to? If my feelings for Tabitha only increased, would it affect my choices to get back home?

CHAPTER TWELVE

We waited until the "evening" of the fifteenth day before either of us even brought up the subject of the beacon. As the day went on, we grew quieter and politer to each other. It felt as though any disruptive noise would wake the bear that rested just inside the Cave of Avoidance we were tiptoeing in front of.

Somehow, late, we had finally managed to find ourselves facing each other in front of the beacon terminal. We stared at each other, Tabitha with a certain uncertainty and lack of assertiveness that actually bothered me. As they progressed, I'd wondered how the last few days would change her, if at all. They must have: something was making her less adamant and sure of her own sense of rightness, and that concerned me. Not only because I have a distrust and disappointment in those who change for another person, but because a change in Tabitha's outlook and attitude solidified the fact that *something* significant was happening between *us* that I didn't want–even though I desired it. I didn't want the responsibility for someone changing because of me, even a tiny bit, especially when, if things worked out, I would be out of their life as soon as possible.

As we looked at each other, waiting for someone to drop a shoe, I tried to examine myself to see if we were changing me.

Before I could come to any conclusion, before either of us could break the silence, an urgent tone on the panel shocked us both into jumping and drifting through the air. We laughed as we righted ourselves, the tension broken, but we quickly got serious again when we discovered what the signal was alerting us to.

* * *

We heard the arriving ship latch onto the node, and the exit hatch creak slightly from what must have been a change in pressure on the other side.

Tabitha and I had thrown on our PECS suits as a precaution. We floated against the back wall, each with a hand gripping one of the wall straps. The other hand entwined in the other's. I looked at Tabitha, and I think she looked back at me–the dim mirrored surface of her face mask reflected a warped, dark blue emergency pod. She squeezed my hand and nodded. She had been vindicated. Her people had arrived before we needed to activate the beacon, and I knew she was relieved. So was I, of course. I hadn't been looking forward to trying to convince her not to wait one more day, as I was pretty sure she'd try to argue for. Then another. And possibly a third until I let her talk me into dying in the pod. There were bright, soft moments when I didn't think I would have minded.

The access panel next to the hatch came alive and provided the room with a little red glow, then yellow, and finally a friendly green. The hatch hissed violently as the seal broke and the last bit of p.s.i. equalized between the pod and the ship, and then slid down into the wall.

The rest happened too quickly to recall exactly what happened. The instant the hatch slid away, the darkness beyond became a blinding nova of light. My mask's comm system must have been jammed as a muffled silence prevented me from hearing anything Tabitha may have been saying, as well as the arrival of soldiers. Rough hands grabbed and tore me from Tabitha and my grip on the wall. I yelled and shouted, but if I was being heard, I was being ignored. They bound my wrists behind my back then pulled me into the vestibule of the attached ship. The gravity in there was activated, and I dropped like a stone onto my face. Fortunately, the PECS face-mask is quite resilient.

Hands again grabbed and forced me to my knees. Something hard and pointed was shoved under my chin, and I felt a slight shock around my face (like the feeling of licking a 9-volt battery but around my head), and my face-mask was ripped off. My ears exploded with a sudden change in pressure and the smell of astringent and burnt plastic flooded my nose.

The blinding light was gone, but I was still blind. After two weeks in near darkness to suddenly have a zillion candlepower Klieg light shock my retina into painful submission, I was concerned whether or not I would ever see normally again. What I *could* see was vague dark-on-dark images of human-like forms pointing things at me. Dots of light bounced here and there. Muffled voices gave and accepted orders.

"What the hell–" in a courageous show of indignation, was all I could get out before I was backhanded by what felt like a brick wrapped in bull hide. No admonition, no command to shut up, just a quick, sharp, physical reminder that I was not in control and, whoever was, had no need to explain it to me.

I did hear a muffled voice say, "Take her to A, him to C. Sergeant, I want this pod swept down to the individual atom. Move!" I heard boots clomp, Tabitha trying to shout through some kind of gag or muzzle, and what sounded like her being dragged off.

The hands grabbed and gripped and pulled. I shouted, "Who are you? What–" and I was thrown onto my face. This time, without the face-mask, my nose cracked against the grip-ribbed floor of the ship. Light once again exploded in my vision, pain tore through my face and a wave of nausea threatened to make me sick on the floor I knew I was pooling blood on. I choked and sputtered.

Once again, no words, no threats, no admonitions. I was picked up by my bound arms and dragged, leaving a trail of blood behind. I felt good about that at least.

* * *

I don't know how long I waited in the cell, or "holding room." It felt like a couple of hours. After the first few minutes of choking on the blood running down the back of my throat, and keeping back the urge to vomit from swallowing blood, I tried to find some kind of position against the floor or a wall where I might be able to pinch my nose, but it was futile. I continued to drain blood until it finally stopped on its own.

My arms had long since gone numb by the time I could begin to really see again. The room I was in was flat white, dimly lit, maybe two meters by two. No chair, nothing. A dim light eked out a dab of illumination from above. It smelled horrible in there, and I knew I was the reason.

So much for my resolution to regain control of my life.

I had started to doze off while sitting propped in one of the corners, the come-down from the adrenaline dump made every muscle (that wasn't numb) ache, but my head was swirling with a sleepy fog when the door slipped open with a jarring suddenness. I jerked and sent waves of pain through my joints and face. Two men in black fatigues (wielding stubby guns that looked a lot like short, blocky submachine guns that went back from the hand-grip toward their bodies, and extended barely an inch out in front of the forwards grip), stood on either side of the door. One barked at me, "Get up! Let's go." And waited.

I looked from one to the other, their expressions set in stone. I slowly creaked to my knees and got to my feet by wedging my shoulder into the corner and pushing up on wobbly legs. I knew I had to look as pathetic and wretched as I felt. I knew that was probably intentional, part of the humiliation to make me submissive. I staggered to the door on legs alive with pins-and-needles. One of the guards went ahead of me, leading me down a cramped, sterile white corridor, while the other followed behind. Close, but obviously not wanting to touch me. I wondered what would happen if I just stopped. I figured he wouldn't have much of a problem touching me with the butt of his weapon. I kept walking.

When we came to a door labeled "Conference Room C," the guard in front touched a button on the panel next to it. I saw him glance up at the top of the door. There was a pin-hole dot of black. Camera most likely. A light on the panel turned green and the door slid aside. Beyond was a woman in a uniform very similar to Captain Escatado's back at the interview room on Gadreus. She was looking down at a slate, typing and pointing and dragging on its face with her fingers. The guard behind me ordered, "Inside."

Without looking up, the woman immediately said, "Please sit down."

I walked in and the door shut behind me, leaving the guards on the other side. Didn't matter. I was pretty certain the room was equipped with various means of killing instantly should I become a threat, and those means were probably trained on me at that moment. I sat in the available chair opposite the woman across the small table.

After a moment, she looked up, and I caught a glance of cold assessment cross her face that lasted such a brief fraction of a second that a video recording would have missed it. I didn't, and it was all I needed to realize that everything that followed was an act. Her face broke into a look of sad shock at my appearance. I knew my face and neck had to be a gruesome mask of clotting blood, snot, and tears. Complete lack of any trace of disgust in her expression and voice simply convinced me of what I saw before. She was *too* good. "Oh this is just terrible," she sighed. "Absolutely unforgivable." She reached into a drawer and pulled out a conveniently stored package of thick, moistened towels and set them in front of me. I kept my eyes on her face and shrugged my shoulders. She tsk'ed and said, "Oh, of course! Here, let me remove those for you." She came around the table and manipulated the binding around my wrists, and I was freed.

She was very good, I thought. That moment of offering me the towels, a sign of compassion and care, an offer of help to restore my appearance and dignity–while at the same time reinforcing to me, with my bound hands, that I was powerless and beholden to her for every iota of pride and humanity. She was playing both roles of Good Cop/Bad Cop on a subliminal level. I was impressed.

"Better, yes?" She smiled at me. Her hair was a golden brown, a shade lighter than her skin. I'd have placed her as Brazilian, if such a place still existed. I could detect a clean, soapy-flower scent from her, cutting through my clogged sinuses and terrible body odor.

"Yeah, thanks," I responded. She nodded and moved gracefully back to her chair, where she sat casually and waited, watching, smiling politely. My arms were on fire from my neck to where they disappeared into the numb nothingness of my hands. I winced the entire time I carefully opened the packet and went through four hand-size towels before I felt I resembled something human.

As I cleaned my face, bringing new tears every time I pressed too hard near my broken nose, she spoke. "My name is Julia Murphy." Charming smile. "Captain Julia Murphy, but there's no need for ceremony." Nice. Friendly but reminding me of our very specific relationships in the situation. "And you?"

I wasted a few seconds before answering, hissing with eyes closed as I rubbed a delicate spot. Then, "Frankletti. Max Frankletti." Screw it. No debate this time whether I was going to cooperate with the authorities or not. They didn't earn my cooperation. This track may let me know if they already know who I am, or knew Frankletti, or . . . it didn't matter, actually. Just screw 'em.

Her porcelain-cast face didn't change a bit. "How was it you came to be in such an unfortunate situation, Max? Stuck in a Pansys node's emergency pod for fifteen seds?"

"Where's–" I almost said her name, "Kara?" I didn't know what Tabitha's story was, or would be, to the captain, if anything at all. They'd know I was lying–if not now, then later. Screw 'em.

Captain Julia expertly furrowed her brow in a look of sympathetic friendship. "She's resting. It seems your ordeal had a rather terrible impact on her." I met Captain Julia's eyes. What was she saying to me? I had a feeling this was a thinly veiled message that she's "resting" up from being beaten as *part* of our continuing ordeal.

I put the last towel on the pile with the others and sat back, rubbing my wrists.

"How long were you on New Torment, Max?"

"I wasn't."

"What happened to your ship, Max?"

I shrugged. "Engine trouble."

She leaned forward and placed her hands in prayer-position on the table in a perfect pose of earnestness. "Max, I think we have a misunderstanding, here. See, when we discovered the two of you in the node, well, my superiors thought you were saboteurs. Now, I *know* that's not the case. You're obviously stranded travelers, right? Just lucky enough to make it to the node before your ship's antimatter containment blew, yes? We just need to know what happened so we can get you back where you belong." Smile. "How 'bout it?"

Oddly specific slip of information, the containment. They obviously studied whatever wreckage was left of *The Bluerock*. I'm sure she counted on me catching that, leaving me to wonder what else they knew. Well, her ploy gave *me* something: I at least knew she knew I wasn't Max Frankletti. Now to see what else she knew. I sighed, "I'm sorry, captain."

Smile. "Julia, please."

"Julia. I'm just, tired, you know. Stranded for days . . . guess it made me a little paranoid." I smiled back. Yeah, you bastards, it has nothing to do with my broken face. "See, we were on the way to New Torment when the sync-delay relay in the cell containment went out. Well, I guess things got out of hand from there–I'm afraid I'm not a ship's mechanic by trade."

"What *do* you do, Max?"

"Food management. Well, cafeterias and diners mostly. I make some mean meatballs." I grinned winningly.

"What were you headed to New Torment for?"

"Work. You know how things are. Gotta get some, where it can be had."

"Know anyone on New Torment?"

"Mmm, not really. Just heard they might be able to take some people on, you know."

She nodded thoughtfully. Then she looked down at her slate for the first time since I sat down. "Then you don't know a . . . Tabitha Kim, then?"

Score. She knew exactly who the resting girl is. Now, how? Did she tell them? Did they beat it out of her? I felt my face get hot and my back tighten as anger started to boil up. Damn, Captain Julia would be blind not to see that tell. I needed to keep calm.

"Hmm, name sounds familiar. You know, I think that's who I maybe spoke to about a job there."

"She's dead, Max."

Even my thinking paused for an instant before I thought, *What's her ploy?* Was she just testing me? Was she telling me the truth, knowing I knew she knew? What exactly did "resting" mean in this case?

"Really? Well, that's a shame. What happened?"

"You know, that's the funny thing, Mitch. We don't exactly know, and we were kind of hoping you could tell us."

"Well, I'm sure I don't know, Julia." Wait. Wait! Did she say . . . did she say. . . .

She saw it in my face. "You really think we wouldn't know who you were,

Mister Creek? You do know that you're recorded the instant you stepped foot on the tarmac back on Gadreus, your face and bio's archived and sent out to every CASS base and ship in the galaxy, don't you?"

"Well, at least you didn't call me 'Jarrod.' About damn time that stopped happening."

"Oh no, we have your father well scanned and archived, as well. We know the difference."

"Uh, what?"

"How about we discuss New Torment, shall we? Why don't you tell me what happened."

"'Father'?"

She studied my face. Slowly, "You don't know, do you."

"I don't see how it's even–"

"New Torment, Mister Creek. What happened?" Friendliness gone like it was never there.

"It bloweded up real good."

A little red in her neck, now. She wasn't quite as in control as she appeared. "Five hundred people, Mister Creek. Dead. Like that. And if you know something, you owe it to them to tell me."

She was angry about the lost lives. I believed her sincerity. I did feel guilty for my taunt at their expense, but at least it convinced me of something I already suspected: the CASS weren't responsible for what happened.

"Look, I don't know anything about it."

"You seem to know enough to know it exploded."

"We saw it happen, before our own ship blew up. That's it."

"No, Mister Creek, that's *far* from 'it'!" she said. I stared.

She leaned back and glanced at her slate. "Okay, I'm going to cut you a little slack, Mitchel. You have no previous record. No prior interaction with the system prior to being picked up on Gadreus a few weeks ago. And so far we can find no record of you in non-CASS-affiliated legal systems. You've either been a very good boy, heretofore, or extremely sneaky. I'm going to take the chance that it's the former."

Interesting, I thought. No mention of time travel, despite what I said to Captain Escatado, which was surely recorded. Even if they thought I was lying, joking, or crazy, one would think she'd bring it up in the context of having no record, even if ironically. "So, this can go really very easy for you. Tell me what you know, everything, and depending on how much you're involved, we may be able to just release you at the nearest port."

"Just like that."

"Why not? You help us, there's no reason why we can't help you, as well."

"And Tabitha? What about her?"

Captain Julia cocked her head. "Do you really know who she is?"

I pictured that one moment when she was coiled around me, under the restrained blanket, her legs over my legs, her head on my chest, telling me about how she left her family on bad terms and felt like she'd deserted the sister who had so often protected her . . . as well as she could. "Yeah, I have a pretty good idea."

"Then you must know that there's nothing we can do for her. She's chosen her path and must accept the consequences of her actions. There's nothing you, or even I, can do for her. But *you* have a chance to go a different way. You can quite easily save yourself, Mitchel. It's really easy; you know what you need to do."

I leaned forward, resting my crossed arms on the desk. I could pick up that soapy-flower scent again. "I'm sorry, Captain Julia, I think we have a misunderstanding. The name's Frankletti. Max Frankletti."

She seemed honestly disappointed. "Shame. He shares the same fate as Miss Kim."

The door hissed open behind me, and those nice strong hands picked me up by the arms and dragged me away.

CHAPTER THIRTEEN

I tried to reset my own nose, but I'm not near as proficient with such things as Tabitha, even if I wasn't making myself blind and nearly unconscious from the pain I was inflicting upon myself. I'm certain they were watching me, and I hoped I was providing them with a good laugh.

I finally gave up after the third time the world started to fade away.

I sat in my empty cell, in a different corner from the one that still had drying blood from my previous visit. I discovered there was a retractable toilet seat and water spigot that provided a steady trickle–which was quite handy as I was in my room for hours (maybe a day or two, I couldn't be certain), before the door opened again. The light never changed in there. It actually wasn't as bad as they probably thought it should be, not after spending two weeks in a slightly *larger* room with an even more annoying constant blue light.

What did make it nearly unbearable, though, was not knowing anything about Tabitha's condition. I kept replaying in my mind the words and inflections Captain Julia used when she talked about her. But, the words and inflections eventually changed in my memory, and I couldn't trust them for any assurance as to what she was implying–if anything.

Some unknown time later the lights went out. I sat, poised, waiting in the darkness for the sound of the door to open, or some disembodied voice to shout a command. However, nothing happened for some period.

After another batch of unknown time, I was lying on my back, making hand puppets in the dark: "Why, yes, Mister Shadow, the water is quite cool this morning."

"Ah, Mister Noir, not like the winter of aught nine. That was a Winter that killed the groundhogs and voles alike."

When the room then exploded in light and a sound like a bad 50s science fiction laser beam set up a couple octaves higher than necessary and perhaps at a hundred, or a thousand, decibels, drilled through my ears. I screamed involuntarily and pressed my hands against my ears, but the sound was penetrating directly through my skull. I was effectively immobilized when they came in and grabbed me, threw a bag and a strap around both my head and hands, and dragged me out of the room. My hands were now forced against the side of my head by the restraint. I tried to feel for the ooze of blood coming from my ears, but I felt nothing.

I was thrown into a chair, my ankles strapped to the chair legs, my torso strapped to the back, then my hands released from the head-bag and strapped behind me. Once I was secured, the bag came off. As with that morning, yesterday, or the day before–whichever it was–I was still blind from the light.

From the darkness, I was struck by something heavy and thick in my stomach.

"WHY'D YOU DO IT?"

"Wha . . . I . . . I didn't–"

Thud!

"WHY'D YOU DO IT?"

I coughed and gasped for breath. "I . . . I. . . ."

Thud!

"WHY'D YOU DO IT?"

I couldn't breathe, couldn't even cough. My body was forcing me to double-over, but the strap around my chest kept me upright. The muscles in my abdomen felt like they were tearing in contraction; my stomach wanted to lurch but could do nothing. My head was thrown back, mouth open in a silent scream as I tried to take in or expel air–my body couldn't figure out what it wanted to do, even if it *could* do it.

Finally, my abdomen relaxed enough that I could scrape some ragged air into my lungs. I coughed and groaned it back out, and did it again once or twice before: "WHY'D YOU DO IT?"

"Please–"

Thud!

And so it went on an uncountable number of times. Each time I wasn't even given a chance to respond to the question. The question was unnecessary, really. Getting an answer wasn't the point of this exercise.

When I got a chance to stop and breathe short, excruciating breaths, I noticed I was in what I was sure was the airlock we had been brought into from the node. The floor was the same grip-ribbing, and I was facing what was obviously an airlock hatch.

The voice boomed from behind me, "Yeah, you see that airlock. That's where we'll throw your body when we're done with it. If you don't TELL US WHY YOU DID IT!"

"No!"

Thud!

* * *

I woke up back in my cell, wet with sweat and urine, unable to take a full breath. I was pretty sure I had at least a couple broken ribs and possibly an abdominal hernia. I lay in a fetal position, in the persistent, dim light, moving each body part as carefully as I could to make sure everything was still there and unbroken. Legs, arms, fingers and toes all better off than my nose and ribs. That was something.

I don't think it was more than an hour before the door opened and I was once again hooded, grabbed up and dragged out, crying out through gritted teeth as it felt like my abdomen was splitting open. In a way, that was much worse than a broken arm. A broken arm is simple, but what the heck might be going on inside of abused and battered torso? Internal bleeding? Ruptured organ? The actual pain was horrific, but the fear of unseen damage was tortuous.

They deposited me in a chair and removed the hood. I rocked, clutching my stomach. I was back in Captain Julia's room.

"Oh, no, Mitchel. You look terrible."

I groaned.

"I can talk to my superiors, on your behalf. You're not a prisoner; you're simply here for questioning about New Torment. There's surely a mistake." She paused. "Can I do that, Mitchel? Can I tell them this has been a mistake? Do you want that?"

I still hadn't been able to look up. I stared at the unmarred white floor. I nodded.

"Mitch, say the words. Talk to me. Tell me 'yes.'"

I told her.

"Good. We're working together now. Cooperating. We've broken that wall between us—can you feel it? Such a powerful, simple word: 'yes.'"

The smell of soap and flowers. She'd come around to sit on the edge of my side of the table.

"You were on New Torment, yes?"

"Yes."

"Mitchel, I'm so happy you've decided to come around and let me help you. Why were you on New Torment?"

"I . . . don't remember." At the moment that was true. I found it difficult to think, and my visit to the asteroid seemed years ago.

"Mitchel, I understand." She pulled something across the table. A glass of clear liquid already poured. She held it in front of me. "Here, drink this.

You'll feel better."

My hands were shaking, but I took the glass and started to bring it to my lips. The thought crossed my mind: truth serum. Sodium penta-something. That's what was used in the old spy movies. Surely, centuries later, they'd have developed something at least as good. They could have used that from the very beginning if they really wanted just answers. I didn't know what I held in my hands–it could have been water, or a drug to reduce inhibitions, or a drug to actually make my stomach better and allow me to think clearly. What I did know, what I was certain of, is they didn't need to torture me. They wanted to. And Captain Good Cop was as active a participant in the sadistic charade as her superiors and the guy with the truncheon.

I opened my hands and let the glass fall. "Fuck. You."

She stood up. "Oh, Mitchel. It was starting to go so well, too."

The door slid open behind me.

* * *

They didn't let me pass out that next time. Whatever they shot me up with kept my mind awake and vibrating through the oozing hours that followed. It's odd that I recall being awake and aware as they electrocuted me such that it felt like the very marrow of my bones were lava and my joints exploded, but I don't remember much about it. I suppose it's a lot like what alcoholic blackouts may be like, except without the fog of inebriation during the events.

I remember being asked questions: both pointed, and absurd and unanswerable. I recall breaking down very quickly and answering—at least when the questions weren't rhetorical (which they often were), or when the question wasn't surreal and I had no way to answer, giving my tormentor reason to rip my skull out through my chest. I remember screaming and crying for both Lori and for Tabitha.

At one point the torture stopped. I doubted the session was over, and the fear of what was to come was unbearable. Then I heard boots march in and Captain Julia appeared like an over-enhanced foreground object in a Photoshopped picture where everything else was blurred. "Why are you insisting you came from the past? Explain this."

"I did . . . I did. I am."

My senses felt sharpened, enhanced by the drugs they gave me. I'm sure it was all the better to feel pain with, my dear. I heard a distant voice insist to Captain No More Good Cop Julia that the scan verified my responses as "not originating from the limbic-hippocampus cluster but from the inf-temp-cingulate regions indicating . . . " I was telling the truth.

"When? What year are you from?" Captain Julia demanded. I told her.

"Impossible," she said, not to me. "He must be lying. Making it up." The distant voice mumbled something. "Then he's cracked." Mumble.

To me, "Alright then, Mitchel. Continue. Tell me everything."

I did.

And while my mouth worked on its own, my voice droning in the background like the undulation of cicadas in the heavy, humid summer air, my mind–perhaps unlocked and bent by whatever they gave me to focus sharply on details while submerged in a cloudy lake of pain–played around the edges of a memory that faded in and out of resolution.

A barn. The barn. My mother's barn. It sits behind the house I grew up in. A barn that is less a barn and more an over-sized barn-shaped shed. The house and barn exist outside Iowa City–closer to the town now than it was when I was born. I'm visiting her, my mother, for my once-a-month "see how you're doing" visit. I go into the barn because she had finally sold the engine block that sat in the middle of the floor. It sat there the entire time I lived there, a fixture as immutable as the house and barn itself, and now someone from Craigslist has it. In its place is a patch on the concrete clean of dirt and discolored by oil that had years to become that faded brown with indistinct edges.

A distinct line runs within the stain, barely perceptible. It's part of a slab within the slabs that form the floor of the barn. It doesn't make sense to be there. I'm intrigued; I investigate. It's a small, square separation previously kept unseen by the engine. A space in the seam of the concrete slabs to receive the crowbar, and I push down on the bar, a cinder block is the fulcrum. The slab lifts and I push it aside. There's a hole going down into darkness. The dim yellow light from the flashlight, long and silver and powered by four D batteries with patches of corrosion on the ends, is stopped several feet below by the surface of something large and white and possibly metallic, or plastic–I can't tell.

The ladder, an A-frame that will fit down the hole only while folded, creaks as I climb down it. The cicadas outside the barn fade as I descend into the darkness, the flashlight thrust into my front pocket. I stand on the surface of this underground object, buried but for this patch exposed to the surface. Something is wrong; I feel dizzy and strange, like my mind is working a second slower than my body as every movement I make feels separated from being my actions.

A crawlspace moves along the surface of this thing and farther under the floor of the barn. Is it a tank? Septic? Water? I crawl behind the anemic light until the off-white thing drops away and reveals an opening into the ground. I consider going back to the house, asking Mom about it, having Lori come check it out with me. But I'm here and I need to see what this is, why this tank appears to be a giant box with an open door and a ramp leading into it, surrounded by cold rock like a cave. The opening leads into a cave within the cave. A storage container? A buried trailer?

The ladder is now down with me, lowered over the edge, and I descend to stand on a ramp looking into a room, maybe a short corridor, with doors leading into other rooms. There are small control panels, electronic control panels with small dim lights beside the doors. Working, modern electronics *buried since at least the mid-70s, untouched for decades. Impossible. I want to believe it was installed during this last week since the engine block was taken away, but I know that's also impossible.*

I walk into the opening, and lights turn on. . . .

I'm strapped down and Captain Julia looked to the unseen people behind me and must have gotten some kind of confirmation. She said, "Alright, get him back to his cell. And clean him up. I don't know what his value is yet, and I don't want him too damaged." She strode away.

I was cleaned up . . . by a high-pressure hose as I rolled and flopped on the floor like a piece of trash being hosed down the driveway. It was after that bit of good-natured fun that they gave me a dermal patch for pain. I figured out already that I was being constantly scanned during my last interrogation and had no serious injuries–just the broken nose, a few cracked ribs that would heal just fine if I don't do anything stupid like roll and flop around on the floor, and some torn abdominal muscles that had the same prognosis.

Dressed in baggy yellow overalls, I was once again dragged by my arms to my cell and unceremoniously discarded. A few minutes later, the first bowl of something food-like was sent in through a panel in the door. I tried to count the number of times I'd slept to calculate how long I'd been there, but it was no good. I couldn't figure out the instances of dozing, sleeping, unconsciousness and make a reasonable estimate. It could all still be one day, maybe three. I did know that I had been hungry for some time, interrupted by instances of nausea and acute stomach pain. I wolfed the dense oatmeal stuff.

Pain relegated to a dull roar, stomach full, I had a chance to wonder what had become of Tabitha. What did the captain mean by "her fate"? There's no doubt the CASS probably saw her and anyone of the synd or their supporters as traitors to their own cause: seditionists, dangerous criminals. No doubt that if they didn't even know who I was and they tortured me, someone like Tabitha was sure to be killed.

I didn't want to make the possibility that it might have already happened too real in my mind. I didn't really mind that they broke me with physical pain, and that all the resolve I had discovered in me when I dropped the glass in the captain interrogation room was washed away by the pain and fear. But the torture of thinking that the last I would ever see of Tabitha was our holding PECS-protected hands in the emergency node pod, hearing her gagged resistance in my blindness, would have been too much to bear and would certainly have crushed my spirit.

So I brought Misters Noir and Shadow back and let them distract me until I felt the ship rock from an explosion.

CHAPTER FOURTEEN

I stood in front of the cell's door, feet wide apart for stability. After the third shudder the ship remained still. There was a faint bleat of an alarm on the other side of the door; I was waiting for it to open with some guard to pop in and tell me what was up and what we were going to do. Thoughts of reactor core breeches and anti-matter containment were forefront in my mind.

The door did eventually open, but it wasn't a guard who stood on the other side: it was some large guy in a black PECS, the face-mask removed and dangling from a strap on the back of his neck. He did have a weapon similar to the CASS guards, however, and he was pointing it at me as a guard would. He shouted, "Who'd you come here with?"

"What?"

"C'mon! Hurry up. Who're you here with?"

"Uh, Tabitha. Tabitha Kim."

"Right. okay, let's go." He ran down the corridor. Someone else in a PECS with the mask still sealed reached in, grabbed me by the jumpsuit, and pulled me into the hallway. There were two more PECS-clad people with guns. One of then grabbed the automatic from one of the two dead or comatose CASS guards on the floor and tossed it to me. It was lighter than I expected it to be, almost like a toy. I held it gently, not quite knowing what to do.

"Who–"

"You heard him," one of the PECS said in a tinny, metallic voice through the suit's speaker, "Let's go."

The three of us jogged up to the one who opened the door. The pain meds were still coursing through my blood, but the jarring of the run-walk pushed the pain in my ribs into consciousness. The corridor lights had gone to a bright but diffuse red. The alarm was insistent but surprisingly not terribly nerve-wracking. At the other end of the corridor was another door like my cell's. One of the PECS stepped up and attached a device next to the door panel and another piece on the door itself. They did a little of this and that, and a sound chimed. The device was removed and the facemaskless guy pressed the open button.

I knew who should be behind the door, but I was afraid to see what state she was in. She was worse than I'd hoped, but better than I'd feared. Tabitha was lying on the floor in a yellow jumpsuit. I rushed past the PECS guy and over to her. She moved slowly, trying to look up at me, groaning. One eye was swollen shut, there was blood in her hair, and her right arm moved limply as she tried to roll over. My heart tore between joy that she was still alive, and agony at the state they put her in.

I brushed hair out of her face. "Tabitha. It's me, Mitch. Tabitha, we're being rescued." I hoped that was true.

She tried to focus on me with her good eye, "Mi . . . " She could barely move her jaw.

One of the masked PECS guys kneeled beside me with a small red bag. "Tabitha, it's Sasha," the mechanized voice said. His hands moved quick and surely, probing the back of her jaw, her arm, lifting eyelids.

"Her shoulder was dislocated a couple weeks ago," I said, "it may be again." Sasha nodded. He started to select dermal patches.

The guy without his mask stood behind me. "Where's the other guy?"

"Huh?"

"The other guy. Tabitha's message said there were three of you. We've already cleared the other holding cells."

Sasha confirmed the dislocation and asked me to help him reset it. Tabitha was still too out of it to even react.

"Ian, yeah. He's dead."

Face guy grunted. He turned to one of the others, "Tell Far' stage two is complete. We're not yet mobile and need to hole up here for the moment." The PECS he spoke to nodded and remained silent. I assumed they were relaying the message through the face-mask comm.

Sasha got the selected derms on and was strapping Tabitha's arm to her side. I helped hold her up. Her head lolled around without resistance.

A female mechanized voice came from face man's message relayer. "He says 'no go,' they're pinned down at junction alpha. They need all hands."

"Damn. Right. You," he said, pointing to me, "guard Tabitha and Sasha. The rest of you, on me. Let's move!" And off they went.

Tabitha started making some moaning sounds, sounding a little more cognizant. Sasha was applying some kind of ointment to her swollen eye, muttering something soothing to her. I had a momentary pang of jealousy.

I shook it off. Ridiculous. I picked the weapon off the floor where I'd laid it. I had shot firearms before: rifles and shotguns in Boy Scouts, a friend's 9mm pistol (and not counting paintball markers and Airsoft replicas). So this, what I assumed was some kind of submachine gun, didn't feel terribly unfamiliar. Except, context changed everything and gave the weapon more weight, more air of dark import. I'd never shot at anything other than paper targets and clay pigeons. I'd never even gone hunting, and never cared to. I got my meat from the grocery store, where I imagined the animals were dispatched with love and fairy dust, not the violence inherent in killing. Holding the gun in my hands made the thick, sticky feeling of Ian's metaphorical blood return to my hands. His death was the result of a heated, emotional act of self-defense. Ironically, doing it with the brutal force of my hand made it seem more justified and honorable to Ian and who he was before he flipped out than the idea of dispassionate throwing of metal at a distance.

"Hey, the hallway," Sasha urged me. I had been staring down at the black metal machinery in my hands.

"Oh, yeah. Sorry." I leaped to my feet and almost fell as pain shot through my sides and abdomen and down into my legs. The meds may have been wearing off, or I'd just been doing a lot of non-recommended recreation. I squatted in the doorway and looked down the red-washed corridor. I tried to listen for any distant gunshots announcing the battle they'd talked about a moment ago, but all I could hear was the continuing alarm. I kept the short muzzle of the gun trained down the corridor and my eyes peeled for movement at the intersection.

I glanced back into the room. Sasha had Tabitha sitting up and drinking something. I tried to see if we could make eye contact, but she kept her head low, a wavy curtain of hair in front of her face.

A clomp down the hall. Someone turned the corner. I instinctively pulled the trigger. Crap, what if it was a synd guy? Too late. . . . But nothing happened. What? No, I now saw the CASS uniform, and they saw me low in the doorway. I pulled the trigger again, nothing. The CASS guard raised a pistol, and I fell painfully into the room as two chunks of the wall behind me exploded. His pistol made no report–that was disturbing.

The safety! I was on my back, my stomach muscles feeling like they do after a hundred sit-ups, when you've only done ten before in your life. I looked where my right-hand thumb naturally gripped the gun; there was a small green patch in the metal. I slid and rubbed my thumb on and around it, and hit the right movement that turned the green to red just as the CASS guard entered the doorway. Point pull trigger fire! The gun barely moved in my hand and made just the slightest clicking noises as it spat a stream of metal into the guard. He fired the pistol in reflex and the shot went into the floor as he fell to the ground. He didn't fly or even fall backward like I expected–he simply fell lifeless, straight down into a clump, revealing a splattering of blood and viscera on the wall and floor behind where he stood, still revoltingly obvious despite the red light.

"Close," Sasha said. He was helping Tabitha to her feet. "Check the hallway!" He'd removed his own face-mask by then, his coffee-dark skin glistening with sweat.

On command, I pulled myself up to my knees and carefully arched over the dead guard. "Clear." I stood out in the corridor as Sasha eased Tabitha over the guard. Halfway over, Tabitha bent down and picked up the guard's pistol, then kept going.

Sasha said, "She's getting stronger, but it's temporary while the drugs are working. She'll crash hard when this is all over; we have to get back to the ship."

"No," Tabitha interrupted. "Forward . . . forward deck. We help." She stood up straight. The puffiness of her left eye had already gone down by half from whatever Sasha did, but the horrible bruising was still there, and the white of her eye was darker red than the hallway lighting should have been responsible for. She looked at me and paused as if she had to think about who I was, then her face softened. She pitched forward but caught herself on my jumpsuit. Her head was heavy against my chest. I put my face down into her beautiful, matted hair. Sasha kept an eye down the hallway.

Tabitha sighed hard, stood back up stronger than before, and gazed at me with the confidence I was used to. She furrowed her brow, questioning. I nodded. She nodded back and started down the corridor, growing confident with each step.

Sasha walked beside Tabitha, "Around here, to the left. That way's the docking rings, down there to con." We headed toward the control deck.

The assault on the ship was already over by the time we reached the command center. The ship, the CAC *Vigilant*, was quite a bit smaller than I had thought. I had it in mind that I was aboard some Star Trek *Enterprise* sized ship. The *Vigilant* was a corvette-class cruiser meant for patrolling and courier missions and had about twenty crew and officers.

Face guy approached us with another guy and a woman in mask-less PECS. He said, "Tabitha, you alright?" She just nodded. "Captain wants to talk with you. Feel up to it?"

"Later," she replied. Now face guy nodded.

"Captain Julia–er, Captain Murphy?" I asked.

"What? No, ours. Who are you, anyway?"

I looked at Tabitha. She was gazing past face guy to the milling of people in the command area. I noticed scorch marks and holes in the wall of the corridor we stood in and wondered if bullets weren't ultimately a bad idea on a spaceship.

"I'm Mitch. I arrived on New Torment with Frankletti," was all I told him.

He glanced at Tabitha, who nodded without looking at him. "Well, good enough for me." He smiled and offered his hand, "Ericsson. Currently the boarding chief for the free ship *Udachi*. We got Tabitha's message and got here as soon as we could. We were delayed by a run-in with another CASS ship–and I think you'll be glad we did."

Tabitha looked away from where she was gazing down the corridor. "Why's that?" Tabitha's voice was raspy and tight. I wondered what more they did to her, a known and wanted criminal in their books, considering what they did to me: an unknown person simply in her company.

We started walking toward the command deck. Ericsson explained, "It was a battle cruiser, alone. If it'd been accompanied per S.O.P., and we hadn't've gotten the drop on it, we wouldn't have a chance. As it was, we had to use the BAG on it. Afterward, Cynta hacked their logs. Seems they were headed to the same place, to intercept and eliminate one CAC *Vigilant* and everyone aboard it, and any salvage in the area."

Tabitha and I looked at each other. "Maybe it *was* CASS at New

Torment," I said, perplexed.

"Doubt it," Ericsson continued. "They also had orders to visit New Torment as a secondary mission and ascertain why they haven't replied to latest CASS communications."

"So," Tabitha began, "why . . . why destroy us?"

Ericsson shrugged. "Dunno. Maybe your Captain Murphy might have an idea. I think she should survive her wounds."

"Hey–" Ericsson stopped. "Tabitha, it's good to see you again. It's been a while." He smiled. Tabitha smiled weakly, but sincerely I'm sure, and gripped his large upper arm affectionately. It was really bothering me how disconnected she appeared. I told myself it was a side-effect of the drugs basically animating what would likely otherwise be the broken and near-comatose woman I first saw in the cell. I was a bit frightened to think about what kinds of new pharmaceuticals have been developed to keep soldiers fighting on a battlefield.

We were in the command deck. It was large, about as big as the storage area on the *Lysander* and dark. Someone had turned off the red night-sight light, and the illumination in the room mainly came from the various console displays. Pops and sparks came randomly from a couple of consoles that got the brunt of gunfire. There were three or four bodies pulled over to one side of the room; Sasha and someone else was working on a wounded synd. Sitting on the floor against a bank of consoles with their hands strapped behind them, and looked over by four armed synd, were six or seven CASS crewmen and officers, including Captain Julia–who had one of her arms blown into a red ragged pine tree of destroyed flesh and bone. Some kind of wide, thick ring with a blinking green light was around her upper arm just under the shoulder. I assumed that thing was keeping her from bleeding out. I turned away, disgusted by the unidentifiable gruesomeness something human can become from violence. The image of the blood and pieces on the wall behind the guard I killed, who just dropped lifeless, as if a switch were turned off, started to turn my stomach.

Ericsson looked back the way we came. "Ah, here comes the captain."

I turned to see three people striding up to us, the one in front had a dark, angular, hairless head. He saw me and we both said, "You!"

"So, you're a bit late," Farrius said.

"Well, I uh, got a bit caught up in something. You understand."

I had told Tabitha about my first encounter in the future, but had forgotten the guy's name. At the time she said, "Hmm, he sounds familiar." Now, she had this slightly, sleepy amused expression. Ericsson said, "What? You two know each other?"

"Not exactly," Farrius said with a smirk, walking up to me. He looked me up and down. "I happened to encounter *solo tanod-gubat* here in Jarrod's ship a few weeks back. You were supposed to have him meet me, friend. I don't like being stood up." (At the time, I caught the last bit from he actually said: "*No me gusta que taong pinagtsilan* shit-zen." The rest I figured out later.) His demeanor took a decidedly more serious aspect. Ericsson seemed intrigued still; Tabitha took a step closer and was no longer a bit amused.

Bolstered by seeing Tabitha having my back, a few weeks of acclimation to my situation, a day or two of torture, and an SMG in my hands, I held my chin up this time, "Look, *captain*, I really couldn't care less what you don't like. I'm not going to explain myself to you, and that's just going to have to work for you. I owe you nothing."

There was a brief pause and gazes were set. The blood had rushed to my head so fast I started to get a little dizzy and my hands shook slightly. Nevertheless, I held my lock on his eyes.

Farrius spoke, his breath smelled like mint and bacon, "Well, captain. T*anod-gubat* here says he doesn't owe you anything."

I squinted in confusion.

A voice from behind him said, "Huh, I would have at least expected a 'thank you' for saving his life. What's this galaxy coming to?"

I leaned to the side and looked past Farrius. The two people that he had come down with were a petite blond woman with what looked like steel balls for eyes and a tall, bearded man. The man walked up to me and Farrius stepped aside with a smirk. "Captain MacVey of the *Udachi*. I'd like an explanation for why it is I just risked my ship and lost two of my crew saving your pale ass."

"I, uhm, thought. . . . Yeah, I'm with Tabitha. I arrived with Frankletti." *Magic words, don't fail me now.*

"We'll see about that." He said it with such finality that I knew no response from me was appropriate. He shifted his glare to Tabitha. "This squares us." She nodded.

He brushed me aside and strode into the command deck. "Alright, let's get the prisoners onto the ship. I want to get undocked in ten minutes and blow this piece of metal in fifteen." The four synds stood the CASS prisoners up and started them for the doorway.

"Not that one." Tabitha was pointing at one male CASS officer. The look on her face was set in stone. Scary in its passiveness. The guy she was pointing to started to look around from companions to synd alike. He had the look of guilt and was trying to hide it. Tabitha gestured her head to the side. The synd guards looked at Captain MacVey. He stood for a moment in thought, then nodded affirmative to the guards. Two of them grabbed the CASS guy by his bound arms and shoved him to the other side of the room, where Tabitha followed, pistol in hand.

I didn't watch. I looked at the remaining CASS prisoners. It was a tableau that, of all the memories from this time, would, without synthetic aid, stay with me in vivid detail. It was a study in humanity. Most of the CASS crew looked down in shame, or fear, perhaps. Others looked angry, curling their lips or shaking their heads. But one person, Captain Julia Murphy, looked at me as I looked at her. She showed neither shame nor anger. She smiled at me with arrogance and pride. She looked at me as if to say, "I have no idea what all this trouble is about, but I'm enjoying myself." Oh but she knew. She knew everything that happened to Tabitha. Ordered it herself, I'm certain.

The pistol only clicked; the rounds made no report. Three clicks. A grunt followed the first and the sound of a collapsed body followed the third. Tabitha strode back to us followed by the two synd guards. They wrangled the prisoners out of the com and down the corridor. Captain Julia and I broke eye contact only after she passed me.

Tabitha put her hand in mine. I was shaken out of my disgust for Captain Julia and looked at Tabitha. She was truly looking into my eyes for the first time since I entered her cell. She looked tired, but not the drugged sleepy way she did earlier. She looked at me like she wanted to tell me something but couldn't find the words. She looked like she wanted to tell me, "I'm here. Now." I squeezed her hand, and she squeezed back. We walked down the corridor to the *Udachi*.

CHAPTER FIFTEEN

The *Vigilant's* explosion was bright and quick, but we were already traveling away fast enough for it to recede and disappear in the distance in a matter of seconds. Normally a synd attack like this (let's face it, a pirate attack if I ever heard of one), would try to leave the attacked ship intact and commandeer it or, if too damaged, "tether" it to a frigate craft to be dismantled for pieces which would usually get used for parts in settlements and colonies. But because of the likelihood of additional CASS ships coming to investigate New Torment, or the missing ship ordered to make the CAC *Vigilant* equally missing, Captain MacVey decided it was too risky to call a frigate in for salvage.

I found out MacVey put us on a course to Tau Ceti, all the way back past Sirius, the way I'd come. "No," I stormed behind him into the *Udachi's* command deck, "we have to go on."

He turned to me, hands planted on his waist. "I'm sorry?" He didn't at all look it.

"We have to keep going. We have to follow whoever blew up New Torment."

He sat down in his command chair. Farrius leaned against a console next to him, arms crossed, smiling. I still had to find out what he was all about. "Really?" the captain sneered. "This ought to be good. Do tell? Explain to me why I should turn this ship around."

Ericsson had offered Tabitha and me the chance to shower and change into some fresh clothes. Tabitha had gone ahead, and I'd lingered just long enough to catch the captain's plan. Now I was alone, confronting this rather scary person on his own ship, surrounded by his crew and someone who'd already threatened me once before. I steeled myself: "Look, I don't mean any disrespect. But I'm guessing you know Max Frankletti. He and Kara, uh . . . Karayitri, may be captive of whoever destroyed New Torment. You took the risk to save Tabitha–surely you can see the reason of going one more step."

"Very good. Did you practice that?"

I remained silent.

He continued, "I owed Tabitha. And I was already on the way before I found out just how complicated this cluster-fuck is. Now I'm sorry about Max, I know Tabitha thought a lot of him and he has history with the synd. But it's going to get awfully crowded around here very soon, and I'd rather not be anywhere near here when they decide to send a whole battle wing instead of just a single ship. We're going to Tau Ceti, where we've got some business going. I have to admit, *whatever* I owe Tabitha, if I hadn't already been coming from Procyon on the way there, I *might* not have bothered to divert to your node. You remember that. You're alive because it was convenient for me to save you. What do I get for my kindness? Farrius?"

"A dead mechanic and reactor technician, four wounded, and a damaged hull." He smiled.

"So, Mister Creek, what can you offer me to make up for my losses? Hmm? What do you have to pay me back for saving your life?" He stood, towering over me. "I owed Tabitha, but I don't even *know* you. You're going to want to settle your current bill before you start ordering additional services. Are we clear?"

Farrius was positively beaming. The girl with the cyberpunk eyeballs was leaning back in a chair, boots propped on a rail. I couldn't read her. Some other guy at a front console position was craning around looking entertained. *Great*, I thought. *Yet another opportunity to be completely ineffectual in a time of necessity for control over my life.*

"Yeah. Yeah, I understand very clearly. Captain."

"Good. Now get off my damn bridge, Mister Creek."

Farrius waved his fingers at me from his crossed arms. This was going to be a swell ride.

I finally found someone to tell me where I was going to be staying: one of the petty officer's suites, which was a four-bunk room in a cluster of five other four-bunk rooms and a shared washroom. Rather palatial compared to a cell. Although, I felt a pang of longing for the node capsule and its cramped and cozy blueness. Well, certain aspects of it, of course.

I found the suite Tabitha was in. She was in one of the lower bunks; the rest were empty. I started, "We have a problem."

She was lying facing the wall, wrapped in a large gray towel, her hair dark, wet and stringy. She put a hand out without looking. "Lie down next to me."

I walked over and sat on the bunk. She had violent bruises on her arms and legs. On either side of her ankles, knees, and elbows, were two-inch wide burns in perfect circles. I couldn't imagine what might have made them. "We need to get that medic, Sasha, to take a thorough look at you, Tabitha," I said quietly. "There could be internal–"

"Please, lie with me." Her hand sought mine and held it against her side. I laid in my yellow coverall against her back, feeling her breathe, caressing her arm. Her still damp shoulder smelled soapy; her hair smelled like earth in the rain.

After some time she said sleepily, "I love you." I replied I loved her as well. I waited until her breathing deepened, then I followed in sleep. If anyone came in or out, we never heard them.

* * *

"I guess it's really your choice," she said as she tried on a pair of boots someone loaned her. I was examining the clothes offered me–not too bad: loose-fitting gray cotton-like shirt and gray-green trousers. Tabitha was given black fatigue pants and a brown sweater. Her eye had swollen back up and she moved stiffly, with occasional groans and hisses, and her right arm was practically immobile. I had to help with her sweater. Thankfully, she had her energy back and I was grateful for that.

"That device, and, more likely, wherever it came from, is the only clue as to how I got here and how I might get home." I helped Tabitha with her boot. They laced up the front for fit, then zipped up the side for quick on and off. With her arm mostly out of commission again, these would be convenient once I got them laced for her. If what I just said bothered her as much as it did a part of me, she didn't let on. "Frankletti and Kara, we might still be able to help them as well." She nodded. "You want that, if we can, don't you?"

Under her breath, she said, "Of course." Then more firmly, "Of course I do." To me, "I do. But MacVey's not going to be easily swayed. He's kind of known for his bull-headed single mindedness." She sounded like that was that.

"I don't get it. You're going to just accept that's the end of it?" I finished lacing her boot, but held her foot in my hands. "Tabitha, he's your friend. A comrade or co-whatever. If there's a chance he can be rescued, you're going to give that up? Even after what you've experienced, have fought through and for?"

"Don't."

"What?"

She pulled her foot away. "This. Don't try to manipulate me into. . . ."

"Into what? Making a decision you know is right?"

"Why?" She stood up, her other boot on but flapped around. "What's right about it? We don't have a single clue whether they're alive or not. No clue who's got them or why. We have something of a clue about how powerful they are, and you want to go chasing after them–where you *think* they've headed–in nothing more than a barge with aspirations of being a battleship."

"The *Udachi* took out two CASS ships, one of them a *real* battleship."

"A battle *cruiser*, a small one at that, and only because they got one-in-a-million lucky." Someone had come into the cabin to grab something from the cabinet below his bunk and avoided eye contact with us until he left.

"Battle-whatever. MacVey saved you because of some debt he owed you. You and Frankletti talked like you were old soldiers in war. Ian was ready to kill you because of the reach and power and influence the synd has and the effects it had–that you're a part of. You can convince MacVey, I know it. And the two of you surely have other contacts nearby."

She squinted at me the way she did sometimes, "You're talking about raising an armada? To what? Take the CASS head on? Because that's what's going to happen if we head back that direction. A mining operation lost, a scout lost, a cruiser lost. What's the next thing they're going to send, do you think?"

"That's exactly why we have to turn around and go *now*. Before they have a chance to get a fleet or battalion or whatever out here."

"And then what happens to us, huh? Assuming all goes according to your plan? You're on your way home, hoorah hoorah, leaving me . . . *us,* behind to . . . I don't know what."

I lowered my voice. "That's it, isn't it."

"Now what."

"What we've avoided talking about since the last couple of days in the node. My leaving you to go back to my family. That's what you're upset about."

She looked at me incredulously. "Screw this," she said, and stormed off with a flapping boot.

I felt the urge to run after her–maybe that's what she hoped I might do. I couldn't move myself to get up. I dropped my head into my hands and dug my fingertips into my scalp. Just what did I expect was going to happen? I was so angry at myself for letting it come to this. I realized then that I hadn't felt guilty about telling Tabitha I loved her until this conversation– and then the guilt was soul-crushing. I wanted to be mad at her for not agreeing with what I thought was a perfectly reasonable course of action, one that I thought she would wholeheartedly support; yet, instead, I was mad that she put me in this position of second-guessing myself because I wanted to follow the course my feelings for her set up.

I got up, stiff and groaning, and headed out of the bunk cluster. I needed to get some answers, even if I wasn't sure of the questions. Except for one question that had been nagging me. I had to at least talk to Captain Julia. (I wasn't surprised to find out there were no "supervisors" on her ship. The buck stopped with her.)

I wandered around the ship. It was certainly the largest ship I'd been on so far–except maybe the *Vigilant*, but I didn't get to see much of *that* one. I passed people here and there, some walking, some conversing, some evidently working–as far as I could tell. No one would go out of their way to acknowledge me; a couple people would at least nod to me as I passed. Finally, I saw Ericsson, and he waved. "Hey, Mitchel. How're you settling in?" He wore a blue canvas shirt with the sleeves rolled high up on the arms, exposing walnut-cracking muscles.

"Oh, fine. Thanks. Say, where are the prisoners being kept?"

"Mitch," he looked serious, "you're not going to kill one of them, are ya?"

"No no, nothing like that. I need to ask the captain some questions. There's not some protocol or rules about questioning, is there?"

He laughed. "*Dios*, no. What do you think we are, CASS? But," he pointed a serious finger at me, "I'm serious about not killing any more of 'em. Lowers the chances of getting ransom."

"Seriously? Ransom?"

His face cracked, and he hit me in the arm with his meat-paw. "What do you think we are, common criminals? No, we'll drop them off outside some settlement. We're vilified and hunted enough just defending ourselves; we don't need a scorched-space campaign against us for being cruel savages. So, you won't mind if I hang around and make sure nothing happens, right?"

"Hmm? No, actually, that's fine. Probably wouldn't hurt having some muscle behind me for implied intimidation."

"Yeah, that's a far sight better than the treatment they gave you guys." We started walking the direction he had come. "How's Tab' doing, anyway?"

"Better." I was still a little hot.

"So, you guys together then, huh?"

"Well, yeah, sort of. Actually, it's kind of complicated."

"M-hm," Ericsson nodded. "Usually is, huh?"

"Not that I'm changing the subject–"

"But you are," he chuckled.

"Yeah. Look, so, I know the synd does things outside the law. . . ."

"Whose law?"

"Natural law?" He gave me a sidelong look. "Kidding. No, what I mean is, Tabitha's told me a lot about how the synd works. Usually by working within a community or settlement, often a new one or a troubled one, and sets up unions and trade arrangements and basically help create apolitical collectives."

"Yeah, mainly."

"And the CASS doesn't like it."

Ericsson huffed, "Yeah, I'd say! When it works out, the people see they don't need the CASS and their puppet politicians to get along and thrive."

"So, then, in a sense, the synd operates outside the law."

"Heh, you must have lived under the CASS for some time, now."

"Well, actually, no. Not really."

Ericsson stopped in the corridor. "Then, what do you think the CASS is?"

I stopped and turned back to him. "What do you mean?"

"I mean, what is it? Is it a law of thermal dynamics?"

"No, no, it's . . . I don't get your point. It's the Confederation of . . . Associated Sovereign Systems, or something like that."

"Right. Is that the fourth Law of Motion?"

I looked up and down the corridor we had stopped in. I hadn't wandered down this one yet before. A woman tapping on a slate walked by. "Well, no. It's a government. Sort of."

"Sure, sort of. Except one difference: it's not at all! It's a myth."

"Tabitha used that term for it once."

"Yeah, probably. It's part of the reason of why we're fighting the invasion of the CASS's influence. It's . . . it's like as if someone grabbed the stories of Zeus and Apollo and decided they were going to start making people believe in them. Why doesn't that work?"

"Actually it might. Where I come from there's people all the time making up new religions and getting followers."

"Well, that gets to my point, but first, if someone started going around getting people to believe in Zeus, does that make Zeus real?"

"No, of course not."

"So, why should it be more real that people go around telling people, 'Hey, there's an all-powerful rulership of the systems, and it's called CASS, and you better follow what it says'?"

"I think I get what you're saying. CASS is an abstraction."

"Sure, okay."

"It's an arbitrary . . . thing that only has power because people give it power."

He broke a wide smile, "There ya go." He started walking again, and I matched his long stride. "They don't have any more 'natural right' to rule over and control people than any of the mythical gods have."

I stopped us this time, thinking, "But, here's sort of where my concern or skepticism starts: how is the synd any different?"

Ericsson looked at me quizzically. "You were trapped in a node with Tabitha for a week or so, and this didn't come up?"

"Well, yeah, it did, but besides the fact I'm trying to get a fuller picture, a lot of times we weren't in the mood to go over basics and ended up skipping right to arguing details."

"Simply, the synd doesn't *rule* anything. It's not a government, or a body of laws people made up and wrote down, it doesn't charge taxes or fees, doesn't tell people how to live."

"Doesn't it? I know the synd restructures communities and will even work to get a community to break ties with CASS. Isn't *that* telling people how to live?"

"No, not really. I mean, we advise people how to live free, without *any* coercion. How to settle community disputes, trade with other communities and worlds. How to collectively manage resources, and, especially, how to do it without taking advantage of people who labor to make goods or provide services."

"That's not telling people how to live?" This was starting to sound like one of the conversations Tabitha and I had had.

"But here's the big difference: If people don't want to do what we advise and offer to help institute, we don't make 'em. We don't force anyone to do what they don't want. The CASS, that's what solidifies them as a government, no matter what they describe themselves as–a confederation or association or whatever–they use force and the threat of force, or at least the power of manipulating economy, to make a world join their confederation. Follow *their* rules and laws. Heh, the financial strong-arm doesn't work so well when a world doesn't use monetary economy." He nodded his head the direction we were headed and started walking again.

"Yeah, this is pretty much what Tabitha and I talked about."

He stopped again. "Are you, what, testing what she's said?"

"Hm? No, not like that. It's just–" I sighed and resigned myself. "You know Tabitha pretty well?"

"Well, sorta. I mean, we'd met a few times and she worked as a social liaison and civil advisor on settlements that I was working martial development with."

"So you've talked?"

"Yeah, a bit. Whatchya getting at?"

"I don't know if you noticed, but she can be rather passionate about her beliefs and doesn't hold back when she talks."

Ericsson gazed up in the air as he slowly replied, "Yeah, I guess that's true. Been a few years, but I guess I recall her being . . . enthusiastic. But, you know, most of us in the synd are pretty gung-ho about what we're fighting for. When the freedom and progress of hundreds of millions of people are at stake, you have to be a *little* fanatical, else nothing gets done."

"No, sure. Good. That's kind of what I was hoping for, in a way, you know, making sure she's not the *only* crazy one, if you know what I mean." I chuckled and started nonchalantly walking again, hoping I was going the right way.

I was glad to hear Ericsson chuckle as well as he caught up beside me. "Yeah, I guess I can see what you mean. If you're lucky enough to not have been caught up with these issues before, and you're thrown in a can with a true believer, I'd probably be wary, as well."

"Uh, which way?"

"Oh, yeah. Here." We came to a hatch where Ericsson needed to submit to a retinal scan to unlock, then entered a small room with three more hatches. Two guys in clothes similar to my own sat at a table with a translucent wall panel that showed a cluster of video displays visible from both sides of the panel, including a shot of the hatchway we just came through as well as a couple showing the CASS prisoners.

"Hey, John. Mo." They nodded back at Ericsson. "We need to speak to their captain."

One of them said, "Orders?"

"Naw. Personal thing."

"Now, we're supposed to keep her unharmed."

"No, no, nothing like that. Mitch here just needs to ask a few things–I'll make sure that's all."

The one who spoke shrugged, but said with a tired sort of mechanical detachment, "Remove all weapons and other loose items on your person." Ericsson removed a pistol from the small of his back and some kind of multi-tool from his belt. I didn't have anything to remove.

From the monitor I could see the prisoners were separated among four rooms, Captain Julia alone in the small one the guard got up to unlock. The electric lock on the hatch disengaged with a thunk, and the guard stepped aside. He kept his weapon down but ready and an eye on one of the displays in the monitor. "Remember, no damage."

"No problem, Mo," Ericsson replied with a smile. As he opened the hatch and let me slip through, Ericsson hissed at me, "No damage."

The room was longer than my cell on the *Vigilant*, but just as narrow. And just as dimly lit. A toilet was bolted to the wall and actual cots sat against two of the walls. The original owners of the *Udachi* thought more of their prisoners than did those of the *Vigilant*. Being in this room made my skin crawl, but that one difference gave me a nearly subconscious greater appreciation for the synd.

On the bed lay Captain Julia. She was on her side, her right arm gone at mid-bicep and the stump wrapped thickly with a black bandage that I'd find out later was specially designed to accelerate cell growth and prevent infections.

Ericsson brought a chair in with him and closed the hatch behind us. He put the chair down next to me and stepped back to stand against the wall, arms crossed. I nodded thanks and sat down. "Captain . . . Captain Murphy."

She sighed. She had been awake but kept her eyes closed. She rolled back and peeled her eyes open, first looking at me, then Ericsson, and back to me. "Mister Creek." She smiled wryly, "I imagine our role reversal amuses you."

"To be honest I'd rather be nowhere near you and try to forget about you and our roles, past or present."

She sat up and moved the remainder of her arm and grimaced. She pushed her loose hair from her face with the other hand. "You look a mess," I told her.

"What is it you want, Mister Creek?"

"You said something . . . earlier. When I mentioned the name Jarrod." She remained silent. "Do you remember?"

"Yes."

"What can you tell me about him?"

She studied me. "Why?"

"Because I asked nicely?"

She looked over my shoulder at Ericsson. "Mister Creek, if what you've told *me* is true, then I can accept that you don't know how things stand. I have nothing to lose. There's nothing you have the power to give me. Why should I help you?"

I scooted my chair closer and leaned in. "I have nothing to offer you, captain. If these people are going to let you go or ransom you: I don't know which, and I have no power to stop them." I heard Ericsson shift behind me. "I have nothing, so I have nothing to give. Except thanks." She looked at me incredulously. "All I want is answers. Right now even more than getting back to where I belong. I'm laying my cards on the table. Sitting here in this chair, I'm as much at your mercy as I was strapped to a table. You can give me nothing, or you can help me out, and, in return, I give you only appreciation more sincere than the hate I feel for what you did to me."

She appeared to think about this. Finally, "Genetic analysis put you as the child of Jarrod Sagson."

"But that's impossible. And you know why."

"If we have to keep talking around in circles, this is going to be a lot harder than it has to be." She was right. I had to make a choice. I decided if I was going to be able to get anywhere, except back to MacVey's whim, I was going to have to trust someone.

I looked over my shoulder. Ericsson still leaned against the wall, looking at me quizzically. To Captain Julia I said, "My father died soon after I was born, over three hundred years ago. And his name wasn't Jarrod Sagson."

She shrugged. "Be that as it may, genetically you're his offspring, with an error margin so low as to be inconsequential. It's more likely, anyway, that you're not from the past than it is he's not your father."

Ericsson shifted again. I said, "What do you mean?"

"I mean you have gene traits that my technician says only developed in the last hundred years or so. So, from my point of view, you're simply insane and *think* you're from the past so convincingly your very brain functions are in on the psycho delusion. Or, your centuries old dad isn't who you think he is. Me, I'm leaning toward the former."

"No, that can't be," I said. "I have no record in the system; you said it yourself."

"Oh, that's not a mystery at all. We don't have but a fraction of the humans in the confederation registered, yet. If you've avoided run-ins with the law up until now, or, for that matter, also avoided regulated forms of intersystem commerce, it's perfectly reasonable you wouldn't be in the system."

"I . . . the ship I awoke on. No way could I get there. Jarrod's ship.

Where's he? And the device. It's related, I know. My memories. . . ."

"I don't know about any of that. All manageable, I'm sure."

I wracked my brain trying to remember those first hours after I awoke. I had spent a day trying to confirm to myself I wasn't dreaming or insane. I hadn't considered the possibility, even then, that where I was, *was* where I belonged and what I remembered before that point wasn't real. That couldn't be possible. My memories stretched back to childhood of being on and growing up on Earth, Iowa, since nineteen seventy-five. School, holidays, mundane moments and special occasions–all on an Earth that, now, essentially doesn't exist.

But then, even I had problems believing in time travel, because everything I was taught about physics told me it was impossible–but that was the only explanation conceivable.

It was now more important than ever that I find out what happened to that device taken from *The Bluerock*.

"Guess that wasn't the answer you were looking for, huh," Captain Julia smirked.

"No, I guess not. But thanks for the info." Without warning, I threw a punch as hard as I had ever thrown in my life, certainly breaking her nose and two of my fingers.

Ericsson grabbed my shoulder and she grabbed her face with her remaining hand as blood started to run down her chin. "Ahhmmpf!?" She cried.

"Oh, you have my forgiveness for what you did to *me*. But I said nothing about what you had done to Tabitha. Burn in hell." I swung around, strode past Ericsson, and banged on the door. John opened right up and let me past. Ericsson followed with the chair. "Mitch," he started, but just shook his head in mock disappointment.

I shrugged. I looked around. "Where's Mo?"

John stood by Captain Julia's relocked hatch. "Smoke break." He seemed to be looking at me the way people lately do when they find out who I am. Or, to be precise, who I say I am.

"Thanks, John," Ericsson told him. "Sorry 'bout the damage." John shrugged and watched us leave.

"Hey," I said when we were on down the corridor, "Could they have listened to us in there?"

"Yeah, probably."

I stopped and faced Ericsson. "What do you think? About what you heard in there."

He looked around as if waiting for an answer to walk by. "I couldn't say."

"Do you think I'm insane?"

"Heh, I just met ya." He smiled.

"Do you . . . do you know of some way someone can implant memories?"

He shrugged. "Anything's possible."

"Like time travel?"

He shrugged again.

"Okay, I'm going to tell you the whole story, and, after that, I'm going to ask you a question." I looked down the corridor. "Is there somewhere we can talk where we won't be listened to?"

"No guarantees, but there's a storage locker over here."

CHAPTER SIXTEEN

Among the shelves of engine parts, I told Ericsson my story up to that moment. "What do you think?"

"Well, I have to admit, that's an interesting tale."

"Do you believe me?" I needed to know not just so I knew *his* position, but so I could possibly feel better about what *I* thought I knew.

"I believe you believe it." That didn't help.

"Look, here's the bottom line: I need to get off this ship and find out who attacked New Torment. Who took the device. Telling this all to you makes me all the more certain of what I believe. Why would CASS want to have me killed and keep it secret? Why would this priory . . . thing, want me killed and steal the device? The answers to everything rest back there."

"How do you even know where to look for them?"

"I don't, for certain. I know where it was according to Frankletti that Jarrod had last been before his logs went weird, and where the logs picked back up from. It's where we were headed when we stopped at New Torment. All I can count on is that if the New Torment attackers didn't go there, then *something* surely *is* there that can help me figure this all out. A clue at least."

"How do you know Murphy isn't lying to you about your dad?"

I thought about that one. "I'm pretty sure she's not. It came up in a time and situation that I don't think she had contrived. She seemed honestly surprised that I was surprised to hear about Jarrod. And I think I had convinced her back there to be honest."

"Yeah, good luck having to go back to her for any more information."
He chuckled. "So, how do you think this Jarrod thing fits in?"

I shook my head, "I have no idea. I have no choice but to believe it. The
supposed resemblance . . . it's the one thing in all this that is most likely to
be the truth, and the one I find hardest to accept, but I suppose I'm going
to have to if it means figuring this all out."

"Don'tchya know what your dad looks like? They have pictures where
you're from?"

I sighed. "I can't tell you how many times through my life I'd begged my
mother to see pictures of my dad. She's always told me she didn't have any,
that he was a very shy man. They'd known each other only a year before
they got married, had me a year later, and he died within a year after that.
Before digital and phone cameras, so I'd always been anything from mad to
annoyed that there weren't any pictures of him–but I believed it. And mom
was always regretful of it herself. She's told me as I got older I looked more
and more like him."

Ericsson waited a moment, then said, "Okay. So, what do we do?"

I looked up at him. He was a good half a head taller than me. "So you're
in? You'll help?"

"Hey, whatever this is, it sounds a lot more exciting than what I'd been
doing lately. This little raid on the *Vigilant* was the most fun I'd had in a
while–got my blood pumping again." His smile was both childlike and
scary.

"What can we do to convince Captain MacVey?"

Ericsson turned serious, "Hmm, depends."

"On?"

"On what he makes of your conversation with Murphy."

"Yeah, I thought so, too. I figure Mo's filling him in." I fiddled with
some moving bit on an unknown part. "How do you think he's going to

use it?"

"Well, I don't know him all too well; I've only served under him for a couple months now. My last ship, the *Saint Christopher*, well, she had to be put down, let's say. I took on with MacVey, and, well, I thought that was going to be more exciting, but he seems to have gone more into business schemes than privateering."

"Wait, what? Privateering? Piracy, right?"

"Only against CASS ships and those who blatantly side with them."

"Yeah, figures," I sighed. "You're not going to just let the prisoners go, are you?"

"No, probably not. But I didn't know where your loyalties lay before. Now, I'm pretty sure you're not CASS."

"Yeah, but I'm not necessarily with the synd, either."

"Ah, but you're not CASS, and that's what's important." He smiled that creepy-child smile.

"Okay, whatever–we can discuss that later. Does Tabitha know? That this is a pirate ship?"

He shrugged. "I don't know, maybe. If she knows the captain or Farrius, possibly. She was one of those political idealists, you know? Believed the whole anarcho-syndicalist thing, but kept it civil and social. Mostly. I guess she's been known to fire a mean rifle now and then. But then some of us, I don't know, just prefer different ways to express politics, you know?"

I thought for a minute. "You know what? I'm not exactly sure I care one way or the other–"

"Oh you should. I can't say I know much, but I've found it sucks a lot more to be killed or maimed or made homeless for no good reason than because you're fighting for some ideal."

"Maybe. But what I mean to say is, I don't really know whether I agree with you, you guys, whatever . . . but you're my best shot at moving forward, so I'm not going to argue."

"Works for me."

"We need to find Tabitha and see if we can figure out what we can do from here. Let's go."

"Aye aye, cap'n," he said without irony. At the time, I didn't know whether to be complimented or worried. "How's that hand?"

I realized I'd been holding my right hand to my chest, the pain a deep throbbing. "Messed up. I'm going to need to get it taped."

As we headed back to the living areas, I asked, "So, Farrius. Who is this guy, anyway?"

"Oh, an independent contractor. He does what MacVey does, except, while we take a little, smuggle a little, kill a little, to *mostly* help the synd or put a thorn in the side of the CASS, Farrius does it *all* for himself."

"Why's he here?"

"Not sure. We picked him up a couple weeks ago or so in the Sirius system. Guess he and MacVey have some deal. Probably having to do with the new venture MacVey's got starting up at Tau Ceti."

We met up with Tabitha in the infirmary. She was sitting up in one of several beds, cinching her belt with one hand. Her right arm was inside her sweater, leaving the sleeve to dangle empty. My immediate unsettling thought was of Captain Julia, but I shook it off. Tabitha looked up as I walked to the side of her bed. Sasha was examining something on a display on the other side of the room. "Hey," I said.

"Hey," she replied, looking back down.

"Had to remove the whole thing, did he?" I joked.

"I have to keep it immobile for a couple of days until the nans've repaired the tissues enough."

"Nansive?"

She finally looked up at me, her expression neutral. "'Nans have.' Nans. Nanobots. They help mend whatever they're designed to, then decay away."

"Nice." I looked around. "Heck of a setup compared to *The Bluerock.*"

She nodded.

"Listen, I need to talk to you."

"Oh?"

"Yeah, we, uh. . . ." I looked over at Sasha, who was easily in earshot, although he was concentrating on his display. "We need to find a place to talk."

"Whatever you have to say, you can say it here."

"No, I really can't."

She glanced at Ericsson, who had come in behind me. "You're not apologizing, are you?"

"Apologizing? For earlier? I. . . . okay, I'm sorry for the way I acted earlier. Maybe I was being a bit presumptuous, but I haven't changed my mind about what I need to do. In fact, if anything, I'm even more certain than I was before. And if you'll let me talk to you, in private, maybe I can convince . . . no, not *convince* you, but get you to understand, just where I'm coming from."

"You're right, you know. I *do* know where you're coming from, and I know that's right where you're going back to."

"Tabitha, look, I'm sorry. I really am." I tried to keep my voice low despite the rising emotion I felt. "I didn't anticipate for . . . us to happen. How could I? I . . . Tabitha–this whole thing, this. . . ." I glanced around the room and lowered my voice again. "Is more than just about you and me, and you know it. Of all people I know, both here and back home, you're probably the most idealistic person I know. I haven't met many people in my life, almost no one where I'm from, who is willing to put their actions behind their words. That's part of what attracted me to you. I'm not sure I agree with everything you believe, but I love that you feel passionate about it and will fight for it." She stared me in the eyes; I couldn't tell what she was thinking, how she was receiving what I was saying.

I took her free hand with my good one. She let me, so I continued, "I wasn't just saying it before; I do love you, and I know what that means for us, and so I hate the fact that I feel this way because of what will happen if . . . what I'm looking to have happen, does." I hated being so frustratingly obscure, but I had no idea if Sasha was listening, and, if he was, what he would make of talk about either time travel or plans of refusing the captain's orders. Ericsson cleared his throat uncomfortably and eased around the corner out of sight. "Part of me doesn't want to be able to return, if it's even possible. And I hate myself for that, as well. But this isn't all about me, or us. It's about Frankletti and Kara and probably a whole lot more, and that's what I'm relying on your idealism for."

She continued to stare for an excruciating eternity. Then, "Apology accepted." She squeezed my hand and let go to move to get up. "We need to find a place to talk." Warm relief washed away the chill of anxiety and fear that had been building through my body.

I helped her sit up and hop down, although I sensed she really didn't need help and was just letting me. My head was still buzzing from emotion, and I tried to change frequencies. "So, you have a clean bill of health?"

Sasha replied, disconcertingly quick, "No major damage, physically. Although she needs to rest for a couple of days and continue to treat the burns." He gave Tabitha a stern look. She smiled with a lot of teeth and took a pouch of derms and ointment sitting on a rolling tray next to the bed.

Then he turned his gaze to me, "Your hand."

"Huh? Oh, yeah, that's why I'm here."

"What happened?" Tabitha asked.

"Oh, stupid accident, really."

"Well, let's get that looked at." Sasha rolled his chair over to me.

Tabitha moved around to sit on the end of the bed. "Well, and I was glad to get out of here." She mock sneered at me. I smiled at her. "Oh, don't think this is over, Mister Creek. I'm still mad at you, and we'll talk about this some more. I'm just going to let you tell me what it is you have in mind." I nodded to her soberly as Sasha's sure and efficient hands moved mine around under a translucent computer slate that showed the insides of my hand.

Keeping a stern look but a soft voice, she said, "I love you back."

* * *

Tabitha, Ericsson, and I found a secluded area of one of the engine rooms. Ericsson's status on the ship seemed to give him a wide run of the craft.

"So, the way I see it," I was concluding, "whatever Captain MacVey is up to probably isn't necessarily in the synd's interests, but finding out about what's going on out here *is*. If there's a new threat to the synd apart from CASS, you're going to want to know, and soon." Tabitha had afforded me the floor to speak my piece uninterrupted. "Now, I admit that my interest is the synd pretty much begins and ends with *your* involvement in the synd," I said, looking at Tabitha, "but that doesn't mean I can't see how we can't have shared interests. Some new threat, which obviously doesn't care about wantonly killing people, destroyed a synd-friendly mining operation, and possibly has friends of ours. People in your organization are going to want to know who they are and what they want. They may be in my way of getting back home. And we may be able to help your friends and people who I owe for helping me out." I paused for effect. "There are too many reasons why we need to turn around and go back, and not enough not to."

"Except," Ericsson began slowly, "if these new people are as well armed as you imply, I'm not sure this ship is up to the job of defending itself against something like that. And I can tell you MacVey will be less than interested."

"Tabitha, what class of ship did Ian say he detected? That fired the missiles?"

"Meade class," she answered, still nailing me with a thoughtful gaze.

"Ian didn't say what else was out there, if anything else at all. How big is a Meade-class battleship? Does it have to be all that major to fling missiles at an asteroid?"

Ericsson shrugged. "Well, a fair size larger than the CASS cruiser we took out getting here. They're capable of full spectrum energy and ballistic shielding, can carry up to eight fighter craft, and have decent number of modular hard points for various weapons systems. Although, they're kinda slow in both standard and Q-thrust. I'm pretty sure this ship can outmaneuver a Meade. Even so," Ericsson said warily, "MacVey is still not going to be very interested in taking one on when he doesn't have anything directly to gain from it."

"You can't convince him?"

"Nope. He took me on board because of my past roles within the organization, but I don't have any personal weight with him."

"Tabitha?"

"He's made it quite clear that he's paid his debt to me and would likely rather have nothing else to do with me."

"Well, then it seems like he wouldn't have any reason not to drop us off at the next friendly base or planet and be done with us, and we can see about finding some other means." I was beginning to believe that her answering my question without protest was tacit agreement with my plans. "How long would it take to get something else?"

She looked into the air above my head. "Depends how far we've gotten, where we get dropped off, who else might be nearby. Best case: we could be dropped right off on a base with berthed synd cruiser with a captain friendly to our cause." Her choice of words made me feel more confident. "Worst case: could be left in desolation and have to wait weeks to find someone fitting the bill to come around."

"The time we spent in the node may already be too long. What about chartering or renting something?"

They both snickered and traded looks with each other. Ericsson said, "Maybe if we pool our money; I have a couple hundred in a few different system's coin and about one-k in an anonymous CASS stick. Tab?"

"Well, I'm afraid anything I had was left on New Torment, and I don't have any standing accounts anywhere."

"Hmm, that leaves us about . . . a half mil' short. Mitch? Whatchya got?"

"Yeah, yeah, I get it," I sneered at the chuckling jesters. Then, "Here's an angle we've been completely overlooking. From what I've observed the entire idea of time travel is as incredible here as it is where I came from. Surely, the possibility of getting some scoop on working time travel would be enough to convince someone to help. Maybe even MacVey?"

"Yeah, that might be a help–I knew a few ships' captains who would love to help for that sake alone, but it could be dangerous knowledge to have leaked out on the Pansys," Tabitha offered.

Ericsson shook his head. "I'm not sure we want MacVey to know about that angle unless we have no choice. He's pretty mercenary, to the point that there could be proof of angels, but unless he can find a way to profit from it, he couldn't care less. And if he did know of a way to profit, he'd find any way possible to exploit the angels 'til they bled milk and honey."

"We may not have any choice in that if your friend, Guard Mo, heard us with Captain Murphy and went to tell MacVey." Ericsson nodded agreement.

I took a breath then said with as much confidence as I could muster, expecting to get laughed at again, "Well, what would it take to take over the ship?"

Ericsson raised an eyebrow; Tabitha looked at me like I was a talking dog. "You're not serious."

"I'm just examining all the options."

"You're talking about mutiny. Do you understand how serious that is?" she asked.

"I may be wrong, but I thought mutiny could only be performed by members of the crew. You and I are not crew members. And it's not new to Ericsson here."

"Hey," he responded reflexively without changing his expression. "I never said anything about mutiny . . . directly. Nothing can be proven. I'd never be able to find respectable work if word got around that I was part of any mutinies, especially *two* of them."

"Which is why you're on the respectable *Udachi*," I quipped. He shrugged.

Then to Tabitha he said, "Besides, you're no stranger to armed rebellions."

"Well, no, but that's not the point. Those situations were entirely different. Revolting against a free ship's captain for no other reason than to countermand his ship is worse than murder . . . especially if murder is involved." I was sure she was actually joking with that, but sometimes I couldn't catch Tabitha's often-dry humor. "We would be marked by synd and even CASS, more than we already are for being synd, and free peoples alike."

"Look, I'm not saying I like the idea, I don't even know if I'm capable of doing such a thing. I just want to know what's possible. Is it? Is taking the ship possible?"

"About five or six on the crew now came over with me from our last ship. . . ."

"Including Mo?"

"Nope."

"Rats."

"Anyway, if we coordinated well and had the element of surprise, we could do it."

"I can't believe you're seriously considering it," Tabitha said.

Ericsson shrugged, "Hey, the man's just looking at the possibilities. I'm here to help."

"Okay, well, just think about that one for a bit. We'll call it Plan C. What's Plan A? I say we give reasoning with Captain MacVey a shot. If we can find the thing that will motivate him to want to help us, that's the best solution for everyone. I think if one of you two were to get him alone, without his crew, he wouldn't have to defend his pride, and it might make him more amenable to consider it."

Tabitha nodded. "Alright, I'll give it a try."

I smiled warmly at her.

Ericsson said, "And Plan B?"

"We convince the captain to let us off the next good place to do so. He really has no reason not to: we're taking space, food, air on his ship for no good benefit."

"And if he *does* know about who you are?"

"We have no choice but to turn that in our favor. Convince him there's money in it somehow. The technology is for the taking, or he could negotiate some service he can provide to whoever developed the tech."

"Assuming our path even leads to the tech's origin, of course," Tabitha reminded me.

"Of course."

"Okay," I continued, "we're set. Tabitha, want me to come with?" I asked as we were getting up from where we were sitting on various pieces of machinery.

"No . . . no, it'll be best if I talk to him alone."

"Alright. Ericsson, can you use a hand?"

"Heh, I think I better handle it. This will take some delicate feeling around."

"Of course, I understand. I'll uh, see if I can find something to eat. Kind of hungry. . . ."

We split up outside the entrance to the lower engine area and went separate ways. I wandered around until I found the galley. At least *this* time I got the chance to eat something before I was accosted and escorted away at gunpoint.

CHAPTER SEVENTEEN

I ate a rehydrated meal in little individualized compartments in a tray in the galley. I couldn't help but be impressed with the *Udachi*. It was very much a military vessel in that it had no luxuries; however, if ships could breed, I'd say its maternal grandmother was a passenger liner. Everything had a sort of finished look to it. For example, the interior walls of *The Bluerock* were bare metal with exposed struts and cabling. The floor had been squares of removable metal tiles. The floors of the *Udachi* were covered in some kind of unusual carpeting that could best be described as velour, but which wasn't worn or faded in the high traffic areas. The walls were light beige segments, with strips along the top of the walls that radiated soft light. This kind of attention to decor was evident throughout the ship, even when its purpose as a military vessel was obvious, like the crew's bunk clusters and the holding cell Ericsson and I visited earlier. Even the engine rooms seemed put together in such a way as to make whoever worked in them feel comfortable and considered. From what I had seen, I agreed that there might have only been twenty to thirty people serving on Captain MacVey's crew, but this ship could easily have held a hundred. I wondered how MacVey came to be in possession of it.

And so unlike *The Bluerock*, which had a single room for eating and the storage and preparing of food, the *Udachi* had a modest dining room and a partitioned off preparation area, where meals could actually be cooked and served by a chef–although it was self-serve while I was there. A couple people were eating and talking when I'd arrived. They looked up at me when I walked in but quickly dismissed me. When I was mostly done with my grainy "vegetable" mush and "meat" plank, someone else walked in, went up to one of the ones talking, whispered something, and they left together, leaving the other talker shrugging to himself.

I took my time finishing up and decided to head back to the crew quarters, and was exiting the mess, when two guys with those short assault rifles marched up to me. The one in front said, "Creek, you're to come with us." His appearance vacillated somewhere between bored and menacing.

"What's this about?"

The other one grabbed my upper arm firmly, but not come-with-me-else-I'll-rip-this-off-and-beat-you-with-it rough, and guided me before him down the passageway toward where I remembered the bridge to be. I found it interesting that I no longer had any fear at being accosted or arrested now that it's happened to me a few times in as many weeks. Oh, I still feared what might come after, but not so much the accosting.

We passed the entryway to the bridge and went on to another door. One of my chaperones pressed a discreet pad beside the door and we waited several seconds. I made eye contact with him. His expression was completely neutral but with an intensity that gave neutral a completely new dimension of texture. I ended up shifting my gaze out of self-preservation.

Finally, the door swished aside and revealed a modest office, most of which was taken up by a sitting area in front of a desk, with upholstery that matched the wall scheme throughout much of the ship. Sitting in one of the padded chairs was Ericsson. He looked at me with a wry, apologetic smirk, and looked away. Captain MacVey sat at a desk unmarred by having any objects resting on it. The two guards stepped in behind and to either side of me as the door whispered shut.

"Where's Tabitha?" I asked.

"You knew she wasn't going to go along with it, didn't you?" Ericsson replied. "She just couldn't stand to be here. Guess she really does have feelings for you, after all."

"What are you saying? Be here for what, exactly?"

"Well aren't you just the industrious one," Captain MacVey said. A long strip of window in the wall behind him framed his head. "You're on board for barely a day and already you're inciting mutiny among my crew." I couldn't decide whether to deny it, which would have been fruitless, or try to shrug it off as an exaggeration. I said nothing, but looked as impassively as I could at Ericsson while my gut tensed and I felt my face grow hot. I felt about as stupid as I ever had, regretting trusting someone I didn't know and already had a history of betraying people. But Tabitha, too? That was harder to believe. Though, I found to my disappointment and surprise, I admitted to myself: *it wasn't impossible.*

The captain continued, "You know, I should be angry, but I'm not." He got up and stepped from around his desk. "This is actually kind of amusing. I almost considered telling Ericsson to let it go on, see how far you'd go. I imagined you the skittering little rat, running from person to person in the shadows, trying to convince them to betray their captain. Rebuffed, and *poing!* Off you go skittering somewhere else to try anew, silly little rat."

I didn't have trouble finding my angle. "That's cute, really. But did you stop to consider maybe you're being played? You're told by someone of fickle loyalty that the new passenger is concocting conspiracies on a ship he knows nothing about, where he knows no one on board, and you believe it? Captain, I hate to tell you, but you're a touch gullible."

He strode up to within inches of my face. "Gullible? No. An idiot for taking you onboard in the first place–that, I'll admit to. I should have just left you in that cell and let you vaporize with it. I never take on passengers, and I broke my own rule out of carelessness. I thought you might be able to serve some kind of use, later. That's my mistake. One that I'm going to remedy by getting rid of you now."

"Really? You don't think a time travel device would be of any use, then?"

MacVey's visage of stoic aggression cracked a little. "What are you talking about?"

I glanced behind his shoulder at Ericsson, who had gotten up from the couch. He gave the tiniest of nods. Everything changed, and I was overwhelmed in that instant by the rush of sublime understanding of events going on around me.

MacVey said, "Whatever, I don't have time for your crap." To the guards behind me, "Take him to the airlock–"

The light, provided by the soft white strip around the top of the walls in that room, dimmed and there was a slight change in the ambient hum of the ship. "What the hell?" the captain said.

"Now," Ericsson said.

Without a thought, I shot my open palm into MacVey's face, jamming his nose upward. Perhaps smarter than another punch, but the force of the blow sent knives up my arm through my injured fingers. The captain, taken completely by surprise, staggered back, one hand on his face and the other reaching for something on his hip. Ericsson was on him, his own pistol against MacVey's temple. "Nope."

I expected a blow from behind me. I step-turned to the side and found one of the guards holding his SMG on the other one, who was already holding his weapon out and away in careful slowness. I just assumed that the offensive guard was on our side, covering the one loyal to the captain, and not the other way around, or else my taking the SMG from the defeated one would have ended rather awkwardly.

"Alright," Ericsson said, "well done. We need to move fast and gain control of the crew before Tabitha loses control of the ship."

"What happened to plans A and B?" I asked.

Ericsson shrugged. "Not as much fun. Besides, we needed surprise if C was going to work at all."

"Tabitha agreed to C from the start? What, as soon as we split off?"

"Yeah, but we can discuss that later. We have to move!" He prodded MacVey with his pistol, "March."

"Fugger," MacVey replied through his hand as he walked to the door; his eyes were already nearly swollen shut. Ericsson went through the door first, into the hallway, then waved the captured guard and MacVey on out. The guard, hands in the air, walked out. Our guard got behind the captain to nudge him on.

Then, before I realized what was going on, the captain turned and grabbed the guard with one hand, and a violent cracking sound nearly deafened me. The captain grunted in pain as angry white and blue light arced out from where he grabbed the guard. The guard jerked and arched his back so far back I heard another wet and muffled crack, then the guard collapsed to the floor. MacVey had deftly retrieved the dead guard's SMG from his hands before he hit the ground, slammed the butt of it into the wall next to the door, causing it to slide shut and dividing us from Ericsson and the other guard, and leveled it at me. I was already throwing myself behind one of the couches.

I barely heard the electric whir as MacVey opened up a stream of metal into the couch. I heard the *pumf-thud* of countless rounds tear into the furniture. I braced my back against it, weapon gripped tight in my hands–or at least tight in one hand as my right was a glowing ball of dull pain. I made sure the safety was off.

The door opened again, and the torrent of bullets stopped. I popped around the side of the couch in that instant and shot reflexively in the direction of MacVey. I shot too low, and my burst tore apart both his shins. He fell to his knees with a growl, swinging his stream of fire back toward me–until Ericsson's shots opened a fountain in the side of his head. He fell forward on his face.

Since the crack of lightning but a minute earlier, sound had constantly filled the room in the flare of activity. Now, it was disturbingly still and silent.

The once-captive guard lay just inside the door, blood pooling around him. The clothing on the arm and chest of our guard was scorched and smoldering. MacVey's arm was blackened. I stood up and saw Ericsson shaking his head, "He must have had a 'last-ditch' hand implant. Risky." I learned it was a one-time-use, high-voltage implant some people got for just such an occasion. The risk came in both that it could sometimes kill the wearer as well as the intended victim, and poor implementation can result in unintentional discharge.

I scanned the carnage that lay about. Risky? I'll say.

"Well," Ericsson said, picking up the other SMG and tucking his pistol into his belt, "one less thing to worry about. Guess there's no turning back now, eh?" He winked and stepped back out into the hallway.

I picked my way around the bodies, trying unsuccessfully not to look at them. "What's the situation, then?"

"Tabitha's holed up in the main computer room with a couple of our people standing guard. We have one securing the weapons locker. Another of us on the bridge, where we should go now. And, well, Marco there," he said, indicating the contorted guard at our feet before leading us down the corridor. As we turned to enter the bridge (my heart still refusing to leave my throat), we came upon a woman, carrying an SMG, standing at the door. She and Ericsson nodded to each other.

There were only three other people on the bridge: someone I didn't recognize sitting in the captain's chair, another fellow at a console, and Silver Eyes (also known as Cynta to everyone else), working furiously at her console, her face set in a scowl. The guy in the chair said, "Ericsson, what was that sound? Do you know what's going on? The ship's controls seem to have gone down and we can't raise the captain."

"Yeah, about that," he replied, "there's been some new developments."

Cynta stopped her activity and turned to us slowly, realization on her face. "It wasn't what was planned, but Captain MacVey's dead."

Cynta kept her chrome fixed on us; the guy in the captain's chair was noticeably uncomfortable, looking to each person in the room. "What happened? What wasn't 'what was planned'? How's he dead?"

"Look, I'm hoping we can do this nice and easy. Peaceful. Well, more than it's been so far. . . ." Ericsson began to look uncomfortable.

The guy at the console spoke, "You're taking over the ship."

"Well, yeah. But, more like, changing leadership is all."

"You killed the captain?" the chair guy accused.

"Yes, yes we did. But, like I said–"

"You can't expect to get away with that."

"This is mutiny!"

Things were beginning to get out of hand. Any moment someone was going to end up firing their gun into the ceiling to get everyone's attention. I was as surprised as anyone to find that *I* was the one to fire the burst into the ceiling. The electric whir and *t-t-t-tak* of the soft rounds flattening against the reinforced ceiling wasn't quite as authoritative as a blast from a gunpowder round, but it shut people up for a second.

"Here's the deal," I began, stepping onto the dais. I made sure to keep the weapon pointed down, unthreatening. "Like it or not, I know *I* don't, we were relieving Captain MacVey of command because–Wait. Let me talk to the ship, everyone. Can you do that?" I looked at Cynta. She raised an eyebrow.

Ericsson spoke into his collar: "Tab', give con the all-open." I heard a quiet *poing-poing* sound. Ericsson nodded at me.

For a moment I couldn't speak; the flash of courage I felt was bottlenecked, my voice locked. I looked around the room, all eyes on me. Except the armed woman at the bridge's entry: she was watching the room. Finally, I shut my thoughts down, didn't try to craft words, and just opened my mouth. I just spoke to the few in front of me: "My name is Mitchel Creek. I, and Tabitha Kim, who some of you know, were until yesterday prisoners on a CASS ship. You rescued us, and it was no easy feat, I understand. I thank you. However, I'm afraid the job isn't finished.

"I don't know how much of the situation Captain MacVey told you, but we have a situation that needs addressing. One in which MacVey was avoiding for purely personal financial reasons–while there are lives, possibly a great many lives, hanging in the balance. We have a duty to go back and make right the situation, to hopefully rescue other fellow synd, possibly from the CASS, possibly another group that's recently gotten involved. We also need to go back to find out what this possibly new threat to all of us is.

"So, we have taken the captain's command away from him and plan on going back. In the process, Captain MacVey was killed. It was not something we planned on, and I regret it happened. But this is how things stand. We don't expect everyone to agree with this move, and I don't plan on forcing anyone who disagrees to go along with us. We will stop at the nearest opportunity to let off anyone who wants to. In the meantime, I would like to encourage a civil atmosphere, for everyone's' sake. That's all." I heard another *poing.*

"Navigator?" I asked in general. The guy at the console responded. I went over to him, SMG slung on my back, and leaned in conversationally, "I need you to set a course to GC colon six-eighty-one point twenty-seven point one-fifteen. And find out all the habitable bases or settlements between here and there."

I could see him thinking about those coordinates already, trying to place them in his mental galactic map. He looked incredulous and gave a cautious, "Yes, sir." He got to work. I glanced over at Silver Eyes as I stood up–she still watched me, impassive. Lights from the console in the dim room reflected in her "eyes." Creepy.

"Alright. What do you all say?" I said to the bridge. "I meant what I said.

We're not going to force anyone and will let anyone who wants, off the ship." I passed a meaningful look to Ericsson. "Who wants out?" I looked to each in turn. Console guy smirked and kept working his charts. Captain's Chair Warmer looked uncertain, and like he was about to say something, then shook his head. Cynta I was worried about. When I looked at her, she didn't respond. I tilted my head at her, inquisitive.

She shrugged. "I'm going to need control back if we're going to go anywhere."

I looked at Ericsson. He spoke in his collar again, "Tab', XO. Give us the stick." Cynta cocked her head, then nodded, and turned to her console.

"Good," I said. "Thank you, all."

I went over to Ericsson and asked in a low voice, "Uhm, couldn't help notice, you called yourself XO. That's like the second in command, right? 'Executive officer'?"

"Yeah, I figured it was either me or Tabitha. And since Tab's more of an intelligence officer type, it'd be me."

I looked around to make sure no one was listening in. "No, I mean, second in command to *whom* exactly?"

He chuckled, "Well, you, exactly."

I grimaced and walked out of the bridge into the corridor, expecting him to follow. I turned to him, "Me? What do you mean, me? I'm not a captain. I don't have any military experience."

"Well, neither do most of the people on this ship. But you don't have to be military to command a ship. Just . . . in command. You know, unless you want to run it in true collectivist form. Which is possible; there're some ships out there that do that. Sometimes it works, sometimes–"

"I thought *you* were going to take over."

"Me? No, I've always thought of myself as the fist behind the captain's power, not the captain himself."

"Okay, what about Tabitha? She's certainly more of a leader than I am.

Heck, she *already* has the experience."

"Look, from what I just saw in there, you're it. Whether you like it or not, you took on the Emperor's Robe."

"Great, thanks. Wonderful choice of metaphor." I looked into the gloom of the bridge. Seat Warmer was standing in between Console Guy and Silver Eyes, looking out at us, pensive. He couldn't hear us, but it was still unnerving.

I turned back to Ericsson, "So, that's it? We just took over the ship? No fighting through the corridors?"

"Oh, it's not over yet, I assure you. I'd watch my back until we drop the riffraff off, if I were you."

"As the fist behind the captain, isn't that your job?"

He smiled his creepy smile. "I'll do what I can."

"Hey, that reminds me, MacVey didn't know about the time device. What *did* he know? What did Mo tell him?"

Ericsson shrugged, "From what I could tell, nothing. I thought the best way to get some guns in there and still have surprise, would be to get you in there under guard–at least one that'd be with us. I told MacVey you were inciting mutiny. He didn't say anything about knowing anything about what you revealed in the brig."

"So, where did Mo go?" Ericsson shrugged. "Can we like, track where he is on the ship? Some kind of bio-reading or computer chip?"

Ericsson raised an eyebrow. "What kind of fascism you think we run here?"

"What's Mo's name? His last name?"

Ericsson shrugged. I turned back to the bridge and asked the SMG woman, "Do you know Mo, the brig guard?"

"Yeah."

"What's his last name?"

"Hernandez."

"You. . . ." I indicated Seat Warmer. "What's your name?"

"Jennings."

"Jennings, have Mo Hernandez report to the bridge."

He nodded, and then pressed a touchpad on the console, "Mo Hernandez, report to con. Mo Hernandez, report to con."

Ericsson followed me to the bridge. I turned to him. "That reminds me too, where's Farrius? If anyone's going to cause us trouble, he's definitely suspect number one." Back to Jennings: "What's your role on the ship?"

"I'm . . . I *was* the XO." (Ericsson said "ouch" under his breath. I said, "Like you didn't know," to him, under mine.)

"What's after XO?"

"First Officer."

"Who's that?"

"Cynta, there."

"Okay, the two of you are going to share the position for the time being." Jennings gave me a look, and Cynta paused what she was doing. "Problem?"

"No, yes. That's, not. . . ."

"Standard? I didn't think this was a military ship."

"Well, it's not. But. . . ."

"Okay, look. Some things are going to be non-standard. At least for a while. I can assure you that before this is over, things are going to get very non-standard. I have to assume you can work with that."

"Yes . . . sir."

Okay, I thought, *that is going to be very hard to get used to.* "So, Farrius—what's his position?"

Jennings replied, "He, uh, doesn't have one."

I looked over at Ericsson. He said, "Yeah, like I said, he kind of came on not long ago and became resident business partner."

"Well, let's find out where he is as well." Jennings paged Farrius on the ship's comm.

Then Cynta spoke, "His ship's gone."

"What's that?"

"The *Tsaul Ki*. It launched about ten minutes ago."

Ericsson stepped to a console and pressed some buttons. "Yeah, normally no ship can leave berth without authorization from con. Looks like he overrode and launched manually."

"How many other ships are docked in this one?" I asked.

"There was Farrius', two reusable shuttles, and ten emergency boats. Actually . . ." Ericsson looked at the ceiling in thought. "Only one operating shuttle, two pods are gone, and two are disabled. At least, last I checked." He looked to Cynta, who cocked her head in a way I saw Ian do now and then when he was communicating with the ship, then she nodded. "Good. So, looks like only Farrius shoved off."

Almost to myself, "And Mo."

"What's that?"

"Mo hasn't returned the page. How much you want to bet he's with Farrius." Ericsson nodded slowly, coming to the same conclusion. "We need to find out who else may be missing."

Ericsson nodded again, then pressed a button, "Section Chiefs, XO. I want a headcount of all your personnel reported to conn, ASAP."

"For not being a military ship, it sure runs like one. Frankletti probably would have walked across the ship to dope-slap me if I tried speaking on the ship's comm so . . . regimentally."

"Hey, some organization and regimenting just works. Serves us well when we have to take over and board CASS ships to free prisoners."

"Not complaining." I smiled. Still, it was going to be hard getting used to.

I looked over at the captain's chair. I'll admit, it was tempting to saunter up and sit rakishly like a Captain Kirk. Nevertheless, I felt I was already straining my luck to the breaking point as it was. Maybe on a pirate ship I'd be expected to spit on the defeated captain and take his hat, but I figured I should play it diplomatically.

"Ericsson," I pulled him aside. "Should we, you know, take care of the captain's body? Store it, give him a funeral, put him in a wood chipper . . . what should we do?"

"Ah, yeah. Don't worry; I'll take care of it." He stepped out into the corridor with the guard for a moment, then came back alone and stood near me.

I looked around: everyone else was doing something. I felt a little uncomfortable with the guard gone, SMG on my back and Ericsson at my side or no. "So. . . ."

Ericsson said, "Yep."

"So *that* happened."

"Yep."

"Not over, you say?"

"Nope."

I paused. "What do we do now?"

He shrugged. "I could go for some tea."

I turned to him, "Really? I would never have pegged you as a tea drinker."

"Something wrong with drinking tea?"

"No, no. I like orange pekoe, myself."

"What's that?"

"A tea, that . . . nevermind."

Console Guy turned around in his chair, "Captain, the coordinates indicate the middle of *tiada yang*. Nothing. There are a few locations along the course: two settlements, including the one at Luyten's Star, two mining bases . . . oh, wait, sorry . . . one mining base now."

"What's the closest?"

"Luyten's Star is five seds away at best. Seven at current speed."

"Alright, then, Mister . . . navigator, engage."

"Sorry?"

"Yeah, let's just go there."

CHAPTER EIGHTEEN

For the next couple of days, wherever I went, either Ericsson or two of his armed friends stayed next to me. I quickly discovered I was treated with an amount of respect by the people overtly on "our side" and a certain fear or deference from the rest. Only a couple of times did I notice a threatening glare, but then, both Ericsson and Tabitha were letting me go to only certain areas on the ship where I was surrounded by friendlies. I was beginning to think Ericsson might have had a self-preservation motive with his nudging me in the position of leader of the revolution. My being unknown by everyone, but supported by Ericsson (well-known brawn) and Tabitha (somewhat known brain), made me a blank slate for people to project any number of rumored identities and motives on. Someone from the lower decks had started some crazy rumor that I was a time traveler. That one got only marginal support.

At both her and Ericsson's insistence, Tabitha and I stayed in the captain's quarters. They were at the end of a "well defended" corridor adjacent to the office he was killed in. Fortunately, the spongy carpeting on the ship was almost impossible to stain so no trace of the fight remained after Ericsson's people took care of the crime scene. The crew had a very short and terse burial in space. I attended, but remained silent and unobtrusive. I thought it would be a good show of respect toward my opponent, which might go some way in placating any faction that might still have it out for me. I was wrong.

Since the mutiny, Tabitha started to warm back up to me. I think political unrest made her happy regardless of what scale it was on. Our angry exchange went ignored in an agreement to focus on the present and let the future take care of itself. An agreement neither of us really wanted, but it was the only thing we could think to do for the time being. She was busy doing her thing with spreading "love Mitch" propaganda and making herself involved with ship's operations, and I was busy with staying out of the way except to make well-timed and decisive actions on the bridge now and again. I was pleased to find that was something I could do without being handled and prompted.

I discovered Sasha was himself pleased by the change in ship's leadership while he was reworking on my hand. While he was injecting some kind of bathroom tile caulk into my arm, he told me, "I haven't actually been under MacVey for very long. Only since I got on at Eridani-E. I've been mostly working as a physician for developing areas, remote settlements, places that could really use a doc."

"Must suck for them when you have to leave a place. Ow!" My bodyguard, the same woman from on the bridge earlier that day, Frelah Hardt (an actual former CASS Marine corporal), eyed what was going on a little closer.

"Yeah, imagine if this stuff didn't have a pain deadener mixed in. Working on bone's never pleasant." He adjusted the medieval lance he jabbed into my hand and continued to slowly inject gray ooze. "Part of what I do during my stay some place is train other people in medicine. People who'll take over when I'm gone."

"Must be tough."

"Can be. Some places already have a medic of some sort—a guy who went to medical school years ago before heading off to a colony, a woman who was a neurosurgeon before being whisked away to be the medic for a refinery settlement. What a lot of these places need is a generalist, an all-round doc-of-all-trades. That's one of my specialties. Quick and dirty meatball medicine."

I looked at him. "That's not something someone wants to hear from the guy shoving pancake batter into his hand."

He laughed, "Don't worry. This is child's play. Remedial, in fact."

"What's this supposed to do, exactly?"

"It's like a cast from the inside. This stuff will molecularly bind with the bones in your hand, harden like cement, and promote bone regeneration."

"Why didn't you do this the first time?"

"Well, besides being painful–"

"Yeah."

"There can be complications."

"Okay, that's something you want to tell someone *before* the procedure. Man."

Sasha smiled. "Well, they're minor. There's a chance of blood clots, but we can prevent that. A chance of bone cancer, but that's also preventable. The most likely negative side-effect might be permanent stiffness after the paste has dissolved. Rare, but possible." He removed the needle and found another location to inject it.

Through gritted teeth, I asked, "You said 'one of your specialties,' what's another?"

"Xenopharmicology and procedures."

"Wow, that sounds cool. That's . . . let me guess . . . strange medicines? Alien medicines."

"Yeah, pretty much. Every single location, every planet, every moon is different. No matter how terraformed it is to look like old Earth or Mars, even subtle changes affect everything. If the atmosphere has two-percent more nitrogen than the plants that settlers, and whoever, transported there are used to, new species develop after several generations, creating, at best, new foods and textiles, and, at worst, new allergies and poisons. There was one world I worked on where the wheat that was brought there from another settlement cross-pollinated with a variety of wheat that had been transplanted there years ago from another location, and created a fatal diuretic."

"Geez. That's . . . yikes."

"That's the unexpected stuff. There's always the issues with native flora and fauna that were deemed harmless by the scouts and frontiersmen, but they're often corporate contractors paid by the discovery, not by the success of the settlement. Well, even with the benefit of the doubt, they're usually not trained or bother with the right equipment to get a true analysis of all the poisons and allergens that could be harmful. Or trace elements in the soil or atmosphere that could take years to cause problems. Even at the genetic level sometimes."

"Wow. I'm impressed that working on that kind of problem is your deal. You must be like a hero to a lot of people."

Sasha shrugged, but kept his hands stone still. "I don't know. Whatever. All I know is that I wish someone like me visited the town I grew up in before it was too late. Sometimes all it takes is the right instrument, and a lot of these settlements could be spared endless troubles and diseases and illness for want of a couple of pieces of electronics and someone who knows how to use them." He pulled the needle out and placed it aside. "Here, keep your hand under this screen until I say. It'll activate the catalyst in the paste. Your hand's going to feel hot, inside, and like it's blowing up several sizes, but don't worry. That's normal."

I kept my gaze on my hand, waiting for any horrific bubbling. "So, what brought you onto the *Udachi*?"

"Vacation."

I gave him a look. "Really? Vacation?"

"Yeah. 'Sabbatical,' maybe. I needed some time on a steady job, recharge my batteries. MacVey assured me that medical needs on the ship would be pretty routine. Of course, that was before our run in with a couple of CASS battleships."

"Yeah, hey, I never did thank you for what you did for us. Especially for Tabitha."

He nodded.

"How long's your vacation supposed to last?"

"I was thinking of seeing how things went here, see if whatever MacVey was setting up on Tau Ceti could use me . . . maybe a year. Maybe I could pick up some new techniques and especially some new equipment I could take with me when I set out again."

"So, this change in plans. Change in management and mission and all that, this doesn't bother you so much?"

"If there's one thing I've gotten good at, it's dealing with change and the unexpected. I kind of have to be. No, I needed MacVey when I came here, but I wasn't getting a good vibe from him."

"Ah. And, what kind of vibe do you get from me?"

He smiled. "Still working on that. But so far so good. At least, I believe you when you say your intent is to save people. Can't really refuse that mission, can I? Probably a lot more pure of a goal than whatever MacVey and his friend were working on. Besides, I might not be a synd man, but I've worked with the synd a lot in my career. Mostly good people with noble intent. In fact, I owe some of them. Including this Frankletti."

"Oh? How's that?"

"I was on Sydney's Folly, a town on a moon in Cygni Beta. One of CASS's early official acquisitions in their association. One day, middle of the night pretty much, all official CASS delegates and ambassadors and whatnot evacuated. Hush-hush. No one would have known in time, until it was too late, if I hadn't already been on my way there to spend some time with an old friend who'd settled there. I arrived in time to discover CASS militia had slaughtered hundreds of people during a riot."

"A riot over what?"

"Plague."

"What? Plague? What kind?"

"The deadly kind." He gave a humorless chuckle. "Some epidemic hit the town. Fast incubation, slow death. I pieced together later that my friend had come up with a vaccine, but the materials needed to mass produce it weren't available. The local governor confiscated her work, inoculated his family and other high-ups, and then barricaded himself in the governor's estate. Food and medical supplies to deal with the infected were supposed to be distributed by the militia, but it fell to chaos, and the governor had no desire to actually govern. He was some appointed trust-fund politician, nephew of a cousin of a corporate robber-baron's son or something. All he cared about was the power and privilege. Couldn't care less what happened to the people he was supposed to be serving." He gestured to my hand. "You can relax your hand now."

"Huh? Oh." I hadn't even noticed that my hand felt like it had turned into an oven-warmed bowling ball, with as much dexterity as one. I turned it over and back. It looked a little red and puffy, but otherwise normal. From the inside, it felt heavy, stiff, and bloated. I was afraid to move it, feeling like I'd bump it against everything. "How long is it going to be immobile?"

"Only a day or so, then it'll just be really stiff for a few days."

I nodded. "So, that's when they rioted?"

"Almost. It started as a protest. Small at first–people demanding food distribution, aid. Then word got out about the vaccine, and the protest turned ugly. The governor told his militia to protect the estate at all costs. And they did. Killed scores of people. Protest turned to riot, and the rich and powerful fled so fast they almost forgot their fine china. Leaving the town to die."

"Well, how long did this all go on? It must have been fast if no one off-world knew about it until you arrived."

"Several weeks from when the virus started to become epidemic, to when all hell broke loose."

"Weeks? I don't get it. How come they didn't send word out for help? Send ships out?"

"The governor didn't want word to get out that his little empire was crumbling."

"I still don't get it. How's that stop word or people from getting out."

Sasha shook his head. "When you own all the Pansys relays on and near the world, and the spaceports, and control mass communications with an iron fist–you pretty much control everything. Word doesn't get out."

"Where is he now? Surely, he didn't expect it to stay a secret. If you hadn't arrived, someone would eventually. Shipments, trade, whatever."

"I can't imagine what he thought, but he did get away with it. Space is a big place, and the ability for big-wig corporate mucks to hide one of their embarrassments is pretty easy. *He's* probably vacationing on some CASS or private-army-guarded resort planet."

"Well, what about the town? How'd Frankletti help?"

"Oh, I arrived in time to see the plague escalate to the point where people died in the streets and no one was able to find anything to do with the bodies anymore. Maybe, two, three thousand out of five-hundred thousand people were left. I was able to hook up with a couple of Libby's, my friend's, peers and see what we could do about creating vaccines enough for some people at least.

"Then Frankletti arrived. Seemed he'd been in the neighborhood, so to speak, and picked up some suspicious chatter from a convoy of ships leaving the system. Thought he'd swing by and check things out."

"How long ago was this?"

Sasha looked at the ceiling in thought. "Mmm, I want to say about twenty years ago? Let's see, I broke up with James in forty-one and flew to the one-twenty-eight colonies to get some work. Was there for a few months, then Cygni. So, yeah, forty-one, forty-two. About twenty years ago.

"Anyway, I had arrived on an interstellar shuttle that took off the second the pilot understood what was going on, leaving me without transportation. I knew a method of being able to synthesize vaccine using these rodent creatures on a planet in a nearby system. Frankletti and his crew made some crazy adjustments to his ship, and flew there and back in just a few days with all the material I needed. Completely trashed his FTS drive and probably irradiated everyone on his ship, stranded him on Cygni for a couple of months doing repairs–but most of the last couple thousand people lived. Plus, he and his synd were able to set up a franchise there, or whatever they call them, and get the people working on living without being under the control of a privileged few–dependent on their noblesse oblige, or lack of, to live, much less progress. Last I heard, Cygni was really beginning to thrive again."

I looked up and bodyguard Hardt was nodding her head as if to say, *Buddy, I know just what you're saying.* "Wow," I said. "That's a heck of a story." Sasha nodded and began collecting his instruments.

* * *

"Mitch! It's happening–the counter attack. Get up, *now!*" Even before my eyes were half opened, the SMG was shoved into my hands. I tried to grip it with my right hand and forgot I could barely move my fingers. I could move my index finger enough to pull a trigger, but I couldn't grip the handle of the weapon. With my brain still sleep-foggy, I switched hands and hoped I could use it left-handed . . . if I had to. I heard a loud, sharp *pop* from the other room, yells, and the *whirr-tatatatata* of SMGs. The fog evaporated.

Tabitha, in a long undershirt and knee-length shorts, was at the door connecting the quarters with the office, pistol in her own injured hand. Her right arm was still bound to her body under her shirt. What a formidable pair we made.

The sounds were coming from the entrance to the offices. I flew out of bed and peeked around the doorway. Ericsson, Hardt, and another guard were around the doorway alternately leaning out or around to fire streams of metal down the corridor. The bullets these weapons fired, and most firearms one would encounter in space, were made of a processed pseudo-metal designed to tear flesh but flatten upon impact against something large and hard . . . like bulkheads and ships' consoles and other things that traditionally don't behave well when shot. The bullets themselves are extremely tiny and difficult to stop by the kind of flexible body armor that dispersed a bullet's energy out and through the garment. Hard body armor could be torn apart by the ten-rounds-per-second barrage. The bullets harmlessly (mostly) flattened themselves when the solid objects they hit have enough mass to dissipate the round's energy out and away completely, without the waves of energy meeting themselves–like around the back of a bulletproof vest.

"Eyes down!" Ericsson yelled as something *tink-tanked* across the floor near them.

Tabitha turned away from the office and threw her arm over her face. "Close your–" Tabitha yelled at me before the world went white. Seeing Tabitha' reaction, I'd instinctively closed my eyes and turned away. If I hadn't been around a corner and shaded by Tabitha, that likely wouldn't have been enough. As it was, the sunburst two rooms away was strong enough to flow through my eyelids as strongly as if I'd glanced into the beam of a flashlight. When I looked around, my vision was touched with a slight pall of gray, and I'd see spots for the next few minutes. I've since seen places where these eye-killers had left a silhouette of people and things unlucky enough to be next to a detonation, flash-burned against various materials.

Ericsson and pals shot continuous bursts down the corridor, hoping to deter anyone taking advantage of effects from the blast. I ran over to them and crouched next to Ericsson, who was randomly leaning his weapon around the corner, in different positions each time. "How many down there?" I asked.

"About four, maybe five I think. We got one or two right as they attacked, and drove them down the end of the hallway."

I noticed his arm was soaked in blood and the fabric of his shirt torn up. He saw me look, shrugged and kept firing. Streams of metal were raining against our end of the corridor, *tik-tak-taking* against the walls and floor. If not for Ericsson's ragged wound, the delicate sound of the bullet and lack of gun reports made the entire scene feel like one of my friend's and my outings at a local paintball field to play with Airsoft replicas which shot 6 mm plastic balls with compressed air. "Who else is wounded?"

Ericsson shrugged. "All of us, but none too bad." I looked: Hardt had holes in, and blood on, her pants leg and a couple of gouges across her face. The third guy's trigger hand was soaked in blood, and I thought I saw pieces dangling. I turned away, grimacing.

"How's this going to end?" I asked.

Ericsson paused his fire. "What do you mean?"

"I mean, this looks like a stand-off. How's it end? One side runs out of ammo and the other swarms them?"

He sprayed more bullets at enemy I still hadn't seen yet. "Yeah, probably. There's no way we can get around behind them. Unless some of the others of us know what's going on and are able to flank 'em–but we haven't been able to raise anyone else."

I turned to Tabitha, who had come up beside me. She nodded and padded to the captain's desk and started poking around on the console. Finally, she said, "Nothing. I have no comm control. No computer access at all! *Punyeta*, how'd they do that? I had installed protections and back-doors exactly in case of this."

"Cynta?" Tabitha shrugged and kept working.

A stream of bullets flitted against the door jamb next to me; some of them took out pieces and chipped the material. Hardt gasped and grimaced, clutching her shoulder. Her neck and face were peppered with blood splatters from her wounded shoulder. She spewed a stream of curses along with her next stream of bullets.

"No," I said.

"What?"

"No, we need to think of something else. I don't want to end up killing them, any more than I want any of us killed."

"Easy for you to say, captain," the third guy said. "You're not the one getting shot up . . . yet. Thanks to us."

Without thinking, I leaned around past Ericsson and held the trigger back with my off-hand, aimlessly shooting down the corridor. I was greeted with a couple of hits against my gun and heard the *vizz* of rounds scream past my ear. "Am I in the club, now?" Third guy looked away from me; Ericsson grinned.

"As I was saying, there has to be some way to take them down without the slaughter. Come on, it's the. . . ." I had to think, "twenty-fourth century. Surely there're some amazing non-lethal counter-measures."

"Yeah, but nothing we have around here."

"Tabitha. . . ." I turned to her. "Any control of the ship at all? Is there any way sections of the corridor can be blocked off? Like on *The Bluerock?* Only, not manually, like on *The Bluerock?*"

"Yeah, each junction can be firewalled off remotely, *if* I can get control."

"Well, that's it, then. If you can do that, what about filling their section with some kind of gas, or removing the air and making them pass out?"

"I . . . yeah, maybe. But I can't do a damn thing at the moment!" She smacked the console with her hand.

"Wait," she said. "Wait . . . something's . . . let me check."

"Oh you're kidding. You did not fix it by hitting it."

"No, no, of course not. But something did change just now. Yeah . . . I have some control back. I don't know. Maybe one of my retro-viruses. . . ."

"Well, whatever the cause, can you do what I suggested?"

Ericsson said, while inserting a new ammo rod capable of providing up to one-thousand shots, "I don't know if that's a good idea. They may have something stronger than eye-killers down there, and might try to blow a hole in a firewall if they're trapped. Might be some effects we don't want–" He was interrupted by two large blasts from down the hall and the destructive tear of wall several inches away from him. "Son of a–! Who the hell brings a shotgun into space?"

Tabitha moved quickly with one hand across the console. I asked, "Can you bring the walls down fast enough, so they don't just run away?"

"These walls are designed to go down in the case of aerosolized toxins. Instances like that, they'll come down fast enough to cut a person in half. Better one person than the entire ship."

"Well, okay, fast but not *that* fast."

She nodded. Then, "Here goes." From down the corridor came a klaxon, a soft *whoof* along with my ears popping, and an end to the shooting. Tabitha looked up and smiled at me. "It worked."

Ericsson leaned and looked down the corridor, "Huh."

"Now, what can we do about knocking them out?"

Cynta's voice came from the comm system, "I recommend flooding the section with carbon dioxide for a few minutes. Reasonably safe and easy clean-up."

CHAPTER NINETEEN

There were a few other pockets of insurgence throughout the ship. The strongest resistance came from the groups that took the bridge and tried to take the captain's suite. They had first taken over the weapons closet by killing the guards we'd placed there and stormed the bridge just as Ericsson was getting the alert about the attack. I was impressed that the less well-armed groups that tried to take over other key areas, such as the shuttle bay and one of the main engineering areas, were put down by other ship's crew and not specifically guards handpicked by Ericsson. That gave me hope and validation.

I looked at the blood on the floor around where Bartes, formerly known as "Console Guy," was shot during the take-over of the bridge. Evidently, he tried resisting and paid for it with a handful of sub-sonic pellets in his gut. After we recovered the bridge we got Bartes down to sick bay where Sasha and his team started working on him, and a few other injured, but it didn't look good–he'd bled out quite a bit while laying on the floor. Tabitha stood beside me. "I don't trust her," she said.

"Hmm?"

"Cynta. I don't trust her."

"She saved our bacon."

"Our what?"

"Our . . . wait. 'Bacon' is no longer a word? Man, I *have* to get back home."

"No, 'bacon' is a word. How do you save it?"

Times like these I just found it annoying trying to translate idioms. "Look, I'm not sure I trust her completely, either. I found her suspicious since I met her. But she did completely stop the re-take-over of the ship."

"And evidently she could have at any time. She was just waiting to see what side she wanted to be on. She's like a god on this ship, holding all the power, distant until she decides which of us mortals she'll deign to assist. She's another Ian."

Thinking of him still turned my gut. "Ian went crazy."

"Anyone can go crazy given the right circumstances. When people like Ian and Cynta have the kind of power they have, when their brains are wired, literally, the way theirs are, they tend to go a little easier. And it's easier for them to take out more people with them. Ian wasn't the first time I'd seen meld-psychosis, and I assure you it won't be the last time *you* see it."

"My last volunteer assessment put me at only a twenty-percent risk." Cynta'd come up behind us.

Tabitha flung around. "What, couldn't hear us well enough over the ship's system?" She glared at herself through Cynta's "eyes."

I shot Tabitha a side-long look. "Cynta, thanks for helping us out back there."

Her face was still pointed at Tabitha's. "You're mad I cut through your firewalls and control routines."

"Yes. No . . . I'm annoyed and curious about that. I'm mad at your timing. If you're really that interested in helping *us*, and you could bypass my work so easily, why didn't you stop the attack before it ended up killing people?"

"From what I hear, you have a body count yourself. Both directly and indirectly. What do you care about a few more?"

I wondered if what Cynta heard and I already knew were the same, or there was more I didn't know.

"I do care when it's needless. Answer my question. Why'd you wait?"

Cynta shrugged, but it seemed as sincerely relaxed as a smile that doesn't reach the eyes seems genuinely happy. "I wanted to see what Cap'n Mitch here would do." Tabitha raised a "go on" eyebrow at her. "Look, what do I care where we go and what we do and why–I just care about who's giving the orders. Do I want to be under a stupid *rufião* who only knows to shoot his way out of a spot? I'd rather someone who can think gave the orders around here."

"Once again, a lot of orders-this and leaders-that for an anarchist ship," I said with a smirk.

Cynta turned to me. "Look, Captain," this time the title sounded a little too mocking, "anarchist doesn't mean chaotic. I'm surprised Tabitha hasn't beat that into your head yet." Tabitha wore a curious expression. "A 'free ship' means any one of us can come and go as we like. Some of us are volunteers, some, like me, were contracted by MacVey and are waiting to see if we're going to renegotiate our jobs or take off at the next port. If a captain is captain because of the vote of the crew or by brute force, if decisions are made by that person or by committee–a ship still needs a single voice representing it, else it's going to just fall apart. Most everyone on this boat realizes that. Most of us don't care to be that voice and want to just do what we're good at. The ones who do want to be that voice you've already killed or I helped knock out. The rest of us are waiting to see if we want *you* representing a purpose we can share in, or we'll jump ship later and sign on with one that does."

Tabitha gave a grudging "Hmm," and started to walk out. On the way, she paused and said, "I still don't trust her."

When she'd gone, Cynta said, "She's just pissed I broke her work. And I can't blame her. It was good work, some of the best I'd seen from a non-enhanced. I'd be pretty pissed if someone cracked my codes and I knew they shouldn't have been able to."

"Yeah," I said cautiously, "probably." I found, looking at Cynta and her emotionless eyes, that I had to consciously work at framing my own emotion on my face. Her unnatural features made my own become less natural and more contrived, even if what I tried to show was exactly how I felt–like at that moment. "But I have to agree with her, that our recent experience with someone else who'd been . . . enhanced, if that's how to put it, has made us kind of wary."

"I heard. Mental break, huh? Heard you had to put him down." Somehow her comment felt like a challenge.

"I don't know how much you know, but I'm more of a visitor here than you probably realize. At first, I really didn't have any choice but to simply accept what I didn't understand, but I'm coming more to the realization that I have the ability, and the right, to change the circumstances I'm finding myself in."

"Welcome to the synd."

"What I mean is: I need help to get where I'm going. I appreciate any help I can get and from whomever. However, I have to be in charge if it's going to happen. I'm glad that you decided that for the time being our paths are going in the same direction. And I hope you'll be willing to help me further on. But if I'm going to be able to both reach my goal *and* do so without unnecessarily harming others, I have to know who I can trust and how far. I can't have constant surprises of changing loyalties or competing agendas. I have to know that I can trust you."

"Okay, can't argue with that. If that's what you want, how about you do something for me."

Leery, I asked, "What?"

"You prove to me I can trust you."

"I thought my non-lethal rebellion-ending plan did that."

"No, that proved to me you weren't a thug. That's halfway there. If you don't want any competing agendas, I'm going to need to know exactly what cap'n's agenda is. You tell me everything, and I can tell you whether to be surprised or not by more rebellions or mass exodus from the ship at the first opportunity."

"How do I know you're not going to use what I know against me and find some way to capitalize from it."

"Funny," she said with hands on her hips, "I had this strange dream just now that we were having a conversation about trust."

I sighed. "You're right. Yeah, you're right."

I looked past her to the wall screen showing a field of stars on black. When you looked at it just right, it had a certain three-dimensional quality to it. The field seemed to dip through the wall the screen was on, and superimposed computer text and graphics hovered inches above the field. Unlike both *The Bluerock* and the *Lysander*, which had actual windows on the bridge and cockpit, the bridge of the *Udachi* was safely well inside the ship, away from possible hull damage. No windows here, only display screens and holo-projections. I couldn't help but feel I was on a set, acting a role.

"Alright. One hour, officers' meeting in the captain's office. It'll all be made clear, and we can, in complete openness, discuss what we're all going to do."

"Sounds great," Cynta said. "Now, who exactly are officers around here?"

* * *

"And I'm saying that before we even listen to what he has to say, we should vote on whether he's legitimately even the captain," Stevens (pronounced "stay-vuhns, gawdammit!"), astro-mech and duly elected Section Chief for the engineering department, was saying. He stood with his arms crossed, against the wall, opposite the couch.

I had decided to bring together the section chiefs and bridge "officers," who, as I inferred the first day when I had rearranged some assignments, weren't officers in any traditional martial capacity. Titles such as "executive officer" and "first officer" were appropriated for division-of-duty purposes. On the couch were current First Officer Jennings, de facto Medical Chief Sasha, and Master-at-Arms Ericsson. The Chief Steward Ah Kum Xiao, more or less in charge of the day-to-day needs of the crew, like food and supplies, sat alone on the smaller couch perpendicular to the larger one. Her black hair flowed unbound from under a brimless cap. She became Chief Steward only thirty minutes earlier when it was realized that the previous Chief was one of the rebels. Tech Chief Cynta sat in the desk chair. And Tabitha, who gave me an exasperated smirk when I called her my cabin-girl, sat in a cushy chair next to where I stood in front of everyone.

"He took the job over from MacVey; he's captain," Jennings said.

"Are we just killing each other now for our roles on the ship? Hells, I'm still not even crystal on what happened. All I know is a couple days ago, we take on some CASS prisoners and a couple of synd advisors, and next thing I know this stranger kills the captain and whoop-dee-doo, we're taking orders from him. How the hells do I know he's not a CASS spy? Murdering the captain to take over the ship, that's not beneath 'em."

"Look, I realize information's been kind of slow and scattered–things have been weird the last couple days, no doubt. All I can say is: here we are now to straighten it out and make sure we're on the same page," I said. "All I can do is assure you I'm not CASS and hope you take my word."

"I'm not crying any tears over MacVey, but as far as I'm concerned, his death marked the end of *him* bein' captain–not the start of *your* bein' captain. Now I didn't go along with the take-over plan because I don't think we need to go all fighting against ourselves, but we need a vote on it else I don't give a damn what you have to say."

Of anyone on the ship, I would have most been afraid to go up against this Stevens. His biceps were bigger than my thigh. Bigger than Ericsson's thigh! Antagonist or not, I was glad he was in favor of democracy over violence. I looked around at mostly friendly faces. "Well, I guess that's fair. I want nothing more than legitimacy in the eyes of the crew. Let's vote."

"Not just us, the whole ship."

Tabitha spoke up, "Normally I couldn't agree with you more, but I don't think that's totally feasible at the moment. We in this room represent all the crew in some fashion; I say we go ahead and vote and accept the result as an ad hoc quorum. We individually discuss what we talk about in here to the crew, and then let the crew vote by whether they stay on or leave at Luyten's Star."

"No, that still gives him control of this ship by default, just a difference of who he has to crew it. I'll go along with an ad hoc for now, to keep things civil, but there has to be a crew vote of who's captain or not before Luyten's."

Jennings said, "We can be there in two seds. We can have the vote tomorrow at mid-sed?"

"Sounds good to me."

"This vote now, does it have to be unanimous or will a majority work for you?" asked Cynta, leaning forward in the chair with her elbows on her knees.

"Hells, there's only seven of us voting. One of us can mean ten crew. I say it should be at least six-to-one or else it's crew vote."

That sounded pretty risky to me, but I really didn't see any other choice if I wanted as much trust and cooperation as I could get. "I think that's only fair, as well."

"Alright," said Tabitha. "All in favor of accepting Mitch as captain of the *Udachi* until such time as a full crew vote can be made, raise your hand."

Tabitha had hers raised as she spoke and kept it up. Sasha. Cynta. Jennings. I looked at Ericsson. He smiled mischievously and raised his hand. Ah Kum shrugged and raised hers. After a pause, Tabitha lowered her hand and said, "All opposed?" All eyes were on Stevens. He didn't raise his hand.

"What? I don't not want him captain; I'm just not sure he should be, either."

"Okay, six yea and one abstention–Mitch remains acknowledged captain of the *Udachi* until tomorrow's crew vote." Tabitha gave me a small nod, and I let out a breath I didn't know I was holding.

"Well, this seems a little surreal."

"So, Captain Creek," Ericsson began.

"Pro tem," Cynta interrupted and winked. That was very disturbing.

"Captain Creek, pro tem. Gonna tell us all what the plan is?" Ericsson smiled. I bet he couldn't wait to see how those who didn't know me would react.

And to their credit, once I told everyone, no one called me insane.

I told them everything that happened to me since waking up weeks ago in Jarrod's ship, skimming over the more personal events. At one point Tabitha rested her hand on my leg.

"And that's why we need to go out there. I'll find answers, and, maybe, a resolution to my being here" (even though I inferred Tabitha was accepting of my mission, I still felt it best to avoid pounding home the Home Nail too much), "and very probably also find some situation of great importance to possibly everyone on this ship." And then I waited.

They wore various expressions of thought. Or maybe it was incredulity. Ericsson looked comfortable, leaning back on the couch and watching the ceiling. Tabitha rested her chin between her fists. Cynta . . . well, I had no idea how to read her. She was impassive and still. Finally, Ah Kum asked Jennings, "Do you know what's out at that region?"

Jennings scrunched up his face, "Are you serious?"

"What?"

"You seriously believe this?"

"I . . . " she looked at me and quickly looked away, "I'm not saying I do. I just think it would be good to know what, if anything, is out there. Help understand."

Jennings looked suspicious at her. Then he turned to me. "Time travel? You expect us to believe you're a time traveler?"

"Well, no, I don't time travel as a continuous thing. It was just that once. Although perhaps once more if things work out that way."

"It's impossible," he said with finality.

Ericsson said, "Obviously, not really."

Jennings turned around to that end of the couch. "I can't believe you believe him."

"Let's say I'm going along with it," he smiled. I raised my eyebrow at him, but he didn't notice.

"I'm telling you it's impossible. The nature of space-time prevents objects from traveling in time. Well, maybe some particles can travel into the past, but not whole objects and certainly not forward."

Cynta piped up, "Aren't we *all* traveling into the future? So to speak?"

I felt it was time to say something. "Jennings, this is the most I've heard you say in a week. I hate to interrupt, but, as I recall, where I'm from it is considered completely, entirely, absolutely impossible for matter to go the speed of light much less *faster* than it. But, you guys can."

"Well, but that's different."

"How?"

"We kind of work around the limitation."

"Tear space, sure. Why couldn't someone have found a way around the impossibility of time travel?"

"I. . . ."

"Stevens, I haven't heard from you yet. What do you think?"

He thought for a moment, keeping eye contact with me. It started to feel uncomfortable, then he said, "Well," at Jennings. "I didn't hear you answer Xiao. Is there anything out that way?"

"You, I . . . no. The charts and records show not a thing."

"Before you ask," Stevens then directed at me, "I'm not sure if I believe your story. I have no reason to. I've no idea who you really are, save for what Ericsson here says, and the scrog still owes me for cards the other night."

"Hey, I'm good for it," Ericsson smiled back.

Stevens continued, "I say so long as there's no big CASS base where you're taking us, we can waste the trip. If nothing's there, well, we'll just kick you off and go find some work that needs doing."

"Now, wait," I put up my hands. "I didn't say I knew for sure that there'd be something there. I'm just saying that's where best guesses point to."

"So, if there's nothing there, you expect to just commandeer this ship for as long as you want, searching for your phantasms?"

"Well, no, I don't suppose I could do that." I secretly hoped, though.

"Then I think the best deal you're going to get is we'll let you take us where we're pointed now, and you catch a comet if it don't pan out." He shrugged, "'Less you know how to work on a ship?"

I wondered if there was a job on a spaceship shoveling coal into the FTS, or washing dishes. "Well, I picked up some skill at astrogation, but I've no idea if I'm. . . ." I let that trail off. Talking like a captain wasn't something I'd gotten used to yet.

I said, "Okay, it's a plan. Jennings, if you'd be so kind, check the charts and logs and whatever for everything we can find out about our destination that might be hidden or obscured." I thought for a beat. "Also, while you're at it, check on Luyten's Star. See if you can compile as much recent information we have available. And then keep the scanners up on high as we get nearer."

He must have understood what I meant, and gave in to the majority, as he shrugged and replied, "Yes, sir."

Cynta said, "We received a Pansys update to our general database a few days ago. I'll make sure it's integrated into our systems."

I nodded. Ah Kum Xiao looked at the floor as she started to speak slowly, "You know, if this is true what you say, about being from the past, this could change things, change the way humanity thinks of existence, like nothing else has."

"Finally," I said, "*someone* gets it." Tabitha gently punched my leg. I smiled at her.

Ericsson furrowed his brows in thought, which was a rare look for him. "What about space travel? I mean, I can't imagine what life must have been like when everyone, ever, anywhere, had to all live on the same rock."

"Yeah," I said, "trust me, it's . . . it was pretty crappy."

Tabitha said, "And yet, it really probably isn't very different, is it?" I looked at her quizzically. "It's like we talked about, back then." That was the term we'd come up with to refer to the time stuck in the node that was only a couple of weeks earlier. To the rest of the room, "I can't imagine things have changed very much, have they? Not at the foundation." I noticed Stevens was nodding. "We still have the same oppression and political power games and exploitation that you had back on old Earth. Only now, it's over a wider area."

Sasha sat forward and said, "I have no clue what old Earth was like, but I can imagine what it's like to be stranded on a planet with no hope for getting off of it. For years I've traveled to and lived among people who are born, live, and die on the same world with no expectation of ever leaving it. Nor the ability even if they wanted to. For most of them, whatever CASS is doing in general, throughout the multisystems, doesn't matter to them as much as the politics and exploitation that's happening right there on their own little rock. To them, *that's* the entire universe."

"Huh," I said, "I'd never thought about it that way, being 'stranded' on Earth, but without our being able to leave it, in my time, that's what we were."

Ericsson said, "Yeah, but I, and I think most of us here, in this room and certainly this ship, have all been to worlds that people don't feel stranded. I mean, don't get me wrong, Sasha, you're a *tiān shǐ* for working with the most . . . what–"

"Victimized?" Tabitha offered.

"Yeah, okay. Most victimized people. But there's a lot of places where people have just said t'hell with everyone's crap, we're going to go live where we just have to deal with our own crap and not have to deal with yours. All you have to do is catch a ship, and you can be off on another world more to your liking. Hells, if you have something to trade, or can work, or even don't take up too much space, a passing synd ship'll take you wherever you want on their route. I don't know, how possible was that on old Earth?"

"Eh, not too sure. I guess if you had the money, you could live anywhere you wanted. Otherwise, you either lived and worked in whatever society you're born in or else you could go be a hermit in the woods away from everyone."

"See," Ericsson pointed to me, as if I were the proof of his argument. "Centuries later, thanks to FTS, and you can have any number of choices of ways to live without having to be a . . . what? 'Hermit?'"

Sasha was shaking his head. He wore a tired look. It was Tabitha who spoke, "That's fine, if you're lucky enough, one: to come in contact with a synd ship. We go wherever we can as often as we can, do exactly that to help as many people as possible to choose the life they want to live. But we're a dust mote in a nebula. And, two: CASS has reached more and more systems, trapping more and more worlds in their web. I can remember, decades ago–" I realized at that moment that I really didn't know her real age. Not that it really mattered to me, but I'd learned that life extension techniques, the most basic of which many people could take advantage of–even the genetic manipulation variety–have allowed people so far to live as long as two hundred years. I had to force myself to refocus on what Tabitha was saying. . . . "When CASS was an annoyance. Now, generations are being born under the culture, politics, economics CASS has created. CASS convinced them that they have no value except what labor they can provide to create wealth and power for the few who use CASS as their police. Their army."

She was on the edge of her seat, wanting to stand up and pace as she talked, as I knew she liked to do out of habit. Sasha and Cynta were paying close attention to her. Ah Kum looked down at her hands. Stevens was still nodding.

She went on, "I've been to worlds, worked with people, who had a history of not having to work under the control of wealth. Not being forced to work for another's profit. And yet, after only a couple of decades of being under the 'protection' and cultural influence of CASS diplomats and emissaries and political operatives, their people had become slaves to their own commodification. Convinced they needed the illusion of supposed prosperity CASS actually forced on them, and that the only way to get it was by working producing ore, or crops, or drugs, or factory products that they themselves would never own! Stuff that would get shipped off to be made into CASS military ships and cities. Military ships that had no purpose except to force more and more worlds to accept their way of doing things. Cities that thrived on the labor of these ensnared worlds, without a single thought as to where that ore, and food, and drugs, and products came from."

She waved her hands in the air, "Oh, but it's okay. These millions of people on dozens of worlds are better for the fact that instead of having their own cultures, being able to work or not as they see fit, for their own benefit, they get to buy into ideas of wealth imposed upon them as something that's 'natural' and 'for their own good.' They appropriate entire worlds of people and force them to work in order to buy into an imposed and foreign culture. So that they, *too*, can become a CASS-ruled city or world-state one day, and can be rich and powerful and make *other* worlds mine their ore and raise their crops and produce their useless products that serve no purpose but to make them feel like they own a lot of stuff–which has become a symbol of power."

She stopped and glared at Ericsson, challenging him. I put my hand on her shoulder. She didn't move. Her muscles were stone.

Ericsson said, "Tab, I'm not arguing with you. That political stuff is your game; you know the score and what the rules are."

"That's the problem. It's *everyone's* 'game.' Everyone is affected by the politics forced upon them by another."

"And what I'm saying is you can avoid that crap, get away from it, better than ever in all history is my guess, with a ship. I did."

"And you think you actually escaped it? You're fooling yourself."

"I . . . I was just saying," Ah Kum raised her voice and then gradually brought the volume down as she spoke, bringing some of the tension in the room down with it, "that with time travel, well, perhaps that can lead to a true, complete escape from all the political systems, no? I don't know . . . how it works? Maybe changes in the past can be made? Maybe people can travel far in the future. It would be a real escape."

Everyone thought about this for a moment. Then Cynta said, "Until someone somewhere finally invents nanogoo," which was met by a round of mumbled agreement.

"Uh," said, "I know nanobots, but nanogoo?"

Stevens gave me an odd look. "Yeah, nanobots are ancient, been around forever. Nanogoo's the stuff that'll make anything from anything."

I turned to Jennings. He obliged, "It's when we are able to use nanobots to break down any matter–like, say, an asteroid–into component subatomic particles and then rebuild them into anything the bots are programmed to make. Rarefied metals, buildings, ships. . . ."

"Food, clothing, literally anything," Tabitha finished. "It will be the complete end to any scarcity. All concepts of wealth disappear when you can make anything you like from rock or stardust."

"Wow. Like, alchemy. Is that really possible?" Everyone nodded.

Cynta said, "Theoretically, absolutely. One research facility announced, what . . . about hundred years ago or so? That they had made a breakthrough."

"What happened?"

I noticed half the room turned to Tabitha. "No one knows for sure. The lab and half the moon it was on were completely obliterated."

There was something unspoken in the air, like no one wanted to be the one to say it. So I said, "You think it's CASS that did that?"

Jennings looked bored, Ericsson remained amused, Ah Kum and Sasha wore curious expressions and looked to Tabitha, Stevens may have rolled his eyes (which pissed me off a little), and Cynta was as unreadable as ever. Tabitha took her cue. "Yes, I do." She looked at Stevens, "Sure, it could have been a catastrophic accident. It's possible. Though who has the most to lose if nanogoo is created? CASS stands to lose literally everything. They cease to matter. Their powerful elite will no longer have the power that controlling things, stuff, has given them. People are controlled by things, whether they're forced to sell their labor to make it or sell their autonomy and identity to own it. Things, commodities, control people. And the people who control the making of things control it all. CASS will do anything to make sure no one can ever rise above scarcity and the systems of arbitrary wealth they create."

Stevens said, "Well, at least we can all agree that when it happens, an' we know it will, that'll be the thing that changes everything well and for good!" Everyone again mumbled agreement.

I took the opportunity. "Okay, this was interesting. I think we covered everything we need to cover right now. I'll make an announcement about the general election, and I'll let you all sort out the logistics of it. Cynta, Jennings, whatever information you find, let me know as soon as you do. Please." I thought I should say something more, something inspiring or at least as weighty as half of what was discussed this evening. But I decided to not risk whatever capital I had gained by sounding like an idiot. "Thank you all for coming." Even that sounded lame to me.

CHAPTER TWENTY

That night in bed, Tabitha and I had an awkward and amusing time trying to figure out the best way to cuddle with our respective injuries. I wore a pair of thin knee-length shorts that looked odd to me, but Tabitha assured me that there wasn't anything weird about them, followed by a: "You and appearances," that I think was meant to sound endearing. She wore only a baggy, brown-colored shirt.

The former captain's quarters were small, Spartan, with walls a slightly lighter tan than the walls throughout the ship. The first day we moved in there, once we replaced the bed cushion, replaced the thin bedding, and force-recycled the air, it was a nice and cozy room. Although we silently agreed to leave open the door to the adjoining office.

When we finally settled in and the room was quiet, I said, "Tabitha, we need to talk."

"Don't worry about the vote," she replied with her eyes closed, "my sense of things is that now that the violent opposition was put down, most everyone else wants to go ahead to Luyten's and see what happens. They'll vote for you as captain. Then, we just don't do anything stupid, and we'll probably keep most of the crew on."

"Well, that's good to know. But what I meant was, we need to talk about us."

She kept her eyes closed, her face impassive, but I felt her stiffen just slightly. "I'm tired."

I had to suppress a chuckle at the stereotype role-reversal. "A couple of days ago you were ready to throw me out an airlock, and now we're cozy again. I don't understand."

"I wasn't *that* upset."

I waited, but she didn't say any more.

I *wanted* to say, "If there's one thing I learned in my marriage with Lori, through all of our rough times, is that communication is of the greatest importance. It saved us on more than one situation." Of course, what I *did* say was, "Talk to me, Tabitha."

She sighed, then opened her eyes. "What do you want me to say?"

"I can't believe you're at a loss for words." I playfully nudged her. She didn't smile.

She turned her head slightly to look at me, just, and said, "I've decided to accept whatever happens." She turned away again. "It's all I've ever done."

"What? That doesn't sound like you at all. If anything, I've learned you jump right in the middle of things, fixing and changing them however you can."

Her voice lost all its edge. I hadn't heard it this soft since the node–but it had a hesitant quality I'd never heard before, "That's when it comes to others' conditions. I've always accepted whatever happened to me. Personally."

"Oh." I wrapped my arm around her middle and spooned myself against her back. "I wish things were different."

"Yeah."

"I can't *do* anything different than what I'm doing. You have to know that."

"I do. That's why I'm just going to accept it. I'll enjoy the now. When you go home, this will have been something that happened to me, and I move on." She sounded unaffected. It was disturbing. It reminded me of how she had shut down after we'd been rescued from the *Vigilant.*"

"Tabitha?"

"Hmm?"

"I . . ." I didn't like being in the same category as her being raped and tortured. Or when she had to sell herself as a teen to survive. I sighed. "I love you."

She put her arm around mine, making me hug her tighter. "Shut up." Her eyes were closed. I lay back into the flat pillow.

Eventually, her breathing deepened and slowed. I lay there, trying to bring memories of Lori and Chloe to mind. They felt centuries away.

* * *

I had started to get the impression that the vote was something of a formality; that my having, in essence, taken the position and getting the tacit approval of the section chiefs, and having put down a rebellion, had by the morning given me a feeling of inevitability. As I learned about how the next day's voting went, my hubris dissolved.

The voting was preceded in every section, every department, by a period of discussion and debate. In most cases, it got heated as some people argued that voting was itself a tyranny of the majority over the whole. Why should they, it was argued, be forced to follow the will of the majority simply because there were more of them? (That made a certain sense to me, and then I realized they were working under a pirate before I took over.) Yet a vote did take place, with many refusing to participate, and the slim majority agreed to recognize me as captain until we reached Luyten's–at which point people were free to come and go as they wished. Some people had nominated other people, like Stevens, to be captain. Some of these people, like Stevens, actually came close to getting a majority vote in their respective departments. And some, like Stevens, got numerous votes across departments.

At the end of it, most of the crew understood that being on a dangerous ship, in the middle of black space, demanded some voluntary surrender of inherent self-sovereignty and agreed to continue working if they didn't get their way in the vote (or non-vote). Some people chose to strike and not work, I learned. So long as someone else could do their job, everyone seemed to support that decision. I made sure that there were no vital jobs left undone and was assured by the section chiefs that everything was being taken care of. The right to strike was truly a respected virtue among these synd and anarchists. And so was being skilled at multiple jobs so that you could take over for a striking comrade if the alternative meant being stranded in space. This acceptance of scab workers, I thought, rather mitigates the point of striking–of putting a wrench in the works of the oppressing power–but I guess it's another concession that has to be made for living in space. As I learned there were contradictions in the oppressive means of production and living under it, there were also contradictions in the alternatives.

I sat in the captain's chair on the bridge (the first time I had done so for more than a couple of symbolic minutes), late in the sed following the final vote. I felt I got there by the skin of my teeth, but at least I was there legitimately. It still felt weird. Jennings and Cynta had been alternately working separately and conferring together for hours.

Finally, Jennings came up to me. "Okay, we have some information on our destination, I think."

"Hit me." (Another idiom I had to explain.)

"Well, all the data we could pull from Pansys archives show nothing past Luyten's Star, relative to Procyon, for at least ten light years. All astronomical surveys show dead space for as far as anyone has been known to travel at Q-thrust. Luyten's is basically at the edge of known space, in that direction."

I sighed. "There's got to be *something*." Tabitha was sitting on a padded rail that ran behind the chair and placed a hand on my shoulder.

"Wait, that's not all, though. Cynta and I ran some deep data scans from various sources, many from unmediated channels and off-the-grid astronomic databases, and some tiny anomalies and discrepancies began to form a picture." I sat up in my seat. Tabitha stood up. I looked over at Cynta, lounging in her chair (which, by that point, I believed was the only way she *could* sit in a chair). She nodded at me. "See, space is big, right?"

"Are you mocking me?"

"No, just establishing basics," Jennings said. I still wondered. "Anything beyond a few kilometers and you pretty much won't see it unless you're looking for it and right at it. When most surveys do a scan, they're either mapping visible stars for navigational purposes, or scanning an extremely narrow field for a blip of something."

"Yeah, go on."

"Well, when you scan a large field for navigation, you don't get a sense of the three dimensions of space unless you make more scans and calculate velocity and take into account red-shift, and–"

"Right, still pretty basic." I started to get impatient. I knew this stuff even before Frankletti started teaching me astrogation.

"Okay, long story short, when you have multiple scans of a large region from many diverse points of origin spanning scores of light years and calculating the effects of relativity, you get a much clearer picture of all those qualities, plus information about objects you *can't* see among them. Especially massive items that affect the movement of, or even just the light from, other objects." He stopped and smirked, waiting to see if I was going to chide him again for being too basic.

"Massive . . . can't see . . . you're talking about a black hole."

"Not just a standard, run-of-the-mill black hole, but a massive black hole. Thousands of solar masses. About as massive as I know of before you start getting to super-size center-of-the-galaxy ones."

"Where? Where is it?"

Cynta piped in, "Best we can tell, it's only about one light year away from Luyten's Star, about forty degrees above the galactic plane."

Tabitha asked, "How can it be so close to a colony, even a frontier colony, and not be seen? Well, detected?"

Jennings shrugged. "Like I said, you kind of have to be looking for it, or do a comprehensive composite analysis of field surveys, like we did. Maybe no one's bothered for that area yet."

"Or," Cynta suggested, "CASS has been keeping it secret."

Jennings sighed, "Not again. Look, I told you before that'd be–"

"That makes sense," Tabitha said. We all turned to her. "You said you searched our Pansys archives. Why didn't you find anything there?"

Cynta turned to Jennings with a smirk. He said, "There just weren't any scans for that region."

"But you found the data you needed from other sources, other databases. Pansys is an unmanaged, unregulated system, but it's the standard for pan-system communication and data transfer–"

"Open source," I said.

"What?"

"Back, where I'm from, it'd be 'open source.' Where maybe someone or a group will come up with an idea but then release it to the public. If it works, it's a good idea, lots of people will use it. And then the public might make changes and improvements and fixes making it better as one giant, unmanaged and unregulated group."

"Exactly. And what group has the reach and ability to interfere with Pansys node archives across the systems? There isn't one except CASS."

Jennings said, as if he'd already said it many times, "But why would they?"

I said, "Depends on what's out there they don't want people to know about."

"But, a black hole? Why? It's not like there aren't black holes elsewhere in the galaxy."

"A black hole is interesting. It draws attention. There's something else there, near there, that they want kept a secret."

Tabitha chewed on the tip of her thumb. "Would be nice to have an idea what we might be getting into before we get there."

"The colony on Luyten's might know," Cynta said.

I nodded. "And they may be close enough to be either compromised or generally not on our side when we get there."

We all thought for a moment, and then I said, "I do have one possibility, though slim, of getting some info before we get there."

* * *

"Are you sure you don't want me to go in with you?" Ericsson asked.

We passed through the first security door and entered the vestibule to the brig. "Yeah . . . why aren't there any guards?"

He shrugged, "One ditched the boosters, you know; the other is taking over for a striker in engineering. Guards're kinda unnecessary, anyway. They're pretty secure in their shiny bungalows."

I "hmmph'ed" and looked at the security monitors. The former crew of the *Vigilant* was in various modes of boredom, exercise, talking. . . . Captain Julia, still alone in her small cell, was reading a physical book.

"Your hand's probably not up for another lesson-teaching; what's your plan?"

I wasn't looking forward to talking to her again. I felt the way we'd parted last time was a fine exit. Walking in there now made me feel like the guy who slammed the door behind himself in righteous indignation, only to find his coat stuck in the door. "I'm going to try talking."

"You know, Sasha goes in there every day, checking on them. Her. He's probably got a rapport. You could ask him to drill her for what she knows."

"Yeah, that's not a bad idea, but I doubt he'd agree to it. If he did, he probably wouldn't push too hard at signs of resistance."

"You gonna push hard?"

I didn't answer. I walked over to her cell's door and poised my hand over the control. I looked at Ericsson. He shrugged and put his hand over the control at the security desk. I opened the door and immediately grimaced at the smell of sweat and mildew that wafted out at me. Captain Julia looked up from the book she held in her one hand and raised an eyebrow. I walked in and Ericsson shut the door behind me.

"And to what do I owe this surprise visit?" she asked.

There was no chair in the room this time. I stood at the end of her bed and looked her up and down. She'd gotten something to tie her hair back since I last saw her, and the tidy condition of her clothes and made-up bed she lay on was a contradiction to the smell of the room. She had some bruising on her face, dark patches under her eyes. "Your nose looks good."

"Sasha does good work. Did you come to undo it?" She didn't appear to be very concerned, just curious.

"No. I came to ask you something."

"Must be pretty important for you to come all this way, especially after how theatrical our last parting was. Must be a blow to your pride."

I hated that she could read me like that, but I refused to let it affect me. I shrugged. "I don't know if it's important or not, just something I thought you might know about. Besides, I was bored."

She smiled. "You're not very good at this game, Mitchel."

"Who says I want to be?"

Her face melted into an odd seriousness I couldn't quite read. "Don't play games you aren't good at when lives are at stake. A little piece of advice."

I thought about that, and nodded. I sat down on the end of her bed. She looked curious again and glanced at the door. She must have suspected I wouldn't come this close to her unless I had a battalion just on the other side of it. "What is out just past Luyten's Star?"

"A lot of space?" she said quickly and flippantly, but I could see she was thinking hard about it. Trying to work out what I knew and wanted to know, I was sure.

"We know there's something out that way CASS wants to remain hidden. We're going to find out what it is soon. You have nothing to lose by letting me know a little ahead of time."

A smile grew on her face. "Nothing to lose? You really believe that?" I cocked my head. She continued, "I know you're not going to kill me, Mitchel. Based on our time together on my ship, our brief talks here, I know this. Sure, you may throw a cheap shot for some feeling of vengeance, but you'll neither kill me nor torture me. In fact, I'm certain that at the nearest opportunity you're going to let me go, or release me to people who may ransom me with the intent of letting me go when they get what they want. You're neither a murderer nor do you believe in letting others murder for you."

I hoped my chagrin didn't show. She was probably right. Of course, I couldn't help but think about Ian as she said that, but I felt a strange sense of absolution as if her words proved to my psyche that his death was the self-defense I knew it was. And the showdown with Captain MacVey was, as well. These were necessities, not murders. Weren't they?

I thought of what Tabitha did to that guard on the bridge of the *Vigilant*. I had wondered over the last several days if I should have tried to stop her. I doubted I *could* have stopped her. I came to the uncomfortable conclusions I didn't *want* to stop her regardless of could and should. If we had that moment to live again, I likely would have let it happen the same all over. But that was Tabitha's right, wasn't it? To get her own revenge? Or did I have an obligation to stop and avoid murder no matter what? Did my lack of attempting to try put that CASS officer's blood on my hands, as well?

It was only in an instant after Julia said what she did that the macro of thoughts and feelings activated in my mind, and I felt a little sick from the flood of them.

"Even so, I still have much to lose. What do you think will happen when I'm reunited with my people?" I shrugged. She said, "A full and complete debriefing. And while they may not use all the same techniques we use on the likes of you, they . . . we, are very thorough in making sure what we report is the truth. The complete truth. Even more than we're aware of consciously."

She continued, "If I tell you anything, they will know what I told you and under what circumstances. If I don't put up a fight, break under anything less than extreme torture, a court martial is possibly the least of my worries."

"Great group you hang out with."

"It's the necessity of war."

"War? War with who?"

"Entropy. Decay. Chaos."

"Okay, seriously? How do you wage war with chaos?"

She chuckled as if I were missing the obvious. "And exactly how does the synd create the chaos and decay that needs to be eliminated?"

"Actually, that's a good question. Enlighten me."

"Your friends travel the confederacy and the frontiers stirring up unrest. They disturb the ability for the race of humanity to work together as one. They limit the chance for peace and harmony. Sure, perhaps that sounds fanciful. But I tell you not because it's some utopian fantasy I've bought into, but because I've seen both sides of the struggle between order and chaos, that the efforts of the synd sow conflict while the CASS brings technology, cooperation, unity."

She examined me and must have seen something in my expression because she put the book down she had still been holding this entire time and sat forward, closer to me. "Mitchel, I was lucky in that I grew up on a world that was able to mine large quantities of ore necessary for building various parts of the infrastructure, the foundation, of civilization, allowing it to flourish. My world had a great deal of wealth. Another world in our same system was less fortunate. They had to struggle more to sustain their economy and develop anything resembling luxury or creature comforts. So when a group of people who were part of the nascent 'synd' came to the system, they easily victimized that world. Convinced by their impassioned rhetoric, the people there threw their own already delicate economy into chaos, made exiles of their fairly appointed government officials and anyone who would dare try to stop them. I was only a girl; this was maybe sixty or seventy years ago. . . ."

I was thrown from her tale for a moment. Captain Julia didn't look a day over thirty-five, forty tops. I promised myself to look into the subject of life-extension technology I kept running across.

She went on, "But I remember clearly when we learned of the self-destruction that finally consumed that world. Civil war, mass poverty, complete collapse of their civilization. When we discovered synd agents among our own society, we rooted them out and eliminated them without haste. And, because of that, my world was spared the chaos that killed our neighbors. When the CASS came to welcome my world into the confederation, we saw the protection they offered against chaos, against self-destruction. I was able to grow up comfortable and well off, where otherwise there would have been decay. So when the time came, and I was given the chance to enlist into CASS, I did so gladly. Thrilled to be able to help others experience prosperity and peace. Democracy and freedom."

She adjusted, tried to hide a wince, and continued, "You may think of me as a monster, Mitchel, for what I did to you. And, honestly, I am sorry you got caught up in all this. I do believe, now, that you *are* caught up in something you didn't intend to be mixed up in. Nevertheless, understand that what pain or discomfort I cause one, two, a handful of people, is a small price for saving the lives of millions, perhaps billions of humans throughout the colonized worlds. Humanity has never been so scattered, so disconnected, so vulnerable, since it was crawling around on different islands on a single world eon ago. Now more than ever, we, as an entire race of creatures in a universe seemingly designed to exterminate us, need ideological unity and cooperation. And the only way we can achieve that, for the good of everyone, is to root out and eliminate the forces that would undermine it. It *is* war, Mitchel, don't let yourself be fooled. You're caught up in a situation, that's to be sure, but it's not too late to do what's right. You could be an important part in helping us preserve and protect humanity." Her eyes were bright and piercing and seemed to float over her olive skin.

I stood and took the couple of steps to the door, feeling a little dizzy and overwhelmed. Ericsson opened it from the other side. I saw him sitting on the security desk, hand still poised over the button, eyeing me carefully. I turned back to Julia, where she still sat looking at me solemnly. I considered for a futile instant asking her again about Luyten's Star.

Ericsson closed the cell door behind me. As I started to leave the security vestibule, he said, "What she said in there, you know it's crap, right?"

I kept walking.

CHAPTER TWENTY-ONE

I informed Tabitha, Jennings, and Cynta that Captain Julia had nothing to offer regarding Luyten's Star; we'd just have to go there ready for anything. I spent the rest of the sed in the captain's office alternately piddling with the computer interface and lounging on the still bullet-riddled couch.

Eventually, Tabitha came in. She stood in the doorway, her arm still bound under her shirt, and she held a computer slate in her hand. The similarity in appearance to Captain Julia made my skin crawl. "When do you get to unbind your arm?" The fact that part of me was asking that question for selfish reasons made me feel even more despondent than I already was.

"Tomorrow." She stepped into the room and sat in the chair at the end of the couch, next to my head.

"Do you want to talk?" she asked in a soft voice. Her careful demeanor was unusual.

I sighed. "No. Not really."

I observed the pause.

"I saw the recording," she said finally.

"What?"

"After Ericsson told me about your talk with Captain Murphy, I watched the recording."

"Are you going to tell me how much of a deceptive and manipulative liar she is?"

"Do you think she is?"

"Me?" I started staring at a different part of the ceiling. "After what she did to us I'd be a fool trust anything she says."

After another pause. "She could be telling the truth."

I craned my neck to look at Tabitha. I sat up. "What?"

"That's what's bothering you, isn't it? That it sounds true? Rings true? Well, she very well could be telling the truth. She *could* be lying, but she may not be. And, in fact, there's really no reason why anything she said has to be a lie."

"As usual, it seems, I don't understand. Everything about everything since I got here has been complicated. Or political. Usually both. Where is normality here? Where are the people who aren't pirates or insurgents or freedom fighters or military? Why is everything I've encountered since landing in Gadreus laden with conflicting politics?"

"Mitch," she said, as if trying to explain bad news to a child, "everything *is* political, even the 'normal.' I'm certain it was where you came from, too, but you were too immersed in the normal you grew up in to see that *everything* is political. Back on New Torment, most of the people who lived and worked there, they lived every day in their normal day, mining asteroids. Sleeping in their beds, eating meals, raising families, watching vids–they weren't freedom fighters or revolutionaries. But they lived in a socio-economic model you find unfamiliar, so perhaps even they wouldn't have looked 'normal' to you. And whether you find it normal or not, *they* did. And they were killed, likely, because *their* normal came into conflict with someone else's."

I stood up, ran my hands through my hair, and walked to the other end of the room. Tabitha continued, "Everyone in the galaxy has their normal. Whether they're farmers or craftsmen or miners or metropolitan or traders, nearly everyone you could possibly meet live their lives through their normal days just like you used to do–unaware of the conflicts that go on all around them, where the spheres of divergent normalities meet. The conflicts and contradictions are the foundation for whatever kind of life they have that they consider normal. Working to farm for their community's prosperity, or to feed another planet exploiting them. Working in an office amidst the clouds or miles underground, playing with numbers and figures that help a corporation maximize their profit and eliminate labor costs–never ever seeing the results of their work on the people they affect. Or the people who live in the cities or the metroships who live off the work of others they'll never meet, or see, or probably even hear about. But politics, and the conflicts between the normals, affect their lives in ways they'll never understand or appreciate. Like *you* probably didn't before you were forced to see different normals."

I turned to her. "I'm not seeing any normals at all, just the conflicts, and that's what I'm getting really sick of."

"You're seeing the truth of things that underlie the various and subjective conditions. What the people who live in them call their 'culture.'"

"And so what of Captain Julia–Murphy? What if she *was* telling the truth? Does it matter at all that two worlds' cultures are thrown into upheaval, one of them crumbles, when a third decides to impose itself on it? Forcing a different normal upon them?"

"Okay, Mitch, the 'normal' thing has to stop. It served a semantic purpose but now it's just confusing the issue."

I crossed my arms and smirked at her. "My question still stands."

She leaned forward and rested her elbow on her knee. "Let's say everything she said was true. At least as she understood it. What she described is something that happens. Not a lot, but it does, here and there."

"You're not helping the case."

"Mitch, I'm not trying to help any case–I'm telling you the truth. The truth isn't a fantasy, it isn't roses, there's no utopia. I'm not here to paint you pretty pictures. You have to understand, and that's what I've been trying to help you to do for days, weeks: There are no pretty pictures. Even the most bucolic and peaceful existence, culture, lifestyle, appears that way only to those who are benefiting from it *being* that way. For everyone else whose labor it's built upon–it's misery and exploitation and excessive poverty and conflict."

Tabitha paused a second, looking back and forth between my eyes. She continued, "In the picture Murphy described, her world was a wealthy, peaceful world grown rich from the mining it produced. Who grew rich, I wonder. Probably whoever owned the mines, and whoever sold the product to other worlds. And maybe some of the wealth was felt by the workers and the people who owned businesses to cater to the workers and their families. But, from what I've seen, I will bet you that the other world she referred to, the one that had to struggle, was struggling to provide her world with agricultural products they needed at alarming rates. I've seen it countless times. One world strikes a boom, gets enormous wealth of some sort, and then uses their power and influence to force other worlds to sell them necessities and luxuries in payment for survival wages. The poorer world is locked now after a generation or two into this one-sided economy that they were forced into and now have to rely upon to live."

She sighed and looked around the room, at nothing in particular, and went on, "And so, yeah, synd or some other person or group may come along and see the needless exploitation by the more powerful world, and try to free the exploited one from the relationship to arbitrary wealth imposed upon it, that has shackled them. But don't think for a second that they do it for a lark and then flee the scene if things go sour. I've known many good people who have given their lives to help entire worlds free themselves from economic enslavement to another world, or the abusive wealthy on their own world. People who put everything they have into it, whatever it takes. Whether a gentle nudge in changing the economy, or full-scale revolution, they're in it to see it through. If it fails, as it does now and then—no one is under the delusion freedom is easy—I've not known a single synd who up and took off. If they didn't lose their life in the struggle, they remained to pick up the pieces and continue the struggle, leaving, if they ever do, only after the world or community they helped, is well on the way to sustainable success. Many stay, even then, having created roots." Tabitha's gaze had grown far away, her face softening. I felt like she wasn't talking to me anymore.

She looked back at me, "Yeah, maybe some freedom fighters, revolutionaries, failed in their attempt to free a world from the economic domination of Murphy's world. Maybe the people of her world did in fact find agents working from the other end to help the cause. Maybe they found some of their own people who had realized what was happening and tried to protest or affect change. And, maybe, all they found were innocent scapegoats her world's leaders needed to pin the ever-present problems on. Likely, some combination of the three. From Murphy's point of view, as a child on the wealthy world, yeah, she was taught and convinced that the world hers was exploiting was a poor, unfortunate world that probably deserved their poverty, never realizing that it was her *own* people *keeping* them in poverty and politically, and militarily, unable to resist being virtual slaves. And she was probably taught and convinced by her culture and politics to hate economic change and progress and anything that would threaten the power the wealthiest of her world maintained with an iron grip. They would have the most to lose by losing their chains around the exploited world. Losing the influence they had by convincing their own people that this way was the only right and true way for people to live. They, the rich and powerful, had everything to lose—and when you're in that position, you'll do anything to keep control. Lies, propaganda, are just one of many ways to craft and maintain what people think of as culture—as . . . the normal."

I sat back down and tried pushing on the coffee-table leg with my foot. It wouldn't budge. "So her culture was threatened by change, by vilified agents of an evil band of thugs and opportunists, and so it's only natural and expected that she would be convinced that the right thing to do would be fight that element that threatened her home," I said as if finishing a joke I'd heard a hundred times. Which, in a way, I had over many days with various setups. "So, what, she's to be forgiven for what she is? What she did?"

"*Chod* no! Are you serious?"

"No. Of course not." I flopped back against the couch back. "I was trying to see where the rubber meets the road, so to speak, in your philosophy."

After having that expression explained to her, Tabitha said, "It doesn't matter even if someone is raised believing violence is normal, when used against someone else it's still a crime against self-sovereignty, human integrity."

"And you've been involved in violence–"

"Not her . . . their . . . kind of violence. Never . . . torture."

"But violence. War? Revolution? Uprisings?"

She looked at me as directly and seriously as she ever had, her gaze moving back and forth between my eyes. Then, "Yes."

"Then by your own rationale, when people feel violence has been done to them, or is threatened, they have a right to defend themselves? To eliminate the threat?"

She sighed, "Yes, I understand your point. And I can't blame people for defending themselves, of course not! What they think of as their 'way of life.' But what Murphy and her CASS do is not defense. It's not some, even misguided but sincere, attempt to protect their lives and fairly earned livelihoods. What they do, as a group or collective, is unwarranted, preemptive, cruel and merciless destruction of anything that threatens their power. Not even *their* power, but the power of those *in* power."

"Christ," I dropped my head into my hands. "Okay, enough." I stood back up and moved aimlessly. I wanted to leave the room, but I despised people who walked out on arguments; even at an impasse, it felt cheap and passive-aggressive. "Look, I need time to think."

"About–"

"I don't know. Maybe not even to think. I just need time. Or to get away. I can't . . . I'm tired."

"I'm sorry." Her voice was again softened. I looked at her; her gaze lowered.

I didn't mean it to jab or prod, but I had to know: "What for?"

She made a little sweep of a gesture with her hand. "You're being here."

My voice sounded like it shook to me, I don't know if it did to her. "What . . . do you mean by that?"

"You don't belong here," she said. "You shouldn't be here. I'd just taken it for granted you were here, and from nearly the moment I met you, we've been thrust together in this situation." She took a deep sigh. "It's been difficult for me, this time, what we've been through. I've lived through worse; I've always figured I'd probably have even more ahead of me. I guess for you, this is a kind of hell, isn't it?"

She finally looked up at me. "Who are you? From my point of view, who are you? You could be from a comfortable, wealthy world, right here in our time, and I've been trying to get you to see the truth of the galaxy you live in. But you're technically not even from this universe." She shook her head. "I've lived hopping from world to world for decades–all my life. You didn't even have more than one world a few weeks ago. What do I know about where you came from, what it must have been like for you? You're centuries old. You speak odd and archaic. You haven't stopped wanting to leave since you got here. And, here you are with me. If I believed in fate, I'd take comfort in that it was meant to be. But it was just dumb, blind chance that you got stuck with an old revolutionary." Her voice dropped further, "And I got stuck falling in love with you."

I went over and knelt in front of her. Her wavy brown hair hid her face. I touched my hand to her cheek and felt dampness. I nudged her face up to look at me. "Tabitha, I . . . I don't regret being stuck with you for one second. I . . . Christ." I pulled her to my chest and hugged her. We were silent for some time.

She said, "Don't go."

"What?"

"If you get the chance, if it's possible, please don't go."

Hearing her say that, plead it, made my heart ache for the vulnerability she never let show. I didn't know what to say. Each day away from Lori and Chloe made missing them easier, and I hated myself for that. Was it because of the extreme circumstances I was in? Was it a coping mechanism? I could do it–I actually *could* decide to stay. She made me want to stay despite the arguments, despite the politics. I couldn't find the words to tell her this, or even if I should. "I love you," was all I could manage to say. I felt her sob, quietly, into my chest. I was awash with self-loathing.

CHAPTER TWENTY-TWO

Late the next day I sat in the captain's chair, fidgeting while others did their jobs, which, to me, looked like a lot of waiting and fidgeting. Finally, Cynta sat up in her chair more alert, looking at whatever it was she alone could see. Her hands played about the console. Tabitha, sitting in an open chair, between Jennings and Cynta, at the long, semi-circular console, noticed the change in activity as well. We shared a look. She started to examine screens and monitors. Jennings finally caught on a moment later, looked from Tabitha to Cynta and back, then at me. Without a word, he turned to his own controls.

In the air between the console and the front wall, projected three-dimensional images of charts and nav controls and readouts appeared and danced around. I was able to figure out a second before Jennings said, "Luyten's Star within standard array range. No other ships detected in the area—we dropped out of FTS as a precaution. We should arrive within . . . two hours at Q-thrust." He stopped, but I saw in the displays an object being surrounded and teased by animated reticules and scan results scrolling next to it.

"What's that?" I said, pointing to it.

Cynta replied, "That's what we're trying to figure out."

"Best guess?"

"A base of some type."

"CASS?"

"Probably," Jennings said.

"How far are both the planet and the probable base?"

"Well, Luyten itself, the only actual planet orbiting the star, is still about a hundred AUs out." It took me a second to calculate in my head using what I'd learned about astrogation that that was about two or three times the distance of Pluto to my old sun. "The . . . base is about another fifty past that."

"What if it is a CASS base? Are we in danger here? We can scan them, surely they're scanning us."

Cynta replied, "At this distance they're not getting anything more detailed about us than we're getting from them, which isn't much. We're just another ship approaching a free system."

"We can rip a *pecu* that way," Tabitha said.

I couldn't stand the edge of the seat anymore; I stood up and tried to saunter over to the console. "What's that?"

"A probe equipped with the bare minimum FTS needed to send it on a one-way trip."

"You can put FTS on something as small as a probe?"

Jennings said, "Sure, if you don't mind it obliterating in an unshielded anti-matter explosion after a billion kilometers."

"Yeah, I don't know about basically firing a missile at a CASS base."

"We don't launch it directly at the base, we send it forty-five degrees out of line and it'll likely blow before it gets near the base. Just close enough for us to get some details long before we're too near," Tabitha explained.

"And they won't mind?"

Cynta shrugged and said, "Well, it's not too unusual for a ship to do that toward an unknown object, especially out along the edges of known space, as *we* are. If they decide to come out and investigate us, they might use it as an excuse to be *gaand chutiya*, though."

"They don't need an excuse," Ericsson said, grinning, as he entered the bridge.

He came up beside me and clapped a hand on my shoulder. "I noticed the change in ship hum and came to see if we're out of FTS. What's up?"

We filled him in on the situation. He said, "Yeah, send a ripper. Why not?"

"Cynta," I said, "once we're in their detail scan range, what'll they get from us? What'll they see? Regardless of the exploding probe, are we, like, radiating the image of criminal element?"

She shook her head. "We're pretty well cloaked. Our differential marker sig shows us as a merchant freighter with a few minor and believable infractions. Enough to not look suspiciously clean, not enough to draw attention–if they don't look too close."

I stared at the holographic dot amidst the projected field of stars, a yellow, pulsing set of brackets around it. *That could be it; that could be the end of the road. Or at least the last stop to the end.* "We need to know. Send the probe."

Cynta nodded and raised an eyebrow slightly. I saw a new set of projected images and scrolling figures appear in the air. A three-dimensional nav chart depicted a system-wide image of Luyten's Star, its only planet and its orbital path shown in a gradient circular line, a plus symbol representing us, a square representing the base, and a dot with an attached label box of rapidly changing data representing the probe as it ripped through space toward the square.

After a few minutes of watching the dot move through the air, Tabitha spoke up: "Do you still want to make for the planet first or head toward the base?"

"Mmm, no, even once we get results back, I still think we ought to stop at the planet first. They'll likely have information we could use to better plan, plus I owe it to the crew to let them take their leave, as promised, before we head into anything too serious." Ericsson grunted approvingly while everyone else remained occupied by whatever they did while waiting.

After a few minutes, Cynta said, "Nothing yet from the *pecu*, but ship scans are confirming a massive gravity well ten-point-three trillion kilometers from current location, plus twelve degrees galactic latitude."

"Black hole?"

"Fits the profile."

I figured there wasn't any point, but I peered around the star field. "Anything visual?"

"No, we don't have resolution enough to display lensing–not enough for *your* eyes." I didn't hear condescension in her voice; she was simply matter-of-fact.

By the time our intended planet was the size of my fist in the display, Cynta said, "*Pecu* has detonated."

I said, "Hmm?" just in time to see a tiny, extremely bright, extremely brief flash of brilliant white light from the edge of the floating display. "That didn't damage the base, did it?"

"No, it was tens of thousands of kilometers from it. It would have been brighter for them if they were looking at it at the right instant, but that's all." She looked at me over her shoulder, "Like I said, it's really no big deal."

"Right. I'll hold you to that."

The remaining interminable time it took us to arrive at Luyten, I constantly eyed the holographic monitor for approaching dots. None ever appeared.

Once the planet, which appeared pale yellow with splotches of red and brown, was large enough in the view to make out mountain ranges, Jennings said, "We're being hailed."

"What're they saying?"

Audible to all now, came a voice, "Luyten Collective to incoming ship: please respond."

"Tell her, I mean, open a channel?" (I was ever pleased that my ersatz astronautical lingo was usually understandable–I was rarely asked what I meant by something I thought sounded like something I should say. The same couldn't be said for the reverse, though.) I heard the *bong* of an open mic. I cleared my throat and said, "Hello. This is acting captain Mitchel Creek on the . . . Free Ship *Udachi*. Uh, requesting permission to land and resupply."

The disembodied voice chuckled. "No need to ask permission, 'acting captain.' You're welcome here, so long as you and yours aren't intending any trouble. I'm sending you the SVN beacon now. We'll see you when you land."

"Thank you." I passed a pleased smile over to Tabitha who smiled back knowingly.

I said to the room, "Okay, that was easy."

Cynta shot a sardonic smile, "You expected we'd have to fight our way in?"

"Well, no, I just . . . didn't expect easy." I sat in the chair, deflated.

As I watched the details on the planet become evident and refined, I was reminded of my approach to Gadreus. I asked the room, "Why no flaming layer of . . . flame as we descend? Or shaking and vibrating? I'm used to seeing kind of violent descents to planets."

I noticed Jennings glance over at Cynta before he turned around to say, "That only happens in uncontrolled falls at high velocity. No one needs to do that unless you're making an emergency landing in a survival pod or something."

"Oh. Well, that's good." I thought for a moment, considering the size and shape of the *Lysander, The Bluerock*, what I knew about what the *Udachi* looked like externally. . . . I took a risk at being humiliated further, "So, I was just wondering, how exactly does a non-rocket-shaped ship take off from a planet? I mean, aren't aeronautics and fuel efficiency important at that point? FTS drive?"

Jennings smirked. I was really starting to get sick of that. "Using the FTS in any substantial atmosphere would quite literally shred the ship and everything inside."

Tabitha was leaning forward on her knees. She said, "Both solid and liquid fuel rockets are used for a lot of small purposes, but for interstellar ships like this, using fractional Q-thrust provides the force needed to climb out of a planet's gravity well with atmosphere being only a minor issue." I nodded to her and we both continued to watch the planet spin under us.

As promised, Cynta and Jennings cruised the ship down to the planet's surface. As we descended, the holographic display expanded to nearly encircle the entire room, acting as a virtual window to the outside, overlaid with continuously updating data and information. The view displayed an off-white and dusty ground with a ridge of mountains to one side and the simple buildings of a town to the other. Once we fully stopped (the fact that I didn't actually *feel* anything even while I saw from the display the effects of touching ground, caused a sort of cognitive dissonance), the display reverted back to a quarter-circle arc in front of the main console.

"Atmosphere good, local weather is good, and all systems check." Cynta looked around at nothing while her hands worked.

"Okay. Well, guess I better let everyone know we're here." I heard the *poing-poing* of the open all-ship channel.

* * *

"Captain Creek, let me introduce Councilor Staand." The smallish man with sun-bleached hair gestured to a thin woman who looked to be in her late 50s. Her ebony skin stood out in contrast to the loose, khaki-colored slacks and shirt she wore.

She smiled warmly and inclined her head, "Welcome to our world, captain. I hope your stay is pleasant." A third person, a young man with a computer slate in hand, made a polite nod.

I nodded back. "Oh, just Jennings. Or Mitch, actually. My commission is sort of a casual thing, I suppose you'd say." The councilor nodded. I continued, "I appreciate your letting us resupply here."

"We share what we have. All we ask in return is that you provide anything you can spare."

"Of course. My . . . one of the first officers is putting together a list of any cargo we have that we can provide, but I also have some crew that'll be getting off here. Most will probably try to head off elsewhere when possible, but some may stay."

Tabitha, who along with Ericsson, came with me to meet our welcoming party at the ship's entrance, spoke up, "I've talked with some, and I can assure you that even those who would like to stay temporarily are more than willing to work their share while they're here, councilor."

"I'm glad to hear that. But, of course, I expect no less from synd," she said with a sincere smile.

"Oh, some of us are synd," Tabitha clarified, "but this is technically not a synd ship."

"I see." She gestured to a small building several yards from the landing platform. "Let's sit somewhere comfortable while we discuss what it is you'll be needing during your stay. Dahari," she indicated the younger man, "will see to providing your crew, and former crew, a place to stay for the time being." Tabitha communicated details back to the section chiefs and, at that point, those who wanted to quit the ship made their leave along with those who just wanted to get out and about.

We followed our hosts to the nearby building that reminded me of a small-town airfield administration building, but significantly more clean and tidy and without the smell of burnt coffee. We sat in the lounge, which had a nicer, more comfortable feel than the utilitarian appearance of everything I'd seen so far. The conversation began with pleasantries and I'd remarked how I'd never seen a sky quite that shade of light orange. Councilor Staand nodded her polite nod. We got around to talking about our stay and Tabitha, comm-linked to Cynta back in the ship, spoke mainly with the young man with the slate regarding details and quid for the quo.

It wasn't until that part of the conversation was over that I realized money had never been brought up; everything was discussed in the form of barter, exchange of labor, and gifting.

Finally, the conversation seemed to open back up for others to participate. I said, "Councilor Staand, there's one other matter. We have some prisoners on board, some counter-revolutionaries." I didn't pause, but I looked to see if the "counter" adjective would be remarked upon. No reaction that I noticed. "There are a couple that are responsible for killings during a mutiny, but most are only guilty of choosing a side. I really have no interest in turning them over to CASS authorities."

"Well, it certainly doesn't sound like their jurisdiction, in any case," the councilor said.

"No. The ones who haven't done any violence, I promised to release as soon as reasonable."

She smiled, "I don't think that will be a problem. We'll have some advisors interview them, and, like the rest of your disembarking crew, the willing and compatible ones will be welcome to stay here, and the rest can stay until someone else can take them off-world."

This time I was the one who gave a polite smile. "Thank you."

"And what would you like done with the more seriously accused?"

"Well, I'm . . . not exactly sure what the normal way of doing things is in that respect."

"Generally, the offended or victimized party, or someone representing them, calls for a trial of peers from any community willing to host it." She seemed to end that statement as a question.

I looked at Tabitha. She nod-shrugged. "Okay, if I may, I'd like to ask for a trial for them here?"

"Our arbiter will gladly review the situation and arrange an interview with all the parties involved."

"Sounds good. Do you have any idea how long of a process that can be?"

"Certainly it varies. But sooner and shorter the better, for all involved."

"Of course."

After that, we spoke of various odd topics. I assured the councilor our stay would be as brief as possible as we had urgent business elsewhere, and we were bid to look around the community and enjoy their hospitality. Hands were shook, and finally Tabitha and I stepped back into the red-tinted glow of Luyten's daylight. Ericsson went back to the ship to continue the ship-refresh. Tabitha and I walked a little way from the building while I decided what I needed to do before we left.

When we were out of earshot of anyone, Tabitha said, "You realize, it's possible that they could claim a counter-accusation against *you*."

That made me pause. "How much weight do you think that would get?"

Tabitha shrugged. "I don't know. Depends on what flavor of ideology the arbiter, and whoever else is involved in the decision making, adhere to."

I sighed. "Well, they all seem reasonable enough. I guess I've no choice but to be honest and hope justice prevails."

"Speaking of which, what about the CASS prisoners."

"Hmm?"

"The CASS prisoners. You didn't mention them. What are you thinking?" she asked, curious, not accusative.

I looked out over the area. Beyond the "airport" buildings, across a field of what looked like short corn, at the buildings of Luyten's Home. People walked here and there, and handful of three and four-wheeled ATVs and carts tooled around. Out to the left of the bulk of buildings was a line of greenhouses, and beyond that, some more fields. Then a ridge of hills marked the short horizon for most of my field of view. A line of four

HUMVEE-sized trucks kicked up dust as they came toward town from the hills.

I noticed the silence. No distant sound of engines, traffic, or machinery. No birds, either. A slight rustle of breeze through whatever the nearby field of corn-weed was. It was pleasant–and a little disconcerting.

I started walking back to the ship. "Not sure. I don't know what's ahead of us, I thought we might need them for leverage."

"Hostages, then?" Again, she sounded more curious than anything, but it stopped me. Hostages? I hadn't much thought of them and what I was keeping them for, not consciously; though, when I did think of it, I used the vague concept of "bargaining chip" at worst. But "hostage" brought to light a whole different aspect–reality–to what I was thinking, and what that made me. I couldn't be a hostage-taker.

"Crap. Crap crap. No. Forget it." I turned to head back toward the office to see if I could catch the councilor or one of her entourage.

"What's wrong?"

"I can't keep hostages."

"What happened to just a minute ago?"

"I came to my senses."

"Wait. No, it's a good plan. If CASS has Frankletti and the others, we may actually make a trade."

"Really? *You* believe that? They'd make a deal and just let us go?"

She sighed. "No, not really."

I nodded. "Then whatever we do it's likely not going to need them, anyway."

"So what are you going to do? Just let them go? After what they did?"

Good point. "What most of them did was just fly a ship. Only a few are really responsible for what happened to us. The rest should get a trial."

"You're awfully cavalier about it."

I turned to Tabitha. "Cavalier? I'm being just. I thought that was something important to you."

"Of course it is. No, of course it is. But so is pragmatism."

"Naturally, using people as currency, as a commodity to be used for their use-value, is pragmatic. And just?"

She looked at me as if she just got a whiff of something sour. She turned to the port office building. "I'll go tell them."

"Frick," I said to no one in particular. I looked around. I was alone.

I looked back out at the circle of hills that put the community and its fields in a sort of basin. Inside the basin, there were only a couple of buildings more than two stories tall. They looked like storage facilities or maybe small factories. From the distance, one looked like a simple apartment building. But for the most part, our ship, and a nearby hanger, were the largest artifacts out in the open. I felt uneasy about that. Especially since I had no idea what, if any, fallout the *pecu* might bring upon us.

I fumbled in my shirt pocket for the comm radio and set the frequency. "Tabitha? . . . Tabitha?"

Finally, "Yeah?"

"What do you think about asking if we can move the ship somewhere less conspicuous?"

Pause.

"Okay."

"What do you think?"

Pause.

"Yeah, not a bad idea."

"Okay. Thanks." I kept my voice light.

The translucent greenhouses shimmered red and orange in alien sunlight. I hoped they were okay with guests as I walked a trail leading to them.

CHAPTER TWENTY-THREE

There were three greenhouses, each the length and breadth of a football field, and I could see a few people moving around in the nearest one. There weren't any signs on the door warning people away or indicating authorized personnel only, so I eased the door open and called, "Hello? Can I come in?" No response.

The outside door opened into a room with boxes and equipment, a couple of desks, and the smell of flowers and ammonia. I walked through the room to the passageway leading into the greenhouse proper and called another, "Hello? S'okay if I come in?"

A woman in an off-white coverall popped up from behind a waist-high track of plants. "Hello? Hi," she said. "Can I help you?"

"Uhm, I was just wondering if I might be able to have a look around? We . . . I'm visiting Luyten's and was curious."

She stood upright and wiped her hands on a nearby rag. "Have time to kill, eh?" She smiled. She, like many on Luyten's, used more of a Spanish-English creole than the all-mixed-up space-farer's lingua franca of most people I'd encountered so far–although her accent had a bit of what sounded Scottish or Welsh or something I couldn't pinpoint. It was an interesting confluence of vocabulary and accent.

"Yeah, pretty much. My wife and I would browse greenhouses and nurseries on weekends. Have something of a garden back home. Not much, but we enjoy it."

"Well, come on in. I'll show you 'round."

"Thanks. Hope I'm not intruding." The floor inside the greenhouse was a grid of rough plastic that allowed water and spilled soil to fall through the slats. I could taste the humidity. Oddly, the light that filtered through the walls and ceiling was a dim, light orange, like the harshest red was being filtered out of the sunlight outside.

"Not at all. Not much of what we grow in here is native to Luyten; you might just recognize a thing or two."

I chuckled. "I don't know about that. What I'm used to is far, far from here." She shrugged. "So," I continued, "you can actually get this much . . . alien plant-life to grow here? Like this? Is the soil imported too?"

"Ah, actually, the soil is almost completely native. Decades of bacterial conditioning, from the day the first settlers landed, have helped convert the soil into usable material. At least, for the specific species and hybrids we have here. Which, of course, have been engineered to thrive in such soil." She pointed to a row of plants an aisle over. "That over there, with the greenish pods? *Vigna pillicus luytana*, or, 'broken bean.' It started out a century ago, native to a world with radically different nitrogen and pH balance, and a white star to live under. Now, here it is. A basic staple of our diet."

"Huh. Cool." I watched as another two women and three men farther down the building were busy doing various things with various plants. Another two people could just be seen at the far end loading boxes through a wide door into a 4-wheeled ATV. A series of misting sprinklers kicked on a few aisles over, for a few seconds, then shut off. This was the closest I felt to home since I got to this time.

"I wonder," I said, "with the soil being engineered and uniform? And the plants all engineered to thrive in this exact soil, if I understand right. . . ."

"Mm-hmm."

"Aren't they susceptible to a really bad disease or fungus or anything?"

She smiled. "You do know a thing or two about growin' things, don't you?" We continued walking, and as my host spoke, she fussed with some leaves of a plant here, absently adjusted stalks there. "Indeed, that is a serious concern. Fortunately, we're pretty cautious when it comes to allowing any off-world plants nearby. There aren't any insect or bird life that can pass pathogen around the crops. And we have some rather powerful and effective remedies that stop any disease before it gets out of hand."

"I noticed the lack of birds. Insects, though? Not even out there?"

She shook her head. "There some native ground crawlers, but Luyten was a pretty dead world before settlers arrived, and no one since has thought to import any bugs here."

"What about pollination?"

"Wind and manual labor, I'm afraid. Works well enough."

"Wow, no mosquitoes or wasps or spiders. Nice." Then I thought. "No fireflies or butterflies, and bees are kind of cute. That's sad." If she knew the bugs I referred to, she didn't mention it.

"I'm Sureth, by the way."

"Oh, sorry. I'm Mitch. Nice to meet you."

"Likewise."

Sureth walked me down a couple of aisles and showed me the computer-controlled water system, the nutrient-rich ivy that grew in the air, suspended from pipes above our heads, and told me the adventurous history of a little plant called "golden ice."

At one point I asked, "So, what's your job here, then?"

"Hmm?"

"Here, at the greenhouses, or farm, or whatever this is."

"Oh, whatever needs to be done. I specialize in the watering system, maintaining it, and I take extra care of the analgesic plants in the house next to this one."

"Oh. So, you don't have a title?"

She gave me a curious smile. "This . . . I don't . . . *work* here, in the sense I think you mean."

I gave *her* a curious smile. "How do I mean?"

"Well, I think you mean in places like the CASS cities and metroships. Go in to the same job every day whether you need to or not, whether you *want* to or not, to do things to make people money."

"Yeah, I guess that's how I mean." We stopped walking next to a section of plants that were nothing more than clusters of giant leaves held up above the soil by the tiniest stems. "So, you volunteer here?"

"I suppose, in a manner of speaking. We all do, if you want to see it that way."

I glanced around at the others in the greenhouse. "All of you here?"

"Not just in here–on Luyten's."

"So, back up. Your work here in the gardens, farm, whatever. How often do you work?"

"Here, take this," she said, handing me a blue watering can with a long spigot. "You need to carefully pour it on the soil under the leaves where the sprinklers can't reach. There you go, until it just starts draining out the bottom." She got her own can from under the rack of plants and also started watering.

"Now," she continued, "how often? Oh, I stop by every day, for probably an hour or two. Sometimes all I need to do is check water pressures, make sure there aren't any breaks in the line. Some days I need to rotate trays around, when Marcus or Jenni are here as well to help out." She nodded her head toward one of the women several sections down, writing something on a clipboard. "There's enough of us who come in like that, that we don't often want for help."

"Why?"

"Hmm?"

"I mean, why do you do it? What motivates you?"

That curious smile again. "I like to. I enjoy it, and I'm decent at it. Besides, it's a change from the other role I have as a surveyor."

"Surveyor? As in a land surveyor? Measuring distance and stuff?"

She chuckled. "Yes, measure and stuff."

"I'd say that was a change. You enjoy that?"

"Very much. Oh, don't worry, you can give more water than that. There you go. Yes, I like being outside and the hiking and using a different part of my brain, I suppose. When I do that, it's usually for most of a day I'm needed, but I don't mind. It's only every couple of days that I do that."

"Huh. Sounds like you get a lot of leisure time."

"Perhaps. I hadn't really thought of it like that. I work as much as is necessary to serve the community, in the roles I can fill. No need to work more than that, is there?"

"I guess I'd never thought of *that*, either. Is that what it's like for everyone here? On Luyten's?"

Sureth shrugged. "More or less. Marcus, I mentioned earlier, he does his work for a little while every few days. Most of his time he spends going around the community, talking to people, checking up on the sick or elderly, seeing if they need anything or just to have someone to talk to. And he paints. Really interesting patterns on the rock, out on the lee-side of south ridge. Now my wife, Renna, she works with the atmo-conditioners. It's hard work, keeps her busy for days at a time, out in the hills."

She had mentioned her wife so casually that I almost didn't notice. Back at home, same-sex marriage was rare, if not outright illegal–determined by the state to be a right adults couldn't have for themselves. The normalcy to the concept, just an every-day idea that wasn't unusual, was itself unusual and refreshing.

"So, she enjoys that, though?"

"Sure. Oh, she complains now and then. Who doesn't? But sure, she loves it. And if she didn't, she wouldn't do it. She'd do something else."

She took my watering can and replaced it with hers below the plant racks, then took some pen-like device from a pocket and began poking it in the soil at various places, looking intently as some readout on its side. "So, Mitch, what is it *you* do?"

"I, well, I guess right now I captain a starship."

"That sounds exciting."

"Yeah, it's been that, I guess."

"It's not what you usually enjoy, though?"

"Well, no, not really. I'm, I used to be, well, I suppose I still am, a network administrator." She looked up at me. "It's part computer system . . . maintenance, part computer programming. Part customer service."

"Oh, that sounds important."

"Yeah, I guess." I thought about what I did forty-five, fifty hours a week, babysitting servers and analyzing logs and setting up and taking down user accounts. But especially the calls I'd get from customers irate about an outage preventing them from logging on to their favorite online game, or blaming us for a virus that trashed their machine because they opened an unexpected attachment. "No, not really important. Kind of unnecessary, really."

"Oh. Then you must enjoy doing it?"

"No, not really."

She looked up at me with a curious frown. "Then, why do you do it?"

"I guess I don't know. Well, to be able to pay the bills, of course. I mean, I didn't *always* hate it. Back when I was teaching myself networking and running my own servers in my basement, it was a blast. Heck, I put more hours into computers back then in two or three days than I do now in a week, and never thought a thing of it."

"What happened?"

I shrugged. "I guess it became a job."

"A job in the sense of–"

"What they do in CASS cities, yeah."

"I see. That's a shame. Is that why you captain a ship now?"

"No, not exactly. That role kind of fell in my lap."

She then said an idiom that, roughly translated, goes something like, "You can't visit the stars, their light comes to you." After she translated it for me, I said, "Ah, I suppose so. Unfortunately, I'm kind of in the process of finding the one star in billions I need."

I crouched down to look at a stretch of plants that resembled miniature heads of cauliflower in loose bunches as big as my fist. A sweet, odd smell, like basil and newsprint, lingered around them.

"You're taking a break then, now? From the search?" Sureth asked.

"Just a refueling stop. Then off we go again."

"Maybe you could come back once you found what you're looking for, stay a bit. Maybe find that passion for what it is you want to do again instead of what you think you need to do? Sometimes, what you *need* to do is exactly what you *want* to do."

I sighed. "Yeah, except what if what you *want* to do unavoidably hurts someone?"

"Surely, if you don't intend–"

Cynta's voice, small and staticy from my radio, broke in. "Mitchel. Incoming ship. Fast. From the direction of the CASS base. I only just now noticed–" and then silence.

To Sureth I said, "Sorry. Sec." Then, into the radio resembling a featureless cell phone, "Cynta, come back? You cut off."

Silence.

"Huh. This probably isn't good."

Sureth, curious, but also perhaps a little suspicious for the first time since I met her, said, "Trouble?"

"Mm, hope not. But I think I better head back just in case. It was really nice to–" And this time I was the one cut off, by the sound of three booms in quick succession, not too far away.

I turned around and peered through the greenhouse wall. Wrinkled and out of focus through the translucent material was the obvious flicker of a raging fire in the distance, back in the direction the ship was. The others in the greenhouse were looking as well, and converging.

I pressed the indicator that caused the radio to broadcast in a wide spectrum. "Tabitha, are you there? Come in, Tabitha." Silence. If there was trouble, there's no way she'd remain silent out of spite or anger; when it was serious, she was professional. "Tabitha, come in." My stomach was an empty pit.

Sureth looked back at me, then at the fire again. "Come, we'll take a rover," she said, calm and direct. She walked quickly to the doors at the back of the building. The others had started walking that way as well. I followed.

By the time we reached the door, the radio kicked back to life. ". . . it . . . signs . . . should be getting through. I broke the jamming; you should be able to hear me now. Mitch?" Cynta's voice sounded tinny and digitally compressed.

"Cynta. What's going on? What was that? You okay?"

"Fine. We'd moved the ship to a quarry. Not sure what's going on; some kind of explosion? All I know is I detected a corvette class ship approaching, later than I should have, and then all the ship's sensors blacked out. Barely got comms back up."

"Yeah, I think I see a new ship out on the landing field. Something's on fire over there, maybe one of the buildings. I think near where Tabitha and the councilor that greeted us were." A squat, white object the size of one of the greenhouses sat about where the *Udachi* had been. There was movement around there: people running. I looked over to the community buildings and saw people running there as well, away from the landing area. The faint staccato of disturbing cracks and pops wafted our way.

The handful of us at the greenhouses were gathered together and talking

in low tones. Someone was saying we needed to go help put the fire out;
someone else, with odd-colored eyes (though not as odd as Cynta's), looked
intently in that direction and said, "Guns. People in gray uniforms. They're
shooting at people!"

We all looked at each other in various flavors of shock.

One of the other women said, "Like hell they are," and sprinted toward
one of two nearby ATVs. "Let's get them!" Two of the men followed. They
climbed on the vehicle and sped toward the town to the sound of an electric
hum.

"Cynta," I was still holding the radio to my face. "Do you have
communications with everyone else?"

"I've open-channel capat."

"Tell . . . where's the ship relative to the farms and the town?"

"The farms are between us and the town."

"Okay, tell everyone willing to, to grab weapons and converge on the
greenhouses. We've got trouble."

"Aye aye."

A second later Cynta relayed the order (or was it thought of as a serious
suggestion?) to everyone with a radio, and presumably on ship.

The far-sighted, so to speak, woman looked to be in her early 20s. She
asked Sureth, "What do we do? I think we're being attacked?"

Sureth furrowed her brow and continued looking at the distant scene
that, to us, still only appeared to be a fire. She told her, "Get on the phone
and see if you can reach anyone at Guard Shack. If so, see if they have any
advice on how we can help." Obviously glad to be able to do something, the
young woman rushed back through the greenhouse.

I said, "I've got some people coming; they should be bringing some
firepower."

CHAPTER TWENTY-FOUR

We watched helplessly as the fire burned on. We no longer saw people moving, but we could still hear the echo of gunfire from the town. I kept trying to raise Tabitha on the radio.

The eye-enhanced woman came back and told us she had to try several times before she was relayed to one of the volunteer security officers the town used for protection. ("Law enforcement," *per se*, didn't exist as Luyten's Home technically had no laws.) Best he could tell, a ship came out of Q-thrust in atmosphere, shot the port buildings, landed, and several men came out of the ship shooting at anyone they saw. Once word spread, citizens began arming themselves and are currently defending the town from their windows and doorways.

Soon, I heard vehicles growling up from the other side of the greenhouses. Four large, mismatched, ATVs full of men and women from the *Udachi* drove up to us. Most were wearing some kind of vest or shirt that looked like body armor, and all had at least one firearm. Naturally, Ericsson was among them, as well as my former bodyguard, Frelah Hardt. Cynta was driving one of the large, six-wheeled machines; Sasha was in the rear vehicle, large black bag on his back–the one he'd had when he treated Tabitha during our rescue. I quick-counted twenty-five or twenty-six people.

Ericsson handed me a snub-nosed SMG like the one I fired briefly during the counter-coup attempt a few days ago. (*Had it really been only a few days?* I wondered, amazed.) "What's the plan, captain?" he asked. His joviality belied a bearing of military-like surety.

"Okay, from what I hear, the attackers have moved into town and are shooting things up. The townspeople are returning fire and have the benefit of cover."

"CASS?"

I shook my head. "I don't think so. Gray uniforms, and no one has described the ship or them as CASS. As of yet."

Ericsson nodded. "Right."

I turned to Sureth, "Are the buildings set up in regular blocks? Streets at right angles pretty regular?"

She furrowed her brow. "Mm, mostly. I mean, the main roads run east-west pretty regular, but most every building is separated by a walkway or a road."

"Okay, if, I think, the attackers are making their way through town, maybe they're after something."

Someone on an ATV suggested, "Maybe us."

I smirked ironically and continued, "And they're meeting resistance from the town as they go along, we'd probably be effective coming up behind them as a single force. You think?"

Ericsson nodded again. "Yeah, sounds right. We should have most of us *kabayo tumakbo* behind them, and a team on roads on either side to either take them from the oblique or cut them off from escaping down between buildings."

"Assuming they're all sticking to one road, too," I grumbled.

"There's that. But we have to start somewhere." Then to one of the guys on the back I never met, "Lewelling. We're going to see if we can find where they're progressing. Tell Cynta, James, and Matlov to follow close, and when we signal, James will follow me. Cynta take hers down the next previous road and Matlov down the next one after us. Check your targets; no accidental local casualties."

"Right," Lewelling said, and then started relaying the info on his radio.

Ericsson asked, "You hopping on or going with one of them?"

I looked at Sureth. "What are your plans?"

"We need to stay here and help protect our food supply. We have a lot in storage, but if anything happens to the farms, it could make things very difficult for us in the long-run."

"Ericsson, have any extra guns?" He nodded. Frelah pulled out a couple of pistols and another SMG and handed them over to Sureth and two others.

Back to Sureth, I said, "Good luck. And, uh, thanks for the tour."

She looked about as nervous as I felt, but hid it half as well as I did. Still, her eyes were steady and her hands sure on the gun. "Good luck to you, too."

I climbed on the wagon-back of the ATV, sandwiched between Frelah and a man with no shirt under his body-armor vest and a stocking cap pulled low over his brow. Ericsson jerked the ATV forward and then gunned it toward the town.

The light had quickly dimmed over the last twenty minutes or so as the sun set. There were no clouds and the sky had a deep crimson glow that graduated from the color of dried blood at one horizon to burning-ember-red toward the direction of town. I held on to the edge of the wagon with one hand while I tried to hold the SMG steady on my lap as each bump jerked me off my already precarious seat. I'd made sure the safety was on three or four times in the couple of minutes between the greenhouses and the first legitimate town building.

I tried to listen for gunfire, but couldn't hear anything over the whine of the ATV's electric engine revved at max, and the crunch of the large knobby tires grinding the rocky ground. I pointed over Frelah's shoulder, giving Ericsson an indication where I thought the invaders may have gone down. The buildings here were all low, plain structures with round windows set in featureless walls cast in shadow.

As we approached town, I saw several bodies in the road and sitting against walls. A couple in unadorned gray uniforms, but most in the simple, loose clothing of the locals. One woman, crouched over one victim, apparently giving aid, caught sight of us as we approached and raised a pistol. She must have recognized us as not being among the attackers, and quickly lowered it before we passed her.

Just as Ericsson careened the ATV around a corner of a building, I got a good look at the landing area–the main building and hanger were devastated infernos, and the smaller buildings around them also ablaze. A squat, pale ship sat almost exactly where the *Udachi* had sat maybe an hour earlier. A ramp in its belly was open and descended.

I tapped Ericsson on the shoulder and he slowed to a stop. "I'm taking a few and checking there," I said, gesturing. He nodded.

I hopped off and ran back to the last ATV, shouting to Cynta in the third one as I went by, "Cynta, grab someone and come with me."

I reached the end. "Sasha, and you," I indicated the muscle next to him, "we're going to check for survivors over there, and then secure their ship." They immediately jumped out; boots crunched the ground. Cynta, Sasha, two others, and I started jogging toward the fire as the ATVs sped off into town.

The nearly blinding inferno made the surrounding twilight appear as dark as midnight by comparison. We could barely get within fifty yards before the heat was too much to bear. The wind the fire generated blew our hair and clothes and I couldn't keep my eyes open from the heat.

The guy Cynta brought was looking back at the town. "Why'd they blast just here? When they coulda blasted the town?"

Cynta answered, "Maybe they want the town for something and figured the landing area would have defenses or other ships they didn't want to deal with. Or, naturally, radar and scanners and other vessel-detecting equipment."

Sasha had an arm over his face, "Mitchel, there's no way anything survived in or around that."

"Tabitha was in there."

He looked up at me, squinting, tears from the intense heat glistened on his face. "Are you certain?"

I nodded. "I sent her back to talk to the councilor about something. Then I left." The building we had been in was burned or blasted to the foundation, the hanger, with whatever other ships and fuel and whatever inside, sent flames impossibly high into the air.

It wasn't real, some part of my mind called out. For the first time since I woke up in the *Lysander*, I felt the disconnect of my experience with reality, and I was certain what I was seeing and where I was standing wasn't real. The heat searing my face was an illusion. The ball of anger and loss welling in my gut was happening to someone else.

I heard Cynta say, from a million miles away, "There, over there. Bodies."

Her eyelids were barely slits. I looked where she was pointing but didn't see anything; the glare from the fire obscured everything around. I started running in that direction anyway, keeping my eyes forward, opened as much as I could. My own tears running down my cheeks.

Finally, I saw shapes on the ground. A few, closer to the burning remains of the administration building were aflame. Farther away, three of them in a group lying in various positions, like discarded rag dolls. One with dark skin and khaki-colored clothes, one I didn't recognize, and another in a familiar green shirt and slightly large boots. I collapsed on my knees next to her, the gun falling from my hands. Her hair was loose and splayed around her head. It was singed and bits curled from heat. Blood oozed freely from a cut on her forehead.

"Tabitha," I said, and cupped her face in my hands. Instantly, a fist shot up grazed my chin. "Gah!" I exclaimed, and fell back in the dirt.

Tabitha tried to sit up and fell back, her head lolled around and she appeared to not be able to see anything. Anger and loss turned to joy and concern.

"Tabitha, it's me. Mitch."

She lay on the ground, blinking, scrunching up her forehead. She kept saying, "Wha . . . wha . . . wha . . . " like a mantra.

I put my hands on her face again, prepared to duck but nothing happened, and spoke calmly into her ear, "Tabitha, Tabitha, it's okay, you're okay. It's me, Mitch. You're okay." I hoped it was true.

Sasha ran to a stop next to me. I looked at him; he nodded to me. He held her head steady and shined a bright light from a finger ring into her eyes. I could see her pupils contract. He pulled what looked like one of several elastic hair bands from his wrist and ran it up to her bicep. A tiny green light on it flicked on, then started blinking. He said, "She was unconscious; it takes a while to reorient. I think she'll be okay. I'll be back." He virtually leaped to the councilor's side and started examining her.

"Tabitha? Can you hear me?"

Her gaze started to land on my face, look around it, and then a look of recognition came on her face. "I . . . wha . . . M– Mitch. That you? What–what happened?"

Cynta and the two guys ran up to us. I nodded to Cynta. She gestured and the two followed her over to the third body not on fire. I said to Tabitha, "We've been attacked." I tried, but I couldn't hear any gunfire over the sound of the nearby roaring fire. "*Being* attacked."

"Who?"

"I don't know. Plain gray uniforms. Know them?"

She shook her head.

"Tabitha? I'm sorry."

She furrowed her brow. "What for?"

I thought, and then chuckled. "Everything. I'm glad you're alive."

She smiled. "Am I?" She sat up, slowly, wincing. I told her to be careful. With a grunt she sat up on her own, her hair a mess around her face. She moved her arms and legs, seeming to test everything.

"How's your arm?"

Tabitha rotated her shoulder, "Still in place. Thankfully." Blood was dripping off her jaw from the rivulet that flowed from just below her hairline. She gingerly felt around the wound, as if testing to make sure she didn't have anything gaping or hanging open, and finally touched the gash.

I tried to rip the tail of my shirt, but it wasn't going to give. I started pulling on the cuff of a sleeve, hoping for a tear. Tabitha smiled and produced a knife, I didn't know she kept, from out of her boot. "Thanks." I cut a ribbon of cloth from the shirt tail, folded it up, and gave it and the blade to her. "I don't think it's too bad," I offered, as she pressed the cloth her head. "Head wounds, you know." She nodded.

We saw Sasha helping the councilor up on her feet. Her clothes were torn, and she stumbled, but she seemed okay. No one was around the third body.

I asked Tabitha, "Do you remember anything?"

"Yeah," she considered the ground between her legs. "I was still talking to the councilor, and I heard someone in the next room saying something about a ship pulling out of Q-thrust too close to the planet. And . . . something, I don't remember. I think I heard Cynta on my radio say something, and I remember yelling at people to get out. Pushing the councilor out the side door. Then . . . you next to me, your face coming out of a fog."

"Well, looks like you saved her life."

Sasha came over and read something off the band he put on her arm, then nodded and made a positive sound. "Vitals okay. Anything broken?"

She shook her head, "Don't think so."

"Abdominal pain? Shortness of breath?" She shook her head. "I'll need to check you for internal bleeding later–sooner if you feel pain or dizzy. Dizzier."

We both nodded. I helped Tabitha to her feet. She seemed steady. We stood for a moment, my hands on her arms. Then, I pulled her into a hug. As usual, she started out stiff but soon melted into me. Her hair smelled like her, and a little burnt. I chuckled into her neck. I knew I should have been mentally and emotionally separating myself from her, but I also knew that would be as possible as lifting this planet with my bare hands. Right then, I never wanted to leave her–or her leave me.

She said into my neck, "What now?"

"Now?" I pulled away and looked at her dirty, smeared, bloody, beautiful face. "We take their freakin' ship, is 'what now.'" I bent and picked up the SMG and called to the group if anyone had a spare gun. One of the guys pulled a pistol from his belt. Tabitha took it, checked the magazine, chambered a round. Her hands shook a little, but I knew it was entirely from the effects of her recovering and not at all from nerves. The professionalism had returned. "Ericsson's leading a contingent to track down the attackers in town. I grabbed us here to find you, and take the ship."

A faint smile sneaked onto her face, I presumed because of my order of priorities. She said, "Where?"

"Other side of that inferno."

"Quicker the better. Let's storm it and not risk a sneak attack." She turned and said, "Cynta, any chance of you're able to scan-hack the ship remotely?"

She shook her head, "Been trying. No signals to rail."

Tabitha turned back to me. "Captain?"

I looked for the councilor and found her sitting next to the third body. I caught Sasha's eye. He said, "She'll be okay there. We're set."

The group of us, Tabitha, Cynta, Sasha, and two fellows who I didn't know but were willing to follow my lead, was a very odd (and a little frightening, I have to say), band of hooligans starkly illuminated by a hellish fire. I was truly afraid for whomever we'd come across. "Here we go."

CHAPTER TWENTY-FIVE

We ran between the inferno and another razed building, which allowed us to make as straight of a line to the ship as possible while giving us some cover. Though still dozens of yards away from the fire, the air around us burned our lungs and made running torture. Once we passed the buildings and the perceptible heat barrier, the shock of cool air gave me a burst of energy that motivated me to sprint the rest of the way to the ship's landing ramp–with everyone else close behind.

I hit the end of the ramp, stopping my inertia by grabbing a post connecting it with the ship, and tried to gasp for air as quietly as possible. Cords of muscle in my legs were on fire and my lungs were filled with sand, but I held my SMG as steady as I could and aimed up through the opening into the ship. No movement. The light coming from inside was dim and cold. My companions circled around the ramp in varieties of similar discomfort, casting their gazes in various directions on the lookout for movement. We took the moment to celebrate our headlong rush into what looked like non-detection by catching our breaths.

After I was able to breathe without making a rasp, I nodded to one of the muscle-guys, and we started up the ramp. The other muscle and Tabitha came up behind us, and Cynta and Sasha took the rear. For the third time, I made sure the safety was off on the weapon, and crept in a semi-crouch that felt like a decent way to creep. The hull of the ship was a good half-foot wide and it took forever to raise my eyes above the inside floor, expecting at any second for a shot to slam into the top of my skull. None came. As soon as I could peer into the ship, I looked all around me, as did Muscle. No threats. I nodded to everyone behind me, and we moved up as a group.

Once we hit the floor inside the ship, we spread out and around the circular . . . rotunda, of sorts. The room was about twenty feet across with three corridor entrances. The air was musty and sour like it had been closed up for weeks without air filtration.

Pointing at Muscle One, I whispered, "He and I will head this way," indicating the middle corridor and the one that looked like it probably led to a bridge or control deck. "Tabitha and you take one of the others. Sasha and Cynta, stay here and cover our backs. Warn us if someone tries coming up from behind." Everyone nodded. Muscle Number One and I began walking, muzzles forward, down the dim corridor with intermittent running lights along the textured floor.

At an impressive door, a secondary airlock, we stopped and examined the control panel. It appeared to indicate the door was unlocked. Muscle Number One and I exchanged looks. He placed his off-hand on the panel and raised his gun, ready. I gripped mine in both hands and bladed my body to present a smaller target, and nodded.

The door *k!shhhhed* open and revealed a large, open room with curved pillars and consoles along curved walls. One of two men in gray uniforms turned casually in a chair, saying, "You did not report your returning–" then saw us and jumped out of his seat, reaching for a sidearm. Bursts from both our weapons riddled his body and plinked the surrounding equipment. He fell against his chair and collapsed to the floor.

His companion jerked at the sound, looked around and saw us, and leapt forward with a roar even as I was yelling, "Hands up!" A Twin tattoo of gunfire and he fell to the floor as if he'd been tripped. The way he had lain, and the first guy was crumpled, allowed part of my psyche to dismiss them as simply two unconscious men.

Until the blood pooled and spread from under the one at our feet. I quickly moved away and composed myself outside the room.

"Yeah, this looks like a bridge. Do you know anything–" I started, and was interrupted by echoes of gunfire from down the corridor.

Muscle and I ran down the passageway. I couldn't see Sasha or Cynta where we'd left them, but I saw the top of a gray-capped head on the ramp, just under the level of the floor we stood on, firing a gun at something on the other side of the rotunda. Muscle saw him too: He stopped, braced his body against the wall of the corridor, and fired a short burst. I heard several *tak-taks* of rounds hitting the floor, and a bloom of red mist in the air. The head had dropped below, out of sight. We kept moving.

The gunfire didn't abate at all. We peered around the corner and found Sasha and Cynta (Cynta with rivulets of blood running down her arm and back of her shoulder), taking cover around the corner to one of the corridors, continuing to fire at unseen assailants down the ramp. They'd come up behind us!

I toggled the radio. "Cynta, what happened?" I saw her glance up at me, and then continue firing. Point taken; they were a bit busy at the moment.

"Tabitha," I called into the comm. "The bridge is clear, but Cynta and Sasha are pinned down at the entryway. What's your status?"

After a second, she replied, "Got . . . our own we're dealing . . . with." The pauses punctuated by gunfire. Damn.

I looked back out at the rotunda. The horizontal entryway above the descended ramp was nearly flush against one wall at its end, but not quite. I got Muscle's attention and made an arching motion around the opening. He nodded. We went around the corner, crouched with our backs against the rotunda's wall, making our way toward the far end of the opening away from where the top of the ramp met the floor. Muscle scooched his way between the opening and the wall to get to the other side. I glanced at Sasha and Cynta, both firing at people outside, just below our feet. Neither looked at us, helping us maintain the element of surprise.

I exaggerated a silent countdown from three, and at one, Muscle and I moved along the edge of the opening toward the top of the ramp. At nearly the same moment, grays came into view off the side's of the ramp. Muscle and I brought them down in a–clichéd but appropriately described–"hail of gunfire."

One was able to turn his aim onto me before I threw enough metal at him, and one of his shots grazed me just below the jaw. All I felt was a gentle caress of flesh-charring heat across my neck. I emptied my magazine into him, primarily out of shock, and a serious need to make sure he wasn't getting back up. Then, with great trepidation, I brought my hand up to my neck and felt pain. And blood. I urgently swallowed several times, thinking subconsciously that if it was a deadly wound, I wouldn't be able to swallow, or I'd be tasting blood. Nothing seemed out of sorts.

I looked up at Muscle, and he must have read the look on my face. I brought my hand away from my neck and looked as inquisitive as I could. He shrugged and said, "Think it's just a graze." I looked down, wincing, and saw blood soaking my shirt collar.

Sasha rushed over and firmly tilted my head up and away. He grunted, pulled a tiny gun out of a front pocket on his tactical vest, and shot a spray of goo onto the wound. I felt it grow warm and move against my skin as it slowed the rising pain. Sasha slapped a self adhering bandage on my neck, over the wound. "Lucky graze. The metaderm will stop the bleeding, prevent infection, and you'll be okay." Those words, coming from him and his certain manner, instantly washed the threatening sea-foam of shock away from enveloping my head.

I glanced down at our victims. It was obvious they'd been in some action before they'd engaged with Sasha and Cynta. I wondered what had happened out in the town.

Then I remembered Tabitha's transmission. "The others," I said. We all turned and ran down the corridor Tabitha and Muscle Number Two had gone down.

I caught Cynta's sleeve. "Cynta, back that way's the bridge. Do you think you can get access to the ship to be able to do like you did back on *Udachi?*"

She nodded, "I'll give it a shot," and she ran back the way we came.

As the rest of us ran down the corridor and around a corner, the sound of gunfire–the traditional kind with gunpowder–rang through the ship. We turned and came upon a giant, open room with Tabitha and Muscle on either side of the doorway, taking turns to fire bursts inside. We stopped just on one side and I put my hand on Tabitha's shoulder. She glanced back and said, "Three targets still–" She was interrupted by the staccato of gunfire from inside and the hammer-against-metal sound of rounds hitting the corridor wall near us. Muscle leaned around and let off a stream of electrically thrown ship-safe pellets, which gave my Muscle Guy the opportunity to sprint across the doorway to the other side where he was able to offer supporting fire.

"Three targets still up and using cover to hop-frog closer. They're about twenty meters inside, spread out. Experienced." She looked around. "Cynta?"

"Working on bridge access."

Tabitha nodded, then glanced around the corner. She waited for a second after The Muscles paused their firing, then she fired two shots before she pulled back, saying, "I'm out." Her pistol, like some firearms in our crew, fired bullets the old fashioned way–using a chemical, gunpowder-like, propellant. Though, unlike what I was used to, there were no spent casings after each shot–nothing to eject. Being out-of-ammo on her pistol was indicated not with a slide locking back, but a simple indicator dot on the rear of the gun.

Muscle Two said, "Two still up."

"Reload?" I asked.

Tabitha shook her head, "All out."

"Cynta," I radioed, "anything, yet?"

After a pause she replied, "Just started. Issues."

Muscle One called over to me, "They're behind a couple of tables." Then, he mimed his hands moving up, apart, and around an imaginary object, finishing with his hands gesturing shooting at the object in the middle of the air.

"Anyone bring any grenades? Or those sunburst things?" I asked.

Sasha replied, "Juan had some."

"Back on the ATV? Right." I sighed.

Muscle One raised an inquisitive eyebrow. There wasn't any way around it; this was the best solution to end the standoff before it'd get decided by whoever runs out of ammo first.

Perhaps aside from coming up the ship's ramp, this was the first time I'd made a conscious choice to act and put myself into eminent danger. In all this time, in every other instance I found myself in combat of some sort, it was a reaction to whatever was going on around me. A thoughtless reaction. The guard back on the CAC *Vigilant*, Captain MacVey in his quarters, the counter-coup–I never had time to think about what I was about to do, what the consequences could be. Even moments earlier when we took out the gray-uniformed invaders on the ramp, we had the element of surprise and I still got shot, an inch or two from being killed. Here I was, considering running directly into gunfire.

And I didn't see any other choice.

In a way, I thought, this was simply a reaction as well.

I nodded to Muscle One. He nodded back and crouched, ready to sprint. I shouted, as loudly as I dared, to Muscle Two, "Suppressing fire, on . . ." and I held up three fingers.

I pulled one down, leaving two.

I checked my weapon's safety, again, and pulled another finger down, leaving one.

It didn't register to me until later, when I thought back on the moment, that there was no gunfire at that moment. I imagine I heard scraping and footsteps, but I don't know if that's my imagination filling in blanks. The complete stop of gunfire should have been a red flag, but I was too focused on the remaining countdown finger.

I brought it down into a fist and paused in my own sprint around the corner long enough for James (Muscle Two's name, I later learned) to pop up and lay down some fire to keep the enemy down while we ran around them. James was no sooner in the doorway when he was mowed down by the two invaders. They'd left their own cover and were in the process of storming the doorway, and were only feet in front of us as Muscle One and I were already subject to momentum.

Mostly as a reflexive response to avoid James, who'd stopped abruptly, I crouch-lunged around him before I saw the two. Already a poor target, I turned the lunge into a fall to the floor and fired as I fell, and continued firing as I slid across the floor. I felt tugs against my clothes, and my side, as one of them tried to follow me with his gunfire before one of my rounds finally found a vital organ and he staggered and fell.

I looked up from the floor and saw Muscle One crouched, back against the wall just inside the doorway. The assailant on his side turned away, took a step, and collapsed. A pool of blood began to form around his body. I made eye-contact with Muscle One. His nod to me this time overflowed with entirely different subtext.

I called, "Room's clear! Sasha!" and Sasha was around the doorway before I finished his name.

CHAPTER TWENTY-SIX

I watched Sasha stop at James, then quickly move to Muscle One. Evidently, it was obvious he didn't need to try to help our fallen comrade. Tabitha came in behind Sasha, took stock of the scene, and came over to me. "Where're you hurt?"

The question didn't make sense at first; why would I be hurt? I realized I was holding my side and blood ran beneath my fingers. Tabitha pulled my hand away then tore my shirt open, the bullet holes making a convenient perforation. I had several tears of my flesh of various depths–at least one looked scarily deep, and there was another, lower on my side, that was an actual round hole in my skin. Blood kept running from the various wounds, making seeing just how bad it was difficult.

Tabitha tore away more of my shirt, folded it, and pressed it against my side with both hands. Her expression was determined and I felt some comfort in that.

"It, it doesn't really hurt. Is that bad?"

"Shock. Don't worry, it will." Her smile was sincere and without pity or a patronizing quality. I was comforted by that even more.

Sasha came to us and said, as his hands replaced Tabitha's, "James is gone. Quon's arm is out of commission for a while, but he'll be fine. What've we got here?" It seemed rhetorical, so I just winced and sucked air through my teeth while he poured water on my side and explored around a bit.

Finally, he said, "Good, not too bad. Looks like one scrapped a rib, probably broke it, but I don't think it's shattered. Will need to examine it later. Got a through-and-through on your hip. Shallow, no organs or arteries. You're one lucky *carbón*." He handed Tabitha one of the removable mini-packs from his tac-vest. "I'll check on our friends." I noticed he deftly kicked away dropped weapons as he approached the fallen assailants.

"That was brave," Tabitha said as she started medicating and bandaging my wounds.

"More like 'stupid'."

She snickered. "They're often confused for each other."

"'Brave' is running into a burning building to save people, not running into gunfire and getting shipmates killed."

She punched me in the arm just hard enough to jostle my side.

"Gah! Crap. What was that for?"

"Sometimes I wonder if you're really that dumb, or clueless enough to just look it."

"What's that supposed to mean?"

"Is bravery only when you're immediately saving another life?"

"Mmmaybe–I don't know."

"Well, you saved *our* lives. And you probably helped save the lives of people in this town. Just accept–"

The rest was cut off when in the same instant the lights cut out, something deep inside the ship rumbled, and several somethings in the room popped with a thick, wet *thump* followed by the sound of tiny wet smacks and patters around the walls and floor. Something sharp and ragged raked across my cheek, like someone scratching me with a ragged fingernail. Tabitha hissed, "*Punyeta*! Something hit my back!"

"Cynta," I touched the comm unit. "What the hell was that?" Nothing. "Cynta?"

A dim half-light fluttered on, casting the room in a littering of stark shadows from tables and chairs. Across the floor, Sasha sat next to the headless remains of one of the invaders, leaning back on an arm. His arm gave out and he fell heavy, his head cracking on the floor.

Tabitha and I scrambled over to him. One side of his face was shredded; his remaining eye was rolled up. His hands were in the air, elbows on the floor, like he wanted to grab at something. Blood pulsed freely from his neck.

"Sasha!? Oh fuck no, Sasha!" My vision swam as my head enveloped in a fog. My guts were ice. I tore the tacky bandaging stuck to my side off and tried pressing it against Sasha's neck.

I recall Tabitha sat on the other side of him, watching me. Her expression was of pity, but I don't think it was for him. "Mitch. . . ." I pushed on the bandage on his mangled throat and it instantly soaked with blood. It poured around my fingers and down to the floor. His hands stopped moving, but remained in the air. His mouth and jaw slacked. Sasha was dead. "Mitchel."

I sat back. I looked at Tabitha, but couldn't read her. I think she was sad—maybe concerned. Her face was dirty from smoke and soot, but blood-free. Her hair, though, was glistening from it. Quon was behind me and said, "Fuck. Me." I looked around at five uniformed, headless bodies littering the floor. The one Sasha had been tending to had been pushed by the explosion at least several inches, leaving a gory trail from the completely unidentifiable remains of a head splayed across the floor.

The room was splattered, streaked, and dotted with blood, brain, flesh, and mats of hair. I see it now, still, this scene of utter horror. My mind froze and my body moved on its own accord, taking itself out of the room slipping only a couple of times on gore. The sight of the bloody horror was magnified by the realization that the cause of it was from explosives embedded in the skulls of each and every attacker, set off simultaneously.

I came to James, lying on his back, eyes half closed. A few moments before, he was a person. Now, he was a body cooling in a pool of blood. He had life and a history that made up who he was, no less important than Sasha just because I didn't know him. Now, he was over–turned off. The room was filled with people who had been ended, and I was the cause. My mission, my goals, my actions, led to death. Led to . . . whatever mind-twisting horror saturating that room was. I was a middle-class nobody with a wife and kid who worked the expected number of hours a day and watched TV, and now I'm a murderer by my own hands and someone who kills others by proxy. Once I was responsible for going to the grocery store twice a week, now I was responsible for the fates of human beings, including their abrupt and violent deaths.

My legs stopped working and I sat on the floor in the corridor outside the room. My brain was a can full of buzzing insects. And a buzzing from my chest. It was the radio. A voice had been coming from it and I couldn't recall how long it'd been calling. Minutes? Only just then? The voice came into focus, "Mitch, respond. Cynta."

With a hand that felt so far away, I touched the radio. "Uh-huh."

"Mitch. Something totally *desmadre* just happened. Do you read?"

"Uh-huh."

"Something just triggered a self-destruct routine. If I hadn't already disabled the core from the main sys-proc, this ship would've just left a crater large enough to wipe out all signs of human life on this rock."

"Yeah."

"And, *tae*, these *raro cabronazo* . . . their heads fucking blew off. They're dead, *then* their heads blew up. Who the *diablos* does that shit? I've got blood all over me."

"Yeah."

"Mitch? Captain?"

Tabitha was next to me. "Mitchel. You're okay."

"What?"

"Look at me. You're okay."

"Yeah."

"No, you're okay, Mitchel. And no, this isn't your fault."

"What? I . . . what?"

"I know what you're thinking. This isn't your fault. Yeah, *you're* responsible for the triggers you pull, *you're* responsible for the actions *you* take, but don't think for a second that you somehow control the universe. That you're somehow the orchestrator of every line of action and reaction of every person you come in contact with. You understand me?" I blinked at her. "Are you so arrogant to think the universe centers around you?" Her voice was both accusative and oddly comforting.

"No. No."

"No, it doesn't. You want to feel guilty about the things you do, fine. I've enough guilt myself for a couple of lifetimes. But if I'm responsible for my own actions, you can't be responsible for them too, you understand? You're not responsible for James, he made his own decisions whether to come or go, fight or flee. You're not responsible for Sasha. He made his own decisions over where he went, with who, and what kind of life to lead. And you're sure as hell not responsible for these assholes and their messed up actions. Right?"

"Right. Yeah . . . yeah right."

"Good. Now, are you here? Are you with me? Or do I need to slap you out of this?"

"No. I mean, yeah, yeah I'm here. I'm here. No slapping needed." And I was–I was there. I looked at Tabitha and her dirty, strong, gorgeous face and the world re-centered itself. "I'm here. I'm good. No, I'm not good, but I'm here."

She smiled, I think a little relieved. "And," I continued. "I love you, Tabitha."

Her hard and concerned expression shifted into one of surprise. "Hell,

Mitch. You're such the romantic." She smiled again. "I love you back. Now, if you're sure you're not going to take a mental vacation on me again, I need you to help me get whatever's lodged into my back out."

"Oh, oh crap. Yeah." And just as quickly as I fell into it, the remaining tendrils of fog that had enveloped my brain dissipated, and using the blood-covered med-pack from Sasha's vest she handed me, I pulled out what I tried not to believe was a piece of skull fragment that had stuck, superficially, in her back.

* * *

"They're all dead," Ericsson told me as he dismounted the bullet-riddled ATV. "I mean, we captured a couple as prisoners, but then–"

"Yeah, I know. Their heads. They killed Sasha that way."

Ericsson stopped and held my gaze, then ran a hand over his head. "Damn."

"Yeah." It was still hard for me not to give in to the fog again. I kept to my role, "Cynta reports the ship was rigged to go micro-singularity at the same time. She got to it in time though."

"Ain't that a thing!"

"Ain't it though," I said un-ironically. "We lost James as well, but otherwise, we got the ship and I think their commander. She stopped the explosion, but the ship's computers're still fried. Not sure she's going to be able to get much intel from it."

Tabitha said, "I can guess they came from the CASS base."

"Probably," I replied, "but that's not where we're going next."

Ericsson raised an eyebrow, but Tabitha said, "The black hole."

"Yep. Whatever CASS was doing out there, I'll guarantee that it's what these guys also want, and it's where we're going to get some answers."

Ericsson said, "Yeah, but obviously, these guys weren't some individual outfit. Uniforms, well-armed, there's more of them. And if you're right, then if we go out there, we might be cruising right into a pack of them."

"I agree," Tabitha said. "If the scans show what we think they do, they took out that base–they may have destroyed whatever else CASS had going. We may be arriving too late and over-matched."

I nodded. "Maybe. Possibly. But I don't have much of a choice."

Tabitha looked at me. "You do have a choice."

"About . . . about you know, yeah. I know I do. And I'll make that choice when the time comes. But I have to know *why*. Why am I here. But more than that, we have to know what's coming. We might be the first to be clued in on some seriously terrible situation that's building, and we have to know that, too. If my choice is that I stay here, if my life is here now, I need to know–we need to know–what's threatening it." I realized I'd put my hands on her arms as I made my case.

Tabitha nodded. "You're right. We do."

Ericsson said, "Well, hell. What are we standing around for? The sooner the better, right?"

"I can't demand anyone comes with. This is my decision, and, I'm responsible for it. Whoever comes with me, it's their choice." I looked at Tabitha and hoped she read in my eyes the thanks I mentally sent her.

"Oh, after this," he replied, "I think everyone has a pretty good idea what they're getting into. Whoever comes with us, they're not going in blind."

I smiled at Ericsson and grabbed his shoulder. "Thanks."

He nodded. "I'll get the order out to all former crew that if they want t'be *current* crew, they better get their asses on board post haste."

I nodded. Then, in the radio, "Cynta."

After a pause, "Yeah."

"How soon can *Udachi* be ready to take off again?"

Another pause. "Thirty minutes. It'll be only partially re-fit and re-ess-and-essed, but it'll be ready enough for us to get to the singularity and back."

"Were you listening?"

"To what?"

"Never mind. Good. Make it so." I grinned at myself. "Oh, and Cynta."

"Yeah?"

"Thanks."

I think I heard her shrug over the radio. "How often does one get to fly-by a black hole?"

"Heh. We're on our way back. Out."

I turned and looked at the invading ship: all lights it had on before were out, making half of it into a black shape blocking out the stars from an incredibly clear night sky. The other side was illuminated by a low, flickering glow from the fire that was still burning on the other end of the landing area. "What do we do with this?"

"Oh now what?" Tabitha exclaimed.

"Huh?" I turned and winced from the wounds in my side as they pulled against the bandages they stuck to. Councilor Staand was limping behind a man with a very determined look as he marched our direction. Around them were four armed townspeople, a couple of which obviously saw action during the defense of their town.

"I'm holding you and your people responsible for the damage to our community!" The man's hair, probably normally slicked back, was flopping in stiff strands as he talked.

Councilor Staand caught up. "This is Councilor Young." She turned to her peer, "Thomas, I told you, we need to convene a council ad hoc and investigate the events before we start holding people responsible."

"I want these people detained for questioning. Immediately."

The four guards looked at each other and at us. The two clean guards slowly started to move toward us while the two disheveled ones remained. Ericsson crossed his arms. "I know it was a whole ten minutes ago, but maybe you forgot we just helped you kill the actual people responsible for all this."

The disheveleds nodded and remained unmoved, but Councilor Young replied, "Everything was quiet and peaceful until you arrived, and then suddenly all hell breaks loose."

"Thomas, listen. They helped save us. They saved me. Whatever brought this second ship, it might be related to them, it might not. But the final result is they fought for us. That's enough to justify delaying blame for anything until we investigate. You know the policies."

"Damn the policies and bureaucracy! You heard me, arrest them." This time all four of the guards looked to Councilor Staand and held their ground. Ericsson smiled.

"Excuse me," I held up my hand. "If I may say something here? I'm willing to admit their coming may have been related to our own," I noticed Councilor Staand furrow her brows and subtly shake her head at me. I gathered she was warning me of some "anything you say can be used against you" policy, but I continued, "And, I'm willing to assist in any kind of investigation of that. But right now, you need to let us get back in the air–"

"What!? There's no way I'm going to let you–"

"You need to let us leave because we're going out to find out where this ship came from and why, and what may be behind them. For all we know, this was just some scout ahead of a fleet. If it's our responsibility they came here, it's our responsibility to find out why and see if we can stop any repeat performance."

Staand moved to between us and Young. "Thomas, you know that's reasonable. And you know when we bring this to a quorum, it would vote in favor."

Some of the bluster seemed to drain from Councilor Young, and his hair. "What's to keep them from flying away and never coming back?"

"I take it my word isn't good enough," I said.

Young scowled. To me, Councilor Staand said, "I'm afraid he does have a point. While I, and I think the majority of the council, will look favorably on you and your actions here, and I believe you regarding what you're wanting to do, I have a duty to make sure a proper inquiry happens and you participate."

Tabitha asked, "Okay, understandable. What do you suggest?"

"We should send a representative of the council with you to monitor what happens, to aid the following investigation, and, discourage any fleeing the investigation."

"What's to stop them from also adding kidnapping to their crimes?" Thomas puffed back up.

"Alleged crimes," I corrected.

"And what do *you* suggest, councilor?" Staand asked.

"We . . . put a tracker on their ship. And, send an armed escort ship along."

Councilor Staand turned back to us and said, almost apologetically, "It is a fair request."

I figured whatever kind of tracking device they could put on the ship, if we needed to, Cynta could make easy work of. Not that I had any intention of not coming back, though, one never knows. The escort ship could be annoying, but could also be a help to us. "The escort, they'd stay out of our way?"

"Unless you did something untoward."

"We're going at least as far as the black hole out on the edge of your neighborhood. Hope that's not too untoward." That seemed to get the entire welcoming party's attention.

"A black hole?" Councilor Staand asked. "Where?"

"About, what was it?" I turned to Tabitha. "About a light year away from here?" She nodded.

Young scowled. "Is that possible? So close and we didn't know it?"

Staand shrugged. "I'm not an astrophysicist; you'd have to ask Dunkirk or Ng. But, I think so. That's much too far to affect us in any way, right? And if it's not . . . eating anything, there's no way to see it."

"That was our original destination anyway, before we stopped here to resupply."

Staand nodded. "Well, I for one look forward to hearing what you discover." She turned to address everyone. "I think we have an accord here. I'll go and arrange for the escort and make a formal report to the council. Captain Creek, Officer Kim," and a nod to Ericsson, "I wish you all good luck." She turned to walk away, and paused to look at Young.

"Fine," he said before glaring at us, then turned on his heel and marched away. Councilor Staand followed along with the guards, who looked relieved to be going.

CHAPTER TWENTY-SEVEN

"Does he look uncomfortable to you?" I nodded my chin at the lanky man easily in his mid-twenties who sat with his hands on his knees on a seat against the back wall of the bridge.

Ericsson shrugged and smiled. "Want me to ask if he wants a refreshment? A pillow maybe?"

"Heh, no. Just thinking he probably doesn't want to be here anymore than we want him here. On a related note, how many of Luyten's did we get who wanted to come?"

"Ten. I'd bet at least a couple of them are just hoping we end up on some other world they can hop off to. We prob'ly got a few more than we otherwise would've from some of those hoping we're going after revenge."

"Hmm. What about former crew that stayed behind?"

"Not counting those we had in the hold that we let go, all but fourteen."

I looked around at Tabitha, Cynta, and, surprisingly, Jennings. "That's including all of us?" He nodded. "Twenty-four. That's enough to crew this ship?"

"Sure. We could get by on seven or eight if we had to. It's just good to have extra so people can take short shifts and make short work of things. Worst to worst, we got the CASS prisoners if we need something to plug hull breaches with." That smile, I never could tell was serious or not.

"Well, let's hope it doesn't come to that." Then, out to the bridge in general, "What's the *Escort* doing?" The escort ship had the unimaginative name of: *Escort*. Very pragmatic, those Luytens.

The contents of the holo-display shifted and changed, and I got boxes of info and visual displays of the small ship that followed us. I'd been informed it was fast, maneuverable, had an impressive collection of cannons on it, and was probably Luyten's only militarized ship. "It's keeping a steady five K behind us." I'd already had a brief conversation with its captain as we left Luyten. Captain Chandrima was soft-spoken with a definite strength in her tone and betrayed no indication of being either unhappy nor content to have this assignment to watch and follow us. I told her our intentions, as far as where we were going, and she thanked me perfunctory. That was the last I heard from her by the time we'd reached half-way to the black hole.

"Three hours until we're in the hole's neighborhood," Jennings let me know.

I was just wondering to myself when we'd finally see something of our destination on the screens, when Cynta said, "Detailed imaging and LR scan of the singularity completed. Hmm, interesting."

"What? What's interesting?" I asked. Everyone turned their attention to her.

"Here, five-thousand times magnification," she said, and half of the curved holo-display changed into a massive image of a star field with various semi-transparent boxes of data I couldn't understand. "The singularity isn't the only gravity well in the area."

"Huh? I . . ." We all peered at the display. In the center of the display, I made out a semi-circular dark area devoid of stars. Once I noticed it, I could make out that it was an object with different shades of black defining a spherical shape. It was like an egg with the narrow point of the oval pinched and pulled out to make a long-tailed comma floating in space.

Jennings asked, "Is that a planet?"

"Primary composition is helium with less than ten-percent hydrogen and carbon. Mass: two-point-three to the twenty-eighth power kilograms.

Diameter: one-hundred sixty-nine thousand kilometers. It's small and no luminosity–it's certainly not a brown dwarf."

I stood up, ignoring the grinding pain in my shot-up side. "Oh my god, is . . . is it being eaten by the black hole? Why can't we see it?"

"We're coming in on the same plane as the singularity. The gravitational lensing of the stars behind it is camouflaging it too well. Here, switching to para-visual filters." Instantly, the planet and the swath of empty space attached to the tail of the comma-planet exploded into view with colors so bright it forced me to squint. The planet was swirled with various shades of yellow and orange, stretched to a line that met up and merged with a wedge composed of streaks of white and blue with a red halo that bulged into the width of the planet, before it reached the end of the display.

A shiver ran up my spine and the hairs on my neck and arms rose. I almost couldn't hear myself say, "Pull back. Show the whole thing." The planet and the wedge slowly shrank while the field of stars behind them didn't budge. The wedge grew longer as more of it revealed in the image, and the planet became a yellow dot–the entire thing looking like an exclamation point turned on its side. Tabitha stood, her face displaying the awe I felt. Once the whole thing was shown, I saw semi-circles of pale blue surrounding the swath's center bulge, with a wispy streak jutting perpendicular to the now visible black hole. "That's Hawking radiation?"

"Black body radiation, yeah."

"We can't see this? With our eyes I mean? It was completely black, invisible before."

Cynta explained, "We're seeing a composite of infrared, ultraviolet, radio, and x-ray emission–all invisible to normal human eyes."

"It's . . . incredible," Tabitha whispered. Even Ericsson looked moved. The Luyten council representative sat with his mouth agape.

"Something, this amazing, beautiful, just floating out here in the nothing . . . this . . . truly awesome, I can't believe a God that cares would make it so we'd never be able to witness it. Keep it invisible to us."

"Maybe," Jennings, said, subdued, "He made it so we couldn't see it until we were ready, deserving of being able to see it." Whatever vague dislike I had of Jennings evaporated at that moment.

"So, the planet," I eased myself back into the center chair, "could they have come from that?"

"No," Cynta said, with just a touch of patronizing edge, "that analysis I read was its actual composition, not its atmosphere. It's a giant extrasolar gas planet."

"There's got to be something else out there. Somewhere."

"The FTS velocity interferes with a lot of scan resolution, but I'm cycling through various modes. The computer has to do a lot of interpolating of the data."

Over the next couple of minutes, layers of color faded from the black hole and its meal until we were back to the star field with a barely perceptible black spot and thin line streaking across the display. The bridge felt colder, smaller, and emptier. Finally, after several minutes, a couple of small boxes of data popped up on the display and started scrolling text. Cynta said, "The distortion from the black hole is messing with scan readings, but I've pinpointed a couple of unnatural objects near the singularity."

"What are they? How big? How far?" I asked. Ericsson chuckled at me.

"No clue what they are yet, but composition and probable shape make them likely to be bases of some kind. Larger than satellites or ships. Hmm, one of them is quickly approaching the event horizon; the other is dangerously close, about one or two hundred kilometers away from it and possibly moving in."

Tabitha asked for me, "Can we get to it?"

Jennings answered, "That's pretty close. The gravity well of the singularity is steep at that distance from the horizon. I think it'll be a pretty big risk."

"We'll know more when we get closer," Cynta added.

The representative piped up, "Uh, I know I'm supposed to be just observing here, but all this talk about approaching a black hole . . . I'm not sure that's a good idea."

I turned around in the chair to face him. "What's your name again?"

"Cheng. Cheng Stonecutter."

I raised an eyebrow. "Cheng, trust me, I know completely how you feel. But there may be a lot at stake here with much to gain and even more to lose if there's something important out there and we don't investigate."

Then, to Jennings, I said, "Alter course to intercept the base farthest from the black hole. Cynta, keep scanning, every way possible, and let us know if the danger becomes too much. Can you, like, measure gravity and whatnot from a distance? You know, determine if the pull is too much somewhere for us to get out safely before we get that far?"

"Yeah, with pretty high accuracy, especially once we leave FTS. Even more if we're not using Q-thrust."

"Well, obviously, let's FTS as long as we can. Cut it once we get too close to be able to know for sure."

"Aye, aye, cap'n. Estimated time to deceleration: two ship-standard hours and forty minutes."

Ericsson yawned. I raised an eyebrow. "Bored?"

"Huh? Hell no; this is all pretty crazy. Been a long day, y'know. Haven't slept in a couple days."

I stared at the star field. Perpetual, endless night. It was easy to completely lose track of time this way. Days never happen–it's all just one continuous night interrupted by occasional periods of sleep when you can't stay awake any longer.

What happened today? Sasha was killed by self-destructing invaders, I was in multiple firefights and got shot, landed on a whole new world and explored a greenhouse full of wondrous plants, I played captain of a ship of socialist anarchists. When does the day end? It was nighttime on Luyten's Home, somewhere around midnight, in fact. Ship's clock has it at half-past five in the afternoon. How incredibly arbitrary time was.

Each star out there in that endless field of black created its own time-frame for any inhabitants its system might hold. Were there any sentient alien races out there? So far, as much as humanity has expanded into our little patch of the galaxy, no evidence had been found. Is the way we measure time, by the passing of shadow over the planet, a uniquely human way to divide our life into segments?

And out there, invisible unless you have the sight of a god, was something so beyond comprehension, it could warp and stop time itself—render it meaningless.

"Kali."

Tabitha and I turned to observer Cheng Stonecutter. I asked, "What?"

"It's Kali, the goddess of time, darkness, destruction. Her name is literally 'the black one.' There she is." Everyone stared at the nothing that consumed in silence.

* * *

"Q-thrust disengaged; fifteen minutes until we dock with the base." Jennings continued to monitor the ship's tracking while making small manual adjustments. The holo-display showed the enhanced image of a base at the end of a series of overlapping grids that disappeared one-by-one as we approached. The base looked like a giant postmodern building ripped from the ground and flung into space. It had no apparent top or bottom, and no lights on it either. I trusted Jennings that he knew where on the thing the ship could dock.

Cynta said, "Gravity effects . . . moderate. External dampeners and artificial gravity compensating at ninety-five percent efficiency. The effects of the gravity well where the base is, is approaching significant turbulence and distortion." She looked up at the holo-display with her inscrutable eyes, and I knew she wasn't looking at it, but rather at the calculations and data only she could see. "At the rate the base is falling into the black hole, it will likely get torn apart by frame dragging within an hour, a full hundred and eighty thousand K before even the event horizon."

"Well, we seem to have incredibly lucky, and incredibly bad, timing." In the previous two hours, we discovered the remains of another base that had already torn apart into a line of debris and fell into the event horizon. It was stuck in the invisible molasses of the outer skin of the black hole where, while in its reality, each piece was being disintegrated and pulled into the spiraling center of an accretion disk we couldn't see, by our perspective, those pieces of the base would stay suspended in space for eons until the light reflected off them blue-shifted away. Space-time is a really effed-up thing.

We witnessed the third base get torn up by the difference in the movement of the fabric of space: that close to a spiraling black hole, one region of space moved at one velocity while, just a meter away, space itself was moving at a different velocity. Again, space-time is a really effed-up thing.

Our scans were picking up an immense amount of noise and fragmented signals all around the black hole, but we found this one remaining base still a reasonable distance away from destruction that we decided, so long as nothing went wrong, we'd have time to dock, do a quick check, and get out. It was better than coming all this way for nothing.

Finally, the holo-display outlined a section on the base that it identified as the docking collar, and the overlapping animated squares on the display adjusted to center on it. "Docking in ten minutes."

I sat in the captain's chair, leaning forward, glad to not feel the crack and pull of dried blood on and around my bullet wounds. Tabitha and I had taken a shower during the trip here. It was a long shower with alternating actions of cleaning each other (being careful to avoid each others' wounds), and tender caresses and embraces. It was an intimate encounter, not sexual, filled with a palpable sense of somber adoration. As the dirt and grime, sweat and dried blood, flowed off us, we felt a sense of return from being soldiers and survivors, to lovers. And a sense that we were saying goodbye. The only sound in the bridge was the *bing* and *ding* alerts of sensor readings and proximity notifications. Each of us was staring intently at the display, watching the base eat semi-transparent green grids as it approached.

"You know," I said, "I was thinking, if our culture determines for us what choices we have and the limits of what decisions we can make for ourselves, that means we each have a limited responsibility for our own actions."

Everyone but Cynta turned to me with various versions of confusion on their expressions. Except Tabitha. She nodded, and said, "Yes, more or less. Depending. But, it worked to get you back, though, didn't it?" She smiled. I smiled back. Everyone turned their attention back to the display with various versions of exasperation on their expressions.

A *kshhh-ding!* came over the room's speakers, followed by Captain Chandrima's voice, "*Escort* to *Udachi*. Captain Creek, our sensors over here are detecting an extreme amount of distortion—we're even getting odd bursts of radio noise on audio. My science officer advises me that we should stop our approach and turn back. I'm inclined to agree. What's your status?"

I glanced at Cheng. He had his elbows on his knees, hands in a ball against his mouth, watching the display. "Cynta, how's it looking?"

"I think we're okay. Also reading unusual amounts of noise, but primarily on the far scans and sensors; the short scans are mostly clean and that's what matters right now."

"Okay, but how's the whole gravity and avoiding death situation?"

She paused, then said, "Ship's at about seventy percent efficiency at compensating for the gravity well's effects, and we still have maybe forty or fifty minutes of calm before frame dragging becomes a real concern."

"*Escort*, we're continuing on with the docking. If we're not out in an hour, we're probably never coming out."

Jennings and Cheng shared a look. Cheng said, "Uh, Captain Creek, when I was assigned to come along and observe, I wasn't told we'd be teasing the edge of a black hole. I . . . well–"

"Well, Mister Stonecutter," I interrupted, "here you are. Don't worry, I'm not expecting anyone else to die for me. I and only volunteers are going about the base. Cynta, the instant things start to get a little worrisome here, leave."

"Are you kidding me? I'm going with you."

"I'll do it," Jennings said, a little too quickly.

I kept my gaze on Jennings as I said, "Cynta, you can monitor the situation up here from down there, yes?"

"Yep."

"Okay, she's going to keep me updated on the condition here. I don't want you leaving before we've had a good search. Right?"

"As you wish, captain." He turned to manage the final docking procedure.

"All ship." *Poing-poing.* "This is the acting captain. First of all, I want to again thank all of you who stayed and those who joined for this trip. I'm hoping it's uneventful and short. We've reached the black hole and are now docking with a base discovered in a degrading orbit around it. We have just under an hour until things get pretty bumpy. I'm going over, and anyone who wants to volunteer, of course, can as well. But be warned, this ship is leaving once it starts getting dangerous, so I wouldn't recommend getting off if you don't want to risk seeing what falling into a black hole is like. If you want to come along and search the base, be at the main airlock in three minutes. And, well, it's been a pleasure. Captain out."

I looked around at the bridge. Jennings was facing the display, which showed the airlock engaging from various camera angles. Cynta and Tabitha were standing. Ericsson, who rarely sat in the first place, stood next to me, arms crossed and a mischievous grin on his face. Cheng looked pale. Behind me, in the corridor, stood four crew-persons watching the display or nodding to me. "Alright, people, let's go 'splorin'."

Including myself, Tabitha, Ericsson, and Cynta, sixteen of us gathered in the corridor leading out of the ship. Cynta had already reported that the air reading on the other side was thin but perfectly breathable; no need for suits or masks. While no one said anything about arms, everyone had a weapon ready–including myself.

"Remember, we're here to see what's going on, get answers. Anything that could be useful: computer data, files or something, people. No shooting until fired upon; we have no idea who could be in here. Could be those gray-suited invaders, could be CASS, and could be no one. Be ready, but be cool. We have. . . ."

"Forty minutes," Cynta offered.

"Forty? It's getting shorter." She shrugged. To the crowd, "Barely more than half an hour to do what we can to find out what this base is for, who operated it, and . . . again, anything. You all have comms. The second Cynta broadcasts that the ship is at risk, head back here, pronto. All clear?" I got various responses from "Yup" to "aye-aye, captain." It was the most diverse collection of people I'd ever seen in front of me–all skin colors, nearly equal numbers of male and female, and expressions ranging from grim determination to gleeful excitement. Something about the sight was inspiring.

I looked at Tabitha. Her hair was once again pulled back into a thick ponytail, and her eyes were bright and gorgeous, like when I first saw her. Like each night the last few nights before she fell asleep. "Are we ready for anything?"

The assembled responded in the affirmative, but it was Tabitha I waited for. She nodded and said, "Yes."

"Cynta, if you would, please open the door."

CHAPTER TWENTY-EIGHT

The air tasted like oil and smelled of electrical fire. It was thin, like when you're hiding too long under the blankets waiting to surprise your little sister and you get a headache from breathing your own air. The compartment we walked into was large, but dark. A single emergency light shone above the airlock door, casting stark shadows of each of us as we crossed the threshold. One by one, those who brought flashlights turned them on and added to both the illumination and the casting of shadows. On the wall, above the airlock, was a logo: three interconnected cobalt blue triangles. It was the same logo that was on the ID badge on the dead guy in the crate on the *Lysander*.

"Okay, I'm going this way," I said, indicating one of the four exits from the room. "Everyone spread out. Let's cover as much ground as possible."

Someone else, I think his name was Morris, said, "Be sure to stay in at least pairs, and keep your comms on." Someone else started gathering people to her before heading through an archway. I was captain on the ship, but once we hit "land," people quickly and smoothly took up various leadership roles and worked like teams within a team. I was a little jealous of my tenuous mantle of authority, but I was more impressed than anything.

Ericsson caught my expression, clapped me on the shoulder, and smiled. "And you didn't want to be a leader." Tabitha smiled at me as well.

"Heh, no, I'm actually glad to see how others work together autonomously. Kind of takes some of the responsibility off, you know? Feels

. . . refreshing."

"Good thing it happened before being king went permanently to your head. Most kings don't retire, you know." He winked.

I smiled up at his scruffy face. "C'mon, we're wasting starlight." He, Tabitha, Cynta, and, I was glad to see, Quon (one arm in a sling and the other holding the largest pistol I'd ever seen) and I started following the stark white light of flashlights bouncing down a corridor.

As we quickly and quietly walked down the smooth, square corridor, I listened to the terse updates from other people on the radio communicating finding a disabled elevator, finding disabled equipment, empty rooms, and a body. Then another body. We exchanged looks and kept following our corridor past open office doors and service corridors. The dead appeared to be technicians and employees of this base, each one cut down by gunfire.

And then, cutting under the acrid smell of burnt electronics, I began to smell urine, methane, and then, blood. Our corridor opened into a command center filled with computer consoles, rolling chairs strewn about and tipped over, and bodies. Twelve, maybe fifteen bodies lying on the floor or sprawled over consoles. Pools of blood covered the floor and splayed across black computer screens. Each instance of gore revealed in the spotlight of our flashlights, like scenes in a play. Here, witness this woman in a lab coat, her hair making a corona around her head. And see this man, slouched in his chair as if he'd fallen asleep after a long day–his unfocused eyes and ripped-apart chest belying the true nature of his repose. I was caught in a quandary of whether I use my light to illuminate them in stark contrast to see my way around them, or try to do so in darkness. I stood where I was.

And almost missed an incredible sight that nearly made me forget the slaughterhouse I was in. Across the room was a window, nearly as wide as a football field, looking out over a room the size of several city blocks. I forced myself to cross the room to look out the window at a line of connected glass and metal donut shapes, each the size of a house, with massive pipes running through the line of them. And across this architectural, mechanical wonder, the "room" was open to the black hole. There, framed like a panoramic painting, was a slice of the barely seen but highly perceptible singularity in the process of consuming a gas giant. The scene brought back emotional recall from the first moment I looked out at the field of space in the *Lysander* and realized where I was. The sense of being without anchor or weight in an endless sea of both nothing and infinite power–it was a sense of the sublime that shook me to the core and altered my perception of the moment, of reality. I felt its pull on me, like a force reaching right through my skin, taking hold of my bones, and pulling me toward it. If I wasn't stopped by half a foot of micro-poly-bond, I can't say I wouldn't have stepped off the floor and allowed myself to be pulled into it.

"Here," I heard Ericsson call from across the sea, "it's a couple of the invaders. With heads. Looks like the base's security gave it a good go. Hmm, CASS soldiers here, and over there . . . . Interesting. Well, I guess we can assume these gray guys aren't working for CASS. Is that good or bad?"

I blinked several times, shook my head like they do on television, to clear my mind. I then noticed Tabitha had been standing next to me. She was looking out as well, then at me. I took her hand, "No matter what happens, this will always be with me."

"The view?"

I smiled but didn't answer.

A long, shuddering creak echoed through the walls and floor of the base, beginning and ending abruptly but leaving distant response groans that were felt through the ship. "Cynta?"

"What? I don't know? I'm not an engineer?" I scowled. She paused and said, "Scans show minor hull cracks. Not good, but not fatal, yet."

"Time?"

"Maybe twenty, thirty minutes? Tops."

"Any hope with these computers?"

She shook her head. "No, the system is dead. No power. No life support. Artificial gravity running on particle inertia only; I expect it'll decay any moment. Unless I can get direct access to the storage devices, I can't pull any data. It's a dead rock."

I started picking my way back to the other side of the room, still feeling the ghostly tug of the infinite force at my back. "Can you do that? Where would they store the data on the base?"

Cynta shrugged. "They probably use some kind of standard holographic media, stored nearby . . ." she swung her light around the room, just above the level of any bodies in chairs or over consoles, and landed on a section of the wall that looked to have been hit by a grenade. "There, most likely."

"Yeah. Figures. Backup location?"

"Certainly, but it'd probably be on the other side of the base. If the other facilities we saw already destroyed were all part of one complex, chances are the data from this one was stored over there–but, also, theirs was stored over here. Safety redundancy."

"Well, let's go looking; we're almost out of– wait a minute, can't we just pull the base with the *Udachi* away from the black hole?"

She shook her head, "No. It's too far in. We'll be able to Q' out of the well, but we can't tow anything like that, and standard thrust isn't powerful enough to drag this thing."

"Fine. Let's move." My command was punctuated by another structural groan and, I'm pretty sure, a distant cracking.

As we went down another corridor off the control room, Cynta said, "Want to hear something weird? Where we are, time for us is already running micro-seconds slower than for the rest on the crew back on the ship."

Quon paused a step and answered, "Yeah, that is kinda weird. Cool."

A voice on the radio broke in, "Jenna, bring the cutting torch to us."

I clicked on. "What's up?"

"Captain? Looks like we found something. Came across a door with spot welds. Knocked on it and got reply knocks. Going to cut it open."

"Careful, could be a trap. Where are you?"

"Uh, third corridor from the airlock, to the left, then down a flight."

"We're on our way." Then to Cynta, "Backups?"

"If they're employees, they'll know where they are and I won't have to search blindly for the next fifteen minutes."

Tabitha was already running.

On the way to the sealed door, we passed more groups of dead invaders and CASS soldiers. I asked, "Think security killed them all?"

"No other ship was docked, so probably not," Tabitha replied.

"Oh, yeah. Duh."

The door was labeled "Maintenance Storage - B3." Three of our people were around the door as one of them was using something that emitted an invisible flame or laser or cutting force of some sort that heated the metal to white hot. She was cutting through the last weld and I stood across the door on the other side of the corridor, nervous, fidgeting with the safety on the SMG I held. "Done," she said, finally, and quickly stepped aside as the seven of us raised our weapons in unison on the door. It moved an inch, a crack into darkness, and then slid the rest of the way open to reveal several wounded and battered people blinking into our various hand-held and gun-mounted lights. A couple of the prisoners wore suits, three were in plain clothes, and one was Frankletti.

Tabitha and I both shouted, "Max!" and "Frankletti!" and rushed in to him. "God, you're alive," I said.

"Barely," he croaked. I noticed then that he wasn't doing well at all. He'd kept his eyes closed, even when the light wasn't on his face, and there were burns around them. He wasn't moving his right arm and it looked like one of his legs was broken.

Tabitha asked, "Where's Kara?"

"Dead. They, they just threw her out the airlock like she was garbage."

"Frankletti," I said, crouching next to him, not looking forward to telling this man what happened to his brother, "Joseph's dead too."

"I saw," he paused to clear his throat, "when they attacked on Torment. Ian?"

Tabitha and I exchanged glances. She answered, "Yeah. And, I'm sorry, *The Bluerock's* gone as well."

He bowed his head; I put a hand on his shoulder. He nodded a tiny nod, then a bigger one. "Right. Well, I can't believe you two escaped them. That's something, all right!"

"Who? Who are they?"

One of the base employees, being helped to his feet, said, "The Priori."

"I don't get it. A priori?"

"No," Frankletti said, "they call themselves *the* Priori. They're religious fanatics, unlike anything I've ever seen, and I've seen fanatics. They came from Earth. They think they're the one true belief. They'd been on Earth since it fell to ruin, and now they're expanding out."

One of the employees, wearing a white polo-like shirt with the interlocking blue triangles logo, said, "They destroyed everything! They destroyed the stations. They broke in, shot the place up and set it to fall into the black hole, and locked us in here to die."

I turned back to Frankletti, "Fanatics of what? What religion?"

"I don't know, they're . . . ."

Another of the prisoners said, "They worship what they called 'the Trinity.' God, Jesus, and Mohammad. They said something about 'a jihad against the unbelievers and the wicked that would pervert God's kingdom beyond the stars.' They plan to kill us all."

Ericsson said, "Well, they're not killing you. Not today. Let's go; our ship's docked and this station hasn't got long left." They started moving out.

"Wait," I stopped them. "This base, this station–what is it?" The others looked at each other. "Whatever it is, it's all over. It's about to fall into the black hole and the other bases already have. You're unemployed so no point in secrecy. What was it?"

Frankletti said, "A time machine." I hoped for, even expected that answer, but it was still a shock to hear it.

I stood and looked at the men and woman who once worked here. "How? How is it a time machine? Can something be done to make it work? Before it's destroyed?"

One of them, the woman technician or scientist, replied, "You said the other bases were destroyed already? Then, no. All six stations and the QPF are needed. They, and the black hole itself, are what make up the time . . . machine."

I felt the blood leave my face and my gut knot up. "I can't believe it. I finally made it, across solar systems, to find the answers, to find my way back home–here I am, and all is lost. I can't even make the decision for myself whether to go or stay. It was all for nothing."

Tabitha stepped next to me and put a hand on my arm. For a brief instant, I wanted to be mad at her. I imagined her being happy that I had no choice. But I looked at her, she looked at me, and I saw sadness. "I'm sorry." I put my hand over hers and squeezed.

Ericsson said, "Uhm, we don't really have time for this." I looked at Cynta who was just standing and scowling. One of the other technicians said, "'Go back home'? You mean. . . ." He looked at Frankletti, then back to me. "It's real, what he told us. You're . . . from the past?"

I looked back at Tabitha, but replied to him, "Yeah. From good ole early twenty-first century. I had hoped they'd brought that thing back here, the device I woke up next to back on the *Lysander*. That maybe it could take me back."

"That thing? It was stolen from here, then brought back by the Priori and thrown into the black hole. That's the QPF: the quantum-point foci."

A long, rumbling shudder, this time like a small earthquake, rolled through. I looked to Cynta who was still unconcerned. "What is that? How did it bring me here?"

The woman stepped closer and stammered, looking for words, "It's, it's like . . . space-time is like a sheet–"

"Right, everyone knows the analogy. The fabric of space is like a rubber sheet. Anything with mass is like something on the sheet, making a dimple, or a well, in the sheet. Gravity is the well and objects aren't pulled to other objects so much as they fall into the gravity well."

She looked a little relieved, but not much. "Right. Well, space-time is like that, but in eleven dimensions and folded upon itself in infinite layers. This system of stations, the Gallifrey Project–"

"Wait, the what?"

"The Gallifrey Project. Named after some ancient mythical god of time."

I chuckled, "Sort of. Go on."

"It creates a well so immense, and incorporating both relativistic and quantum forces, that it, essentially, bends the fabric of space-time through to another layer. The QPF is like the very tip of the pencil pushing through the fabric. It breaks through our layer and exists in the next–" The station shook startlingly.

"Okay, Cynta, what's the deal?" She didn't respond and I was immediately filled with a sick dread I hadn't felt since my last moments with Ian. "Cynta!" I grabbed her arms, and she fell to the floor. Everyone that was from the *Udachi* stepped closer.

"I. . . ." she groaned. She blinked rapidly over her silver eyes, like she was just waking up. "What. . . ."

"Cynta, what the hell's going on?"

"I'm cut off. I'm, locked out. I'm locked out!"

There were various sounds of dread from the *Udachi* crew as realization of what this meant washed over everyone. I hit the radio, "Jennings? What the hell?" Nothing. "Jennings, answer me!"

"I'm sorry, captain. I have a responsibility to the ship and its crew."

"Goddamit, Jennings, half the crew is *here*."

I frantically gestured everyone out as Ericsson and one of the other search party leaders motivated people to make it back to the airlock with extreme haste. The station staff that had trouble walking were helped along while Tabitha and someone else helped Frankletti.

As we scrambled along, I called, "*Escort*, come in *Escort*."

Cynta, her awareness slowly coming back, said, "All the communications goes through the ship, and he's got it locked down. They can't hear you."

"What the hell is he doing?" Then, "Jennings, for God's sake don't you dare murder all of us. You come back here now before it gets too late. Jennings? Are you listening? Anyone on the bridge, can you hear this? Don't let him kill us! Dammit."

We reached the airlock and the sound of creaks and structural groaning was at a constant pitch here, while other, larger groans and cracks could be heard through the ship. When we noticed the air becoming noticeably thinner, a lot of worried, and angry, looks were exchanged.

"Jennings," I formed my voice into a calm register, "it's not too late. You do the right thing, you come back here and get us, and I'll understand. I'll be reasonable. Nothing can't be forgiven, *if*, it's corrected before it's too late. I'm not kidding. Jennings? Can you hear me?"

"Mitch," Tabitha was staring at the airlock door.

"What?"

"The airlock connector had no power, we had to connect manually."

"Right."

"Look," she said, pointing to a mechanical indicator beside the door, "it's still engaged. The ship's still attached."

Someone else said, "That creaking. He's trying to tear away from the station."

"Ho-ly. . . . Jennings? We know you're still docked. Open the airlock, Jennings." No response.

Then, after a few seconds, the door slid open and a gush of fresh (well, fresher), air rushed over us. Lanky Cheng stood beside the door.

"You?" I said.

He shrugged. "I was the only one else on the bridge. "

I smiled and clapped him on the shoulder as we all rushed through the airlock back into our ship.

Cynta staggered and paused, smiled and said, "I'm back. I'm back online." Then, her expression fell. "Oh, *punyeta*. We're being attacked." She sprinted back to the bridge with Tabitha and I two steps behind.

CHAPTER TWENTY-NINE

"Status!" I yelled as we entered the bridge. Jennings was at his seat with his head in his hands. Cynta crashed into her chair and, immediately, images and boxes of data and reticules appeared on the massive holo-display.

"Two . . . unknown ships, within fifty kilometers, firing mostly upon the *Escort*. Mostly particle canons, some beam weapons, though, as well."

I glared at the back of Jenning's head and growled, "Jennings, you better be doing anything and everything within your power to help Cynta get this ship undocked and away or so help me I'll do whatever the equivalent of keel-hauling you is."

Then I said into the air, "*Escort*, this is *Udachi*. What's your status?"

After a pause, Captain Chandrima replied, "Welcome back, Captain Creek. We're trying to draw their fire until you can get your shielding back online, but if you don't get going within a couple more minutes, there's nothing we can do; we have no choice but to flee."

"What's she mean about the shielding?"

Tabitha, sitting at the console she'd made hers, answered, "While we're docked, we can't create a field around the ship. We just have to rely on the charged plating, which isn't much of anything at all."

"Okay, the big question: Why can't we undock?"

"It's torqued," Jennings mumbled through his hands.

"You, shut up and get working. Cynta?"

"It's torqued. The effects from the black hole, the structural damage on the base, the station, has basically made the coupling all *desmadre.*"

"Suggestions?"

"I tried to tear the ship away," Jennings moaned again into his hands. "It's too late. There's nothing we can do."

"Cynta?"

"I . . . I don't know."

"People, you're not helping me feel very confident." I turned back to the back wall. Again, a few crew members stood at the back of the bridge, observing. Cheng had come back and was decidedly pale. I looked over at Tabitha. She was chewing her bottom lip, then stopped when she looked back at me. She shook her head.

"Incoming ship," Cynta reported. On the holo-display, one of the three distant dots arced and grew incrementally, slowly, larger. Various data boxes and different colored reticules followed it, except for one pale red one that indicated a weapon's targeting system.

"As if we're not dead enough," Ericsson said in an even voice.

"Well, fire on that ship," I suggested.

"Firing pattern already locked in. It's not going to do much good, even once they're in range. We have no maneuverability."

I stared at the pale red reticule. Something teased the back of my mind. "That weapon targeting indicator, at the bottom-left. Which one is that?"

Jennings glanced up, "It's the BAG."

"Two minutes until the ship's in range to destroy us, three minutes before the station pulls us beyond a change at escape velocity," Cynta reminded.

"The BAG." I asked Ericsson, "That's the weapon you said you took out the CASS battle cruiser with, right?"

He nodded. "Yeah, it could take out that runner no problem. Except, like Cynta said, we can't move. It's a fixed-position cannon–we aim it with the ship itself."

"Because it's so huge, right?"

"Goddang massive."

"And with a massive kick?" I asked. Tabitha, watching the conversation, stood up.

"Well, yeah, except the inertia dampeners compensate so we can hardly feel it."

"Jennings, can we use thrusters enough to move us, and the station, a little?"

He turned and looked at me like I was an alien. "At full burn, sure, but barely."

"Enough that we can align that indicator on the incoming ship?"

He turned to look and slowly replied, "Yeah."

Tabitha stepped forward, "Disengage inertia compensation!"

Cynta replied, with new energy in her voice, "Disengaged, and calculating probable tumble recovery, shielding restoration, dampener re-engagement, and Q-thrust trajectory all for a one-second window."

Jennings swung back around. "Are you kidding me?"

"Jennings, get *this* ship charged up and in position to BAG the hell out of *that* ship. Now."

"You can't be ser–"

"I said '*now*!'"

Ericsson stepped behind me and sat in the captain's chair, laughing. "This, is going to be interesting."

Jennings fired the maneuvering thrusters on maximum power. We could feel the vibration of the engines through the ship, but the reticule didn't move.

"Thirty seconds until they're in range, a minute thirty until we're pulled in."

"All ship," I called. "Crew of the *Udachi*. By now, I'm certain everyone knows our situation. Well, we don't have time for speeches. All I want to say is . . ." I looked into Tabitha's deep eyes, and basked in her Mona Lisa smile. "Well, I want to tell you that it's been a hell of a ride and I appreciate every one of you for coming along. I hope it goes on a little bit longer."

"Fifteen seconds," Cynta called out. The indicator began to sluggishly move across the display as the approaching ship inched across to meet it. I knew increased thrust equaled increased momentum–now that we were moving, along with the entire station, it was only a matter of waiting until the ship was in position before we fired.

I continued, "Everyone clear the compartments far away from the starboard-side airlock. Make sure all bulkhead doors between you and it are sealed. And, hold onto something. Acting captain Mitchel Creek, out." I looked around; everyone who was hanging out had left to find someplace to strap themselves down to.

"Five seconds."

"Don't fire until we're aligned, unless we're too close to the point of no escaping the black hole. We've one chance"

"Like trying to move a planet with a fire hose," Jennings said through clenched teeth as he made adjustments. The ship and reticule were seconds away from touching.

"The recoil could send us farther into the gravity well . . ." Tabitha warned.

"I know I know shuddup," Cynta said, fingers flying over the controls. Her far-away look was intense enough to give me sympathetic aneurysm. "Ship in range. Alignment in five seconds."

As if to prove her point, a spark separated itself from the Priori ship and sped at us. Tabitha read off the holo-display, "Incoming missile." I sat in the seat next to Ericsson and clipped the safety belts.

The missile hit the ship, shaking it violently. The lights dimmed and the holo-display scattered for an instant.

"*Anak puta,*" Cynta gritted.

"Another incoming."

Four seconds later, it hit, rocking the ship harder and cutting out the lights and holo-display completely. Dim emergency lights came up and everyone turned to their respective console displays.

Jennings said, "We can't take another. It'll take the BAG offline at best, tear us up most likely."

"Incoming missile." Tabitha's voice hardly broke.

"Almost there," I watched the increasingly larger ship break the edge of the reticule.

"Impact in–"

"*Fire!*"

I like to think the blast from the BAG incinerated the missile as it erupted from the *Udachi* and destroyed the Priori ship, but I don't know if it did. Within the same instant, the monitors exploded in white light before cutting out, the ship lurched up and back so violently that the world grayed out from the g-force change. A sickening explosive crack rumbled through the ship as it was ripped away from the station, leaving some of her behind. Within half a second, though it felt like ten, the dampeners came back online, the shielding came online, just in time for the Q-thrust to rocket us hundreds of kilometers a second away from the black hole.

"Status," I groaned.

Cynta had a ragged gash on her forehead, bleeding down into her left eye . . . thing. It was very disturbing. "We're out of immediate danger from the black hole. Only one ship detected out there, it's . . . it's the *Escort.* They destroyed the ship we didn't hit."

Ericsson rubbed the back of his neck and moved his head around. Tabitha was bleeding from her lip where, as I found out, the recoil made her bash her mouth against her own knee. She looked over at me and I followed her gaze. My side had opened back up and I was seeping blood through my shirt and pants. I didn't think it was too bad, but I was going to need to get the wounds re-sealed.

I looked back up at her, and we smiled at each other. We made it.

Cynta unbuckled and stood, a little shaky. "Permission to take Jennings to the infirmary, captain?"

"Jennings? Why, what's wrong?"

Jennings as well looked worried as he examined himself for wounds. "What? What?"

When she reached him, Cynta pulled back and threw a right hook so hard I heard a tooth hit the floor and Jennings was left slouching, buckled in his chair, semi-conscious. Ericsson laughed and I couldn't help but smile.

"Okay, I think he got the message. Ericsson, would you mind helping Cynta get–"

She held up a hand to pause me and looked into the air at her invisible numbers and words.

The comm *pinged* on. "*Udachi, Escort.* Impressive recovery. But, I'm afraid we're picking something on the long-range–something, troubling. Can you confirm?"

"Cynta?"

"Ship indications detected. Coming around the black hole, distance roughly two-point-four million kilometers. Interference, but estimated ship classes include scouts and corvettes, battle cruisers, destroyers . . . and capital ships."

Ericsson, Tabitha, and I looked at each other, all previous mirth drained away. Tabitha asked, "How many?"

Cynta returned her attention to the room, and looked at us. For the first time, despite the lack of pupils in her eyes, I felt her looking right at me. "Over one thousand."

CHAPTER THIRTY

"We returned to Luyten's Star as fast as the damaged *Udachi* would allow," I told the council of Luyten's Home.

I sat at a large round table in a brightly lit room. The windows were open and a breeze fluttered the thin, open curtains. "We have no idea how fast an armada of that size can travel, but chances are good they're going to send more of their scout ships ahead, at least."

"Captain Creek," an elderly man in a powder blue shirt said, "Do you know if they were headed this direction?"

I turned in my chair to look at Cynta, who sat with a few others from our ship in the council hall–including Tabitha, Frankletti . . . and Cheng. She replied, "We left before we could get any reliable triangulation. But, this area in general, yes."

"I confirm that," Captain Chandrima said. She sat next to me at the table. Around the table were the man in blue, councilors Staand and Young, and four others I hadn't met before.

Councilor Staand, cleaned and bandaged, asked, "And you're positive about their intentions?"

I craned back around the other way to look at the surviving members of the CASS station. "Yes," I told her, "it's their intention to eliminate us all, or die trying. It'll be yesterday's attack on Luyten, but on a galactic scale."

One of the other councilors shook her head. "I can't even grasp just how horrific this sounds. Do we evacuate the town? Go to the mountain caves or go off-world?"

"If I may, councilors, we can take as many as we can in our ship. As many as two hundred, I believe," I said.

"That is greatly appreciated, captain," Councilor Staand said. "But, where will you go? A force that size is going to be a threat even to CASS. Where can you go, where can we go, that will be safe from them?"

I had no answer, and not because I didn't know the possible colonized worlds.

Councilor Young, significantly more mild than last I saw him, said, in a tired voice, "Can we be certain that this threat is real? That we're at risk?"

"Councilor Young, even if the testimony of all these witnesses weren't unimpeachable, we have the scan logs from the two vessels," the councilor in blue chided.

To his credit, Young nodded and looked concerned. "Perhaps the caverns would be best. Maybe, if any arrive, they'll see us gone and assume we went off-world, and move on."

Another councilor said, "Obviously we need to allow the populace to decide for themselves. Even with the *Udachi's* assistance, we don't have near the ships needed to get the entire population off the planet–some people will *have* to take refuge in the caves."

"We must move quickly," Councilor Staand advised. "We'll make the announcements, activate all marshals and civil officers. First, call to all ship captains to ready their vessels." Assistants and secretaries sitting beside and behind the councilors moved from taking notes to talking quietly on comm devices. "Captain Creek, we thank you for your efforts–if you hadn't gone to do what you needed to do, we might not have seen this coming until far too late. And thank you for your assistance." I nodded. "I wish there was something we can do for you. We'll make sure you're completely stocked with food and supplies."

"Thank you, councilors. Naturally, I'd like to be able to leave as soon as possible. If you can have who and whatever's coming with us to be at the ship within two hours, I'll call us square."

"I understand. You're dismissed. And, captain, good luck."

I nodded, rose, and met Tabitha, who pushed Frankletti in a wheelchair, in the aisle as we left.

Once we walked into the bright orange sunlight, I asked them both, "What do you think? Is flying away the wise thing? Or do we hole up?"

Frankletti, blinded eyes behind wraps for his burns, said, "There are many places we have available, far away, that will allow us to work with other synd communities while we get more information on what's happening. Help us decide our move."

"The ship's pretty messed up. How far can we get?"

"It's a military ship," Frankletti said, "that model is compartmentalized and built to take a lot of damage before it gives out. Don't worry. If we can get out far enough ahead of the advance, we'll be able to get her fixed up. Or, a different ship, even. We have friends out there."

"I don't know. I'm kind of attached to the *Udachi*, now. We've gone through a lot recently." Tabitha and I shared a smile.

We walked, and rode, in silence. As we approached the port side ramp, Frankletti said, "So, captain, eh? I have to say, I'm not sure I'd have predicted that."

"*Acting* captain, actually. My commission was sort of supposed to end at our return, but it looks like I may be keeping the position for a little longer. But, it's a democratic command."

"How are you with the way your quest turned out?"

I thought about that as we mounted the ramp and passed various crew members prepping the ship. On our way back from the black hole, I had sat with Frankletti, Tabitha, and the station survivors in sick bay while a couple of medically proficient crew members worked on wounds.

"So," I had said, "you were talking about how the QPF was the tip of a time-space well, touching another layer of time-space?"

"Listen, Doctor Tabor," one of the suits interrupted, "you're still under contract with Science Division, which includes a strict non-disclosure policy. Now, I'm prepared to let go what you said earlier because of the whole nearly dying experience–all of us were under a great deal of stress and shock. But, now, I think you need to consider what you're going to say very carefully."

"Is it true, about the invasion fleet?" Doctor Tabor asked me. "Is it as big as I heard?"

I nodded, "At least a thousand ships, mostly destroyers or worse."

She looked away for a moment, watching a young man treat Frankletti's burns. Then said, "Mister Carr, I have very carefully considered that you're an ass and you and your precious regulations can take a leap out an airlock." Mister Carr began a retort, but Tabor continued, "I watched nearly everyone I've known for ten years murdered, and was shoved in a hole for days waiting to die. The culmination of my work is destroyed, and it's very possible it will never be rebuilt. I'm going to damn well say whatever I please, and you are free to report me to the next CASS security officer. Which, unless I miss my assessment of this ship and its people, we're not going to be seeing for quite some time."

Mister Carr's mouth opened and closed several times. I think he even made a squeak. Then, he got up, pulled his torn and bloody suit jacket straight, and marched out. The other suit, watched him go, then leaned back in his chair and folded his hands on his knees.

Tabitha, beaming, said, "Doctor Tabor, please continue."

Doctor Tabor resumed, "Well, yes. The QPF, it essentially is the very pinpoint that opens the hole to allow something from our time to enter another. Your time. But the power it needs requires both the energy and the mass of an active black hole."

I sighed, refocusing myself on the conversation. "Okay, so, if I understand, Jarrod, my . . . father, acquired this QPF and followed its pinprick into my layer of time-space."

"Stole," said the eldest scientist of the bunch. "No offense, but he stole it."

"None taken, I didn't know him." Tabitha subtly put her hand in mine. "He, the Jarrod these people knew, I never met and . . . my father, died while I was very young. My mother told me he was mysterious, charming, and secretive. No kidding. But, how did it, I don't know, activate?"

"The build-up of mass and energy takes weeks, and once it reaches a critical point, there's no stopping it," Tabor explained. "The QPF, well, it actually doesn't physically need to be near the system . . . it's difficult to explain. But the fact is he and his partner broke in and stole it right from under us."

"How is that even possible?"

"He had agents on the inside to help him."

"Other synd?"

"No," she said, "Priori."

I sat up. "What?"

Frankletti, his face covered in some kind of medical goo, spoke up, "I can't imagine he knew he was working for them. He took all kinds of jobs for all kinds of people, but I knew him–there's no way he'd work for people like that. Willingly. That other guy, you found in the ship, Mitch, that Jon Ronald? He was Priori. I figure once they got away, Ronald revealed what he was and tried to take over the *Lysander*. Or, a Priori ship was approaching for rendezvous. Whatever. Jarrod protected himself. Then, at some point, poof! The QPF activated."

I noticed that half of the station employees had name badges similar to Ronald's, with the blue triangles. "So, okay, I get all that. Now, how'd I get here?"

The technicians looked at each other. Tabor spoke again. "Well, basically, it snapped back. The QPF, the dimple in space-time, it finally snapped back. What was probably a very short time for *this* layer, hours? Days? Passed relatively slow on yours. I'm guessing, what, fifty, fifty-five years?"

I scowled and looked from her to Tabitha and the others, and back. "Are, are you talking about my age?"

Frankletti chuckled. "Tabor, no life extension where he's from."

"I'm thirty-two." I glanced at Tabitha to see if she had a reaction, but she didn't show one.

"Oh. Interesting," Doctor Tabor said. "Well, anyway, the QPF and the mass that pushed it, essentially, were just bouncing back. It was bound to, it had to, but something must have triggered it. You were in the ship? The QPF rebounded with what it took back with it in the first place and you got caught in the rebound."

"Huh. What triggered it?"

The elder scientist piped in, "Well, it's supposed to return automatically, but something must have gone wrong for it to have not done so . . . until you got to it. What did you do? When you found it?"

For the hundred and fiftieth time I tried to remember the moments surrounding being in that ship. "I'm sorry, I just don't remember. The only . . . only thing that I've been able to remember, is I was visiting my mother's house, outside of town. She has, had, a large shed. Almost a barn, really. I'd gone into it a million times as a kid. She'd sold this engine block that'd been there since before I was born and I'd gone in there to look . . . all I can recall is the ship was somehow in there, hidden below the floor. It'd been there for decades and, when I found it . . . I don't know. That's all I can remember and even that much was gone from my mind until recent events pulled it up."

A couple of the technicians sighed. The elder said, "Well, nothing to be done about that, I suppose. The event must have deactivated, or even reversed, the neural encoding that made up your short-term memory of the encounter."

"Wait, the body. Ronald. There was no way *it* was thirty-some years old. It was only days old when I discovered it."

"Like I said," Tabor replied, "the QPF and its immediate locus, exists here, in this time-space layer. Days, here, did only pass. It, and evidently the ship it brought with it, was still existing in this time-space layer even as it was stretched, so to speak, into yours."

"Wow. Trippy." I tried to wrap my head around that one for a moment.

Then, I said, "Okay, so, what I really want to know is, is there a way to get back?"

Again, they all shared looks among each other. The elder scientist started, "Well, see, I–"

"I'm sorry, captain," Tabor began.

"Please, Mitch."

She sat forward, "Mitch, I don't think so."

"What if it was rebuilt? For all you know, actually, maybe your entire project was being mirrored at another black hole and it's out there now."

She smiled, mostly pleasantly, but with a hint of condescension, like she was speaking to a child, "That's not possible. But even if it were, I don't think it would work."

I expected, in my day dreams of this moment, when I thought about what would happen if I had to convince someone to send me back, or explain why they couldn't, that I would be emotional and have to keep calm. To my surprise, I found I didn't have to work at it. Oh, I felt upset and disappointed, but they were vague, shadows of feelings. I was surprised to discover I wasn't as upset about not being able to go back as I thought I might be. I looked at Tabitha, and I nodded to her and smiled. I caressed her hand, the rough palm and incredibly soft top of her hand, and sat back. I think she understood that I really had accepted what happened, was happening, and I was okay with it.

But still, for no other reason than curiosity, I had to know. Casually, I asked, "Why?"

Doctor Tabor, I think, read my behavior and she relaxed her posture as well. "All analogies fail, at some point, you know. We use analogies to try to illustrate a concept or an event that, to be properly explained, takes gigabytes of documents to do so."

"I understand."

She nodded. "If the QPF was the tip of a pencil, or, a hook let's say, that came down and touched your layer, you're a particle that it pulled up with it."

"Well, shouldn't I snap back then, like the QPF?"

"No, it's completely different. The QPF was, in a manner of speaking, pushed into your layer by a process that, by its nature, would have to rebound. You are something that got ripped away from your layer, without the process of stretching time-space behind you. Like that upper rubber sheet pushed down to touch the lower one, and a bug on the lower one happened to crawl onto the touching upper sheet just before it bounced back. You now exist wholly in this layer."

"Nice. I'm a bug."

"No, I–"

I smiled, "I get it. I was joking." And then we sat there for a moment while volunteer medics tended to the pulls, sprains, bruises, and cuts that resulted from our stunt with the BAG-method of undocking from a space station.

Back on Luyten, after the meeting with the council and the walk back to the *Udachi*, Tabitha, Ericsson, a couple of others, and I took stock of the people and supplies that boarded the ship. A couple of those people were Sureth and her wife, Renna. Sureth brought with her crates of fresh food, herbs, and medicinal plants. In the commotion, it took a moment for us to recognize each other, even though our meeting had only been little more than a day ago.

"Oh, Mitch, isn't it?" she said, shaking my hand. "I'd like you to meet Renna."

"Oh right. Something with terraforming, right?"

Renna shook my hand, "Atmosphere conditioners, yeah."

"Well, welcome aboard. I'm Mitch. Acting captain. This is my . . . girlfriend, Tabitha. Sureth here is one of Luyten's agri-experts."

Tabitha gave me a curious smile and shook their hands. "Nice to meet you. We're hoping this will be just a little vacation for you all. But, well. . . ."

"Yeah," Renna said.

Sureth broke the awkwardness, "Well, I need to oversee the loading of the crates. Here's a list of items with crate number and weight."

"Wow, efficient." She smiled and shrugged. "Well, welcome aboard. Again."

Tabitha and I moved off to receive what looked like tanks of something flammable. "'Girlfriend'?"

"What? Is that insulting? You prefer 'partner'?" I asked, sincerely.

She smiled. "No, no that's fine. I've been quite a few things, but I've never been a 'girlfriend.' Guess I can try that label on for a while."

Cynta came in over the comm, "We're set to take off the instant you're loaded-up down there."

"Right," I said and looked over the dozen or so people and handful of large items left. "Twenty minutes, I think."

"Aye, cap'n."

"Well, shall we?" Tabitha gestured up the ramp.

"Let's get this thing far, far away before next we sleep." To Ericsson I said, "Finish up here, if you would. We're heading to the bridge."

"I'll let you know when we're locked and sealed."

I clapped him on the shoulder and smiled. Then, Tabitha and I walked up the ramp.

"What'd Frankletti suggest?" I asked. "Some place called Pasture? Sounds nice."

Tabitha smirked. "It's colony on a world covered with acidic rivers and is tidally locked with its sun, so, it's always gloomy."

I sighed. "It's the *final* frontier because it's out to kill you."

"What?"

"Nevermind," I chuckled, grimly. "Off we go."

End Book One

* * *

About the author:

Liam has degrees in English and Theatre . . . and yet has spent most of his adult life working in I.T. He grew up in the shadows of the Rocky Mountains, but moved to the Ozarks with his family where he's made a home with his incredible wife, amazing daughter, and a neglected guitar. Publishing this novel and beginning Tragic Sans Press is the culmination of a lifetime of dreaming, planning, and finally, doing–the oft forgotten step by so many.

Discover other works by Liam R.W. Doyle, such as:

First Hand of the Night: A Collection of Five Early Stories,
at Tragic-Sans.com.

Connect with the author online:

Twitter: twitter.com/tragicsans
Blog: www.tragic-sans.com
Goodreads: www.goodreads.com/tragicsans
Facebook: www.facebook.com/LiamRWDoyle